UNHOLY SINS

SAINT VIEW STRIP #2

ELLE THORPE

ELLE THORPE PTY LTD

For Louise,
For all the years of beta reads and helping to make my books
the best they can be.

PROLOGUE
ZEPH

I could still hear her cries as the girl fell on her knees in the confessional booth.

The agony in her voice while she confessed and repented for being a sexual temptation.

The grinding of my molars and the crack of my knuckles when I forced myself to remain seated and murmur scripted words of forgiveness.

With my words, I'd forgiven a sin that wasn't hers but instead belonged to the man who lay sleeping peacefully in his bed in front of me now. Blissfully ignorant of the trauma he'd caused. Completely unaware I watched him with hate in my heart.

She was fourteen years old. Four-fucking-teen.

The room around me was not unlike my own. A cross nailed on the peeling wall above the bed. Rectangular prayer cards depicting saints on the bedside table. A well-used Bible with a creased spine and tattered pages within arm's reach on the queen-sized bed. Like he'd been reading it before he'd fallen asleep, filling his head with promises of good, when his soul was black as the night outside.

In and out. His chest rose and fell as he breathed.

In and out for the last time.

I moved silently, my footsteps soft on the carpet until I loomed over him. My fingers itched, knowing what they needed to do.

The church would do nothing if I reported it. They'd sweep it under the rug, like they had so many times before. His unholy sins would go unpunished.

I couldn't let that happen. Not again.

Like he sensed his impending doom, the priest's eyes flew open. He blinked rapidly in the dim light, his vision trying to adjust, clearly attempting to make sense of the hooded, masked figure who stood over him, fingers wrapped lightly around his thick neck.

Panic set in, filling his gaze, then my soul.

I liked it. The confusion in his eyes. The smell of his fear.

I tightened my grip, enough that his fat hands grabbed my wrists in terror, but not so tight he couldn't speak.

"Help!"

It was supposed to be a scream, that much was clear, but it came out a gurgled noise, as pathetic as the man who'd made it.

Anger mixed with the hate. I leaned in closer. "Is that what she said? Did she beg someone to help while you used her? Did she cry, the way you are now?"

Water puddled in his eyes, perhaps tears of fear and regret, or perhaps just a bodily response to me cutting off his airflow. Either way, they had no effect on me. I loosened my grip, playing with my prey, even though I knew I shouldn't.

The scent of piss filled the air.

"Who are you? I've done nothing. Please. Don't—"

Another squeeze when I leaned in, lips to his ear. "Liar, liar, pants on fire." The words were deep. Dark. Deadly. His lame attempt at excuses only fueled the rage that had nowhere else to go except through my fingers, pressing against his jugular.

"I never hurt her. She wanted it!"

"Stop. Talking." Squeezed. Waited for him to turn purple. Released.

"I know you...your voice..."

He did. I knew him, too, and many others just like him.

I'd joined the priesthood because I didn't want to be like him. I wanted to do good.

Yet here I was, about to commit a mortal sin.

I squeezed one last time. Tight, until he gave up the fight, his body went limp, and the life drained from his watery eyes.

It took all my effort to pry my fingers from the lifeless fuck who'd thought nothing of ruining a young girl's life. Taking his wasn't even close to making amends for the trauma she'd experienced.

As silently as I'd come, I turned and crossed the room, using the sleeve of my black hoodie to open the door so my fingerprints wouldn't be found on it.

I slipped from the rectory and started the long walk home.

I waited for it. The guilt. The realization I'd killed a man.

But when I stepped into my own church, up the dark aisle, and dropped to my knees at the altar, the words that came out of my mouth weren't the ones I'd expected.

"Bless me, Father, for I have sinned...and I don't think I care."

1

LYRIC

"How much for a private dance?"

I dropped into a squat, spreading my knees wide, winding my hips provocatively in time with the beat of the music. Scooping up the few bills that had been thrown onto the stage, I considered the man's request.

It was late. Or rather, early. We'd close the club at five when the sun started its morning rise, so there were only thirty minutes until my shift was over. I was tired. My feet hurt from wearing impossibly tall heels for hours. I wanted to go home and sleep for a week.

But like too many other nights lately, my wad of cash was thin. I'd danced my damn ass off, putting everything into my performance. It had all fallen flat. The men had all been regulars, and they'd seen my act dozens of times before. They threw single-dollar bills instead of fifties, talking more amongst themselves, or drowning their sorrows in the bottom of a glass, rather than really paying attention to anything I was doing.

The man waved a fifty in front of my face enticingly. It was the biggest bill I'd seen all night.

"Seventy-five," I countered, giving him a flirty wink that was all for show, because I certainly didn't find him attractive.

He was older, probably in his early fifties. His pot belly hung over his belt, and his arms were covered in thick, dark hair. He had a baseball cap pulled low on his forehead which just screamed, "I'm balding and wearing this to cover it up!"

But money was money when you didn't have enough of it.

When you had people counting on you to pay the bills.

He ponied up the extra cash I'd requested, and I plucked it from his hairy fingers before he could try to shove it in my G-string. I straightened and then strutted off the stage, motioning for the man to follow me.

He did, a little too eagerly for my liking. His breath warmed the back of my neck, and I gave a slight shudder of disgust. "You need the cash, Lyric. It's twenty minutes, just get it over with," I mumbled to myself.

"What was that?" He took the opportunity to move close enough for his beer belly to brush the small of my back.

I pasted on a fake smile, glancing over my shoulder at him. "I just asked if you have any special requests?"

The private rooms at the back of the club were designed to look like intimate living spaces. Couches, lamps, rugs. A mini refrigerator for refreshments that might want to be purchased. A speaker system where the clients could choose their own music, since the rooms were practically soundproof and whatever was playing in the club only barely filtered through the walls.

I held the door open for the man and motioned for him to walk in ahead of me.

He did, gazing around the room while he strolled to the couch. He turned and sank down into it, spreading one arm along the back, letting his gaze roll over my body.

I shut the door behind me, switching the lock to engaged so the others would know not to try to come in here with one of their own private clients. "You can choose the music. Or a drink…"

He held up another fifty-dollar bill. "I have requests that don't involve music or drinks."

I fought the urge to wrinkle my nose at him. I had a pretty good idea what at least one of his requests would be and I wouldn't do it. But I could really use that extra fifty. It would go a long way to saving what had been a pathetic night. Maybe he would accept a compromise. "I take requests. Within reason."

"I want you fully naked."

I nodded. That was already assumed when you paid for a private dance, but clearly, he was new at this, and I wouldn't correct him. I'd seen him at the club before, but he'd never asked me to take him back to a room.

"That's fine." I reached down and pulled off my G-string. It was all I was wearing anyway, the rest of my clothes already removed out on the main floor. I had no problem with nudity. I took the extra fifty from his fingers and stashed it in a little cubby hole by the door, along with the rest of his money.

"There's more of that if you put your hair into pigtails."

I paused before I turned to look at him again.

His dick had tented his pants.

Ew. But I just let out a laugh that was nothing like the noise I made when I was truly amused. "You like the schoolgirl vibe?"

He just held up another bill.

I finger-parted my hair down the middle and then quickly braided each side. "I don't have hair ties to keep it like this, sorry."

He reached into his pocket. "Here."

He'd come prepared. So gross. But in the scheme of things I'd been asked to do, it wasn't the worst. So I took the hair ties and wrapped them around the ends of the pigtails I'd just created.

"Now dance."

That I could do. I put some music on the speakers and swayed my hips back and forth. My tits bounced with the movements, and the man's eyes drew down, focusing on the boob job I'd paid for back before I had a kid and a sick grandparent to worry about.

"Come closer."

It was a fair request for the money he'd paid. I strutted over to him and leaned in, so my tits were in his face. With my hands either side of him on the wall, I rolled my body up and down, careful not to actually touch him.

Of course, he went for the sneaky boob grab.

I caught his wrist before he could make contact. "No." There was no messing about in my words. They were sharp, and I meant business. "No touching."

"I'll pay extra."

"Not interested."

"You finger your pussy then, and I'll watch."

I straightened, irritated. "That's not what we do here. We don't offer sex. Of any sort."

He mumbled something that sounded like cussing me out, but I ignored it and went back to dancing. He wasn't the first man who had assumed I'd do more than put on a show. He wouldn't be the last.

When he went back to watching instead of asking me for sexual favors, I relaxed and let the music get inside my head. I tuned him out completely, picturing a tall, dark-haired, tatted-up stranger in his position instead.

It was something I did often to make my job a little more bearable.

Moment by moment, the dark-haired stranger morphed into an image I recognized from other fantasies. A chain appeared around his neck, a cross dangling from the end. A scar through his left eyebrow developed. A Bible appeared, but instead of opening and reading from it, he put it aside, his attention focused on me.

One glimpse of an oddly attractive priest a couple of months back, and he'd had a starring role in my fantasies ever since.

I was so going to Hell.

But what kind of priest had tattoos so far down his arm they were visible when his sleeve rode up just the tiniest amount?

A groan of pleasure shattered the illusion.

The sexy, twenty-something priest was replaced with the middle-aged man who'd just come all over his hand.

Anger filled me. I stormed over to the doorway and

flicked on the light, illuminating the mess he'd made on himself while I'd been lost in my unholy daydream. "Are you fucking kidding me? This isn't a sex club. I told you that." I pointed to the door. "Get out."

His gaze narrowed on me. "I paid."

"For a dance," I snapped. "Not for sex. *Of any kind.* Those were my exact words. You think I want to see you pump your tiny dick until it explodes? No, sir, you did not pay me for that, because there is not enough money in the world."

His gaze narrowed into slits. "What did you think was going to happen when you dance like that?"

Oh, he was one of *those* guys. The ones who thought it was my fault they couldn't keep their dicks in their pants. Literally. I'd had a lifetime of them. Men who thought that my long auburn hair was there for them to touch. That I'd had my boobs done just so they could grope. That I wore tight shirts and short skirts so they'd want me. The anger turned into rage. "Get. The. Fuck. Out."

"I need a tissue."

I glared at him. "I don't care. Wipe it on your damn jeans and leave."

He shot me a cold stare and then zipped himself up.

I opened the door wide and stepped aside, while he stormed out into the main room and straight to the exit.

"Good riddance," I mumbled, glad he hadn't resisted. I was too stubbornly prideful to call security, unless it was a matter of life and death. I didn't want anyone to think I couldn't handle my own business.

Eve, the owner of the club and self-appointed mother hen to all her employees, watched over the commotion from where she was wrapped around her boyfriend,

Boston. The club was otherwise empty, and they had probably just been waiting for me to finish so they could go home. Boston glanced at me, untangled himself, and respectfully mumbled an excuse to leave, disappearing down the corridor that led to Eve's office and our changing rooms.

Eve didn't even blink an eye that I was fully naked. In our line of work, we were used to it. "What happened?"

I crossed my arms beneath my breasts. "The usual. He thought this place was something it's not."

"Asshole."

I shrugged. "Nothing I haven't seen before. At least he paid well." I leaned back into the room and fumbled for the cubby on the wall where I'd left the cash he'd paid me.

There was nothing there. The shelf was empty.

No fucking way.

Leaving Eve bewildered, I ran for the door, storming out into the parking lot, still without a stitch of clothing. "Son of a bitch!"

Terry, our security guy, stared at me with big eyes. "What happened? Are you okay?"

"That bastard stole my money!"

Terry jumped up and ran to the edge of the building, looking both ways for the man, but he'd clearly disappeared. "There's no one there, sweetheart."

"Argh!" I spun on my heel, storming back inside the club. Anger balled up in my throat, making it difficult to swallow down the emotion swamping me.

I would not cry. I would not give that creep the satisfaction. But damn if I didn't want to. I really needed that money. Every cent I could get.

Boston and Eve met me at the doorway, Boston silently holding out a robe.

I took it gratefully, shrugging it on and tying the belt around my waist. "Shame not all guys are as decent as you are, Cop."

We all still called him that, even though he'd quit his police force position and started a security company of his own.

Eve put an arm around me and guided me to the bar. Echo, our bartender, sympathetically pushed across a shot of whiskey.

I downed it in one, letting the liquid extinguish some of the fire inside me that was so hot I just wanted to let it out. Preferably in the form of punching someone.

Shame the only people here were ones I liked.

"I barely made bus fare without that guy's money," I complained before I could stop myself.

Eve was the world's greatest, most supportive boss, and my best friend. I didn't like complaining that this job did not always make ends meet. Lately, it didn't even come close.

"I know. I'm sorry. It was dead in here tonight. I've been working on ideas to bring in some new blood." She gazed down at her hands, her words softening. "Nothing will be as good as Fawn's Pin the Penis on the Politician party, though."

The mention of Fawn's name created a rock in the pit of my stomach.

At twenty-two, Fawn was the youngest member of the ragtag family we'd created here at the club. She'd been missing for weeks, taken against her will by her ex. Fawn was the sweetest, kindest, most innocent woman I'd ever met. She was beautiful, and we'd all taken her beneath our wings, like the little sister we couldn't get enough of.

Her disappearance hurt like nothing else.

"Is there any news?" I asked, but the words weren't hopeful. They were flat and dejected, because I already knew what the answer would be.

Boston shook his head. He'd taken it upon himself to investigate Fawn's whereabouts when the police had all but swept it into the 'don't give a shit' pile. "Nothing."

I nodded, knowing he was doing his best.

With feet like lead, I trudged back to the changing rooms and pulled on a tracksuit. After placing my robe back in the beat-up locker with my name on the front, I grabbed my purse and fished out my keys.

Eve was still where I'd left her, sad in the main room.

I bent to kiss her cheek, knowing she was lost in the memories of the night she and Fawn had been snatched. Eve had been lucky to escape, but her survivor guilt was killing her. I could see it on her face, only worsening as the time dragged on and still there was no sign of our friend. "See you tomorrow."

She lifted her head, fixing sad eyes on me. "I'll come up with something to get more people in here. I promise."

I nodded and walked out into the cruddy parking lot, where my shitbox of a car waited for me. I wanted Eve's promises to be true, but without Fawn's creativity, I wasn't sure Eve could pull off something big enough to really make a difference to my earnings. Not to mention the fact we were down a dancer, and the men had really liked the doe-eyed, innocent thing Fawn had going on. Neither me nor Eve could fake that. We'd both seen too much.

I got in the driver's seat, stuck my key in the ignition, and turned it.

The rusted Subaru gave a weak splutter before falling silent again.

I dropped my head to the wheel with a groan.

There was no denying it. I needed a new car. And another job.

2

ZEPH

 aint View Strip Club's neon-pink sign flickered out every thirty-seven seconds. It went black for three seconds, before returning to its lit-up state, advertising the club's existence to the street. The cycle repeated endlessly, all through the early hours of the morning.

I knew because I'd timed it. Many a night. It never changed. Thirty-seven on. Three off. Repeat.

I'd collected all sorts of data on things that happened here on the Strip. How long the traffic lights took to go green. How many men versus how many women lined up to enter the club and how long it took for each of them to be let inside. There was little else to do, sitting in my car five nights a week, watching the club.

Watching and waiting.

A short, potbellied man with a baseball cap pulled low rushed out of the doors without looking at the burly bouncer sitting on a stool, playing a game on his phone. The patron wiped his hands on his jeans, before shoving them deep into his pockets, and disappeared into the shadows farther down the street.

I checked the time, noting it was ten minutes until the typical closing time, and made a mark on my notepad, recording the man's exit and calculating he was the last patron inside the club.

Excitement swirled in the depths of my gut. The last patron out meant the club would soon be closed, and I'd get to see her.

Lyric, with her long red hair and fiery eyes.

Lyric, with a body just made for sin.

It had been weeks since the first time our eyes had locked at a political rally held on the lawn of my church. I'd stood behind the mayoral candidate's family, a silent statue of support, though I hadn't voted for the man. His views on the Strip had irked me from the get-go, but the church had picked where our alliance would lie, and my personal opinions on the matter hadn't been considered.

Lyric had been there with friends from the club, protesting loudly, drawing all gazes their way.

Including mine.

She looked like Annie.

But other members of the congregation hadn't shared my fascination. They'd tutted at Lyric and her friends for the way they'd dressed and the language they'd used.

But I couldn't stop watching her.

While her face and hair bore a striking similarity to the girl I'd once known, tattoos swirled down her arms, creating a full sleeve on her left. Her voice was loud and proud as she shouted about what she believed in, no hint of Annie's soft, respectful tones. When she'd turned my way, her gaze lingering on mine for a moment longer than it should have, desire had roared through my blood, hot and out of place.

I'd spent years learning how to fight back my inappropriate urges. Years in therapy, only for them to tell me I needed God.

I'd listened.

I'd done the right thing and joined the priesthood, praying God would forgive my sins. Praying every day that my urges would go away.

For the longest time, they had. I'd suppressed everything, wrapping it up in a nice little package tied up with trauma and trust issues, and buried them deep.

Until her.

One glimpse had set me to unraveling. It had only gotten worse since.

To the point where now, I couldn't have her, but I couldn't give her up either.

I lived in some in-between world, where I watched her life from afar, wishing it could be more, while knowing it never would.

I blinked when the door to the club slammed open again. That was quick. It normally took them between fourteen and twenty-seven minutes after the last patron left before the staff emerged.

They also normally emerged with clothes on.

Not tonight.

Lyric's completely naked body froze me to my seat. She ran out onto the curbside with nothing but high heels on and her long red hair cascading down her back as she looked back and forth. She said something to the bouncer, who jumped off his seat and ran a way down the street, searching for something.

My gaze drew down her body, over high, round breasts, a flat stomach, and completely bare snatch.

"Fuck," I muttered, sinking lower in my seat.

I was being tempted. I was sure of it. Why else would God create a woman like her, so perfectly suited for someone like me?

The urge to get out of the car, storm across the street, and claim her was strong.

I wanted to feel her naked body beneath mine.

Touch her curves and her skin and all her intimate places.

Put my fingers around her neck and squeeze while she writhed in ecstasy.

I jolted, along with the slam of the door, and realized she'd disappeared back inside.

Good.

She was safer there—in a place I couldn't go.

I picked up a chain of rosary beads, chanting the familiar prayers over and over until they seeped through the haze of lust and need surrounding me. My erection died. The heat in my blood turned cold.

The numbness settled in.

I picked up my notebook and recorded the unusual event, until my careful note-taking turned into a sketch of Lyric's naked body.

It would become the inspiration for a new sculpture. I was already itching to get home and get started on it.

Ten minutes later, at five on the dot, she emerged again. This time fully clothed and with a scowl that had me leaning forward, resting my elbows on the steering wheel, and peering through the windshield at her.

She stormed around the back of the club to where I knew she kept her car.

I waited for it to emerge.

My shift here was nearly done. I'd follow her home, wait until she was inside her apartment building, and then I'd leave as silently as I'd arrived.

Minutes passed. They ticked on, and with each one, a growing sense of unease rattled me.

What was taking her so long? I knew her by now. She was always ready to get home, never dawdling or even bothering to check her phone. The bouncer had gone inside, and the Strip was empty and as quiet as it ever was.

Completely absent of Lyric and her rusted blue Subaru Impreza.

I wound the window down a crack, listening for her.

The curses she let out as she came back onto the street without her car filtered back to me in the quiet night air. I frowned when she pulled her hoodie up and stomped down the street, away from the safety of the club.

I sat shocked for a moment, wondering what she was doing, waiting for her to turn around and come back.

She didn't.

I squinted, watching her form get smaller and smaller.

She wasn't coming back. What was she planning on doing? Walking home? The thought of her walking alone, unprotected at night, was maddening.

Especially since the person she most needed protection from was me.

The desire to chase her, grab her roughly, and slip

into an alleyway where I could take her hard and fast washed over me. To make her scream my name. To have her fight me, only to submit when she realized how good I could make her feel.

"Those desires aren't normal, Zepherin," I muttered to myself. "The joining of a man and a woman is a holy act."

There was nothing holy about the desires I kept inside. I'd been told that over and over again, until I'd shut them up for good.

At least I thought I had.

No other woman had shaken the binds I'd tied around myself. None but her.

All because she was so much like Annie.

I started the car, ready to follow her, when movement caught my eye.

A man emerged from the shadows. Masked and moving quietly, following behind Lyric. The pot belly and hands so hairy I could see it from a distance gave him away as the last patron to leave the club.

The one Lyric had chased after, naked and with her face a storm cloud.

A length of thin rope was wound around his fat fingers.

I could tie her up with that rope. Keep her in my bed, spread-eagled and well satisfied, going down on her for hours until she begged me to let her come...

I was pretty sure that wasn't this asshole's intention.

A deadly sort of anger obliterated all other feelings. Instead of starting the car, I opened the door and got out, slipping into the night, on the tail of a man up to no good.

As silently as a cat, I crept down the street behind

him, stalking a stalker. I kept to the shadows, avoiding the patches of light cast by streetlamps and the occasional car.

Lyric never turned around. She was completely oblivious to the men behind her, watching her every move. A fresh round of anger filled me, this time at her for being so careless. No, not careless. If I'd garnered anything about Lyric's personality from nights of watching her, it was she was stubborn and independent to a fault. She had a club full of friends. She could have asked one of them for a lift if her car wouldn't start.

But she hadn't. Instead, she'd refused to ask for help and put herself in a dangerous situation.

It made me mad enough to want to punish her. Pull her panties down over her curvy ass, lay her out over my lap, and spank her until she cried out for forgiveness for putting herself in this situation.

I squeezed my eyes shut for the tiniest of seconds, trying to erase the erotic image of her pussy peeking out between her thighs. Trying to stop the tingle in my palm that wanted to pinken her ass cheeks. Trying to keep my dick from getting hard over thoughts that were so inappropriate and intense they were dangerous.

Lyric moved past a bricked building, her strides jerky and stiff with irritation. She reached the corner and disappeared around it.

I held my breath, halting in my tracks, waiting for her to notice the man in front of me, who'd also paused, his body tensed as he probably waited for the same.

I waited for her scream of terror. For her to run when she realized she wasn't alone.

It never came. She walked off down the side street without even glancing around.

I was done waiting.

The stalker picked up his pace, edging toward the corner of the building and the street Lyric had turned down. But there was no way he was taking another step after her. I rushed him, easily catching the shorter man, and pinning him to the wall.

His head cracked off the brick with a satisfying thud, but I covered his mouth to muffle his shout of surprise, or pain, I didn't care which. I didn't bother removing his mask. I didn't care who the man was or what he looked like. As much as I would have liked to choke him to death right here and now for even glancing in her direction, I couldn't. This was still the main road that ran through Saint View, and even if it was quiet at this early hour, it wouldn't be for long. There'd be no time to dispose of a body. It was too messy. Too unplanned. It wasn't how I rolled.

Instead, I leaned in, putting my lips to the man's ear as I removed the piece of rope from his now slack fingers. "What were you going to do with this, friend? Tie her up? Or wrap it around her neck?"

I was the biggest hypocrite in the world, because both ideas excited me.

The only thing that made me any better than the cretin beneath me was that I wanted her to like it, too. At least I hoped that made me better than him.

Despite asking a question, I didn't give him the chance to answer. I dangled the thin length of rope in front of his eyes and leaned in harder on his chest, stealing his air. "Run away, now," I whispered. "Run far, far away. She doesn't belong to you. You understand?"

The man gave the tiniest of nods, and I let him go.

He didn't waste any time. He staggered away, back the way we'd come, shooting fearful glances over his shoulder in my direction, making sure I wasn't following.

I shoved the rope deep into the pocket of my hoodie, semi-disappointed with myself for not ending the man's life right then and there. Because I knew he'd try again. Maybe not with Lyric, if he were smart. She wouldn't be his last, and the thought made me sick to my stomach.

I wouldn't be watching out for the next woman.

But the thought of Lyric walking the rest of the way home unprotected was worse.

I rounded the corner in a hurry, quickening my steps to catch up with her.

Her fist connected squarely with my nose.

Pain splintered through my face, blood gushed onto my lips, and I blinked, trying to clear my vision, just in time to see her come at me again.

The second punch hurt worse. I let out a howl of pain that reverberated right through my skull.

The punches just kept coming. She landed a third with a rebel yell that would have made me stand up and applaud her, if there wasn't a good chance she'd just broken my face. I caught her wrist on her fourth attempt, dragging her in tight and spinning her so her back was to my chest, my arms wrapped around hers, pinning them to her sides so she couldn't have another go at destroying me.

That didn't subdue her. She writhed in my arms, fighting my every movement, trying to elbow me in the gut while she stomped on my feet in Ugg boots that did little for her cause. I had to clamp a hand over her mouth to quiet her shouts for fear she'd draw attention to us.

It wouldn't exactly be easy to explain what was going on here.

Despite the blood gushing from my nose and the general pain in my face, I couldn't help but grin into the darkness. I dodged the back of her head slamming back, and it hit me in the shoulder instead of the face, which she'd clearly been aiming for.

She was feisty. There was no real skill or finesse behind her attack, but that was even better. She was wild. Feral, even.

Every inch of me liked it.

A certain part of me liked it way too much. So much I had to let her go before she felt it.

She leaped away the moment I loosened my grip, spinning around and dropping into a fighter's stance, hands up, ready to protect herself.

Confusion appeared in her eyes as her gaze flickered over my bleeding face. "You aren't the man who was following me."

I was, but I was just better at it than the fool with the rope. But I knew what she meant. "No. I wasn't."

Her gaze dropped to my midsection, and then darted to my hands. "No gut. No hair." Her fists dropped a little, curiosity replacing the fear and anger. "So you weren't trying to attack me?"

I shook my head. "I just wanted to make sure you were okay. I didn't think you'd seen him."

She scowled at me, shaking out her no doubt bruised fists that would match the marks on my face. "I can look after myself. I'm not that unobservant."

It was on the tip of my tongue to say she'd never noticed me in all the weeks I'd been watching her. But okay.

She eyed my bloody nose then sighed, opening the purse she had slung across her chest and taking out a package of baby wet wipes to offer them to me. "I don't have a tissue, but these might help."

I took them from her, careful not to touch her again, and retrieved a couple from the packet before giving it back to her. "Thank you." I dabbed gingerly at my nose, wincing at the pain.

She rolled her eyes. "It's always the big guys who are the biggest wimps," she muttered, taking the wipes from my hand. "Give them here. You're making it worse. Hold still."

Like she hadn't just been the cause of my injuries, and moments earlier fighting me off with everything she had, she stepped in close, pressed up on her toes, and peered at me in the dawning light while she cleaned blood off my face. "I was just doing what I thought I had to do to survive, you know. I had no way of knowing you weren't the guy following me. You can't fault me for that."

"I didn't ask for an apology."

"Good. Because I'm not offering one."

The woman was baffling with her confidence. How quickly she'd gone from thinking me the enemy to now tending to me like I was an old friend who needed her help. I suspected there was guilt behind her actions, even if she did refuse to apologize.

I didn't need one. There were mere inches between us, and her warm breath misted over my lips. My dick kicked to life again, loving how close she was. Desire roared through me at the way she'd felt in my arms and the fight she'd put up. Fuck, she was beautiful, even more so than Annie had been. Where Annie had been quiet and docile, Lyric was sassy and strong.

The urge to dominate her and tame her sass was a bellow in my ears.

A flash of recognition lit her eyes. "I know you."

And that was the end of it. Three little words that reminded me I was out of place. I'd moved instinctually when she'd been in danger, but that was over now.

I shook my head, turning away. "No, you don't."

Because nobody did. Not the real me.

Maybe she remembered the priest who'd watched her from a distance.

Not the monster who lived inside.

3

LYRIC

There was a man passed out in the hallway.

I didn't recognize him, but his head tilted on an angle that made my neck twinge in sympathy. The scent of booze poured off him, sickly and unpleasant at this time of the morning. I poked him with the toe of the Ugg boots I'd worn home from the club, and he twitched, mumbling something incoherent. Satisfied I didn't need to call the cops for a dead body, I continued to my apartment. It was ground floor, not ideal in the Saint View slums, but it was all I could afford.

A roof over our heads—any roof—was better than the alternative.

Peggy lifted her head from her morning crossword puzzle, smiling at me over the top of her newspaper. She was old-school like that, refusing to do them on her phone. "Morning, girl. You look like you had a hell of a night." Her gaze narrowed on my busted-up fist, but she didn't comment.

I slumped into a chair at the little round dining table

I'd gotten for thirty dollars on Craigslist. It was scratched and beat to hell but steady, thanks to the folded newspaper shoved under one leg. "Don't ask."

Peggy folded her paper and gently placed it inside her oversized purse. "Sorry to pile on, honey. But your gran had a rough night, too." The older woman gazed at me with kind eyes. "She's getting worse."

I sighed heavily. "I know. She didn't recognize Amelia yesterday. Thought she was me as a little girl. It was upsetting. Amelia doesn't understand, no matter how often I try to explain."

Peggy crossed the room to put her hand on my arm, squeezing it gently. "Dementia is cruel."

It was a bitch. It had been killing my grandmother slowly for the past two years, rapidly progressing from general forgetfulness to her being incapable of listening out for Amelia while I was at work. I'd had to hire Peggy to care for them both five nights a week, for fear Gran would leave the gas stove top on and burn the place down with the two of them in it.

"Hang in there. You're doing a good job, kid."

Peggy's words of praise created tears in the backs of my eyes, but I turned away quickly. I didn't cry. I didn't show emotion at all. I was the tough nut at the club. The one who called it as I saw it and gave no shits about the consequences. The one who thought nothing of going up against a man twice my size, my fingers clenched into fists, ready to fight.

I was tough as nails. Strong as steel. This place had forced me into that role, because weak people didn't survive here.

There was no respite from it. I never got to let my guard down. Tonight had been proof of that.

So instead of crying over how tired I was, how scared I was about my grandmother's health, and how terrifying it was to be raising a little girl in this sort of environment, I pulled my shoulders back, said goodbye to Peggy, and strode into the room I shared with Amelia.

I'd done the best I could to make her side of the room cute, with a rainbow poster, pink bedspread, and glow stars stuck to the ceiling.

I crawled into bed, knowing it was a mistake, but my gritty eyes demanded I take the one hour of sleep before my alarm would go off and I'd have to get up to dress Amelia for daycare.

I fell asleep with the tattooed arms of a priest on my mind.

I'd recognized him as soon as I'd stopped laying into him.

His image seeped its way into my dreams, which were dark and violent. I tossed and turned, sleeping for only minutes at a time, until the creeping sensation of being watched took over and I woke with a start.

I almost welcomed my alarm going off, but analyzing my dreams didn't improve my mood any. I hadn't even apologized to the man. He'd scared off that creep from the club, and I hadn't even said thank you. What was wrong with me?

I glanced over at Amelia and smiled at the little bundle, still sleeping soundly in the home I'd provided for her. I knew it wasn't much. I knew we weren't always safe here, but I was doing my best. My girl was thriving despite our shitty circumstances.

I dragged myself up and perched on the edge of her bed, brushing my fingertips over her forehead and cheeks gently, smoothing back hair that was the exact same color as mine. "Hey, Slugger. It's morning time."

She blinked sleepy eyes twice, before focusing on me. Her grin spread across her rounded face like a wildfire, and she was suddenly awake and full of energy. "Mommy!"

She sprang up from beneath the mess of bedclothes and threw her arms around me. "I had a dream about a serpent, but when he tried to bite me, I ran away real fast. He couldn't catch me 'cause I ran like the wind. Just like you taught me."

I grinned down at her. "You are really fast now."

She nodded proudly. "I won a race at daycare. I beat all the boys and everything."

"That's my girl. Speaking of, it's time to get ready. Get up, brush your teeth, and we'll find you some clothes. We're going to have to leave early and get the bus because my car isn't working."

She trotted off to the bathroom, not questioning why my car was off the road again. It happened so often she was likely used to it.

I sorted through her drawers, frowning at the few T-shirts Amelia owned. They were all clean. It wasn't part of Peggy's job, but the woman was a literal saint on earth and had taken to doing laundry while Gran and Amelia slept. But even with Peggy's scrubbing and the swirling of the washing machine, Amelia's clothes all looked grubby. They might have smelled fresh, but they'd been worn hard and showed the evidence of blueberry stains, red food coloring, and general yellowing because even to begin with, they were old hand-me-downs I'd gotten free from someone in a buy, sell, swap group.

I sighed. That money I'd lost tonight could have bought my daughter a lot of new clothes. Now, I'd have to spend what I had made on Peggy's paycheck.

But there was no use crying over spilled milk. I chose an outfit that was the least stained and pulled it on over my daughter's head when she reappeared from the bathroom. We both knew the drill, and within minutes, she was dressed, shoes on, hair braided neat and tidy. She grabbed a banana and a Pop-Tart from the kitchen while I ducked next door to tell Geraldine I was leaving. She listened out for my gran when Peggy wasn't here. In return, I vacuumed her floors and cleaned her bathroom once a week.

It was a great deal for her, less so for me, but it did give me peace of mind and saved me from taking my grandma with me everywhere I went. And it didn't cost me anything but my time.

By the time Amelia and I got out the door, my eyes were drooping again. I slapped myself twice, trying to wake up. Getting on a bus to take her to daycare was the last thing I felt like doing, but if I kept her home, there was no way at all I'd get any sleep because she would be bouncing around the place and needing my supervision.

I almost wept with joy when my car was in its usual parking spot, a note beneath the windshield wipers from Terry, the club bouncer.

Saw it still in the lot when I was leaving.

Got it going well enough for now. You're in trouble for walking home instead of letting one of us help though. Eve is going to have your head. Key's in your mailbox. Terry x

I kissed the note since Terry wasn't around, detoured via the row of mailboxes, and retrieved the key sitting inside on a pile of unpaid bills. Ignoring those, I strapped Amelia in tight, gave her a picture book to flip through, then drove through Saint View to the neighboring town of Providence.

Providence was everything Saint View wasn't, with its big houses, expensive cars, and obvious wealth. Amelia's daycare was right in the heart of it.

Everybody applauded me for sending her there. She was the poor kid in the fancy school, and all my friends were so proud of me when I'd said I wanted to break the cycle, make sure she got the very best education and every advantage I hadn't had.

What I hadn't told them was my ex was paying for it.

The place was great though. It was state of the art, with qualified teachers, lots of resources, and perfect for my little smarty pants, who could already write her name and read some basic books. She had friends here, the other kids not seeing her grubby, simple clothes and cheap shoes. At least not yet. She was happy and learning, and that was all I cared about.

I got her out of the back seat and smiled at her skipping toward the gated entrance. Her backpack jostled on her slim shoulders, and her ponytail swung side to side.

When I caught up, I pushed the security buzzer and waited to be let in.

"Lyric?"

"Yep. It's us," I told the static-laced intercom.

"Uhhh…"

I frowned at the speaker and then pressed the button again when there was no further reply. "Sarah? Is everything okay?"

"Hang on a second, I'm coming out."

Weird. Normally they just unlocked the doors, and we walked right in.

The young woman appeared a moment later, slipping through the doorway onto the covered patio with us. She patted Amelia on the head when she threw herself at the woman's legs, wrapping her arms around them in a greeting hug.

"My grandma forgot my name yesterday, Sarah. She kept calling me Lyric. But that's Mom's name."

Sarah smiled down at my tiny daughter, but it didn't meet her eyes, nor did she respond to Amelia's tales. "Have you spoken to Lleyton?" she asked me.

I cocked my head to one side at the mention of my daughter's father. "I try not to make a habit of that."

Sarah grimaced, and I knew I should have said something else, but I was tired and snappy and so ready for bed, the words were out before I'd even thought of them.

She cleared her throat. "This is awkward, but he didn't pay her fees. As such, Amelia's spot was cancelled as of last Friday."

"What?" I roared.

Zero to a hundred in seconds. That was me all over.

Sarah winced. "Please don't shoot the messenger. It

wasn't my decision."

I took a deep breath, because it wasn't Sarah I was angry at. "No, no, I'm sorry. It's him I want to yell at, not you. Is there anything I can do to fix this? How much does he owe? I could pay some of it now…"

Like, the seventy-five dollars I made stripping last night. I had a feeling he was quite a bit more than seventy-five behind though, if it was bad enough for them to kick Amelia out.

Sarah covered my hand as I rifled through my purse for the money I'd made last night.

"Even if you had the money to pay the debt entirely, we've already given the position to another child."

My heart sank. "You can't have. It's only been a weekend since she was last here."

"We have a very long waiting list. The first person we called accepted the position."

I groaned. I couldn't blame the school or the parent who'd snapped up Amelia's spot. I would have done the same.

I could blame my pain-in-the-ass, irresponsible ex, though.

"What's going on, Mommy? I want to go play with Julie."

I squatted to Amelia's height and took her arms in my hands so I had her full attention. "I know, honey. We just need to sort something out with Miss Sarah. I'll call your daddy, and we'll get it fixed. Just hold tight, okay?"

A car pulled into the parking lot behind me, the tires squeaking on the blacktop.

Amelia raised an excited hand and waved. "Daddy! Katherine!"

I glanced over my shoulder with a decidedly less friendly expression for my ex and his girlfriend, emerging from her sleek red convertible with the obnoxious plates that read KAT WOW.

Lleyton got out of the car and rushed over to us, looking like he'd just fallen out of bed. "I'm sorry! I'm sorry! Jesus, Lyric, stop glaring at me like that. If looks could kill, I'd be dead on the ground at your feet."

Wouldn't that have been nice.

Katherine, all six feet of willowy goddess that she was, got out of the car and rushed after him. "We're so sorry, Lyric. I thought Lleyton told you about the change in plans. And he thought I told you. We didn't work it out 'til just now, and then you weren't answering your phone..."

Her posh English accent was pretty even when she was rattled. I had to give her that. Not that it did anything to diminish my anger with the two of them for screwing up the *one* thing they were in charge of when it came to our daughter.

"I was sleeping, so my phone was on Do Not Disturb. And what change in plans?" I ground out. "They won't let Amelia in because you didn't pay the bills. That's your one responsibility, Lleyton."

Lleyton shrugged in the frustrating way only a male who came from money could. "It was a misunderstanding. I never saw the bills until after they'd already cancelled her spot. I'm going to pay it today."

I turned hopeful eyes on Sarah. "Does that mean she can come back in?"

Sarah shook her head regretfully. "I'm so sorry. We're

completely full. I can't take her back; we'd be over limit. If you want to put her on the waiting list…"

I lost my patience. "It took us over twelve months to get her off the waiting list in the first place! How long will it take now?"

Sarah cringed. "Eighteen months probably, it's quite long."

I stared at her. "Amelia will be in school by then."

"I'm really sorry."

I spun on Lleyton. "What the hell am I supposed to do now? I've been working all night. I need her to be in care so I can sleep!"

Lleyton rolled his eyes like I was being completely overdramatic. "Settle down. We already found her a spot at another place. Katherine researched it and says the new place is better than this one anyway."

I doubted there was such a thing. This daycare was amazing, even after Amelia's favorite teacher, Bethany-Melissa, had quit a few months back. I'd spent months researching all the centers in the area back when she'd been a toddler. As soon as I'd realized how intelligent she was, I'd wanted her in the best pre-schooling environment I could find.

Clearly, she didn't get her smarts from her father, who was apparently so entitled he didn't even think it was weird he wasn't paying for his daughter's care until they'd kicked her out and he had to cough up in order to avoid being taken to a debt collector. Which was probably what it had come to, knowing him. I was sure they'd sent him ample reminders that were probably buried in his overflowing inbox. Everything with him was all chill and easy and 'don't worry about it!' Until his attitude came back to bite him.

And me.

This was what happened when you got pregnant during a one-night stand.

Katherine cleared her throat, blinking at me with her big, pretty eyes. "You don't need to worry. The center is new but fantastic. It's run by the church—"

Oh hell, no. "Are you joking? So they're going to be shoving God and Jesus shit down her throat all day long? I don't think so." I folded my arms across my chest. "I'm her mother. You don't think this is the sort of thing you should have discussed with me?"

Katherine bristled at my heathenism. "We're all her parents, Lyric. We all want what's best for our Milly girl. She needs the church's influence to offset the things she sees and hears in Saint View."

My mouth dropped open in outrage. She had a nerve, implying where I lived and raised my daughter was somehow below standard. Even if I was a hypocrite since just thirty minutes ago, I'd walked my four-year-old over a stranger passed-out drunk in our hallway.

This woman didn't know that.

She tossed her glossy hair, miffed I didn't immediately agree to her plans like my dumbass ex clearly did.

Katherine threw in one last barb, really just twisting the sharp points so they hurt. "And frankly, we're the ones paying for her education, so there's no requirement for us to inform you of any decisions we make about it."

I'd been itching for a fight all night. Without even thinking about who was watching, I let my temper and exhaustion and worry get the better of me. I launched myself at Katherine, only to be caught around the middle by Lleyton.

"Jesus, Lyric," he muttered, lifting me off my feet and walking me back five paces from his judgmental bitch of a girlfriend. "You're proving her point right now. Knock it off. Amelia is right there."

The fight went out of me instantly, and I held back the snarl at watching Katherine pick up Amelia's hand to lead her toward our cars.

"The daycare at the church will be good," Lleyton promised. "It's the only one in town with a spot available, so we don't really have much choice anyway."

"This is your fault," I accused in a whisper-shout. "I'm not religious, Lleyton. In fact, I'm the complete opposite. Those people are going to fill our daughter's head with bullshit about how I'm going to Hell for taking my clothes off for men."

Katherine would never work as a stripper. She was tall and graceful and everything Lleyton's parents expected in his partner. Everything I wasn't, nor had any desire to ever be. His parents hated my guts, and I couldn't help but think they might have somehow had a hand in this. They were God-loving, front-pew-on-Sunday sort of people too, even if their son wasn't.

But Lleyton was right. I needed care for Amelia. If the church was the only place I was going to get it, then there wasn't anything I could do about it.

"The minute she comes home and tells me I'm going to Hell; I'm burning the place down."

Lleyton just shook his head, well used to my brand of crazy after four years of co-parenting. "I don't even doubt it for a second."

4

———

ZEPH

The homeless shelter kitchen had an aroma all of its own. It wasn't just the vegetables, meats, and spices the cooks threw into big metal pots, getting meals ready for that night's service. Or the thick slabs of toasted bread we slapped butter onto. It was the unwashed bodies of the people who came in. The smoggy pollution that wafted in after them from the main street. A couple of little dogs had been snuck in, their owner feeding them scraps from his own plate, adding to the chaos.

Liam and I both pretended not to see them, because I for one didn't want to see a hungry dog any more than I wanted to see a hungry human. I went back to plunging a ladle into the soup and carefully pouring it into thick Styrofoam cups. Liam went back to handing out bowls and spoons.

"You want soup? Chicken or tomato?" I asked the next woman in line. "This is left over from last night, but if you keep shuffling down the line, Liam has breakfast cereals, juices, and milk if you prefer a more traditional breakfast at this time of day."

"Soup please, sir." She shifted a toddler on her hip who wriggled to get down. "Though we're grateful for either. Just something warm would be lovely." She reached out a spare hand to her slightly older child, who still couldn't have been older than four, grabbing the back of his shirt before he could wander off. "Daniel. Stay close, you'll get lost."

Daniel let out a racking cough but stepped closer to his mother for the time being.

A baby in a stroller gave a squawk of impatience, twisting in his seat, clearly impatient to get out and join his older siblings.

The woman's lower lip trembled slightly when she tried to smile at me. "Do you have any trays you could put them on? These three are kind of a handful."

I finished pouring one cup but motioned to the tables behind her. "Why don't you go sit? I can bring this over for you."

"Are you sure? All these people are waiting…"

I nodded at her. "Go. I'm here to help. The soup is hot. It'll be safer if I give it to you when the boys are all sitting. Nobody needs a trip to the ER for a burn this morning."

She shifted the toddler on her hip back into position, and he wailed about not being let down to join his older brother. "Thank you."

"We have some highchairs over there." I pointed to the corner of the room, and she headed in that direction.

I watched her grab a highchair and drag it over to the nearest table as I finished pouring soup for her family. I added some slightly spotted bananas and wrapped a couple of cookies in a napkin before adding those too.

"Playing favorites?" Liam grinned at me. He had an apron tied over a starched business shirt and suit pants. His sleeves were rolled to his elbows, but it was clear he was headed to his law firm straight after this. "Since when do we do table service and sneaky treats during the breakfast shift?"

He was only teasing though. He would have done it as well, even though the rules were that we didn't leave the safety of the kitchen area. For insurance purposes, they liked us to keep our distance from those who came in off the streets.

"She needs a hand. You would have done the same." I picked up the tray laden down with food and moved around him toward the locked door.

"Yeah, but I regularly get in trouble for breaking the rules." He reached over and pushed down the door handle for me. "So, what's one more, right?"

I gave him a nod, in acknowledgement for him holding the door for me, and carried my tray of food over to the woman and her family.

She glanced up at me gratefully when I approached. "I can't thank you enough. I know it probably doesn't seem like much to you, but I really needed someone to see me this morning."

I placed the tray down carefully and handed her boys soup spoons as their mother gave them their meals.

The toddler, now sitting in a highchair, wolfed down the temperature-tested soup his mother handed him. He was messy and cute, with tomato-flavored liquid dribbling down his chin.

But the older boy, Daniel, poked at the chicken pieces floating in broth without taking a bite.

"You don't like chicken?" I asked him.

He looked away quickly, going shy. A coughing fit caught him again, his little shoulders shaking while his chest spasmed.

I could hear his wheezing from where I stood, even above the low din of the crowd.

"He has asthma?" I asked the woman.

She'd been watching him cough with a frown too. "Yes."

"Does he have an inhaler? It sounds like he needs it."

Guilt filled her eyes, swiftly followed by tears. "I can't afford one. I know that makes me a terrible mother. He had one. But it ran out. I lost my job at the supermarket last month. They said I wasn't reliable enough because I said no to an extra shift in the evenings. But I have no one to watch the boys at night. I can't take them with me. Their father isn't around. If I don't pay the rent, the landlord will throw us out, but when I do pay the rent there's no money for anything else. Not food. Not medicine."

She handed the baby half a banana, but the defeat in her posture was heartbreaking.

Daniel started coughing again.

"He barely eats," the woman said quietly. "He's so small for his age. I don't know what to do."

A tear slipped down her cheek. She made no move to brush it away, until Daniel looked over at her. Another bout of coughs caught him in their grips.

I shoved my hand in my pocket, brushing over the rope that was still there from my little altercation in Saint

View earlier that morning, and pulled out my own inhaler, offering it to her. "Here. Take this."

She pushed my hand away and shook her head. "I can't pay you."

"I have others," I assured her. "I'll be fine. He needs to be able to breathe. When you need another, come back in and see me. I'm here often."

Her eyes glistened, but she took the inhaler from my hand. "Thank you..."

"Zepherin," I filled in, supplying my name.

"I'm Tammie. Daniel is my eldest. Toby in the highchair. Mathew in the stroller."

"It was lovely to meet you all. Is there anything else I can help you with?"

She laughed, but it didn't meet her eyes. "Can you make the supermarket give me my job back? We were doing real well until then. Now I can barely even get an interview. As soon as I say I can't do nights or weekends because I don't have anyone to watch the kids, they shut me right down. The last woman I interviewed with told me if I couldn't be a team player, then I wasn't what they were searching for. They want the teenagers with no responsibilities who they can pay less for working at all hours of the night and day."

A muscle ticked in my jaw. Her story triggered a deep-rooted anger that I'd spent a lifetime trying to repress. "Which supermarket?"

"Checkers? They're on The Strip."

I knew the place. They were franchised all around the state, and there was one in Providence too.

I pointed to the wrapped-up cookies. "I brought some treats. Enjoy them."

With that, I left the downtrodden family to their meal. But the anger didn't lift. It carried on right through the two-hour-long shift while I kept one eye on the people I was serving and one eye on Tammie and her boys. By the time I walked out into the parking lot, I was fuming.

Liam caught up to me, looking much more lawyer-ish now that he'd put on his suit jacket. "You okay? That woman and her kids got to you, huh?"

"They all get to me. All the people who need help."

"Some more than others, though."

I nodded in agreement. "The charity is overrun with the homeless. Every night, the beds are full and we have to turn people away. How long until that woman and her children are the ones we have to send back to the streets because we're full? She already has no money for food or her son's medicine. It's a miracle she's kept a roof over their heads this long without a job."

"Breaks my heart."

"Mine too." A thick feeling of helplessness blanketed me.

Liam seemed just as dejected when he changed the subject. "You going to tell me now what the hell happened to your face? 'Cause you're black and blue, brother."

I shook my head. I liked Liam. Considered him a friend even, after getting to know each other a little while we volunteered at the shelter. But I didn't have it in me today to share that a gorgeous stripper who reminded me of my high school sweetheart had probably broken her knuckles on my nose. Nobody had the energy for that story at eight in the morning. "Another time. See you next week?"

"I'll be here."

We both got in our cars, his flashy and shiny, mine much more modest. I drove from Saint View back to Providence, the buildings getting bigger and more expensive with every passing street. Outside my windows, teenagers walked to school in expensive Edgely Academy uniforms with blazers, their tuition probably enough to feed a small third world country. Gardeners worked at pruning trees and bushes for people too busy or self-important to do it themselves. An open garage door showed off several motorbikes and a boat.

There was so much wealth and privilege in this town it was sickening. How these people could come and go from their million-dollar houses when mere minutes away a town suffered in poverty was beyond me.

Didn't they care?

Didn't they feel the responsibility to help, the way I did? I'd had selflessness drilled into me for the past few years, since I'd become a priest, but it had been the easiest part for me. Helping– protecting—came naturally to me. As naturally as breathing.

At the church, I parked my car in my usual spot. Another car stopped at the same time I did, a sleek red convertible with personalized plates reading KAT WOW.

Steal it.

The intrusive thought held on.

Dump the plates and switch them out for a less obvious set.

I knew a guy who would take care of it for me. Who'd split the cash fifty-fifty.

That money would be life-changing for Tammie and her boys.

I got out of the car slowly, eyeing the convertible with its dark tinted windows and mag wheels, before I came to my senses. "It's broad daylight, Zeph, and there's a ton of people around. Stop being an idiot," I mumbled to myself.

Now wasn't the time or the place.

But later...

I dragged my soup-spattered T-shirt off and used it to wipe at a splodge of dried tomato soup on my arm.

The slam of a door had me turning back in that direction.

And then doing a double take.

Her.

The woman emerged from a second car I hadn't noticed behind the convertible, but I would have recognized her shock of reddish-golden hair anywhere.

She glanced over my face, but then looked to my chest, and then dipped her eyes to my stomach. Her gaze slowed to crawling pace, wandering over every tattoo that inked my skin.

If it had been anyone else, I would have instantly turned away and covered up.

But not her.

A shot of heat burst through me, fiery hot and unexpected, though after our encounter hours earlier, maybe I should have been prepared for the way my body reacted to hers.

It took everything in me to put on my black shirt, button it up, and slip on the white priest collar that marked me as a member of the clergy.

Her eyes widened, a blush popping up on her cheeks before she turned away.

"Father Zepherin...oh my gosh, what happened to your face?"

I dragged my gaze away from the pretty redhead in an old tracksuit and Ugg boots, to her taller friend in a flowing dress. The woman was familiar. Katherine, her name was, though I might have forgotten it if the Kat on her license plate hadn't been a helpful reminder. She was at my sermons regularly, but I had a lot of parishioners, and it wasn't easy to remember every single one of them.

I approached the woman, careful not to look at her shorter friend for fear my face would give away every thought I'd had about her in the last few hours. In the cold hard light of day, I was sure every inch of my attraction to her was written all over my expression. "Nothing exciting. I do some boxing. Not well, clearly."

Lyric snorted back a laugh. "Understatement, much? You got your behind handed to you, judging by those bruises."

Katherine admonished her with an annoyed glare but continued peppering me with questions. "Do your opponents know you're a priest? Surely punching a man of the cloth is morally wrong. I could never!"

Lyric rolled her eyes even though she wasn't directly involved in the conversation. "I don't know. I think I'd be more morally offended by someone taking three punches before they got their shit together enough to fight back. I could fight better than that in the third grade."

"Lyric! Will you please stop, for just one second?" Katherine snapped in exasperation. "Don't be so rude. I'm sure it wasn't three punches anyway."

I eyed Lyric, fighting back amusement. "My opponent this morning took me by surprise. Won't happen again."

She raised an eyebrow. "Oh yeah?"

Katherine glanced between the two of us like she was at a tennis match and eventually offered up an introduction. "Lyric, this is Father Zepherin. He's our parish priest and oversees the new daycare program."

I held my hand out to her. "You can call me Zeph."

I blinked. I had no idea where that had come from. Not one of my parishioners called me that. Nobody did, apart from friends I'd had in high school.

Lyric wasn't a friend, and somehow, with one look, I'd determined she would be.

Lyric watched me, her gaze lingering on my priest collar before she took my hand. "We've met before."

Her grip was strong, her fingers were calloused and rough, probably from pole dancing, but who knew for sure? I'd been following her for weeks but I was under no assumptions I knew this woman. The punches to the face that morning had definitely come as a surprise.

The other woman let out a tittering laugh. "Oh, I don't think so. You and Father Zepherin don't run in the same circles, I'm sure."

Katherine's tone irritated me and a strong desire to defend Lyric rose inside me. "She's right. We have met on a previous occasion. Twice, actually. Not officially though, until now."

Lyric had the grace not to say, "I told you so," to Katherine, but there was the sense of it in the air anyway.

A man reached through the middle of the two women, a little red-haired girl in his arms. "Hey," he said awkwardly. "Uh, I'm Lleyton. This is our daughter, Amelia."

Though it was clear the girl was Lyric's biological

child, Katherine beamed. "She's starting here today, and she's just a gem of a child. So smart and kind and respectful. She'll be an absolute delight."

I wasn't much of a smiler in general, but there was a soft spot in my heart for kids. Maybe because I knew I'd never have any of my own.

"Hello," I said to her, offering the little girl a high five. "I'm Father Zepherin."

She cocked her head to one side. "Father?"

I nodded.

"So I call you Daddy?"

"No, but I might," Lyric quipped beneath her breath, but plenty loud enough for all of us to hear.

Katherine choked and spluttered.

I checked to see if she was okay.

Lleyton shot Lyric a long-suffering glare.

Katherine, apparently recovered from Lyric's crassness, reached out for Amelia and took her from his arms. "Come on, sweetie. Let's go show you around and introduce you to your teachers." She shot a glare over her shoulder at Lyric. "Perhaps your mother will learn how to act appropriately while we're gone."

Katherine, Amelia, and Lleyton walked off to the daycare that ran on the church grounds, leaving me alone with Lyric.

She gazed up at me. "Sorry. Kat Wow is right. That was inappropriate and uncalled for. I'm really sorry if I made you uncomfortable. As you might remember, I kind of had a night, so can we please pretend I actually do have a brain-to-mouth filter?"

"It's fine." She wasn't the first woman to make such a comment. I heard a lot of things people thought they were keeping quiet. The parking lot outside of mass on a Sunday morning was a hive for gossip, and my name often floated back to me above the chatter.

She nudged me with her elbow. "As a priest, you're not supposed to lie, you know."

We walked side by side, slowly toward the buildings. I put my hands in my pockets, digging them in deep. "It's honestly not a problem."

She stared at me incredulously, but there was also curiosity in her eyes. "Did you not hear what I said? I totally objectified you. I'm surprised God didn't just strike me down for disrespecting you on your holy lands."

I chuckled at her dramatic ideas. "That's not really how it works."

"Still. I shouldn't have said that. My kid isn't nearly as rough around the edges as I am, I promise. Don't give her a D because I'm a dick." She clapped a hand over her mouth, then mumbled from behind it, "Sorry. Again."

I pressed my lips together to keep from smiling. "So you apologize for being crass but not for punching me in the face when I'm just trying to save you from creeps?"

She grinned. "Sounds about right."

"Duly noted." I pointed toward the childcare center that had only opened a few weeks earlier. "Would you like a tour?"

She stifled a yawn, covering her mouth with the back of her hand. "I'm sure Katherine already had someone tell her everything."

"But you're Amelia's mother. I'm sure you have questions..."

She made a little 'oh' noise when she yawned for the second time.

"...Or it can wait until pickup time, after you've had some sleep."

In the light, the dark circles beneath her eyes were evident. An uncomfortable feeling settled over me, seeing them this close up. She didn't take care of herself and didn't seem to have anyone to do it for her. I hated seeing people in need. I just wanted to fix things for them. I wanted to pick her up, tuck her against my chest, and carry her to a bed. Then stand guard outside the door for however long she slept, to keep anyone from waking her.

The idea of punishing her for not taking care of herself popped into my head again, but I banished it before I could think about all the impossible ways I'd like that scenario to play out.

Lyric nodded wearily. "I'll just say goodbye to Amelia. If you're still around this afternoon and can spare a minute to show me the place, when I can actually see through my bleary eyes, then that would be great."

I hated how exhausted she seemed. And the fact she was going to get back in her car and drive home.

But before I could voice a protest, she'd ducked inside the childcare doors. I followed close behind.

On the other side of the doors, Katherine and Lleyton were on their way out.

"She's loving it," Katherine told Lyric. "I knew she would. This center will be so much better for her, just wait and see."

Lyric's gaze bounced around the room for her daughter, but it was Katherine she spoke to. "We'll see." Her gaze flickered to Lleyton. "Do you plan on paying the bills for this one?"

He scowled at her. "You could always help, you know, if you have so many opinions on the subject."

Lyric stared down at her feet.

Lleyton sighed, his voice softening. "See you soon, okay? We need to talk about my custody arrangement."

She lifted her head sharply. "What about it?"

"It's outdated," Katherine supplied. But then she noticed I was still standing behind Lyric and cleared her throat. "Anyway, that's a private matter, best not discussed in public. We'll talk soon. But in the meantime, you're welcome."

Amelia spotted Lyric and came running, which was just as well, because Lyric looked ready to murder her ex's new partner.

I held the door open for Lleyton and Katherine, while Lyric swept Amelia into her arms.

"What do you think of this place?" she whispered. "You say the word, and I'll rustle you outta here. We'll take to the road like Thelma and Louise. Just you and me. No one will ever find us."

Amelia giggled, patting Lyric on the face. "You're silly. Can I stay? They have musical instruments, and the lady said I could choose whichever one I wanted to play."

Lyric kissed her daughter's head. "Sure thing, Slugger. You go bang some drums. I'll be back to pick you up at three."

Amelia ran off happily.

"She'll be fine," I assured Lyric.

"Oh, I know. She's my kid. She adapts to whatever is thrown at her. Doesn't mean I'm happy about the circumstances that led us here." A blush rose on her cheeks as I walked her to the door. She stopped me in the doorway.

"I want to pay half of Amelia's fees. Will that be a problem?"

I shook my head. "Not at all. We do split accounts often."

She nodded determinedly, then winced. "How much is this place?"

I reached over to a board full of pamphlets and flyers. Most were helpful tips that parents might need to know about allergies, choking, the benefits of exercise, and the like. But there was also some information on the center itself. I plucked the one with our daily fees and handed it over to her.

She glanced down at it, then her head jerked up, her eyes wide. "Are you serious?"

"Unfortunately, yes."

"Is this a daycare or college?"

I didn't disagree. The prices were ridiculous. They reflected the affluent area, the money the church had spent on the center, and the high quality of the teachers and programs that were run here. But it was an eye-watering fee. More than any of the other centers around, as far as I knew.

There was no charity from the church here.

For the most part, people seemed to like that the fees were so exorbitant. I was sure they saw it as yet another status of wealth and importance in a town that seemed to thrive on it.

But it clearly wasn't like that for Lyric.

"Lleyton and Katherine have committed to paying the full amount. You don't have to—"

She glared at me with fiery eyes. "I need to have a say in my daughter's education. I said I'll pay half." The anger dropped from her expression. "Right after I sell a kidney."

Her attitude was admirable. But it was clear this was going to put her under financial strain, and that gnawed away at me. I wanted to help her. She wasn't Tammie and her boys. She wasn't a stone's throw away from living on the streets. But she still needed help. Her ex and his girlfriend clearly got to run the show when it came to money, and that left Lyric in a vulnerable position.

I instantly knew though, if I showed up with a bag of money, perhaps gained by chopping up a certain shiny red convertible and selling it for parts, she would reject it.

Helping her wouldn't be as easy as helping Tammie.

A tattered flyer on the board caught my attention, and I pulled it down and handed it to her. "We need a cleaner, if you're interested in picking up some extra work."

She gazed down at the paper in her hand, then back up at me with a wrinkled nose. "How much does it pay?"

It paid minimum wage, because Father Byron, who oversaw all the churches in the district, was cheap.

"Not much," I admitted. "But it does come with the bonus of your children being able to attend for free."

"Seriously?"

I nodded, making a mental note to work that into the contract which currently said no such thing.

Her face fell.

"Problem? You don't have to interview. If you want the job, it's yours. We really need someone." I mentally added in, "So I can stop cleaning the bathrooms every night."

"No. No problem. It's petty, really."

"What?"

"Promise you won't judge me."

I raised three fingers. "Scout's honor."

"A part of me wants to say no, because then Lleyton doesn't have to pay for anything. He doesn't pay me child support. He's supposed to, but I made a deal with him that he didn't have to if he got Amelia into daycare in Providence. In hindsight, that was stupid. It gave him total control over her education, and that's too big a thing to let him make all the decisions on." She looked me up and down. "No offence, but if I'd had a say in it, I wouldn't have put my kid into daycare here with all the Jesus loving. I'm kind of an atheist."

"I respect that."

Her eyebrow shot sky-high. "You aren't going to try to convince me otherwise?"

"No. What and who you believe in isn't my business."

"Huh. I thought it was your job to turn me into a believer."

I could understand why. So many religious people did push their beliefs onto others. I wasn't one of them. "People make lots of assumptions about priests, Lyric. Most don't come close to being the truth."

People assumed priests were all good, noble, and holy. Sometimes that was the truth. Some of the people I'd met after joining the priesthood were good right down to their toes.

But there were always rotten apples.

Men who used their positions of power for evil instead of good.

They could stare you right in the eye, smile, and preach from their Bibles. Everyone assumed they were decent, humble men.

Lies. All of it.

Not that I could talk.

I was sure people looked at me and took in the priest collar, the neat, tidy clothes, and quiet demeanor, and assumed I was one of the good ones too.

Not a man who'd put his hands around a priest's throat two nights earlier and squeezed until the color drained from his face. And not a man who had the most impure thoughts about a woman.

Everybody had their secrets. Including me.

"Take the job, and the free care. Open a new bank account and give me the number. I'll have Lleyton put his payments into that. Consider it child support."

Her mouth dropped open. "What? That's illegal."

So were a lot of things I did in the name of righting wrongs. "I know," I said simply.

She took a step back, holding up one hand. "What's the catch?" She eyed me up and down, suddenly wary of me. "You aren't just going to take that money and put it in my account without me owing you something." Her gaze narrowed. "I won't suck your dick, if that's what you're thinking."

"You won't…" I squinted at her. "Why would you think I want that? You're doing me a favor in cleaning this place. I'm doing you one in return."

Getting a blow job hadn't been my intention. Far from it.

But now the idea planted itself in my head, in bold, vibrant color. What she'd look like, kneeling before me, submissive and sweet, naked, her lips slightly parted, ready for me.

I squeezed my eyes shut, sucking in a sharp breath. "I just want to help."

It was all I ever wanted. To be the sort of person who did good and helped make this fucked-up world a little bit better for the people who deserved it.

Lleyton and Katherine could keep their obnoxious convertible if Lyric let me help her in this way instead. The legalities of it didn't concern me. As far as I was concerned, I was in the right here. I was settling a wrong. Giving a woman and her child what should have been freely given from the girl's father.

God would have liked that, I think.

It was a selfless act.

Apart from the fact getting to see Lyric every day felt like the most selfish, decadent act of all.

5

ZEPH

Father Byron's elderly mother was a regular at our meetings. The woman had to be in her eighties but took the greatest pride in serving each of her son's friends homemade cupcakes and little sandwiches cut into triangles. She moved around the room quietly while he read from the Bible, insisting that each of us try the food she'd prepared.

I thanked her profusely, taking one of each when she offered the tray to me. "These are going to be delicious, Nancy. You take care of us too well."

The woman flushed pink at my compliment, then an odd shade of blue, followed by red. It took me a second to realize it wasn't her but police lights flashing around the room, illuminating the aging faces around me.

Father Byron paused in his scripture reading and glanced out the window. "What's going on out there? Is that the police?"

He stood and crossed to the window, while the rest of us stayed in our seats as obediently as if we were children and he our headmaster. A frown deepened the lines on his forehead.

"Are they headed into Saint View again?" Father Peter called out. "I hear there's been a lot of trouble there lately. Gangs and shootings and undesirables."

There was a ripple of agreement from the other men in the room, and I forced myself to nod along so as to not draw attention to myself. There were 'undesirables' everywhere. The only difference between here and Saint View was the police tended to overlook the crimes committed by people who could afford to pay them off.

Father Byron shook his head. "There's two officers coming to the door." He brushed his hands over his knitted cardigan. "Everybody, sit tight. You'll perhaps use this time to pray."

I narrowed my gaze in on the backs of his hands, covered with dark hair.

Just like the guy from the Strip who'd followed Lyric.

Father Peter, older than me by at least forty years, snapped his fingers in front of my face.

I blinked at him, noticing the dark hair on the back of his hand too, and frowned. Clearly that was something that happened as men aged, and not a telltale sign that someone was a perverted creep who followed women home from strip clubs.

I rolled my head to crack my neck, releasing some of the tension.

I tended to keep to myself as much as possible, never quite feeling like I one-hundred-percent fit in because I was so much younger than most of the others, but if I was to say I had friends, Peter and Byron were the two I would have said came closest. I liked them both. They were committed to their faith and welcoming to all, including me, the young, messed-up asshole who'd arrived on their doorstep four years ago, completely and utterly lost and in desperate need of guidance. They'd taken me in without question, and I owed them a lot for the fact I was even still here, when I'd been so intent on ending it all.

Shame crept up the back of my neck for even considering either of them were anything but what they appeared, hairy hands or not.

Father Peter looked at me questioningly.

"I'm sorry," I murmured, rubbing my fingers absently along the rope I'd taken to keeping in my pocket at all times. It reminded me of Lyric. Of protecting her. It was an odd thing to find comfort in, but I was well aware not many of the things I did were considered normal. "Did you ask me something? I wasn't paying attention."

He jerked his head toward the door Father Byron had left through to greet the approaching police officers. "What do you think that's all about?"

I lifted a shoulder in a shrug. "I've no idea. Can't be anything good."

He clasped his hands together and bowed his head. "You're right. We should pray while we wait. Just like Byron said."

I mirrored his actions, dropping my gaze obediently, but prayers weren't on my mind.

Getting out of here and back to the church because Lyric would be cleaning there was though. We'd agreed she'd either clean before or after her shifts at the club. She already had someone lined up for the evenings, and extending her hours slightly wouldn't be too inconvenient.

But the only gloves we had were sized to fit my hands. I'd need to stop off at the store and get her a pair that would fit her. I wished I knew what sort of snacks and drinks she liked. I'd get an array of different ones while I was there, so she had a choice.

A throat clearing from the doorway caught my attention.

"Excuse me for interrupting your prayers," Father Byron announced, with two burly police officers standing behind him. "But the gentleman from Providence PD would like a word." He stepped aside, motioning for the officers to enter the room.

The uniformed man, probably in his mid-fifties with a pot belly straining at his shirt buttons, moved to the front. "It's good I've caught you all here at once. I was prepared to come see all of you individually because this matter is of some importance."

I forced my face to remain neutral, but I had a feeling I knew what his next words would be.

"We found the body of a man yesterday. He's been identified as Father Simon Collier."

A shocked gasp rippled around the room, and too slowly, I added a fake one of my own.

"We'd wondered where he was," Father Peter spoke up. "He was supposed to be here at this meeting."

They might have wondered, but I hadn't. I knew the man was cold and limp in the morgue, probably awaiting an autopsy. I was surprised it had taken this long for someone to notify us.

Of course, I wasn't going to say any of that. "What happened?" I asked instead, over the top of the upset murmurs of the other men.

The officer glanced over at me. "His cause of death has not officially been confirmed, but all signs point to foul play. We believe him to be murdered. Strangled in the same way of Father—"

"Jones," Byron said on a hushed whisper. "Father Jones was strangled. God rest his soul."

We all made the sign of the cross hastily. Me, because any mention of Jones and his penchant for altar boys made my skin crawl. He'd been my first kill, and frankly, it was a little annoying to not be able to brag about it. If they all knew what he'd done, they'd be throwing me a parade for removing his pathetic existence.

Officer Johnson nodded, mouth pulled into a grim line. "Yes. One murder we wouldn't make any assumptions, but two priests gone, and we have to consider that your profession is being targeted."

I fought back the urge to scoff. I was hardly targeting the profession. The profession was just fine. But Jones had a computer full of rage-inducing images of children doing things no child should ever be forced to do. And Collier? Well, that teenager who had come to confession, crying and thinking she was the problem? I couldn't allow him to do that again.

It was dramatic of them to assume I was some sort of priest serial killer though.

"We'd like you all to consider not going out alone, or at night. I'm recommending security be increased at all sites..."

The officer droned on with his warnings, but I'd already lost interest and was ready to wrap this thing up.

"There's no need to fear, brothers. If we are good and true at heart, God will see that and protect us."

The officer frowned in my direction, but the others all nodded at my words.

"Father Zepherin is right. The Lord will see the danger and protect those who believe." Byron tipped his head in my direction, a silent show of appreciation for my efforts to calm the men.

Even after years of training, I found statements like that difficult to comprehend, but I truly knew no one here, doing the right thing, had anything to worry about.

I pushed to my feet, regarding the men remaining in the room. "I have other obligations tonight, gentlemen. If we're done here, I need to be on my way. We have a new cleaner starting, and I need to be there to show her around."

Father Byron glanced at Officer Johnson, who dismissed me with a flick of his hairy hand. I shook my head in wonder as I left the room. Was that what I had to look forward to in my later years? Growing copious amounts of hair in places I didn't really want it? Odd the things you don't notice, until you do.

I drove straight to a store I knew stayed open late and grabbed a cart from their designated position near the entrance. Leaning heavily on the handles, I meandered around the store, buying gloves and snacks and drinks for Lyric. There were few people here at this time of night, but I took my time, knowing I wouldn't be able to sleep once I went home anyway.

My little church in Providence was cloaked in darkness when I arrived. The daycare had long closed, and all masses had been wrapped up hours earlier. All parishioners had left the premises, and I was officially off the clock until I had to meet Lyric in the early hours of the morning.

My heart stopped when I spotted her, waiting on the doorstep, her face lit up only by the dull light of her phone. I stopped in my tracks. "What are you doing here?"

She jerked her head up. "'Bout time you showed up. I've been knocking for ten minutes. I was just about to call you!"

I checked my watch, but it definitely said 9:00 p.m. "I thought you were coming after your shift?"

"I left a message on the church's answering service. Eve said I could start late. The place has been dead lately, so she has it covered. I assumed you'd be here."

"I didn't get your message. I'm sorry. I was out."

She eyed the shopping bags clutched in my hands. "Clearly, but no harm, no foul. You do your own shopping?"

I squinted at her. "Of course. Why wouldn't I?"

She looked me up and down. "Honestly? I kind of thought people would just bring stuff to you. Like all your God-loving groupies who live to serve you. Or you'd have some...heavenly messenger who delivered." She laughed at her own ridiculousness.

It amused me, too. "I do consider Uber Eats a heavenly messenger some nights."

She grinned. "Me too. Man, me too. Nothing better than getting Thai food delivered to your door at eleven at night when you have a craving." She rubbed at her bare arms briskly in the cool night air. "So, I can start now, right? You aren't going to make me come back at our scheduled time?"

I narrowed my gaze on the goosebumps popping up on her bare skin. She was dressed in casual shorts and a T-shirt, one with bleach spots giving away they were her cleaning clothes. But it wasn't summer anymore, and though it rarely, if ever, snowed in Providence or Saint View, that didn't mean you could wear beach gear year-round.

"You're cold," I accused, ignoring her question.

She glanced down at her arms wrapped around her middle. Like her posture was a surprise. "A bit," she admitted. "But I'll warm up as soon as I have a mop in my hand. Want to give me the lowdown?"

I couldn't stop staring at her clearly chilled arms. It riled up that idea I'd had earlier, that she wasn't looking out for herself. An urge to demand she pay attention to her own body and needs rose in me, but I already knew her well enough to know she'd argue with me if I made my accusations out loud.

That would drive me insane. I dropped my shopping bags to the ground at my feet and shrugged out of my lightweight jacket. "Here."

She shook her head. "No, seriously, I'm fine."

I didn't move my hand.

She quirked an eyebrow at me. "I said, I'm fine."

But an involuntary shiver gave away that she was bluffing.

I clenched my fingers into the fabric of the jacket because putting her over my lap and spanking her ass 'til it was pink wasn't an option. Nor were any of the other ways I wanted to punish her.

We were at odds, neither of us willing to back down.

Slowly, a smile crept across her pretty face. "I'm really annoying you right now, aren't I?"

"A bit," I admitted.

She reached up and slapped me gently a couple of times on the cheek. "Get used to it, Zephy. I'm a hard pill to swallow."

She ducked beneath my arm to grab the shopping bags full of cleaning supplies from the ground and strode across the lawn to the church. "I'll start in here."

Had she really just called me Zephy? I had never been called that in my life. Zeph, sure, but only rarely and by friends I'd lost contact with once I'd joined the church. To my family and parishioners I was always Zepherin.

I followed her in some sort of Lyric-whirlwind shock, and by the time I got out the key to the church door, she was already rifling through the bag of supplies I'd bought.

"Ugh. Pine-scented disinfectant, Zeph? Worst scent in my opinion. But oh! Purple gloves? That's my favorite color, you know?"

I knew. Or at least, I'd assumed. She often came out of the club wearing purple sweatshirts or pants. "So, this is the church," I said dumbly, but thinking clearly around her wasn't easy. I pulled out a cloth. "Sorry about the pine scent. I didn't know it offended you. Here. I'll help."

She snatched it out of my hand. "No, you won't. I'm here to do a job and get paid for it."

"I didn't mean I wouldn't pay you."

"No, but I can't take it from you if I don't feel like I earned it."

"Admirable, but I don't mind. I have nothing else to do tonight."

She'd already spritzed the liquid all over the first pew and was busily wiping it down with a cloth. "Go watch TV or read a book."

She was more interesting than either of those options, not that I could say that. "It's your first night..."

She stopped her scrubbing and lifted her gaze to meet mine. "Scared I'm going to steal from your piggy bank?"

I blanched. "What? No. Not at all." She might have been broke and from Saint View, but I instinctually knew Lyric wasn't a thief.

Thieves could spot other thieves a mile away.

She shoved her hands on the curve of her hips. "Zeph, if you just want to hang out 'cause your perfectly priestly house is boring, you can just say so."

I stifled a smile. "It's not boring. Just—"

"Lonely?"

I nodded.

Something in her softened. "Fine." She pointed to the pew she'd just cleaned. "Sit. Talk while I work. I forgot my headphones anyway."

I didn't like she wasn't letting me help. But I sat where she indicated and held onto the hard wooden pew so my fingers wouldn't go searching for a rag to help her dust.

Her gaze narrowed in on my hands wrapped around the seat either side of me.

Blushing, I pulled my sleeve down to cover up the tattoo that wound itself around my wrist and edged the back of my hand.

"Why did you become a priest?" She looked away, like she knew she might be crossing a line but still really wanted to know.

Clearly, I hadn't been quick enough to cover up the tat. The thing always invited conversation I didn't particularly want to have. So I said nothing. The silence drew out between us, only the squeaks of her cleaning cloth filling the air.

"Touchy subject?"

"Yes."

I assumed that would be enough for her to just let the subject drop. That's what other people did.

But Lyric watched me while she dusted, the curiosity in her expression only intensifying. "So just say yes or no to my questions then. Okay? Good."

She hadn't even given me a chance to respond before she continued.

"You came from a churchy background?"

I could tell she wasn't going to take my silence on the matter as an answer. "True."

She nodded. "Thought as much. Your parents are probably front row at all your sermons in their Sunday best, am I right? Married for decades. Three grown kids with probably a grandkid or two. Nice house with a dog in the backyard, somewhere in Providence?"

That was pretty much my family to a T. She even had the details, right down to my older brother, Jonathan, my sister, Kelly, and her tribe of kids. It wasn't the entire story, of course. Because nobody's life was as perfect as they made out, but she wasn't far off. "True."

Her grin was triumphant, like she was enjoying figuring me out with next to no help from me. "You became a priest because you love God so much you never imagined doing anything else?"

Oh, if only that were true. "Not exactly."

She cocked her head to one side in surprise. "Really? You wanted to be something other than a priest?"

If she'd started her cleaning in my quarters, she would have worked that out sooner probably. Though I'd tucked my finished pieces away from prying eyes, the evidence of their existence was still in my room for people to see. There was no hiding the huge bag of clay I'd purchased, or the kiln I had set up. "I wanted to be an artist."

"You paint?"

"Sculpt, mostly."

"I'd love to see your work sometime."

Heat flushed through me at the thought of showing her the pieces I'd worked on lately. That was never going to happen.

She clapped her gloved hands together, temporarily abandoning her scrubbing in favor of working me out. "Okay, the art thing caught me by surprise but still doesn't solve the mystery of why you joined the church. You're secretly gay and don't want to admit it?"

"No. But I've much respect for the LGBTQ community."

"Isn't that against your beliefs?

I sighed because she wasn't entirely wrong. If I had been gay, it would have been a problem for my family, and for all their friends, most of whom were members of the church community. I heard the comments some of the other priests made, mostly out of fear and ignorance, their justifications weak at best. "Depends on your interpretation of the Bible, I guess. I choose to embrace all members of my flock."

Unless one was a horrible human being and strayed too far. Then I had no problem ending them.

Which made me a horrible human being who should probably see himself out. But I couldn't help the lack of guilt I felt over it. I'd never once hurt a person who didn't deserve much worse. I'd taken from the rich to give to people like Tammie and Lyric, women who society held down and took advantage of.

"Ah, so you embrace all the chicks then? Not just me? The old birds get your attention too?" She laughed at her own joke.

"Chicks, old birds, flock. Very funny, Lyric," I deadpanned.

She laughed harder at my response before pulling herself together. "Okay, okay. So you just decided to ditch art and become a celibate priest? There was nothing that prompted it?"

No. There had been a prompt. One so powerful it had sent me straight to the church's door in the pouring rain, begging for forgiveness. I forced the memories of that night away, pushing them back into the dark, twisted depths of my soul where I'd fought to keep them locked for the longest time.

I was safe within the walls of the church. Safe behind vows of poverty and celibacy.

What I was doing here with Lyric wasn't safe at all.

It was dancing a line of danger, playing with a fire that was going to burn us both.

And yet she was so much like Annie I couldn't stop.

I didn't want to play her game anymore. She was edging too close to the truth. Stoking the embers until they'd erupt into flames. "Why did you become a stripper?"

The words came out harsher than I'd intended. Deflecting from her questions about me. Heat burned the back of my neck, both in embarrassment and irritation with myself for letting her get so close.

She heard it. The change in my tone.

Her eyes narrowed. "I don't need your judgment."

Her sharp words were a reminder it was me in the wrong here. Me who'd let her in only to slam down the doors when she got too close to the truth. It wasn't her. I ran a hand through my hair, frustrated and angry with myself. "I'm the last person to judge you. We're all sinners."

That clearly wasn't the right thing to say either.

She bristled visibly, putting the cleaning liquid down with a jolt. "I'm not hurting anyone. I take my clothes off for men, and I dance. That's it. I'm hardly out on the street shooting drugs into the arms of prostitutes and pimping them out for money." She glared at me with fire in her gaze. "I'm not lying or cheating or stealing or murdering."

I wished I could say the same.

6

LYRIC

Mondays and Tuesdays were my normal nights off from the club. But Tuesdays were family night, and Eve put on a big meal for anyone she deemed special. She'd cook her ass off for hours before, and I always felt like an asshole if I didn't show. Plus, it was important for Amelia to be surrounded by so many adults who loved her. If Gran was having a good day, it got her out of the apartment too. Sometimes Eve would sing with her band, and you never knew who would turn up, so it was always interesting.

It meant Mondays were really the only night I had at home with Amelia and Gran. But I didn't even really have that anymore since I now had to go clean at the church. At least it was only for an hour or two, and Zeph was flexible on what time I got there each day, as long as the work got done.

I was in a good mood when I got a text from Zeph, asking me to meet him at the store that evening instead of at the church. So I sent him back a thumbs-up emoji without really thinking about it while I picked Amelia up from daycare. I glanced over in the direction of Zeph's house on the church grounds, but his car was missing from the driveway, so he probably wasn't home.

Amelia sprinted across the daycare to throw herself at my legs, her happy little face beaming up at me. "Hi, Mommy. What's for dinner?"

I hadn't even thought about that yet, though the question did make me cringe internally because I knew there wasn't much in the refrigerator, and I'd made chump change all last week at the club. I was hanging out for my church payment to come in, which Zeph had said would happen at the end of the month.

I'd forgotten how much it sucked to have to wait for a paycheck. I'd spent years picking up mine off the club stage or plucking it from my G-string.

I patted Amelia's sweet head. "I don't know, Slugger. I'll work something out."

Amelia's teacher, a short-haired, middle-aged woman who had a penchant for pearls and wore them daily, smiled at me. "I'm sure whatever you make will be delicious and full of healthy vegetables that Amelia will just gobble up."

Amelia crinkled her nose.

I fought the urge to do the same. "Thanks for today. See you tomorrow."

"Oh, wait, Lyric." The woman grabbed my arm.

I stopped, waiting for her to explain.

She dropped her hand from my biceps and picked up a leaf of paper, handing it over to me with her wide teacher smile firmly in place. "I wanted to give you this. It's information about our dress-up day on Friday."

Amelia jumped up and down, babbling in excitement and twisting my arm to try to look at the paper while I tried to do the same. "Wait a second, kid. I gotta read it first." I skimmed over the paper, irritation prickling at me with every line. I wanted to groan. "She needs a costume that represents her emotions?" I was sure my forehead was so furrowed with lines I'd need a shot of Botox. "What exactly does that mean?"

The woman laughed like I wasn't being completely serious.

I just stared at her until her laughter died off.

"Oh, you know, get her to use her creativity. We really want this to be a project both parents and their children work on together."

"So no just ducking into Walmart for a Spider-Man costume then?"

The woman laughed even harder. "Oh gosh, no, can you imagine? What would that teach them?"

"That Marvel rocks," I muttered, shoving the paper into my back pocket.

"What was that?"

I forced a smile as fake as hers. This was the downside of sending my kid to a fancy-pants school, and now I was going to have to suck it up and deal. "I said I can't wait to get into it. Amelia's costume will be the best you've ever seen."

Amelia let out a cheer, and the smile I gave her was genuine.

We were halfway across the parking lot when my phone rang, my neighbor's name flashing up on the screen. Dread swamped me, and I stabbed at the 'answer' button frantically. She never called me, not unless Gran was causing a problem. "Geraldine? What's wrong? Is she okay?"

"She's fine, but I just wanted to find out which days you'll need me next week because Jordan has a week full of practices and appointments. I don't want to leave you high and dry, but I really don't think I'll be around much. Can Peggy help?"

I sank into the driver's seat and dropped my head down onto the steering wheel. "All week? That sucks."

Geraldine felt bad, I knew, but there was nothing she could do about it.

"It's okay," I assured her. "I'll work something out. You're still good for tonight, though? It's just an hour or two while I'm at work."

"Yep, no problem. I'll turn the monitor on."

We'd hooked up a baby monitor so Geraldine could still be at her place while Gran and Amelia slept. Nine times out of ten, neither would make a peep, but the monitor meant my neighbor could just duck over if either of them woke.

Gran looked at me in confusion when we walked through the door, but her face lit up when she spotted Amelia. "Lyric! How was school?"

The sadness hit me in the gut like a freight train. Peggy had said just last week that Gran was getting worse, and here was the proof of it, right in my face yet again.

Amelia's expression turned sad. "I'm Amelia, Nanny. Not Lyric. That's Lyric." She pointed up at me.

"Hey, Gran." I lifted a hand in a half-hearted wave.

Gran's face furrowed in confusion, but then she laughed and hushed my daughter. "Silly girl. Always trying to trick me. Tell me how your day was."

Amelia launched into tales of crafts and writing practice and sensory play, while I tried to fight down a wave of exhaustion. By the time I met Zeph at the store, I was in a foul mood, annoyed with everyone and everything and wishing I could just take a holiday from my life. I followed him down the cleaning product aisle, dragging my feet as exhaustion and sadness and decision fatigue consumed me.

"Lemon lime or strawberry sunburst scent?" Zeph held up two bottles of disinfectant for my inspection.

I stared at him. Why the hell was he asking me? Why was I even here? This was a ridiculous waste of time to end a day that had already been spectacularly shitty.

"What?" he asked. "Would you prefer wild berry? They have that too."

I couldn't make another decision today. I just couldn't. The ticking time bomb inside me exploded. "You know what?" I threw my hands up in the air. "I don't care, Zeph! I don't care if you pick tutti-fucking-fruitti and wear it as aftershave. I don't care if they have five hundred different scents. It's the stuff we clean the damn toilets with, they're going to smell like shit no matter what you do. So please. For the love of your fucking God, can you just decide yourself?"

It was really my gran or Amelia or Amelia's teacher or my neighbor, or a combination of all four who had built me up to this point, but I couldn't yell at any of them. Amelia was a baby. My grandmother didn't understand. It was my choice to send Amelia to a school that had high expectations, and I had to deal with the repercussions. I certainly couldn't yell at Geraldine next door when she was helping me out.

But Zeph? I could yell at him.

And apparently, I had. Loud enough for the entire store to hear, because every person within earshot was staring in our direction.

Zeph put two bottles of disinfectant back on the shelf and focused on me. "I only asked because you said you didn't like the one we have at the church." Concern was written all over his face. Not anger that I had just yelled at him in the middle of a supermarket. Not embarrassment or irritation because he had done nothing except try to do something nice for me.

It was as bad as kicking a puppy. I may as well have kicked him right in the balls. I hadn't even considered he might have brought me down here so I could choose a scent I liked better than the obnoxious pine that churned my stomach.

I groaned out loud and buried my face in my hands. "Ugh, Zeph. Can you just argue back?"

He leaned on the shelving, blocking me from view of the other shoppers. "I suppose I could. Or you could just tell me what's wrong." He threw me a smile, even though I was being a bitch.

"You're painfully nice."

"That's what's wrong? I'm too nice to argue with you?"

I shook my head. My damn eyes felt like someone had rubbed them with sandpaper. "I just want someone else to make decisions for me once in a while. I have so many to make, all the damn time. What's for dinner? What will Amelia wear for her daycare dress-up day? What am I going to do with my gran when she forgets me entirely?" A sob welled up in my throat at that thought, but I swallowed it down before it could set my eyes to watering. I wouldn't cry. Not in front of Zeph. Not in front of anyone. Crying was something I didn't do. Ever.

Zeph picked up the lemon-lime-scented cleaner and added it to his cart. He steered it wordlessly toward the checkouts and started scanning his purchases.

I followed along miserably, feeling like an asshole who was very probably going to lose her job.

When he'd finished paying, we went out to the parking lot, Zeph following me to my car. I opened it and slid behind the wheel.

He braced his hands above me on the doorjamb and leaned down so we were eye height. "Lyric."

I didn't even want to look at him. I'd yelled at the poor man. Not even just a man. A softly spoken priest, no less, in front of a supermarket full of people.

"Lyric. Look at me."

It wasn't a question. It wasn't even a request. It was a growl of a demand that relaxed something inside me so much it was almost pleasurable.

I did as I was told. For once, I shut my mouth, didn't argue back, and did as someone told me to.

His eyes were beautiful. I hadn't really noticed them before, but the color was startling up close, a deep brown that was nearly as dark as his pupils. He smelled good too, like he'd showered before coming down here. The corner of my eye caught another tattoo creeping out of the neckline of his shirt.

Another one.

I so wanted to know how many he had. Whether they covered his body or if the one on his arm and this new one were his only two. I'd gotten a glimpse of him in the parking lot a few days back, but it hadn't been enough to properly document his art collection.

"You're not working tonight."

His statement shook me out of my tattoo wondering. "No," I confirmed. "It's my night off from the club. I just have the church to do."

He shook his head. "I know that. But that's not what I meant. You're taking the night off."

I opened my mouth to protest, but he held up a hand. "Don't. You're going to go home, run a bubble bath, soak in it, and then you're going to go to bed. You're going to sleep. For as long as you need to."

I fought off a sigh, because that sounded like a luxury I could only dream of. But it couldn't happen. "Amelia has daycare in the morning."

"I'll be there to get her ready and drop her off."

I frowned. "What?"

"You heard me."

I had, but I just couldn't quite comprehend the words. "Why?"

"Why?" He seemed confused. "Because you're so exhausted and overwhelmed that you yelled at a priest in the middle of a supermarket." The corner of his mouth flickered up cheekily.

I squinted at him. "I did do that, didn't I?"

He nodded. "Can you please let me help? Amelia knows me. I'm at the daycare center every day. She won't be scared. But I am scared of the state you're working yourself into."

"I'm fine."

"Lying to a priest now?"

I chuckled.

He reached over and rubbed his thumb over my lip with a smile on his.

Both of us froze.

Me, because his touch sent tingles straight from my mouth, all the way south until they settled in a very unholy position.

Him because, well, probably because he'd just touched me pretty intimately.

He coughed, turning away quickly. "I'll be there at six. You better be fast asleep and smelling of raspberry bubbles." He stepped back and closed the door.

It hit the frame of the car with a thud that I felt right through my very confused body.

"I don't have any raspberry bubbles," I said softly, eyes trained on the big man whose secrets I really wanted to know.

He reached into his shopping bag and pulled out a red bottle. 'Raspberry scented bubble bath' was printed on the label. "Now you do."

I went home, tagged out Geraldine, and checked on Amelia and my gran, all with the bottle of bubbles clutched in my fingers. Both my grandmother and daughter slept peacefully, their breathing even and steady. The apartment was quiet, for once, the rough neighborhood outside was calm, and I was essentially alone.

I hadn't taken a bath in years. My showers were short and functional, never a time for relaxation because I was always in a hurry and so short on free time it was sob-worthy. If I lingered in the shower, it was only because I was washing my hair, which was so long now that task took forever, or shaving my legs.

I wanted sleep. My bed was calling me.

But Zeph's demands burned my ears. Somehow, I knew that if I didn't take the bath, he'd know.

I slipped into the bathroom, quietly closing the door behind me, then turned to the faucet. Water filled the tub slowly, and I squeezed a generous dollop of the red bubble mixture beneath the flow. The scent rose instantly, deliciously fruity. I trailed my fingers through the warm, soapy water and decided Zeph had excellent ideas and taste in bath fragrances.

I stood to pull my shirt over my head, my sweatpants and underwear following to the floor straight after. Before the bath was even full, I stepped in and sank down into the warmth of the sudsy water.

It was bliss.

Pure, freaking, warm, nice-smelling bliss, even if the bath itself was a little on the small side. It was nothing that couldn't be corrected by bending my knees so I could sink my shoulders right down.

I tipped my head back, resting it on the rounded porcelain edge, and stared up at the yellowing ceiling that really needed a fresh coat of paint I couldn't afford. "Good idea, Zeph," I said to the quiet room. "Great, even."

If he showed up and got Amelia ready for school tomorrow morning, he might even become my new favorite person.

I ran my hands beneath my arms and behind my knees, washing the day's grime from my body. I swept my fingers across my abdomen, then higher across my breasts.

I shuddered at the touch of slippery, soapy fingers on aching nipples.

How long had it been since I'd had sex?

I couldn't even remember. It was an embarrassingly long time, that much was for sure. It had been weeks since I'd even had a chance to make myself come. There was always somebody here, either my gran or Amelia or the hired help. And I shared my room with a four-year-old. It wasn't like I ever had the chance to go out and get laid. Or even have a little solo pleasure time.

But Zeph had forced it on me today. He hadn't specifically said, "Go make yourself come, Lyric. You're a grumpy bitch who needs the release." Hell, as a priest, he probably knew next to nothing about female orgasms. A total waste when the man looked the way he did. But I had the opportunity now, and if I didn't take it, how long would it be before I got another? My pussy would probably have grown a new hymen by that point.

I tweaked my nipple, enjoying the feel of my body lighting up, even if it was at my own hands and not at Zeph's.

I froze at the thought.

Not a partner.

Zeph.

Oh, I was so going to Hell. It was one thing to dream about the man with his broad shoulders and secret tattoos and sweetly sexy eyes. That was out of my control. I couldn't help what my subconscious did while I was asleep.

But masturbating while I thought about him? That was an entirely different sort of sin.

Eh. I was an atheist anyway, so that probably meant I didn't believe in sins or Heaven or Hell.

I couldn't stop thinking about him.

I slipped a hand beneath the water and between my thighs. I was hair-free down there, you had to be in my line of work. My knees dropped outward so they rested on the sides of the bath, and I found my clit.

Closing my eyes, I imagined my hand was Zeph's, his strong fingers rubbing my most sensitive of places. The reality was the man probably had no idea where a clit was, but in my head, he knew exactly what he was doing. He clamped one hand on my thigh, holding my legs open to him while he drank in the sight of my wet, slicked pussy.

I let out a tiny moan, rubbing my clit harder until I had to throw an arm over my face to muffle the sounds I was making. I ached to be filled. Ached for Zeph to slide into the bath with me, wrap my legs around his hips, and plunge inside me.

I made do with my fingers, two of them reaching inside to stroke my G-spot. A shudder racked my body, one desperately filled with need. I ground down on my fingers and bit my lip so I could use my other hand to go back to my clit. The two movements combined dragged every ounce of tension from my body. An orgasm spiraled up from somewhere deep inside me, and I drew it out, slowing my movement, playing with myself because in my head, it was Zeph, and I didn't want it to end.

He'd be big. The man was huge, and I knew his cock would be too. In a bath together I'd be able to see every inch of him, every tattoo on display for me to admire and trace and lick.

I imagined his tongue tracing my tattoos, especially the one that trailed down my hip bones to swirl across my mound.

I dunked my head beneath the water while I came, so I didn't wake the house with shouts of pleasure. The water sloshed around me as my orgasm barreled through, igniting every nerve ending, warming its way through my body like silk.

I fell asleep that night with relaxed muscles, warm tingles, and a beautiful, but completely off-limits man on my mind.

7

ZEPH

I didn't need to search for Lyric's address on her employment paperwork. I'd followed her home from the club enough times to recognize the run-down apartments she called home, but I'd never gotten this close. Normally I parked down the street but today I stopped in front of the building and eyed the bottom floor, which I knew to be her place.

It wasn't safe. That was a glaring red flag that caused the hairs on the back of my neck to stand up straight. In the cold hard light of day, the building was in even worse state than I'd first imagined. Windows were broken and hastily boarded up. A burned-out car shell was abandoned on the sidewalk. Old mattresses and couches were piled up to the side of the door, left by tenants who probably couldn't afford removal services.

It was bleak and made my sparsely furnished home at the church seem like a palace.

I got out of the car and picked my way across the uneven path, frowning at the complete lack of security to the building. There were no locks, no buzzers, no gates or codes. "Jesus Christ, Lyric," I muttered, not caring that I was taking the Lord's name in vain since there was no one here to reprimand me for it.

No wonder she was as tough as she was. She had to be to survive in this environment.

Her windows faced the street, so with a bit of mental math, I worked out which door was hers and rapped my knuckles quietly over the wood.

Noises floated out from within, including an old Elvis Presley song, the running of little feet, and an argument between two women, one who sounded suspiciously like Lyric, despite me telling her to sleep in this morning.

It was 6:00 a.m. No person sleeping in should be awake right now.

Sure enough, when the door flew open, it was Lyric standing there, her long hair pulled up in a messy bun, soft tendrils falling around her face. She was makeup-free, fresh-faced, and clearly not wearing a bra beneath her thin sleep top. Her pert pink nipples hardened beneath my gaze before I could drag my eyes back up to her face.

Fuck.

She had one eyebrow raised, zero shame that I'd caused a reaction in her, but clearly bemused by the fact I'd been looking in the first place.

Instead of trying to explain myself, I moved past her, put my sunglasses down on her kitchen counter, and barked out a question to cover the fact my cock would have liked me to stare some more. "Why are you awake?"

She shoved one hand on the curve of her hip, which I tried not to notice. The more I got to know her, the more I realized she was very different from Annie. Lyric had freckles across the bridge of her nose that Annie had never had. Lyric had curves in places that did things to me, where Annie had been more straight up and down. And Lyric had a sass and confidence about her that Annie would never have in a million years. Their hair and eyes might have been the same color, and they might have both had similar features, but beneath those surface qualities, the two women were night and day.

Except in the way I was attracted to them. Annie a long, long time ago, though sometimes it felt like yesterday. Lyric right here and right now, and just as intense, for the short time I'd known her.

"I'm not used to relying on anyone, Zeph. How was I supposed to know you'd actually show?"

I ground my molars. "I keep my word."

She looked me up and down, a slow appraisal that left me breathing faster than normal.

I was playing with fire with her. I'd known that from the moment I'd laid eyes on her and yet I couldn't stop.

"I guess you do," she said quietly.

"Daddy Zepherin!" Amelia screeched, spotting me from a bedroom just off the main living area which also housed the kitchen. She came running out in My Little Pony pajamas, her red hair almost as wild as her mother's. She stopped short in front of me and peered up with a wide grin full of cute baby teeth.

"Father Zepherin," I corrected her gently, high-fiving her and ignoring Lyric's quiet laughter at her daughter's slip. "But when we aren't at school, you can just call me Zeph like your mommy does."

"Mommy might like to call you Daddy, too, if you

keep staring at her the way you did just now," Lyric muttered.

I glanced over at her with a raised eyebrow of my own, and she laughed some more, holding up her hands in mock surrender. "Inappropriate, I know. I'll see myself out."

"How about you see yourself to your bedroom."

She raised a flirty eyebrow back at me.

Christ. "To sleep, Lyric." I turned away and gazed down at Amelia before Lyric could notice the blush creeping up my cheeks. "Can I take you to school today, little one?"

"I'm not little." She shoved her hands on her hips, in much the same way Lyric was fond of, and pouted at me.

"You're right. You're not, I only meant it as a nickname."

"Mommy calls me Slugger."

"Do you like that?"

She nodded. "'Cause slugs are cute and so I am."

Lyric ruffled her daughter's already messed-up hair. "You think I call you Slugger 'cause you look like a garden worm? You're way cuter than those slimy things. Slugger is just a term of affection. My grandad used to call me that, and I thought it suited you better than a girly nick-name like princess."

Amelia batted her mother's hand away from her hair but spoke with all the love and affection in the world. "You're a Slugger too, Mommy. Percival girls are tough."

"And cute like slugs, apparently," I added in.

"Did you just call me cute, Father Zepherin?" Lyric brushed past me, her bare arm touching mine and setting off sparks of awareness.

It was lucky the only witness to our exchange was a four-year-old who didn't understand flirting. Because I wasn't sure we could have denied that's what we were doing to anyone else.

"Harry?"

The smile on Lyric's face fell.

An older woman emerged from further down the hall, cautiously making her way toward us, peering up at me uncertainly.

"Gran, this is Father Zepherin. Zeph, this is my grandmother, Cheryl."

Cheryl's face crumpled in confusion. "Harry?" she asked again, ignoring her granddaughter's introduction. "I haven't seen you in so long."

I glanced at Lyric, who seemed bitterly unhappy.

"This is why I can't just sleep in," she said quietly, low enough that her gran and Amelia wouldn't hear. "She has dementia. I'm sorry. Harry was her husband. My grandfather."

Instantly, the woman's behavior made sense. While I didn't have a lot of experience with dementia, I did have some parishioners with the condition. I knew sometimes it was kinder to go along with whoever they thought you were, rather than causing further confusion by correcting them. So, I chose my words carefully. "It's lovely to see you, Cheryl."

I blinked in surprise when a tear rolled down her cheek and she wrapped bony arms around my middle.

"Sorry," Lyric mouthed.

I shook my head and patted the older woman on the back gently. "Cheryl, would it be okay if I hung out with you and Amelia this morning? Lyric seems tired, and I really think she could use a few extra hours' sleep."

Lyric opened her mouth to argue, even though the dark circles beneath her eyes told me she was as tired as I thought.

But her grandmother cut her off with a sharp nod. "Oh, yes please, Harry. We have a lot to catch up on." Elvis Presley still played over the speakers, and Cheryl swayed with the tune. "Do you remember this song? We used to play it all the time in that old brown car you had. What was it again?" She laughed girlishly and held her hands out to me. "Dance?"

Lyric grabbed her grandmother's hand. "Gran, no. Come on. Zeph isn't going to da—"

"I'd love to."

Cheryl's face lit up like I'd just offered her a million dollars.

I pulled her into my arms with a warm smile and spun her around the small kitchen like it was a dance floor. She beamed up at me, pure delight and comfort in her aging features.

For a moment, I could imagine the woman she must have been in her youth, hopelessly in love with Lyric's grandfather.

Amelia clapped her pudgy hands together and then reached them out to me. "Me next, Daddy Zepherin!"

With a chuckle, I swung Cheryl past the couch Amelia perched on like a tiny bird. I scooped her up into one arm, jostling her around onto my hip so she could join the dance.

"I wish we still had that record player, Harry. You shouldn't have thrown it out with the trash last week."

Cheryl smiled at Amelia. "You liked it too, didn't you, Lyric?"

Amelia scowled at her great-grandmother. "Amelia, Nanny. Not Lyric."

Confusion, and then fear flooded Cheryl's eyes. She peered up at me again, this time not with the look of love she'd had earlier, but with uncertainty.

"You're right," I assured her quickly. "I shouldn't have thrown it out. All songs sound better on vinyl."

The tension drooped out of Cheryl's shoulders. "That's what I said!"

"You were definitely right." I glanced over at Lyric.

She watched on with misty eyes and an upturn of her lips.

"Go," I told her. "Sleep. I have this. You don't have to do everything yourself. I've got them."

And maybe for the first time since I'd met her, Lyric did as she was told.

Some part of me, the dark, forbidden part I tried so hard to bury, was pleased.

8

—————

ZEPH

The sculpture was obscene.

I knew it. If I'd shown it to anyone else, they would have known it too. Yet, every time I sat down in the corner of my room, that was the piece I was drawn to. The only thing my muse wanted to work with.

The curve of a woman's hips and breasts and thighs. Her legs spread around the chiseled waist of a man—the slightest hint of a cross on a chain around his neck. Not caring I was spreading orange-red clay on my bare chest; I fingered the cross around my own neck. "You're sick, Zeph. You need fucking help."

The woman was Lyric. Even though I'd tried to convince myself the two figures were just general symbols of a romantic joining, they weren't. The fact I kept creating them, each sculpture more graphic than the last, only made me hate myself more.

I shoved the table away angrily and dropped to my knees on the hard wooden floor. I linked my fingers together and stared up at the crucifix on my wall. "Why?"

I begged the symbol. "I don't want this. Is this a test of faith?"

There was no answer from the inanimate object.

No voice of some almighty being in my head.

The judgment all came from within, thick and fast and overwhelming.

I wanted to fit in here. I wanted to be good and pure and never think about a woman in the way I thought about Lyric. No good came from thoughts as dark and disturbed as mine. My parents had told me that. The therapists had told me that. So had the priests. Over and over again. The shame I'd felt confessing the things I'd done with Annie.

There was a reason I'd blocked out my needs for so long. The urges. The desires.

I was older. No longer a teenager with no idea what he was doing and barely through puberty. I should have been able to control the needs I had. Yet every time I looked at Lyric, I wanted them all the more.

My phone rang, rattling around on my bedside table. I rocked back onto my heels and pushed up onto bare feet, padding across the room in only an old pair of jeans, ripped and stained with the evidence of various artworks I'd created over the years. "Hello?"

"Zepherin. Liam. Sorry to disturb."

My friend from the homeless shelter we both volunteered at was a surprise call. We were friendly during our shifts, chatting about my life with the church, and his life with multiple partners and a couple of kids, all of them living in one house. We were as different as night and day, and yet we got along like we had everything in common. But we didn't hang out. As far as I could remember, I'd never given him my number. But it would have been easy enough for him to get from the staff records.

"Is something wrong? Are you okay?"

"Yeah, fine. Good. But I'm at the shelter tonight...a woman came in asking for you. Said her name was Tammie? Had a couple of small boys with her."

"I remember her." I gripped the phone tighter.

"Anyway, she got quite distressed when we said you weren't here—"

"Did she need another inhaler for her little boy? Was he coughing a lot?"

"Yeah, he was. He didn't look very well. I offered to drive her to Emergency Care, but she said she doesn't have insurance."

"Is she still there?"

"We have no extra beds tonight. I found her some food, but it's curfew soon, and I'm going to have to turn them out once it hits ten."

I knew the rules. They were there to keep people safe. The center could only take a certain amount of people each night, and each night it was first in, first served. If Tammie and her boys were too late, they couldn't be allowed to stay. I didn't even know if they needed a place, but I was sure she did need a new inhaler for her boy. The one I'd given them was half used. If he'd burned through that in the week or so since I'd seen them last, he must be really struggling.

I yanked on a T-shirt and shoved my feet into a pair of Converse. "Don't let them leave, Liam. Not 'til I get there, okay?"

There was a late-night pharmacy attached to Saint

View Hospital. I could get him another inhaler there and be over at the shelter in fifteen minutes.

"I'll do what I can."

Despite Liam's assurances, I was sure I'd be too late to catch them. It was five past ten, and Liam should have by all rights cleared the center of anyone who hadn't been assigned a bed. But when I barged my way in through the security doors, new inhaler still nestled in its packaging clutched in my hand, I found him sitting with the family in the office.

Tammie patted her son's back as he coughed, each one shuddering through his skinny body.

I thrust the package in her direction. "Here."

She took it without a word, but her eyes held all the thank-yous I didn't need.

The boy sucked on the inhaler, his relief near instant.

"He needs to be in the hospital," I said quietly.

Tammie only nodded.

"Can I take you? They can send me the bill."

She raised big eyes in my direction. "You can't pay all his bills, Zepherin. He needs ongoing care. I think we both know that."

I'd vowed to live in poverty, so I didn't have a lot of money. I didn't really need it, since the church paid for my accommodations, my car, and food. Anything else was considered a luxury I probably didn't need, and apart from sculpting supplies, my wage generally sat untouched in my bank account. I would give that up to them in a heartbeat, but Tammie was right. It probably wouldn't be enough. "He needs to go anyway. We'll have to work out what to do about paying the bills later."

She nodded wearily, tucking her toddler into the flap

of her jacket. "I know. Let's go. At least it will be somewhere warm to sleep tonight."

My heart sank. "You've been sleeping on the streets?"

She shook her head. "I managed to pay another week on the rent, but there was no money for heating. It's okay, though. It's not too cold..."

Yet.

The word hung in the air between us. It wasn't terribly cold yet, but clearly she'd been feeling it. In a few weeks, it would be winter and a whole lot more unpleasant to live in those conditions. Daniel's cough wasn't going to get any better if he wasn't warm and dry at night.

I drove her silently to the hospital, dropping her at Emergency. I offered to come inside with them, but she shook her head. "Please don't. I don't want to feel any more indebted to you than I already do."

I tried to argue, but she wouldn't hear it, and eventually I let her go, watching the small family trudge inside the hospital. Where no doubt Daniel would get the care he needed, and Tammie would be issued a hefty bill she couldn't afford.

The entire situation broke me.

I drove back to Providence, staring up at the houses that got bigger and more expensive the farther I moved away from the Saint View border. The injustice followed me, like a trail of dirty black smoke. The people who lived in these houses had no idea what went on in their own backyard. Saint View was mere minutes away, and yet it was like a different world. There was an invisible gate between the two towns, but the separation was real.

I slowed and then stopped outside one of the biggest

houses in town. A multistory property with balconies off the top floors, a circular drive, and immaculate gardens that gave a feeling of opulence. The place was nine bedrooms, four bathrooms, and had a swimming pool in the back with a diving board.

I knew because I'd been inside once before, accompanying my mother on one of her charity missions she ran for the hospital where she volunteered. Her job was to hit up wealthy people like the Laudertons and seek donations or sponsorship for new equipment.

She was good at her job. She got people talking about themselves, and the lives they lived, which in this part of town always included things like jet-skiing or taking expensive, overseas vacations. She'd lure them in with her assurances that she loved those things too. Then she'd hit them with the guilt trip.

It basically went along the lines of, "You've just admitted how much money you have to spend on frivolous things. What kind of person are you if you don't give some of that to the needy?"

It almost always worked.

That day I'd been here, I'd listened as Mrs. Lauderton prattled on over tea and cookies, all about her husband and how hard he worked, running their very successful chain of supermarkets.

Supermarkets called Checkers—the same chain Tammie had been let go from because she couldn't work evenings with three children at her feet. The same chain store who preferred to employ barely working-age children because they could pay them less. The same chain store who had turned over a multimillion-dollar profit in the last year and had yet refused to donate to my mother's charity because it wasn't in the budget.

They'd turned my mother's requests down with no hint of guilt.

Greed practically seeped from the brickwork of the overdone home.

From the trunk of the car, I pulled a dark jacket, gloves, and balaclava. I filled my pockets with a few other things that often came in handy, brushing over Lyric's rope deep at the bottom. Then just like I had the night I'd followed Lyric and her stalker, or the night I'd ended a perverted priest who couldn't keep his penis in his pants, I melted into the shadows.

With practiced ease, I moved through the darkness, watching for security cameras or dogs, not surprised when there were none to be found since I had already cased the place when I'd been here months ago.

The front of the house had enough locks and bolts to rival Fort Knox, but the back was another story. It was minimal effort to jump a fence that was more decorative than functional and slip around to the glass doors that led from the building to the outdoor entertaining area and then to the pool area beyond.

Glass doors were always a weak point in any security system, and this one was no different. I shoved my hand into my pocket, ready with a pick that had helped me open many a locked door in the past, but I didn't even need it. One tiny tug on the door, a slight lift to get it unlatched, and the thing was open, giving me wide and full access to the dark, sleeping house beyond.

All money and no sense. I slipped inside, pausing to let my eyes adjust to the darkness.

A curious yip from a small dog I hadn't seen last time was instantly quieted with a treat from my pocket. He sat obediently, waiting for more, and I rewarded him several more times with food and pats on the head until he lost interest and went back to his bed on the edge of the kitchen.

I waited a moment to be sure he was relaxed around me and couldn't help the smile when the creature almost instantly fell asleep and started snoring. Cute mutt.

Dog detail out of the way, I gazed around the huge room, fighting off the urge to whistle at how grand it was.

And at how many expensive things they had lying around, just waiting for someone to steal.

Or redistribute, as I liked to think of it. I doubted Paris and Clyde Lauderton would even notice if I took a few things to give to someone who needed them more than they did. In fact, I was sure they'd agree wholeheartedly that their ex-employee deserved some compensation for putting up with their pompous asses.

Cash and jewelry were my two objectives. They were small and easy, and if Paris didn't go out often, she might not even notice the missing pieces for a while, which would give me more time to sell them without the risk of the police watching the pawn stores.

Some light from the street outside filtered through open windows, eliminating the need for the mini flash-light in my pocket. I crept up the stairs in search of the master bedroom. Or more specifically, a wardrobe or dressing area where jewelry would likely be kept.

The stairs led me onto a landing, with doors either side leading to bedrooms. From memory, the Laudertons had no children. In any case, there had been no sign of toys or school notes or clothes on the ground floor. Snores came from behind one door, and it seemed like the place to start.

It opened silently, revealing a huge bed, much bigger than a standard king-size with a canopy of gauzy fabric hanging over it. The mattress was covered with silky sheets and a white bedspread partially obscured by the two occupants.

Clyde was smaller than I'd expected, at least a few inches shorter than me, and flat on his back with his mouth open.

His wife was familiar, though the last time I'd seen her she'd been made up to within an inch of her life and dressed in a smart skirt and fitted blouse, pearls fastened around her throat.

Paris slept naked, her cleavage exposed to the night air, one nipple hidden beneath a sheet, the other on display for anyone to walk in off the street and see.

I waited for the same jolt of lust I'd had when I'd noticed Lyric's nipples through her thin pajama shirt.

It didn't come. Not until the sleeping woman's blond hair morphed into Lyric's auburn red. Not until her features rearranged themselves into Lyric's pert nose and full, pink lips.

The moment the woman became Lyric in my head, the trajectory of my thoughts changed.

Need roared in. Lust swirled, dark and hungry.

I wanted to drag the sheet off her naked body, spread her thighs, and put my mouth on the folds between her legs.

I wanted to lick her and taste her and tease her. Wrap my fingers around her wrists and pin her to the bed as I slid inside her before she was even awake. Fuck her hard until her cries of surprise turned into moans of pleasure.

Clyde's snore startled me out of my thoughts. Shame took the place of desire.

This was why I'd joined the priesthood.

The things I wanted weren't normal. Weren't desirable. Weren't safe.

I never wanted to hurt anyone, and yet, I was scared I would.

I'd terrified Annie, and back then, the things I wanted to do were tame compared to the thoughts I had about Lyric. I was better off never being alone with a woman.

I scurried into the walk-in closet, swiped a handful of expensive-looking jewelry from a box, and a couple of hundred-dollar bills on a makeup table. With the money I'd get from a pawnshop, it should be enough to pay at least some of Daniel's hospital bill, or for the rent and heat.

I left the room without looking back at Paris. Without again imagining her to be Lyric. I hightailed it back the way I'd come, only stopping when I noticed an old-fashioned record player in the corner of the living room.

It wasn't something I normally would have taken. It was probably not worth much, and it looked heavy and bulky. A waste of effort.

But Lyric's gran's comment about her husband throwing out her record player sat heavy in my memory. The song, and my presence, had made her so happy, in what had to be a confusing and scary time for her.

I unplugged the thing and hefted it into my arms. With a final pat on the sleeping dog's head, I slipped out into the yard once more. My pockets full of jewelry to sell and give to a woman who needed it to pay her kid's medical bills. And a damn record player that would make an old woman happy.

Maybe, if I was lucky, it would have the same effect on her granddaughter. I was quickly addicted to Lyric's smiles. I wasn't sure I could give them up just yet.

9

ZEPH

I was no stranger to Saint View Hospital. My mom had volunteered here since I was a kid, and sometimes she would bring us with her if there was a boy my age in the children's ward who needed to feel normal for a few hours. I'd never minded much, because they had a PlayStation, which I was never allowed to have at home.

As a priest, last rites were often administered in the palliative care wards, so I was often summoned down here to absolve people of their sins while they lay dying.

I hated it. Hated the confessions I heard when people knew they weren't going home. The sins they confessed were always the deepest, darkest ones. The ones that made me want to put my hands around their frail throats and choke the last breaths right out of them.

I refused to utter words of forgiveness to those people. If no one else was around, I let them die with a guilty conscience.

But today I wore street clothes, not here on any official church business. I hadn't slept well, worrying about Tammie and her boy. I needed to know he was okay. I gave the woman at reception Daniel's name, and she gave me a floor and room number in exchange. After a quick jog up the stairs, I pushed open the door to the pediatric ward and ran near smack into my mother.

"Zepherin!" she exclaimed with an *oof* as I steadied her. "Goodness, boy, where are you going in such a hurry?"

"To visit a friend's son. He was admitted last night."

Her fingers clutched around her clipboard, and she glanced down at the list of names with room numbers printed neatly beside them. "Do you know which room?"

"Reception told me. He's eight-oh-three."

"Oh. The boy with the asthma?"

I nodded.

"They're friends of yours?"

"Yes."

She clucked her tongue in that disapproving way I'd grown used to as a child.

I sighed. "What, Mom?"

She shook her head. "Nothing. But you always did pick the strays as a child. Nothing seems to have changed as an adult. That family looks like they came in off the streets."

"They did. I drove them here from the homeless shelter. Was that wrong? Should I have left him to die in a gutter somewhere?"

She scowled at me. "You're so overly sensitive. I have work to do."

I shook my head, and she hurried down the hall away from me. I followed, because that was the direction of

Daniel's room, but at a much slower pace, putting some distance between my mother and me.

At the entrance to room 803, I smiled at Daniel propped up in a bed and watching the tiny TV that hung above it. He put a finger to his lips and pointed at his youngest brother, asleep in a stroller, and then at his mom who had her arms folded on the end of her bed, her head down on top of them. She breathed evenly, fast asleep.

"They were real tired," Daniel informed me as I edged around his two snoozing family members.

"Where's your other brother?" I questioned.

Daniel pointed to the doorway. "Toby's out there somewhere. A nurse lady came and took him to play. She said Mom looked like she'd had enough."

I nodded in understanding. "Hospitals are tough for parents."

"Especially when you only have a mom."

I nodded and patted him on the leg. "Especially then. But your mom is a tough one. Don't you worry about her. You just worry about getting better."

His eyes drooped and he nodded.

"You tired, too?" I asked him.

"I guess."

"No one got much sleep last night," Tammie said softly.

I glanced over at her, cringing apologetically. "Sorry if we woke you."

She stood and moved to her son's side, smoothing back his hair as his eyes closed. "You didn't. Sleep now, baby. Rest."

Daniel snuggled into the pure-white hospital sheets and drifted off.

Tammie sat back down in the hard plastic chair beside mine and sighed.

I reached over and squeezed her fingers. "You're doing great."

But tears filled her eyes. "I'm not, though." She buried her face in her hands. "I'm so ashamed."

I grabbed her hands, pulling them away from her face. "Hey, why? You've done nothing wrong. The only thing wrong here is your boss for not being flexible enough to give single parents a go, and the abysmal state of our healthcare system which doesn't protect our most vulnerable."

She lifted her head with tears rolling down her cheeks. "It's not just that. I need to go to confession. I've done something I'm not proud of."

I squeezed her fingers. "You don't need to worry about that right now."

She shook her head miserably. "I slept with a man a few nights ago."

I raised an eyebrow. "That's not against the law, Tammie. Despite what the Bible says, I like to think that God isn't actually watching our every move. You deserve someone to love you."

The hope drained out of her eyes. "It's not like that. It's... I didn't know him. He offered me money...my boys were asleep the whole time, Zeph. I swear it. They didn't even know he was there."

Someone cleared their throat from the doorway, and Tammie and I both jumped.

Tammie plastered on an embarrassed smile. "Hey, Toby!"

I glanced over my shoulder to find my mother holding hands with the toddler. Her face was pink, telling me she'd probably heard every word of Tammie's confession.

"The nurses asked me to bring him back. He wanted a snack, but we weren't sure of allergies."

Tammie pushed to her feet and picked up the little boy with a bright smile for my mother. "Thank you so much. I'll go get him a cookie from the vending machine. Zepherin, can you stay here with the other boys for a moment, please?"

"Of course."

She smiled again and slipped past my mother with Toby on her hip.

My mother's smile fell. "That's your new friend? A prostitute?"

Daniel chose that moment to start coughing, and the fit lasted so long it drew the attention of the nurses outside at their station. They rushed in, adjusting some dials on the wall behind him that presumably controlled his oxygen flow. Tammie raced back in behind them, passing Toby over to me. By the time Daniel was settled again, and I'd said goodbye to Tammie, I couldn't see my mother anywhere.

I wasn't particularly sad to avoid another reminder I was a constant disappointment to her.

10

LYRIC

It turned out orgasms were good for my mood. Even a couple of days after my solo time in the bathroom, the glow lingered.

Or perhaps it was that I'd seen Zeph every day since.

The man always found a reason to hang out with me while I cleaned or was lingering in the daycare parking lot when I picked up Amelia.

If it had been anyone else, I might have found that behavior creepy, but he intrigued me in a way no other man had in a long time. Every piece of himself that he revealed only made me want to know more. I wanted to get beneath his skin, delve inside his head, and work out why the most gorgeous man I'd ever met had committed to a life few others ever would.

I wanted to know why he'd given up sex and love and companionship. Especially when the vibe between us felt anything but platonic at times. He was attracted to me. I was sure of it. Which only made the mystery of his profession deeper.

If I was being honest with myself, the fact he was off-limits only made me want to unravel him more.

I shook my hips in time to the beat of the song playing on my portable speaker, while my grandmother frowned at me.

"It would have sounded better on the record player. But Harry threw it out."

Even my worry over her couldn't get me down today. "I know, Gran. But at least we have music, right?"

She turned away to stare out the window.

I kissed her weathered cheek and picked up my keys from the kitchen counter. "I'm going to go get Amelia and bring her home, but I've called Peggy to come in early because I can't stay. Eve called a meeting and needs me to come into the club early."

Gran nodded. "Okay, then. Amelia and I will be fine. Zepherin left his sunglasses here the other day, though. Could you take them to him?"

I blinked in surprise at her sudden rush of clarity. I didn't know she'd even been aware that Zeph wasn't my grandfather.

"Sure. Where are they?"

She pointed them out, and I grabbed them from a shelf in the kitchen. I hadn't even noticed them, so Gran or maybe Peggy must have put them there for safe-keeping.

Much to my disappointment, Zeph wasn't lingering in the parking lot. Nor was he inside the daycare when I picked up my grubby daughter who had to have rolled around in the sandbox, the painting area, and spilled half her lunch all over herself.

"You've had a good day!" I greeted her with a laugh.

She scowled up at me.

I cringed at her expression. "Or not. What's wrong?"

She folded her little arms over her chest. "Nothing!"

I glanced over at her teacher with a raised eyebrow, silently asking if she knew why my normally sunshiny girl was suddenly all storm clouds and death looks.

"No nap today," she explained.

Ah. That would do it. Amelia had always loved to sleep. With my weird work schedule, she often went to bed late and was up early. It had never mattered because she could have that nap at daycare. That would have to change when she started school but worked just fine for now. As long as she actually took the nap.

"I don't like naps!" Amelia stormed to the front door but was too short to let herself out. "Naps are for babies."

Distraction was the best technique when she was like this. So I found her little backpack, thanked her teacher, and picked up Amelia's hand. "Guess what? Zeph left his sunglasses at our apartment. I've got them to give back to him. Shall we go see if he's home?"

Her face brightened. "Yes, please. Can I give them to him?"

"Sure you can." I led her over toward the priest's residence, but the open doors of the church and conversation floating out caught my attention. I pointed it out to Amelia. "You know, Slugger. I think he might be in there."

We changed direction and headed that way, pausing in the doorway.

Zeph lifted his dark-brown eyes, and a smile flickered across his face.

"Daddy Zepherin! We have your sunglasses!" Amelia's

little-girl voice echoed around the stone walls of the church.

Pink flushed Zeph's cheeks, as it always did when my daughter called him the wrong name.

But the older couple he was speaking with turned around, the woman's lips pursed together in annoyance.

A sassy retort to her dirty look scalded the tip of my tongue, but I was aware this was Zeph's workplace and I didn't want to get him in any trouble.

"We'll just leave them here," I called to him. "Sorry to interrupt. Amelia, just put them on the seat there."

But Zeph motioned me over. "No, wait. Lyric, come here."

I didn't know why his deep-voiced commands always did things to my insides, especially when I hated commands from any sort of authority figure. But I found myself walking up the aisle to meet Zeph and the couple halfway.

His arm brushed mine, sending ripples of attraction through my heated skin.

"Hey." He smiled at me.

"Hey, yourself."

I couldn't stop watching him. The urge to reach up and hug him was strong, but that wasn't something either of us did. It would be weird. And yet, I wanted to feel his arms around me.

The woman cleared her throat, and I realized Zeph and I had been staring at each other for an unusual amount of time.

Zeph snapped his gaze away from mine and focused back on the other woman. "I'm sorry. Mom, Dad. This is

Lyric." He smiled down at Amelia who had gone shy and was hiding behind my legs. "And that's Amelia."

I widened my eyes, instantly self-conscious. I wasn't exactly dressed for meeting anyone's parents, especially not Zeph's since I knew they were churchy. I tugged my booty shorts down and reached one hand out to his mother. "Lovely to meet you. I've heard a lot about you."

That wasn't exactly true, but I'd heard something, and it seemed like the thing to say.

Especially because she wasn't saying anything.

Nor was she taking my hand.

I dropped it limply at my side.

"Mom," Zeph said in a low voice. "You're being rude."

She looked me up and down, taking in the ripped T-shirt, with holes designed to show off my cleavage and my belly.

Irritation poked a hole in my good mood. She wasn't the first woman to stare at me like that, and she wouldn't be the last, but I never took it well. If we hadn't been in Zeph's church, and she hadn't been his mother, I would have already told her where to go.

She ignored Zeph's warning, her gaze focusing in on Amelia. Or more specifically, the stains on her shirt from a long day of daycare. "Your daughter needs a bath."

I prickled but tried to rein in my temper. "I'm aware. But thank you for your concern."

Perhaps it came out a tad sharper than I intended, because the woman clucked her tongue at me.

"Women of your profession should not be allowed to have children," she mumbled, turning away.

I gaped at her, any pretense of being polite obliterated

with that statement. "Excuse me? What the hell does that mean?"

She threw her hands up in the air, clearly exasperated with me. "And she says the H word in a church? What kind of woman raised you?"

I ground my molars and my fingers instinctively closed into fists, ready for a fight. It was one thing to criticize me and my choices, but it was an entirely different kettle of fish to insult my daughter and my grandmother. Gran had taken me in when my hopeless mother had decided babies cried too much when I was only six months old, and we'd rarely seen her since. Gran was my mother. She and Amelia were my two soft spots, and in the space of thirty seconds, this woman had managed to kick both of them.

Anger radiated from Zeph when he stepped between us. For a second, I was ready to lay a fist into him, because how dare he? How dare he get pissed because I wasn't speaking politely to a woman who was so derogatory to me? I was all for respecting my elders, but only where it was deserved. This woman didn't deserve an ounce of it.

But then his arm swept me and Amelia behind him as he faced-off with his mother, his broad chest and back blocking us from her sight.

Something inside me lit up with pleasure at the protective gesture.

His mother clearly saw it as such, too, and when I peeked around Zeph's broad frame, the ire in her eyes was almost amusing.

She ignored the triumphant grin I shot her.

"It's admirable of you to counsel prostitutes, but when

a child is involved, they should just be removed from the mother entirely."

That wiped the grin right off my face.

"Mommy?" Amelia pulled on the hem of my shorts. "What does that mean? I want to stay with you."

My heart splintered, half aching for my daughter who had just been dealt a cruel blow of reality before she was ready for it. The other half pure fury at the woman who'd delivered it.

Zeph's fingers dug into my hip, keeping me in place. His voice lowered to a deadly whisper. "Don't talk to her like that. She's not a prostitute. Even if she were, your judgment in a holy place is unwanted. I think you should leave."

But I was the one who didn't want to be there anymore. I untangled his fingers from my hip and picked Amelia up, holding her close to my chest even though she hadn't really liked being held like that for a while. Today, though, she burrowed in, wrapping her arms around my neck and tucking her face into my neck.

"Don't bother. I'm taking my daughter home."

I turned and left before Zeph could stop me.

Though I wasn't even sure he would have. With a mother like that, perhaps deep-rooted judgment and bigotry were the secrets Zeph hid inside.

11

———

EVE

*L*yric stormed into my office, walked right up to the small couch I kept here, and rammed a closed fist into a cushion. "Argh!" She punched it a few more times, until the cushion was well and truly pummeled.

I let her go, not unused to Lyric's outbursts of anger. She'd been fiery as long as I'd known her. She would talk when she was ready.

Eventually, she sank down onto the couch, pulling the flattened pillow onto her lap and smoothing it out again.

"Wanna tell me what the cushion did to you?"

She sighed heavily. "Can I not? I don't really want to get into it right now. Just know the cushion deserved it."

I shrugged. "It was definitely asking for it, just sitting over there, minding its own business. How dare it?"

She grinned at me. "What's the meeting about?"

The smile fell off my face. "I'll tell you in a minute when the others get here. But hey, I ran into Lleyton when I was getting my haircut in Providence yesterday..."

Lyric groaned. "Was his perfect girlfriend with him?"

"Well, yes, actually. He was picking her up from her appointment. But that's not the point. He said Amelia is doing really well in her new daycare."

Lyric scrunched up her face, probably because she knew what I was going to say next. "You didn't tell me you'd changed daycares. You were so happy with her last school. What happened?"

Lyric sighed heavily. "Lleyton happened. He didn't pay her fees, and she lost her spot. She's at the church daycare now."

I squinted at her. "I thought you paid her fees? I didn't think Lleyton was in the picture much at all?" Guilt swamped me. I'd been so caught up in my own business the last few weeks, I had barely even checked in with Lyric. That wasn't how I rolled. I was the mother hen. The matriarch of this little family we'd created here. And I'd let the loss of one affect all the others.

Lyric shrugged. "He's around when he feels like being a parent. He says he wants to discuss his custody arrangement, so I don't know, maybe he wants to be more involved. But not paying Amelia's fees didn't exactly get that conversation off to a good start. Though maybe I don't have a leg to stand on because I couldn't afford them either."

I slouched down in my chair. "Because the club has been so quiet lately."

Lyric fiddled with a loose thread on the cushion, plucking at it with her red-polished fingernails. "That, and all the other things I have to pay for. Peggy's wage to look after Gran and Amelia being the big one. But rent went up. Food costs more. It's tough right now."

I hated that. I just wanted to fix everything for everyone, and I didn't know how. Not without Fawn. Ever since she'd been taken, I was lost at sea, floating in a storm with no lifejacket or way of getting back to shore.

Augie traipsed into my office and slumped down on the seat across from my desk, grunting a hello. Phoenix appeared a moment later, filling the doorway with his big, wall-of-a-man presence. He politely knocked, unlike Lyric and Augie, and I nodded at him to come in. He edged into the room, leaning on the back wall, quietly waiting.

I loved the three of them hard. Their pain and problems hurt me. "I need help coming up with ways of getting fresh traffic in here. My ideas suck. I just have nothing that would even make a dent. Promotions. Events. If I could afford a coordinator, I would. But I can't. So it's on us."

"What about like, meat raffles?" Lyric offered, cracking a piece of gum between her teeth. She folded her arms across her chest.

"Meat raffles? Are we stripping at the old folks' home? Who comes to a strip club for meat raffles?" Augie glanced over at her, his glossy blond hair flopping in his eye.

It was a different look for him, after shaving his head for as long as I'd known him. The stubble around his jaw was new too, and while it suited him, because he was runway-model-gorgeous no matter what he did, his new scruffier appearance made my heart hurt.

Because I knew it had more to do with Fawn's disappearance than a conscious fashion choice. He'd been close with her, maybe even closer than I was, and the strain of not knowing was getting to him.

Lyric flipped him the bird. "You got any better ideas?"

"Let's just do the politician dick party thing again. It worked last time."

I shook my head. The Pin the Penis on the Politician party had been huge for us, especially with Fawn taking the reins to plan it all out. But I didn't think it would work twice. Or maybe I just didn't want to do it again without Fawn when it had been her brainchild. "It doesn't make sense. The elections are over. We need something new."

Phoenix cleared his throat, and I glanced up in surprise. He was a man of few words and quite the opposite of Lyric and Augie who always had something to say. None of us knew much about Phoenix, other than he was loyal to a fault and the type of guy you could call in the middle of the night if your car broke down. He'd drive across the country to get you if he had to. But words were not really his thing, and I hadn't expected him to contribute to the discussion, even though I never would have left him out by not inviting him to the meeting. I might have owned the club, but we all got a say in how it ran.

"What about an Opposites Attract party? For both guys and girls. We give everyone a card on entry, and they have to find the person with the matching pair?"

I quirked my head in interest. "That's different."

He shrugged. "We need different. That's what was good about Fawn's party. It brought in a new crowd. We need to think further than just the lonely guys who show up and drown their sorrows in cheap beer. We can still put on a show, but maybe we class it up a bit. Less stripping, more show." He stared down at his feet. "Or not. Probably a stupid idea."

Lyric tossed her wadded-up gum wrapper at him. "Or it's genius. It'll get the crowd moving around, talking to each other. Making new friends..."

"Fuck friends, you mean," Augie drawled.

Lyric rolled her eyes at him. "Not everyone is as big a slut as you are, Aug."

He wasn't fazed by her insult. Probably because it was true.

"It's kind of like speed dating though, right? I think I like it. Maybe we're a strip club four nights a week and something else on the fifth night. A place to meet people." A kernel of excitement lit me up as the idea took hold. "Each week could have a different theme, but all geared around getting people meeting up in person. Everyone bitches about how much they hate the dating and hookup apps, why can't we go back to basics? But with a little help to get them mingling."

Lyric nodded. "We have to try new things. We'll never know what works and what doesn't. What about a fancy-dress night? Maybe to coincide with the Opposites Attract party. Dressing up is more fun with a theme."

I grinned. "If it's Opposites Attract, Boston and I could come as a stripper and security guard without even getting a costume."

Augie sniggered.

"Zeph and I could come as a priest and a prostitute without dressing up either," Lyric mumbled.

I looked at her sharply. "You are not a prostitute."

"Depends who you ask, apparently."

I wanted to argue with her, but she gave me a quiet

shake of her head, silently asking me not to push any further.

I mused on the idea some more. "If we could do one really big night per week it would make the other slower nights less painful." But deep down, I knew it wasn't enough. "We still need to hire a new act though. These parties are great, but we need bodies in here every night of the week. Without Fawn's sweet-and-innocent thing, I feel like the customers are dropping like flies."

Lyric hunched in her seat. I waited for her to react as violently as she had in the past when I'd mentioned needing to hire a new stripper. But this time, she nodded. "Maybe you're right."

Augie shoved his chair back viciously and got to his feet. His hands trembled with anger, or maybe hurt, but I wasn't scared. Augie was tough as nails on the outside, and few people saw the soft, marshmallow center he sheltered behind crass words and an 'I don't give a fuck' attitude.

But I saw him.

I knew his reaction was solely to do with the way he cared about Fawn. It was brotherly love, on his side at least. But it was strong.

"She's coming back, Eve," he growled. "And her job needs to be here waiting for her."

Tears pricked the backs of my eyes, feeling his pain mixed in with my own. "Aug, Lyric needs the cash. She's got Amelia—"

His fist came down hard on my desk, his eyes flashing. "Amelia has a roof over her head, a mother who adores her, and all of us. What the fuck does Fawn have? An abusive ex who's keeping her prisoner somewhere? We aren't giving up on her! Not fucking happening. I'm not out there searching for her every damn day for no reason. I don't care if you've all given up, I haven't!"

Lyric glared at him. "Nobody's given up on her."

"Sure sounds like you care more about money than Fawn."

I cringed at the two of them bickering with each other. It was their normal state of being, and it normally came from a place of love. The two of them were like brother and sister. But everyone's emotions had been running high for weeks, especially mine, though I tried to hide it. I pinched the bridge of my nose. "Okay, enough. Go get ready for the doors to open. Or go home. Augie, I'm talking about you, specifically. You can't be here if I think you're going to explode the first time a customer looks at you wrong."

Augie shouldered past Phoenix. "Fine by me. I'm going to go search for my friend. Again. The one you all seem to have written off."

Phoenix, Lyric, and I all watched him go. Phoenix looked to me. "Should I go after him? He's pretty worked up."

I shook my head. "Let him go. He needs to cool off. I'll talk to him again tomorrow."

Phoenix nodded. He paused awkwardly by the door. "He'll come around. We all know you love Fawn and that she can't be replaced, even if we do hire a new staff member."

I pressed my lips together, grateful for the way he understood me. "Thank you."

With a quiet nod, he disappeared into the club.

Lyric stood slowly, shouldering the gym bag she used

when she needed to take costumes home to wash. The two of us locked eyes, and it was like I could see right inside her brain, even before she said the words we were both thinking.

"Do you think she's dead?" she whispered.

I swallowed the ball of emotion that lodged itself in my throat every time I thought of Fawn and the way she'd been taken from us. I forced down the thought I'd abandoned her when our kidnappers had returned me without her. All because my father was a politician who could have made life difficult for them. I had no idea who Fawn's family was, she never talked about them, but they clearly weren't people Fawn's ex feared.

I couldn't stop thinking about how scared she'd been. How scared I'd been. And now Fawn was alone.

Exhaustion swamped me hard. Every night when I fell asleep, the memories played over as dreams. Both of us trapped. Hurt. Terrified.

I said the words I never wanted to say, because I couldn't lie to Lyric. Not anymore. "I think she might be."

Lyric sniffed and wiped her eyes with the back of her hand. "I do too."

We both stared at each other, water filling our eyes, until she turned away.

"I need to go get ready."

"Okay," I whispered, remembering the last time Fawn had walked out of this office to do the same, and wishing I could replay that last day with her over and over.

Lyric closed the door behind her, and I put my head down on my desk to let the tears fall silently.

"Hey, Evil."

I glanced up at my boyfriend's soft greeting, already

knowing it was him because nobody else called me that. It had once been said in hate, but now it was a term of endearment. I hadn't even heard him open the door. I just stared at him miserably, letting the tears fall down my cheeks.

"Oh, baby." He padded across my office floor and tugged me up out of my seat so he could wrap his arms around me.

He didn't question what was wrong. He knew. He'd been there with me through all the nightmares and the questions, and the fear. He knew her disappearance, and the fact we may never get closure, ate away at me every day. I had survivor's guilt so badly it was near crippling.

He smoothed his hand up and down my back in calm, gentle motions, always my pillar of strength whenever I couldn't hold it together anymore. I cried into his shoulder until I felt bone-dry and my head hurt.

"I hate seeing you like this," he said into my neck. "It fucking guts me."

"I'm sorry."

"Not what I meant. I understand, I just hate how stressed you are. And that there's never any reprieve."

I lifted my eyes to look into his startling blue ones. "You're my reprieve." I pressed my lips to his softly. "I hurt less when you're here."

He kissed me again, lips gentle. It was a kiss full of love. He'd delivered me so many of those since we'd admitted how we felt about each other. But I could never have enough of them. I opened my mouth, tongue darting out to touch his.

He paused, drawing back so he could look at me.

When I said he was my reprieve, a big part of that was

the sex. It was really hard to think about anything else when he was deep inside me and an orgasm was wiping out all coherent thought. It was a daily thing with us. Sometimes more than once a day, because it was the only time I could get Fawn off my mind.

"Kiss me," I begged him, lips against his, insistent and needy. "Please."

He knew I meant a lot more than just kiss me. I meant touch me. Lick me. Suck me. Fuck me until all that existed was him and me and the connection between us.

He glanced over his shoulder at the office door, slightly open. "We're at work. You'll have a club full of people out there soon."

I stepped back and lifted my dress over my head. I wasn't wearing a bra beneath.

Boston's gaze went straight to my tits. He stepped in, cupping one, squeezing my nipple between his thumb and forefinger. He lowered his head to the other to suck it into his mouth.

I dropped my head back with a moan, letting my long dark hair dangle down my back.

His fingers slipped inside my panties, delving between my thighs and my folds, swiping through the silky wetness there. "You're wet, baby."

It was partial arousal.

Partial something else. "I'm ovulating."

He pulled back. "So..."

"So, that baby you want..."

His breath hitched, and he shook his head slightly, like he didn't quite know what to make of me. "What are you saying?"

I pushed his finger up inside my wet core and whispered the words I'd been thinking about for weeks, ever since he'd first broached the subject of wanting babies with me. Neither of us were spring chickens. We were both in our thirties. We'd both messed around with enough other relationships to know a good thing when we had it.

Boston was a good thing. The very best thing.

Though his initial idea of having a baby had come as a surprise, and I'd put it down to his fear in losing me the night Fawn had been taken, now it felt right. He was right. *We* were right. In a storm where everything else felt wrong and out of control, this was one thing we had that no one else could touch. Him. Me. And a little family we could create together. Right now, because my body said we could, if he just agreed.

"Make a baby with me, Josh. I love you, that's all I know. I need more love. More light. Something to hope for. We all need that. I'm ready. Fuck, I'm so ready to be someone's mom. And I'm scared. Terrified really. But every time I get scared, I picture you there by my side..."

"Fucking it up right alongside you?" He laughed.

I grinned. "Fucking it up. Doing it all wrong. But doing it together. Loving that baby like nobody else could." I swallowed thickly. "Being a family."

His smile turned wide, and he shook his head slowly as he bent it to speak against my lips. "I love you. So fucking much. And I'm gonna love our baby even more."

Butterflies lit me up inside. A flood of hope and happiness I hadn't felt in weeks washed over me, and I drew him closer. "We're doing this?" I asked, eyes wide. "Really? We aren't just fucking around?"

His grip on me tightened. "It's never been just fucking around for me, Eve. I'd marry you right—"

I put my finger to his lips. "Shh. Don't say that. We just agreed to make a baby. Let's just have that for now. Anything more makes it feel too good to be true."

He nodded, kissing my fingertip. "Then take these panties off and lean over the desk, Evil. Because you aren't getting knocked up by my finger."

I grinned into his mouth as he kissed me deeply, his fingers hooking into the side of my panties to drag them over my ass and down my legs. He spun me, doing exactly as he'd promised, bending me over the desk, face to the wooden top, ass in the air while he undid his belt buckle.

He knew I loved it from behind, and my knees trembled with the anticipation. My nipples were hard against the desktop, and my core ached, dripping with need for him.

I craned my head to watch him undress, until he was as naked as I was. His dick was thick and hard, erect and just waiting to spear inside me.

He never did that though. He always had to test me first. Bring me to the edge and draw it out, because the longer he played my body, the longer I didn't think. He knelt on the threadbare carpet and spread my thighs.

"I never get sick of the sight of you bared to me like this, Eve. Never."

My legs trembled, but his mouth on my core had me moaning in pleasure. I gripped the edge of the table, shamelessly grinding back against his face and then his hand when he gave me two fingers to ride.

He brought me to the edge of orgasm quickly, because

the man knew my body inside out and could make me come practically on command. His every touch was determined and well placed. His tongue perfection.

He was mine. Made for me in every way possible, and when he leaned over me and drove his cock inside me, it only cemented how perfect he was. He slammed into me over and over until I was on the verge of coming. When I moaned his name, no care given to who might hear, he pulled out, spun me around, and lifted me onto the desk.

The move took me by surprise, because our normal was to finish in doggy. We both loved it. But when I looked at him questioningly, he just tugged my ass to the edge of the desk and wrapped my legs around him, lining himself up with my opening.

"I want to be kissing you when I come, Eve. I want to know our baby was made while I held his mother tight and promised her forever."

A sudden sob welled up in my throat and I nodded, gripping both sides of his face. "Okay."

He rocked himself back and forth inside me, thrusting slowly now, each press of his dick hitting my G-spot, his pubic bone rubbing against my clit until my pending orgasm was back and begging for release.

"I love you," he whispered, jacking up the pace.

"I love you too."

His mouth connected with mine, and it was beautiful and sweet and hot. I spiraled over the edge into an orgasm with a rush of color and need and desire, his cock deep inside me, ready to do the same.

"Oh, for Christ's sake, you two," Lyric called from the other side of the door. "Could you quit fucking where I can see it? Dry as the Sahara over here, you know." She yanked the handle, closing the door the rest of the way.

I burst into laughter, and Boston laughed, but he wasn't stopping for anyone, best friend or not.

"We aren't fucking," I yelled back to her. "We're making a baby!"

There was a shocked silence, and then a whoop of a cheer. A second later, more cheers joined hers, Phoenix, and Echo, our bartender, as well as Lucinda, our DJ, joining in the party. I thought I even heard Terry the bouncer's voice in there, but I hoped not because he was kind of like my surrogate dad.

Terry listening or not, Boston came with the cheers of our found family outside the door, and nothing could have been more perfect.

12

LYRIC

Saturday afternoons were family time. While for other families, that probably meant an outing of some sort, maybe to the movies or an amusement park, none of that was in my budget. But it was special to me anyway, and I was sure Gran and Amelia enjoyed it too. Sometimes, if the weather was bad, we just snuggled up on the couch. If the weather was nicer, we'd walk Amelia down the road to the park, even if it did mean checking the ground for broken glass or worse, before she was allowed to run off and play.

But today she wanted to play a board game, and her current favorite was a thrift shop copy of Operation. So Amelia, Gran, and I had spent the last forty minutes giggling at the buzzing noise the game made as we not so deftly tried to pick little plastic body parts from the game board with wonky tweezers.

"I'm going to be a doctor one day," Amelia declared after winning the first round.

I was so freaking proud of my kid, there was no doubt

in my mind when I said, "You can be whatever you want to be, Slugger. You're so clever, you'd make an amazing surgeon. You'd save lots of lives."

"And earn lots of money so I can go on fancy vacations and buy you a new house, Mommy."

Two things I'd probably never be able to give her. As much as I didn't want it to, the comment plucked a painful string inside me.

My gran glanced up at me, and seeing the hurt look on my face, addressed Amelia. "That's a nice goal to have. But your mommy provides a very nice home for you right now though, don't you think? You have games and toys and lots of food in the cupboard. We're safe and warm and most importantly, together."

I had never been more grateful that today was one of her more lucid days. I'd needed that pep talk.

"Yeah, but it doesn't have a pool. I want to swim."

I pulled myself together, knowing my daughter hadn't meant anything malicious by her words and that she was just a kid. Plus, who didn't want a pool when Saint View sweltered in the summertime? I ruffled her hair. "Me too, Slugger. Me too. Study hard at school and you'll be floating around in no time."

A pounding on the door interrupted, and I got to my feet to answer it. I peered through the peephole since I wasn't expecting anyone, and random strangers loved to bang on my door at all hours of the night. Curses of the ground-floor apartment.

But the man outside the door was one I knew well, as was his beautiful tall girlfriend who clutched her purse to her chest and shot worried glances up and down the empty hall like someone might jump out and mug her at any moment.

I opened the door. "What are you doing here, Lleyton? Hi, Kat."

Lleyton leaned on the doorjamb and grinned at me. It was the same stupid, charming, all-American-boy grin that had led me to bed with him in the first place. It did nothing for me now. His blond hair and blue eyes held no interest in comparison to Zeph's dark ones.

"Came to see my baby girl."

"Daddy!" Amelia sprinted from the living room and threw herself at her father. She circled skinny arms around his legs, and he hoisted her into his arms, wrapping her in a tight bear hug and peppering her face with kisses.

It was nice to see. Amelia was such a great kid, and Lleyton wasn't the worst. He was mostly a good guy, even if he was too irresponsible to be a parent, as indicated by his inability to pay school fees on time. Or, you know, turn up for visitation on a regular basis. But it wasn't his fault he was a spoiled trust-fund baby who had never had to grow up. It could have been so much worse. He was always happy and carefree, and I did wholeheartedly believe he loved Amelia, even if he couldn't be a full-time parent.

Kat crowded the two of them, brushing a loving hand over Amelia's long hair. "Hey, cutie pie."

Amelia grinned at her. "We're playing the doctor game! Want to play?"

Kat shook her head and looked to Lleyton who looked to me.

A sinking feeling rose in my chest. "Why do I feel like I'm about to really not like whatever you're about to say?"

Lleyton tugged at my shirtsleeve. "Don't be like that. We decided to take a trip. Just a short one for the next few nights. We want Amelia to come with us."

I frowned. He'd barely taken her overnight at all, let alone for a few nights in a row. She had daycare on Monday. But Amelia was already squirming excitedly in his arms.

"Where? Is there a pool? I like to swim!"

Kat was nodding excitedly. "There is not only a heated pool, but a waterslide!"

Amelia's eyes went huge. "I've never been on one of those. But I want to. Can I go, Mom? Please. Please. Please. Please?"

I ground my teeth. This was what I meant with Lleyton being a good guy but too irresponsible to be a parent. The idea of taking Amelia on a holiday was nice, especially if they'd picked a place that was as child friendly as what Kat was making out. But he should have asked me alone. Now I had no choice but to say yes or be the bad guy.

Lleyton knew it too. He gave me a sheepish smile that probably worked on his mother and Kat but didn't on me. I'd tell him off later. In private, where our daughter couldn't hear.

"Where is this place? I need an address, Lleyton. When will you bring her back? Where will she sleep?"

To his credit, he answered each of my questions without complaint. So instead of throttling him, I lifted my daughter's chin so I could look her in the eye.

"You want to go stay with your dad and Kat for a few nights? Nanny and I won't be there."

"That's okay, Mommy. I'm big now. Dad and Kat will take care of me."

My heart broke a little, but she was right. I couldn't stand in the way of her spending more time with them if that was what she wanted. "Okay, Slugger. You can go."

Amelia squealed and leaned so far out of Lleyton's arms toward me that I had to catch her. I took her from him, and she put her arms around my neck and whispered in my ear, "It's okay, Mommy. I'll leave my bear for you, so you don't miss me too much."

I snuggled her back, enjoying the cuddle. "Gonna miss you anyway." The thought of her being away from me at all wasn't pleasant, but I knew it had to happen eventually. I set her down on her feet. "Go start putting some clothes and pajamas and underwear into a bag, okay? I'll come help you in a minute."

"I'll help her," Gran said, following her down the hallway to my bedroom.

I shot her a grateful smile and waited until the door closed behind them before I glared at Lleyton. "Seriously? A little warning wouldn't have gone astray!"

He laughed like I was joking. "What can I say? We're spontaneous."

"Spontaneous. Irresponsible. Same, same," I muttered.

He slung a brotherly arm around my shoulders. "Come on. Don't be like that. Amelia is excited."

I shrugged his arm off me. "That's the only reason I'm not strangling you right now."

"Good. Because we have one other thing to ask you."

I crossed my arms over my chest. "I'm not going to like this either, am I?"

Lleyton didn't answer and glanced to his girlfriend, waiting for her to fill me in.

Coward.

Kat cleared her long, delicate, swanlike throat. "We were wondering if we could ask a favor?"

I raised one eyebrow but said nothing, waiting for her to continue.

"I have two cats." She took out her wallet from her purse and flipped it open.

I blinked at the plastic photo holder that dropped out, more than half filled with photos of two gray-and-white, very fluffy cats. The rest of the photos were of her and Lleyton making lovesick faces at each other.

Barf.

But that didn't explain why they were telling me any of this.

"We were hoping you might be able to feed them for us while we're gone?"

I snorted. "Uh, no."

Kat's face fell, but Lleyton rolled his eyes.

"Come on, Lyric. Please? We can't go if there's no one to feed the cats. My parents are away, and all of Kat's family live in England."

"So ask a friend."

"I thought we were," Kat said softly.

I glanced at her, sure she was pulling my leg, but the woman actually did seem hurt.

Guilt roared in, and I really wasn't sure why. I didn't owe either of them anything and yet I found myself sighing and then nodding. I held out my hand in Kat's direction. "Fine," I huffed. "Give me the key."

Kat clapped her hands while Lleyton smiled on proudly, like he'd been the one to fix all of her problems.

Double barf.

From the depths of Kat's purse came a set of keys on a dangling sunflower chain. She placed it gently in my hand and then listed off a Providence address, just around the corner from Lleyton's parents' place. "If you could water the plants, bring in the mail, and check Monsoon's eye twice a day, that would be great."

Twice a freaking day? For fuck's sake. Like I had nothing better to do, between work and Gran and the church. But Amelia and Gran came back out, a small bag on Amelia's back and her pillow clutched in her arms.

"I'm ready!"

So, I said nothing and simply hugged my daughter goodbye, knowing it would be the longest days ever without her.

The door closed behind them, and Gran looked at me. "I can't believe you agreed to feed her cats."

I shook my head at how whipped I was for the little human I'd birthed. "Neither can I, Gran. Neither can I."

13

ZEPH

It only took me a few days to sell the stolen jewelry, and I was pleasantly surprised by how much money I was able to hand over to Tammie and her boys. Her eldest was looking much better after a short stay in the hospital, and when Tammie opened the thick envelope she gasped, staring up at me with incredulous eyes.

"Where did all of this come from?"

"We passed a plate around for you at church last weekend. Everybody was very generous." It was a lie, of course. The church would have never let me pass around a plate for a specific person in need. All donations were accepted by the church, then a board determined how to distribute the money. Tammie and her boys didn't have time to wait around for a bunch of priests and nuns and other official church members to determine whether she and her family deserved a cut of the funds. She needed the money now.

Tears rolled down the woman's cheeks. "I don't even know how to thank you. You've done so much for us."

I accepted the hug she offered and patted her eldest on the head. "It's just good to see him healthy again."

I waved goodbye and left Tammie marveling over the cash in the envelope while her boys ran back to the play equipment, none the wiser to what we'd been discussing. In my car again, I turned to the stolen record player sitting on the passenger-side seat. "Last delivery of the day."

I parked my car outside Lyric's apartment at the same time an obnoxious red sports car with the number plates KAT WOW was leaving. Recognizing it as Katherine and Lleyton, I raised a hand in greeting through the windshield, but neither of them noticed me. I took their parking spot and hefted the player into my arms to carry it down the sidewalk. I had only knocked once when Lyric's door flew open.

"What did you forget?" She frowned, recognition dawning in her eyes. "Oh. You aren't Lleyton."

I shifted the record player into my other arm. "No. They were just leaving as I pulled in."

She opened the door wider and waved me in. "Come in. They took Amelia for a couple days, so it's just me and Gran."

"And a couple of pussies," Cheryl called out gaily, a snigger of delight in her tone.

I blinked. "Excuse me?"

Lyric burst into laughter and threw a couch cushion at her grandmother. "Stop. You're embarrassing him." She twisted back to me to offer an explanation. "Lleyton and

Kat just dumped her two cats on me for the next couple days while they take Amelia on vacation." She pointed to a set of keys sitting on the coffee table in front of her. "I've got the keys to the Kat Wow mansion and am expected to show up twice a day to feed her possibly sickly kitties."

"You never told me Amelia was taking time off school." Not that she had to tell me anything, but I'd seen the woman practically every day. Seemed odd she hadn't even mentioned Amelia going away.

"I didn't know 'til just now. They completely sprang it on me."

Irritation at Lleyton prickled the back of my neck. I didn't like the way he just walked into Lyric's life and made demands of her. From everything I'd seen of him, the man was a spoiled, rich brat. "That wasn't very polite of them. Did they at least offer you some compensation for your time?"

Lyric sniggered. "No. It was more of a, 'Do this for us or we can't go and then Amelia misses out,' sort of situation."

She was smiling, but I was irked Lleyton and Kat would take advantage of her like that. Especially when they clearly knew how she lived. With one glance around her apartment, I could see a dozen things she needed fixed. The faucet dripped. The walls needed painting. There was a section of carpet that had been nearly worn through. All things Kat and Lleyton would have replaced or fixed within a moment's notice because they had the money to just call someone up and do it. And yet they hadn't even offered Lyric compensation for going out of her way?

If she'd been mine, I would have taken any opportunity to help her. To provide for her and for Amelia. Lleyton had the chance and the money and chose not to.

My irritation flared into anger. Instead of letting it get the better of me, I thrust the record player toward Cheryl. "I brought you this."

Her gaze flickered over the gift, and she stood, taking it from my arms, her mouth a little round 'O' of surprise. "It's for me?"

I nodded.

Lyric's eyebrows bunched together. "You didn't buy that for us, did you? It looks expensive."

I shook my head, thinking fast to come up with an excuse. "No. It was lying around at the church and never gets used. I thought it would do better over here with you two." I didn't like lying to her, but I knew she wouldn't accept it if I'd told her I'd bought it. If I'd explained I'd lifted it from some rich asshole's house, she probably wouldn't believe me.

Cheryl, no such qualms about accepting my gift, was already busily plugging the thing in. She grinned up at me from her hands and knees on the floor, plug grasped between her fingers. "My husband and I used to have one of these. Oh, how I loved it. Until he threw it out one day after we had an argument. I'm still cross about that."

"She's having a good day," Lyric whispered in explanation.

Cheryl crawled slowly out from beneath the table, player now plugged into the wall outlet, and she smiled happily. "I wish I had some of my old records. We'll have to go to the thrift stores to try to find some."

I held up a plastic bag hung around my wrist. "Beat

you to it. But of course, the thrift store has more if you don't like these."

Lyric's gaze warmed me as she tracked me across the room, watching quietly. I handed her grandmother the bag, and she rifled through it. I'd searched four thrift shops, going as far as the city to source the Elvis Presley album I knew she loved. I'd put it right on the top so she couldn't miss it.

She pulled it from the bag, a small gasp on her thin lips. Slowly, she lowered the bag with the rest of the records and glanced up at me. "My husband used to play this record to me. We'd dance for hours in the living room."

Even though she was lucid this time and knew I wasn't Lyric's father, I pointed to the record player. "Put it on and dance with me?"

She put it on but then pointed at her granddaughter. "Her grandaddy used to dance with her before he died too. I think she'd like to dance with you now."

With a small smile on her lips, she hummed her way down the hallway to her bedroom, closing the door behind her.

I glanced at Lyric, surprised by her expression.

Her cheeks and the tip of her nose were pink. "That was a really nice thing you did. Thank you. Sometimes music is the only way to keep her calm on her bad days. This will help."

I held a hand out to her and lifted her to her feet. She wasn't a short woman, probably five foot five, but she had to crane her neck back to look up at me. With one hand clutched around hers, I brushed her hips with my other. The chemistry between us crackled, and my palm itched to connect with the tiny strip of skin showing between her sweats and cropped T-shirt.

Her gaze turned heated, eyes lowering to half-mast. "What are we doing here, Zeph?"

The question was a whisper, but a loaded one. I knew she was asking more than just what we were doing in that very moment. But I didn't have an answer for that. So I answered the question as if she'd asked it literally. "I think we're dancing."

"You need to hold me properly then." She put her arms around my neck, and mine slid to the curve of her hips, unable to resist, and then to her lower back, palms pressing just above her ass.

I stared down at her, heart thumping too fast because there was no way I could have explained this to anyone in the priesthood. There was no way I could have explained this to myself, other than I was doing what felt good and natural for the first time in so fucking long.

I didn't want to stop.

We swayed together in her run-down living room, Elvis Presley crooning in my ear, Lyric's warm breath misting across the open neck of my shirt and so sweetly brushing my skin. I inhaled the scent of her hair, marking it to memory, and tugged her just a little closer.

"I don't like that Lleyton and Kat are taking advantage of you."

Lyric sighed and twisted her head to lay it on my chest. "He's Amelia's dad. He's trying."

"He's doing the bare minimum."

"It's better than him doing nothing at all. He's not a bad guy."

I stiffened at her praising Lleyton. Jealousy coursed through me.

She gazed up at me, curious. "Why did you just go all frosty and hard?"

"I didn't."

A smile played about her mouth. "Yeah, Zeph. You did. I said Lleyton was a good guy, and you went stiff as a board."

I stepped back, knowing she was right and knowing exactly why I'd done it.

Because I hated hearing her talk about another man.

Hated knowing he'd touched her. Gotten her naked. Kissed her pretty lips and sank his cock inside her pussy.

I hated knowing that asshole had done all the things I so desperately wanted to do.

"I should go. I just wanted to drop the player off, but I have mass tonight."

Lyric grinned at me, like she could read every dirty thought in my head. "Mmm-hmm. Sure you do. See you later."

I turned and left the apartment, dick hard for wanting her and as stiff as the rest of me.

I'd need a week straight of masses to forgive the violence I wanted to rain down on Lleyton just because he was the lucky asshole she'd chosen to go to bed with.

14

LYRIC

"You look like shit, Augie."

I wouldn't normally greet someone with such a blunt insult, but he was getting worse by the day. He'd always had the high cheekbones and chiseled jaw of a model, but lately, his cheeks had hollowed out to an unhealthy degree, and dark circles took up the space beneath his sea-blue eyes. Harsh frown lines had become a permanent fixture on his paling face, which made me think he hadn't even been surfing lately.

As much as he and I bickered, I couldn't handle seeing him like this.

"Hello to you, too, sunshine." He opened his locker with such force it slammed back against mine with a clang of metal on metal. "Are we starting the night off with insults? Your hair extensions are cheap."

Normally I would have flipped him the bird and insulted him right back because that was how he and I rolled. But tonight, my worry for him overcame the need for smart-ass retorts. "You're late."

He shrugged. "So? You Eve now? What do you care?"

I narrowed my gaze at him. "I care because we were worried something happened to you. That you crashed your stupid bike on the way here or something. We called you a bunch of times."

He slammed his locker shut again and spun to glare at me, arms spread wide. "Well, I'm here now, aren't I? Still in one fucking piece. Get off my case, Lyric."

Oh, he was such an asshole. I loved him like a brother, but I could also punch him like one too. I stood and shoved two hands against his chest. "Where were you?"

He was clearly startled by the force of the shove. His shoulder blades hit the lockers, and his eyes turned dark. "Not your business."

I shoved him again. "Yeah, asshole. It is my business because you're the brother I never fucking wanted, which means it's my job to go all sisterly on you. Which means telling you the fucking truth. You. Look. Like. Shit. You reek of booze and smokes and women."

He shrugged. "I party, Lyric. This isn't new. And you aren't my fucking family."

I took a step back, hurt by the accusation. He was right. Augie liked a good time, and it was no secret he supplemented his stripping income with additional sources of the less legal variety. He was a ridiculously attractive man who welcomed both men and women into his bed at night, as long as they paid well. I didn't judge him for it. We all did what we had to do, and until recently, Augie had seemed to enjoy his lifestyle, so we'd all left him to it.

But that had changed when Fawn went missing.

Everything had changed, and none of it for the better. None of us were moving on. How could we, when there was no closure and every moment was filled with questions and fear? Eve was burying herself in Boston. I was distracting myself with Zeph. Augie seemed hell-bent on drinking and smoking and fucking himself into an early grave.

"I *am* your family, asshole. You can try to deny it, but that's what we are here. Like it or not, you're a part of that. I'm not letting you do this."

He glared at me with an expression that probably would have had me withering on the spot if I hadn't known him as well as I did. He had all his defenses up, pushing all of us away so he could destroy himself without any of us trying to stop him.

"I have no family, Lyric. All I have is parents who never gave a shit. A brother who hates my guts, and rightfully fucking so, after the things I did to him. And this fucking shithole." He motioned around the room. "This fucking club that's falling to pieces because someone fucking took the only ray of sunshine in it."

He slouched down on the bench seat, some of the fight and anger going out of him.

Which dulled a little of my fire too. I sat back down beside him, shoulders slumped. "You never told me your brother hates you. Or that your parents weren't in the picture." I knew a little something about that, after being left to my grandmother when I was a kid.

He shrugged. "They were right to dump me. Bad shit happens to anyone I get close to. Banjo. Fawn."

I put a hand on his leg and squeezed. "I don't know

what happened with your brother, but Fawn wasn't your fault."

He shook his head. "I should have been there to protect her."

"You couldn't be with her twenty-four seven."

His eyes turned anguished. "I knew her ex was bad news, but I thought she was being paranoid. I should have just fucking listened when she said she was scared."

"We all should have listened," I assured him. "This isn't all on you."

He scrubbed his hands over his weary face. "She was in love with me, wasn't she?"

I peered at him curiously, surprised he'd brought that up. "I don't know that she was in love with you. She definitely had a crush."

He sighed.

"Do you love her back? Is that why you're beating yourself up over this so bad?"

He sighed heavily, gaze tortured. "It was never like that for me. It still isn't. She's barely more than a kid, Lyric. She actually reminds me of Banjo and how fucking good and sweet and innocent he is." He groaned, dropping his face down into the palms of his hands. "She felt like a second chance to be the brother I wasn't to him. But then I found out about those fucking dildos you guys got…"

Months ago, I'd dragged Fawn into a sex toy store, and the attendant had talked us into buying personalized vibrators. He'd suggested that most women put the name of a partner or crush on their toy. I'd refused, putting my own name on mine because I didn't need no man to get me off. But Fawn had put Augie's, and we'd laughed as we'd bought one for Eve with Boston's name on it.

But both had caused problems we could have never anticipated at the time. "I wish we'd never done that now."

Augie shook his head. "I should have just talked to her about it. Explained the way I felt and let her down gently. She deserves a good guy, someone who can give her everything she needs." He glanced over at me with tears in his eyes. "I really wanted that for her, Lyric. I can't handle the thought of her not being happy."

I put my arm around him, realizing exactly what he was. "You're a parent, Aug. That's how I feel about Amelia."

He nodded miserably. "I swear, if I'd just been in love with her, it might have been easier to get over. But I do feel fatherly toward her and I swear that's a different sort of love. One I can't let go of just because I know she's probably dead. I let my brother go, because I could see he was happy and safe and I was only dragging him down. But it's not the same with Fawn. I can't just give up or accept she's not coming back."

We sat side by side in silence, with muffled music from the club seeping through the walls. Eventually, Eve came back, frantically searching for us because there was no one on the stage, and Augie and I had no choice but to get our shit together and go through the motions. But that's all it was.

The Strip had lost its sunshine, and without her, none of us were going to be okay.

I texted Peggy on my way out of the club as the sun was rising. I was late, because I'd stayed back to help Eve clean up a bunch of glasses that some visiting college frat boys had smashed. We'd moved practically in slow motion while I'd spilled out everything Augie had said in the locker rooms, and Eve tutted over how worried she was about him. Then accused me of being no better, because apparently, I looked like shit too.

Eve was bossy, especially when she was tired and overwhelmed. Especially when it came to those she considered family.

Peggy replied to my message instantly and with an enthusiasm I wasn't sure anyone but her could truly feel at five-thirty in the morning.

PEGGY

> Sure, hon. I've got nothing on, and your g-ma is still asleep. See you in an hour or two.

I tucked my phone away and got in the car, praying it would start because I couldn't afford an emergency mechanic's bill. Terry had fixed it for me after it last broke down, but he'd warned it was basically held together with duct tape and really needed to be sent to the scrapyard one day soon.

Today wasn't that day though, because the car did start, and I steered it through the quiet Sunday morning streets of Saint View and into Providence. I parked it up in the church lot, in between BMWs and Mercedes, and then followed the other early morning churchgoers inside for the 6:00 a.m. mass.

I'd once stood outside this church and told Eve I'd probably be struck down by lightning if I ever set a foot inside. Today, I'd sought it out, needing a comfort I'd heard some people found here.

Or maybe I'd just been seeking him.

He stood at the front of the altar, watching people find their places. He nodded good morning to those who called out a greeting to him, and I ducked my head, finding a seat in the back row where I could be as unobtrusive as possible.

He still saw me.

His gaze centered on me, fully and without hesitation.

A warmth flickered inside me as our gazes collided, his unreadable. Eventually, not knowing what else to do but aware people were starting to glance in my direction to see what he was staring at, I flicked my head up a notch and slightly to the right, indicating he needed to keep on with his preparations and not stare at me anymore.

Even if I did like it.

He caught on and started the mass, while I sank my tired body down against the hard wooden pew and let Zeph's deep voice wash over me. I had no idea what was going on, but I followed the people around me when they stood or when they kneeled, and moment by moment, a peace settled over me. I didn't hear his individual words or sentences. It all just became background noise, but in a nice way. One where I felt calm and peaceful even though the sadness lingered.

At the end, I let everyone else leave the church while I sat still.

He came to me.

Just like I knew he would.

He sat, his robes brushing my leg. "I didn't expect to see you here today."

"Or ever," I filled in for him with a smile.

He nodded. "Church isn't really your thing."

Was it his? That's what I wanted to ask, because something about the way he looked at me, and the connection that had sparked between us, had me questioning everything about him. But I couldn't say that to him. Not here, after watching him in action. The last hour had me wondering whether every moment I'd thought we'd had was even real, because he'd led that mass with a conviction I hadn't seen from him before. Nobody around me was sitting there, trying to read into his words the way I was. To everybody in that room, he was a priest, one fully committed and believing in the Bible verses he preached.

I pointed up at the altar. "You're good at your job."

"Thank you. But that doesn't explain what you're doing here. Or why your eyes are red like you've been crying."

He was always so observant. So tuned in to me in a way no other man ever had been. "You believe in Heaven, right?"

He paused for a long moment, then nodded. "I do."

"I think Fawn is dead. It's killing us all slowly. Augie especially."

"You've had no closure."

I nodded.

He settled back beside me, our arms touching, his

warmth seeping into me so welcome I wished there was more of it to wrap me entirely.

"I believe in souls. And that death is beautiful."

I glanced at him. "Odd thing to say."

He lifted a shoulder. "There's a beauty in endings. In someone being out of pain and in a better place. Of new life taking its place."

"Where's the beauty in someone being taken too soon? And so brutally?" I stared up at him, practically begging him to make it make sense.

I hadn't even realized I was crying until he tenderly brushed away a tear from my cheek. "Maybe it's in the people left behind and what they do next. The connections they forge in the face of grief. The way they change their lives so hers wasn't in vain. The way you go on and teach the next generation to do better."

I didn't know if I agreed when everything just felt so unfair. I'd already lost Fawn, and it was inevitable I'd lose my grandmother at some point in the not-too-distant future as well.

The thought left me cold. "I wouldn't wish this on my worst enemy, Zeph. The not knowing with Fawn. The daily struggles I have to watch my grandma go through. This life is fucking cruel. It breaks me, day by day, until I don't even know what's left. How am I supposed to raise Amelia and explain all of this stuff to her when none of it makes sense to me?"

His fingers covered mine. "You could have faith. That someone or something bigger than you has a plan. Let them take the reins for a little while. You don't have to do everything alone, Lyric, even though you think you do.

There are people who want to have your back." He cleared his throat. "I want to have your back."

His words were meant to soothe me, and until that last sentence had slipped out of his mouth, they had. But him saying he wanted to be there for me? That he was someone I could lean on? It wrapped its way around me and squeezed until all I felt was confusion and breathlessness.

"You can't make promises like that," I said quietly.

"I already did."

I wanted him to put his arms around me, draw me tight against his solid chest, and hold me. I wanted to tilt my chin up and feel his lips press down on mine.

I wanted all manner of things I couldn't have with him, and I was torturing myself by continuing this when I knew it couldn't lead anywhere. I needed to change the subject. "You ever want to spill what's on your mind? You spend all day listening to other people's problems, who listens to yours?"

"I go to confession, I guess."

"In the little boxes with the peephole? They still have those? I thought they were some ancient relic that was done away with back in the caveman times."

He chuckled and pointed to the booth-type structure to the right-hand side of the church. At this time of morning, it was bathed in early sunlight and looked quite warm and inviting, but I couldn't imagine walking in there, pouring out all the things I'd done that made me a shitty human. Of course, nothing Zeph did was shitty. But I wondered if he'd told anyone about the chemistry between us.

"Do you pretend you're someone else so your boss

doesn't know it's you?" I asked curiously.

He raised an eyebrow, then said in his deep, so-sexy voice, "I don't think that would work well."

It wouldn't. His voice was too toe-curling to be mistaken for someone else.

"So you just spill all your secrets? And trust that he won't judge you?"

He paused, gaze firmly on me. "Not all of them."

A breath rushed out of me.

I was sure I was the secret he wasn't confessing. He was as good as admitting there was more between the two of us than just friendship.

His gaze flickered to my lips, lingering on them longer than they should have. His fingers tightened around mine, and his head moved toward me, so slowly it was maddening because all I wanted to do was lean and close the distance.

But I didn't dare for fear of scaring him off.

I wanted his kiss. His lips on mine. His tongue in my mouth and my fingers in his hair.

I should have cared that kissing me would be going against everything he believed in. But in the moment, I didn't. All I could want was right there in front of me, with a heat and desire in his eyes that stole my breath.

"Father Zepherin? Are you still in here?"

We jumped apart like we'd been electrocuted, right before an elderly woman with a walking stick stuck her head around the entrance. Her frown smoothed out into a warm smile.

"Oh, there you are. Are you coming out? There are a few people still milling around, and Mr. Thompson would like a word before he leaves."

Zeph stood stiffly, wiping his palms on his robe. "Of course, Mrs. Dodds. I'll be right there."

I slunk down in my pew, wishing I could slither onto the floor like a snake. My face burned at being caught.

All we'd been doing was looking at each other, but it had felt like so much more. I felt exposed. Like old Mrs. Dodds had walked in on me and Zeph, naked and making love on the altar.

Oh fuck. There was something wrong with me that I found the idea such a turn-on.

Zeph was equally stiff, and I wondered if he was playing out the same fantasies. But then he held a hand out to me. "Come. You can't sit in here all day."

He was right, I needed to get home so Peggy could leave but I could barely get my breathing under control.

"Your face is pink, Lyric."

"I wonder why!"

"We weren't doing anything..."

The unspoken 'yet' hung in the air between us, as loudly as if he'd shouted it.

But I took his hand and let him pull me to my feet.

He held it until the very last second, when we emerged into the light of the morning.

Brain short-circuiting, I followed him through the still lingering parishioners, standing around in groups on the church lawn, chatting and gossiping like this was their favorite Sunday morning activity.

"...I still don't know how they even got in," one woman complained. She was maybe early forties and dressed in a very proper knee-length skirt and short-sleeved blouse. She caught sight of Zeph and called him over.

He very briefly touched the small of my back, steering me in her direction, a suddenly warm smile on his face for the older woman.

"Mrs. Lauderton. Good morning."

The woman glanced at me but quickly refocused on Zeph without saying anything. Couldn't blame her really. I couldn't stop staring at him either.

"I was just telling Tracey here about our house break-in."

Tracey, clearly wanting Zeph's attention too, butted in, stealing her friend's story. "All they stole was her jewelry, some cash, and a record player. Now, I can understand the jewelry and cash. But why a record player?"

The memory of Zeph and I slow dancing in my living room while a gifted record player spun was still fresh in my mind. I looked sharply at him.

The movement caught his eye, and he turned in my direction. My eyes had to be huge.

"What?" he asked.

I studied him for a fraction of a second while the other two women watched us with interest. But I pushed the idea from my head. "Nothing," I assured him. "Sorry. I should get going. See you later when I come in to clean."

He nodded and went back to the other two women, like nothing was wrong. I shook my head. I'd already convinced myself so many ridiculous things about this man.

He was a priest, not a cat burglar.

But the nagging feeling didn't go away. Especially not when I glanced back at Zeph and found him watching my every move.

15

LYRIC

*P*eggy pounced on me the minute I got home. She grabbed my arm and towed me inside my apartment, her smile ear to ear. "I have a surprise for you."

I followed her—like I had any other choice with the way she was dragging me—but eyed her warily. "I don't like surprises."

She waved her hand around like she was brushing off a pesky fly. "Pfft. You'll like this. Amelia is gone until Tuesday, right?"

I swiped my hand back and used it to yank the tie out of my hair, my scalp tingling in relief. "Yeah. That's what Lleyton said anyway."

Peggy clapped her hands together. "I was talking to one of my friends last night who works in a respite facility, and she said they just had a cancellation for Monday night. I took it. For your gran. So you can have a night completely to yourself. You can go stay in that fancy house that you're babysitting for your ex's girlfriend, have a bubble bath, order some food in, dance around in your underwear, give yourself an orgasm, whatever you want. No responsibilities for once!"

I pinched the bridge of my nose between two fingers, fighting off the impending headache. "That's really lovely of you, but I can't afford it. Those places are so expensive. Gran would hate it—"

Peggy pressed a finger to my lips. "The spot is already paid for. They cancelled too late to get their money back. And Cheryl will love it. She needs to get out a bit, Lyric. She's stuck inside all the time, and I'm not saying that's your fault, I know how difficult it is to get her out when you have Amelia too. But she'll be picked up and dropped off by trained staff, and you don't need to do anything. I'll see her off tomorrow after my shift before you even get home from work." She took me by my shoulders and forced me to face her. "Please let me do this for you. And for her."

Zeph's words about there being people in my life who wanted to have my back rang true in my ears. Here was Peggy doing a beautiful thing for me, and I was about to turn her down because I was so stupidly independent and wanted to be everything to everyone.

Peggy and Zeph were both right. I was burning the candle at both ends and eventually I was going to set myself on fire. I wasn't doing anything wrong by taking one night off, not only from work but from my life.

The prospect twinkled in front of me like it was made of gold. Why the hell shouldn't I use Kat's gorgeous place as my own for one night? I deserved some sort of compensation for dealing with her cat's sticky eye gunk. I needed to go over there later and deal with that again before I went back to the club for my Sunday night shift. Maybe while I was there, I'd investigate where she kept the bubble bath so I was set for a Monday night sleepover.

I gave Peggy a little nod.

She squealed. "Is that a yes? Are you actually agreeing to this, oh stubborn one?"

I laughed and shoved her toward the door. "Yes, I'm agreeing. Get out of here before I change my mind."

She leaned in and kissed my cheek then grabbed her purse and let herself out.

A second later, I opened the door again. "Peggy?" I called down the hallway after her.

She stopped and looked back. "Mmm?"

"Thank you," I said softly. "I really need this."

She blew me a kiss. "I know, sugar. I know."

16

ZEPH

After my Sunday evening mass, I staked out Kat's house. From my car, parked a little down the street, I made notes on my pad of paper about the comings and goings of the neighborhood. The security cameras I needed to be aware of, the dogs that might cause a fuss if they noticed a strange man, stalking around in a balaclava in the middle of the night, any person who might do shift work.

And I waited for Lyric to show up to feed the cats, correctly guessing she'd be there in the evening, before her shift at the club started.

In the dark, my breath sped up. Her long, bare legs were the first of her to emerge from her car, followed by shapely thighs, toned from long nights dancing and performing on the pole, no doubt. She had booty shorts on that clung to her perfect ass, and a baggy T-shirt that had seen better days. The faded fabric was worn in and cozy though, and really did nothing to stop me thinking about her body beneath it. Her auburn hair glinted in the streetlight as she moved to the front door of Kat's extrava-gant house, keys swinging from her index finger.

I noted the time down on my notepad, then sat back and watched her move around the property, switching on lights as she went. I cocked my head to one side, wondering why every light in the place periodically turned on then off, then grinned at the realization she was probably snooping around Kat's belongings. I couldn't blame her. It wasn't like I didn't do the same anytime I broke into a house to steal. The things people kept in their homes, especially the places that nobody else ever saw, were inherently interesting.

Eventually, it was only the downstairs living area light that remained on, and through the open windows, I watched her fill water and food bowls for two cats who twined themselves around her feet, waiting for their dinner.

I checked my watch again. She'd been there fifteen minutes, and with her job done, I expected her to lock up and come back outside. My pen hovered over my notepad, ready to jot down her leaving time, but I sat forward when instead she went over to a sound system and switched it on. Her shoulders instantly shimmied to the beat of whatever she'd put on, and when she straight-ened into a standing position, her hips swayed seductively.

I swallowed thickly, a lump suddenly lodged in my throat when she ran her palms over the curve of her hips and up her rib cage. Her T-shirt lifted, flashing me her toned, flat belly, before dropping again to settle around the tops of her thighs.

I'd thought so many times about what she must look

like when she was working. How her body would move, undulating to a sensual beat. How she must make eye contact with the men who watched her take her clothes off.

And yet I'd never allowed myself to walk inside the club while she was working. Not once, even though I'd envisioned her there a hundred times since I'd learned what she did for work.

I'd want to kill every other man in the room for looking at her. Watching them leer at her, maybe even try to touch her, there was no way I'd be able to stay in my seat. I respected her choice of job, but from the minute I'd laid eyes on her, I'd known I'd never be able to watch her perform.

Unless it was just for me.

A solo dance for no other man. One she performed with lust in her eyes, all of it centered in my direction.

But that was something I'd never be able to ask her for, and so I'd resigned myself to sitting in my car, watching the building where she worked, imagining all the ways I wanted her to dance for me, and only for me.

Like the perverted stalker I knew I was.

Only I wondered if she'd like it. If she knew I was out here, watching her dance.

I blinked as the curtains were abruptly pulled shut.

"Fuck." Had she seen me? I waited a moment, watching for the front door to fly open and for her to storm down the driveway, gorgeous hair flying about behind her and expression full of outrage. I waited for her to slam her hands on her hips and yell at me for being a pervert.

I waited a good long minute. But the door never

opened. Lyric's silhouette danced behind the light-colored curtains.

I groaned and circled my fingers tight around the steering wheel. "Stay in the car, Zeph. Even better, turn the car on and drive away."

I got out of the car, crossed the immaculately kept lawn and the pools of streetlight, to stand in the shadows.

She hadn't quite closed the curtains all the way. This close to the house, there was a gap big enough to catch glimpses of her naked tits and a lacy red G-string, nestled between the plump cheeks of her ass.

My mouth went dry, my dick hard.

Lyric was lost in a world of her own, eyes closed, moving to the sultry music I could now hear even though the windows were closed. The T-shirt and shorts had been discarded to the floor; a bra that matched the panties flung to the couch while she practiced her routine.

My dick wept with precum. I wasn't sure I'd ever been so hard. Her breasts were full and round and high, nipples dark pink and erect, just begging for my mouth.

Fuck. I wanted that so bad. My tongue on every inch of her. Her mouth. Her neck. Her tits. Her bare mound, leisurely being exposed as she torturously slowly removed her underwear to dance naked.

I refused to touch myself, though the urge to reach inside my pants and stroke my cock roared loud in my ears.

But I watched. Hating myself with every breath but unable to walk away.

It was like being strangled, moment by moment, each one more torturous than the last.

It had been a very long time since I'd seen a naked woman. Never one who moved the way Lyric did, with a complete and utter self-confidence that was so inherently sexy I wanted to come even without the added friction of my hand.

Her hands had roamed over her tits more than once, but I froze when she stopped and pinched her nipples. I was sure my soul up and left my body when those fingers inched lower and pinched her clit.

Her moan of pleasure was loud enough for me to hear on the other side of the windows.

Like my feet had a mind of their own, I inched forward, unable to stop myself until I was as close to the masturbating woman as I could get. Was I still protected by the shadows? I had no idea. Not when all I could do was watch her fingers slip between her folds and lower to plunge inside herself.

A noise slipped from my mouth. A groan of primal need and desire, one I couldn't have held back even if I'd been aware of it building.

Her head snapped in my direction.

Our gazes collided.

Neither of us moved. Me, caught out, watching her through a window. Her, fingers lost between her thighs.

Her mouth opened as if to scream.

I braced myself for it. Tried to come up with some sort of excuse as to what the hell I was doing, but we both knew there was none. Nothing other than I was a man who wanted her in ways I wouldn't ever be allowed.

Her mouth closed, recognition lighting in her expression. For the longest moment, neither of us moved.

Neither of us said a word. What was there to say? We'd both been caught.

Lyric recovered before I did. But instead of grabbing for her T-shirt or trying to hide herself, her hands dropped, defiance mixed with lust in her eyes.

I finally had the decency to look away. Shame and guilt and hate for myself swirled through my system, and once again I was reminded why I'd joined the priesthood. Because this was what I fucking did when I let my desires get the better of me. I was a walking red flag and I knew it. Not safe to be around women, and apparently even joining the priesthood wasn't enough.

I'd have to confess. To beg for forgiveness. I was beyond needing a therapist. I probably needed to be committed. Again.

Somehow, what I was doing right now was so much worse than when I'd put my fingers around a man's neck and choked the life out of him. That had meaning. A purpose. He'd been a bad person, and the world was safer without him.

This was for my own sick pleasure.

The two weren't the same.

Lyric shifting to the couch caught my eye. She sat on the edge, watching me, and then swiveled to lie down, head on the armrest, red hair splayed out around her. Her feet toward me, knees pressed together and slightly bent.

Her perky tits pointed at the ceiling, bare and perfect. With agonizing slowness, she took one in her hand, rolling her nipple between her thumb and forefinger again. At the same time, her knees fell out to the sides.

I sucked in a breath, my gaze locked on her pussy, wet and gorgeous and completely on display.

For me.

It was all for me. She knew I was there, and she wasn't running away. Wasn't coming out to yell at me. Wasn't even trying to cover up.

She knew who I was. What I was. And just maybe, what I needed.

Her gaze dipped to my cock, straining behind my pants. I had no idea if she could see how tented I was, how hard she made me, but the slight smile that appeared on her lips told me she probably could.

Her fingers slipped through the arousal at her core, and then she nodded at me, smile becoming flirty as she raised her voice loud enough for me to hear through the windows. "If you're going to stand there watching me, Zeph, you could at least give me something to watch too."

Oh Jesus. My dick kicked hard at the invitation, straining to get in on the action.

It was wrong. Dirty. Forbidden. Taboo.

And yet it was me who'd started this. Me who'd let my desires rule my head. Now there was no turning back. We both knew it. I wanted her too much.

I undid my jeans and put my hand inside my boxer briefs, stroking the thick, warm length of my cock twice before exposing it to her.

Her eyes turned hungry, and that low, possessive growl grumbled through me. I practically purred beneath her gaze, the need for her only increasing with every stroke of my hand and every plunge of her fingers. They came out soaking every time, and her arousal coated the insides of her smooth thighs. I wondered if she was always that wet when she made herself come, or if some of it had to do with me watching.

I wanted it to be because of me.

Watching her writhe on a couch, body so perfect, pussy on full display, moans loud enough for me to hear, was a punishment in itself. One I would never get enough of. I pumped myself harder, faster, matching the pace she used. Her pants became loud, her legs shook with the force of her impending orgasm, and I watched every inch of her so intently I was probably cross-eyed.

I'd never watched a woman come. Annie had never let me try, and I'd been too young and inexperienced anyway to have a real idea of what I was doing. But Lyric cemented everything I needed to know about how she liked to be touched. I learned what turned her on, how many fingers she liked inside her, how fast and hard to work her clit until she was a trembling mess on a couch that wasn't hers.

My own orgasm built deep in my balls, sending spine-tingling pleasure through my entire body. But I held off, waiting for her, watching her every movement, until I knew she was on the verge. Her head tipped back, pressing into the back of the couch, and before I could stop myself, I was rasping my knuckles across the glass.

Her head snapped back up.

"Watch me," I demanded, low, dark, and possessive.

Her orgasm shuddered through her, and she cried out, not with words, or my name, which I ached to hear on her lips, but with pleasure and desire and her gaze solidly on me.

She watched as my own climax took over, thick, hot cum spurting from my tip and over my hand, every drop of it for her and the way she turned me on. I pumped myself torturously slow, drawing it out as long as I could, not wanting it to end.

It had been so long since I'd felt like this. Felt this need for another person. Felt anything other than shame when I put my hand around my cock.

But the feeling was short-lived. When I looked up again, Lyric was on her knees, still naked and beautiful, her hand pressed to the glass.

The truth of who I was, and the things I needed, was never far from the surface. I'd turned it off for a moment, but the realization of that glass being the only thing keeping me from pinning her to the couch and sinking my dick inside her sweet, hot pussy was too much.

I yanked my pants up and escaped back to my car.

17

LYRIC

J avoided the church on Monday. I was supposed to clean, but after Sunday night with Zeph, I couldn't bring myself to go anywhere near the place. Embarrassment heated my cheeks every time I thought about it, which wasn't a regular experience for me. Normally, I didn't give a shit, or at least, I could try to convince myself I didn't.

But what had happened with Zeph had been next level and so kinky I'd been wet for the past twenty-four hours, his dick and the way he'd watched me permanently on my mind. It was a damn miracle I hadn't slipped straight off the pole with how lubed up I was just from the memory. I still didn't know how I'd gotten through my shift. I'd told Eve every detail, and her expression was one I didn't know she could make. I'd thought I'd known all her faces, after working together for years, but one little sentence, "I made myself come in front of a priest," had her needing a sit down and stiff drink.

I couldn't blame her. I still couldn't believe it either.

I was never going to the church again. I was definitely quitting. It was still months away, but thank God Amelia started school after summer and wouldn't need daycare anymore. I was pretty sure Zeph would make himself scarce at pickup and drop-off times for the rest of the school year. Neither of us would want the reminder we'd completely lost our minds for a minute there.

On Monday, with both Amelia and my gran taken care of, and the club closed, I thought really hard about not going to Kat's place at all. I'd been working all day to keep the image of Zeph's dick, hard with need, and then slick with his cum, out of my head, and going back to the scene of the crime was bound to set me right back at zero on the 'forget that you did kinky shit with a priest' scale.

But as much as I could be a bitch, I liked animals and I really couldn't sleep well knowing there were two cats who might have knocked over their water or run out of food.

I went out to my car and almost changed my mind on going again when the stupid engine spluttered instead of turning over. But Peggy would be upset if I told her I'd spent my one child- and parent-free night eating leftover pizza by myself in my shitty apartment while police sirens wailed outside. So I caught an Uber, grabbing some Thai takeout on the way.

Kat's place was a luxury I'd never known. Her carpets were white and so pristine that I was sure Amelia had never come here when they'd had custody of her. There wasn't a spaghetti or Jell-O stain in sight, and everything was painfully clean and tidy. She must have had incense sticks somewhere because even with two cats in the house, it smelled lovely.

Said cats saw me coming and scurried beneath the couch. I peered under it, pretending that couch hadn't seen things last night, and two sets of cat eyes shined back. "I've come here multiple times now, guys. I'm staying all night. Do we have to keep pretending you don't love me? You know you're both going to be all over me the minute I get the food out."

Neither cat made a move. I'd had to pull the gunk-eyed one out by the scruff of his neck the last two days so I could insert his drops, but at least I wouldn't have to do that today. Since I was hanging around all night, I had the luxury of waiting for him to decide to trust me.

So I got their food ready and put their bowls where they could reach them. Ate my own dinner in the kitchen where I couldn't see the living room. I grabbed a duster and scurried around the place like a cleaning fairy. Took a bubble bath in Kat's huge tub that had water jets. The gunk-eyed cat came searching for me once his belly was full, and I managed to get his eye drops in before he went feral again and tried to claw my eyes out.

I didn't go downstairs again though. I got into bed in Kat's room since her spare was set up as an office. There was a pull-out bed in the third bedroom, but I turned my nose up at that. I didn't come over here to have a shitty sleep on a foldaway bed when Kat's looked like an inviting mountain of marshmallow.

I'd wash the sheets and remake the bed before I left in the morning. It was early when I turned out all the lights and got into bed. I'd promised Peggy an orgasm, but if she knew what I'd done here last night, I was sure she'd give me an out on that. These walls had seen enough of my antics.

I watched some TV on my phone, snuggled into the heaven that was Kat's bed. Her mattress was like lying on a cloud, and I spread out right across the middle of it, enjoying the space. It wasn't long before the show couldn't keep my interest and my eyes tried to close. I fought it for a little while, wanting to make the most of my responsibility-free night, but eventually gave in, with the thought that getting a decent night's sleep would actually be pretty nice.

The house was still and silent as I drifted off. No neighbors having a domestic. No drunks out on the street talking shit at the tops of their lungs. No police sirens or lights.

So when I woke to noises downstairs, it took me a moment to work out what was going on. I blinked in the darkness, trying to make out the shape of the room while I listened again for whatever had woken me.

The cats' food dish skittered along the floor making a scratching noise, and I settled back into the pillows, trying to get back to sleep.

The twisting of the bedroom door handle was most definitely not done by a cat though.

I froze, fear coursing through me.

Then pure fucking annoyance.

I'd lived in goddamn Saint View my entire life and had somehow managed to never have some asshole break into my place, at least not while I was in it. I come to Providence for one night, and *that's* the night this asshole decides to break in?

I forced myself to breathe slowly and deeply, faking

sleep while my brain whirred a million miles an hour, trying to come up with a way to get out of this so I could kill Kat and Lleyton later. First thought was that it would be easiest if the guy saw me sleeping and hightailed it out of the house. Presumably he thought the house was empty, and I silently cursed my stupid car for choosing tonight to break down again. If it had been parked in the driveway, this asshole might have thought twice about trying a break and enter.

Through my eyelashes, the man froze, his gaze on me. He glanced back toward the door, and I silently pleaded with him to just go. Because one look at him had tripled the fear I felt inside. He was huge. Broad-shouldered and dressed all in black. The thing that really freaked me out though, was the balaclava. There was something about not being able to see his face that made the entire thing so much worse. No matter how much I would fight, because I would, to the damn death if I had to, the strength in his body was clear. His hoodie clung to his solid chest, his pants hugging muscular thighs.

I just wanted him to leave. For him to decide that robbing a house with a sleeping woman inside was a really bad idea and for him to just turn around and walk out.

I really didn't want to consider that he might have been pleased to find me here alone.

The man moved past me, toward the en suite, disappearing inside it, and I had to make a split-second decision. Stay and pretend to be sleeping only to potentially have him pin me to this bed and rape me?

Or make a freaking run for it.

I was no good at hanging around, waiting for things to

happen to me. I liked to be the one in control of my own destiny.

As soon as I heard him rifling through Kat's things in the bathroom, I soundlessly got off the bed, silently thanking her for buying a good quality frame that didn't squeak, and inched toward the door.

I just needed to get outside the house. If I was outside, I could scream. In a neighborhood like this, where middle-of-the-night screams weren't a standard evening event, people would notice. They'd call the cops.

I was halfway down the stairs and celebrating prematurely before his booted footsteps sounded heavy on the second-floor landing.

All pretenses of sneaking out were thrown out the window, and I let adrenaline take over. It crashed through my system like a bull in a china shop, breaking everything in its sight. I threw myself down the last three stairs and sprinted for the front door, knowing the damn locks I'd so cautiously set were now going to be the thing that slowed me down.

I hit the living area, running at full pace, bare feet sinking into Kat's thick carpet, panicked sweat breaking out across my body. A scream ripped involuntarily from my lungs, but it was too soon for the neighbors to hear it, tucked safely in their warm beds on the other side of the large property. Too soon for it to do me any good because the man grabbed me at the door before my fingers even got to the locks.

His hand slapped over my mouth before I could scream again, and his big body pressed me into the wooden door face-first, his chest hard against my back, pinning me in place so I couldn't move.

Fuck that.

There was no way I was giving in that easily. I bit his finger, and he let out a yelp of pain, yanking his hand back. I twisted against his hold, managing to get around to face him, then wishing I hadn't because his eyes were so dark, they were terrifying.

I raised a leg to try to knee him, but he was quicker than I was. He ground his entire body against mine. His chest. His thighs. His hips.

He was hard. Big. Thick and hard. Terror rose in me once more, but the fight did little good. He was too big. Too strong. Surrounding me completely with his hand back over my mouth, my feeble attempts and fending him off completely useless.

The fight went out of me.

I stared into his dark eyes, both of us breathing heavily, our chests rising and falling in unison.

It went on too long.

So long that the fear subsided and curiosity set in.

Slowly, the man released his hand from my mouth.

I didn't scream.

The rest of him still pinned me, but slowly, moment by moment, a different feeling took the place of the terror. A lick of heat rolled through my spine. I reached for him, and he let me. I tucked my fingers into the neck of his mask and inched it over his head.

"What the actual fuck, Zeph?" I whispered, staring into his deep-brown eyes that were suddenly no longer horrifying but mesmerizing.

He pushed off me abruptly, like I'd broken some sort of spell by uttering his name. He turned around and stalked away. "I'm sorry." He scrubbed his hands through his balaclava-mussed hair. "Fuck, Lyric. I'm so fucking sorry. I didn't realize you were here or I never would have done this tonight. This is so messed up. *I'm messed up.*"

I stared at the man, big-eyed while the adrenaline tried to find some place to go now that I knew I wasn't in danger. Because whatever Zeph was, whatever messed-up things we did together, I wasn't scared of him.

Of course, the adrenaline turned into a thick, lusty desire, and everything we'd done through the window the night before came rushing back.

"We're both messed up," I assured him.

He didn't answer, but he didn't move to leave either. He just paced up and down the living room, gaze anywhere but on me.

"Do you want a drink?" I offered, because fuck knows I needed one. But then I realized what I'd said. "Oh, you can't drink, right? That lets in the Devil?"

He sank down on the couch I'd spent hours trying not to pay attention to. "We're allowed alcohol. Cigarettes too, if we don't smoke in front of the congregation. Can't set a bad example, you know?"

I went over to the cabinets at the side of the room and started opening them, searching for alcohol and glasses. In the second I found a half-drunk bottle of whiskey and grabbed it by the neck.

Behind it was a baggie of something that looked suspiciously like weed. I sniggered at the surprising find, not picking Kat and her perfect princess getup as someone who would also enjoy getting high. Then again, maybe it wasn't hers. Maybe it was Lleyton's. All the more reason to smoke it myself.

"What about weed?" I held out the bag in his direction. "Does the church have any strong feelings on that?"

He lifted a shoulder. "Never asked."

I brought both back to the couch and settled down next to him. Kat's couch was long and wide, but I found myself sitting close enough that our arms brushed.

He didn't move away.

I passed him the bottle of whiskey, and he downed a long swallow while I rolled a joint.

"Don't judge me." I glanced over my shoulder at him while I worked. "I haven't smoked this stuff since before I had Amelia."

He took the offered joint from my fingers and turned it over in his hand while I searched around for a lighter. "I'm not really in a position to judge anyone for anything right now."

I grinned in triumph when I found a lighter in a little ornamental box on a side table. I tossed it over to him. "No, sir, you are not. Are we going to talk about that?"

He squeezed his eyes shut and stuck the joint in his mouth, so his hand was free to light it. He sparked the lighter and touched the joint to the flame while he inhaled.

I expected coughing and spluttering, but he held it in, and then slowly let it out, closing his eyes like he'd completely enjoyed the experience. "Maybe when I've had a few more pulls on this."

I laughed quietly, taking it from his hand and taking a hit myself. The old familiar scent of pot wafted around us. I was vaguely aware that it would probably linger, and Kat would know we'd been smoking her stash, but hey, she owed me.

We were one joint and several shots of whiskey down when he finally spoke again. "This isn't the first house I've broken into."

I leaned back on the couch, wanting my arm to be in contact with his. The whiskey coursed through me pleasantly. I twisted my head in his direction but rested the back of it on the couch. "I didn't think it was. You were all the way in the bedroom before I even really worked out what was going on. That speaks of experience since my grandmother always says I sleep with one ear open. You kinda have to when you live in a ground-floor apartment in Saint View. Can't ever let your guard down."

He exhaled a plume of smoke slowly, then turned his head toward me. "I don't like when people with money or power take advantage of those who have none. Sometimes I find myself doing things to even the score. Your ex and his girlfriend pissed me off with the way they treat you."

I nudged him with my elbow, oddly pleased by the fact he was here robbing a house because he didn't like the way someone had treated me. "Aren't you just a barrel of surprises? Priest by day, sweary, pot-smoking, 'Robin Hood stealing from the rich to give to the poor' by night." I reached for the bottle again, even though I was getting lightheaded from the combo of alcohol and drugs and really needed to slow down.

But he was making me giddy. Despite my vow to avoid him forever after the show I'd given him last night, there was no denying the chemistry between us, or the way I wanted him. The fact he was so forbidden only made the need worse. Every time he gave me a scrap of a hint I could have more from him, I wanted to pounce on it and unravel his secrets until I knew everything about him. "Watching women get themselves off... Making them watch you when they come."

I expected him to go red. Or to shove to his feet and leave because I'd pushed him too far. Maybe it was the pot or the whiskey talking, but instead of running away, he moved closer. The backs of his knuckles brushed over the side of my face. His eyes darkened and locked with mine.

"Did you like it?"

His voice was low and raspy. Deeply sexy and reverbed in places low within me.

I should have said no. I should have said that I never let people boss me around, either in the bedroom or outside of it. Yet something in the way he watched me made lying impossible.

Because I hadn't just liked his demands.

I'd craved them.

I'd come harder than I'd ever come before. All I'd been able to think of since was if his words had that much power over me, how would I feel if it were his fingers inside me? His tongue on my clit? His cock in my mouth?

Every inch of me wanted to find out, and yet I was terrified of asking for what I wanted because of who he was and what he did. We were at the edge of the danger zone that one tiny slip would send us spiraling into it headfirst. "I liked it," I whispered to him. "If I wasn't so scared of the way you'd react, I'd do it again now."

He groaned and closed his eyes. "Jesus, fuck, Lyric. Don't talk like that."

I took a chance. A chance he was holding back while

wanting as much as I did. He was so frigging hot with his dark hair and tanned skin. Stubble on his cheeks because he hadn't had mass that day. The lengths of his hair curled at the ends, and I scraped my fingernails along his scalp gently as I straddled his lap.

He leaned into my touch. He put the joint down and his hands came to my back, flattening between my shoulders and guiding me down until there were mere inches between us. His dick went hard beneath me again, and slowly, he opened his eyes.

"I want to kiss you so bad," he whispered.

I couldn't help it. I rocked over his lap a little, squirming so the hard ridge of his cock pressed up against my clit. I wanted so much more than kissing. I wanted to yank his pants off and kneel between his thighs, take his dick in my mouth, then ride it while he sucked my nipples. I wanted to feel him everywhere. So deep I'd scream his name when I came. I leaned in until my mouth was a mere inch from his, his breath on my lips.

"I can't," he murmured. "I want to. But I can't. I took an oath."

An oath I was sure he'd already broken a good few times in the last twenty-four hours, but I backed off anyway. Because if there was one thing I'd learned from working in the club, it was that no meant no, no matter who you were. If it wasn't an enthusiastic yes, it was still a no.

I went to climb off his lap, but he grabbed my hips, holding me on his still-hard cock.

"Zeph..." He needed to let me go. I couldn't sit here on his lap, grinding my sleep shorts against his jeans because we were both getting off on it. "I should go. Or you should."

I tried again to get off his lap and got as far as one foot on the floor before I was swept right off it and thrown down on the couch. The soft cushions bounced beneath my weight, and I stared up at him. I barely breathed for the need coursing through me. He pinned my wrists to the fabric beneath me. He nudged my legs apart so he was between them, and I wrapped my legs around him on instinct, connecting my core to his cock once more and hating that clothes separated us.

He hovered over me, gaze searching mine, though all he would find there was lust and need and a desire so strong it was practically on its knees begging. "I can't walk away from you, Lyric. I don't fucking know how."

His mouth slamming down on mine was anticipated. The pull between us too strong for either of us to resist forever. But the way Zeph kissed shocked me to my very core.

He kissed like he had all the experience in the world. His lips were warm and his tongue hot, searching for entrance, licking at my mouth until I opened willingly for him. Our mouths met in an explosion of feeling, and it was like being fifteen again, kissing on the back seat of a car for the first time. When sex was off the table, so any connection was desperate and raw and new.

His weight pressed down on me, delicious and strong, and he kissed me until my head spun in dizzying circles, each rotation sending me further and further into a lust spiral that began and ended with him. I ran my fingers through his hair, tugging on the ends until he groaned and ground against me, shamelessly dry humping like horny teenagers.

It was him who pulled away. I would have kissed him for hours more, right until the sun came up and our real lives snuck back in.

But Zeph stared down at me with kiss-swollen lips and messed-up hair, breathing hard. "I should go."

I knew it too. If he stayed any longer, I'd be begging him to get me naked, and he'd already crossed so many lines tonight that I knew he'd probably regret. I didn't want sex to be one of them. "Okay."

His face turned tortured. "If you ask me to stay...if you ask me for more, I won't say no, Lyric. I can't. I want you so fucking bad."

My insides liquefied at the need in his voice. At the barely held restraint.

I wanted to give him that permission to let go. To do the things he so badly wanted to do, and yet I couldn't be the one to do that for him. It had to be his decision.

"You should go, Zeph. I'll see you soon." I unwound my legs from around his waist, releasing him.

He nodded stiffly, pushing up off the couch. His gaze wandered over me for a long, hot minute, and then he was gone, as abruptly as he'd arrived.

I was left wondering what the hell had just happened, and who Zeph really was when he wasn't hiding behind one of his masks.

18

AUGIE

My brother was a good dad. It shouldn't have been a surprise because Banjo was a good man. Except every time I sat on my bike, watching him chase his small dark-haired daughter around the park, all I could think about was how had he turned out so well, while I...

While I was a fucking prick. A screwed-up loser who dragged everyone around him down into the mud as well.

I took a long inhale on the cigarette, letting the smoke sit in my lungs until it burned and forced its way out. I'd given up the fucking things not long after Banjo had walked himself out of my life. But when Fawn had gone missing, I'd found myself craving them again.

And not just the smokes. Alcohol. Sex. Party drugs. Whatever the hell got me through and eased the pain of knowing I'd fucked up yet again.

Luna was so cute with her pigtails flying out behind her while she ran around on chubby kid legs, giggling hysterically at my brother or one of his partners. God, she seemed happy. So carefree. No idea of the shit Banjo and I had gone through as kids with parents who didn't give a fuck, and foster parents who were worse. That little girl was so loved and well taken care of; she probably didn't have a worry in the world.

Banjo caught her around the waist and hefted her up into the air, catching her as she fell back down into his arms. He threw her a few more times while she laughed hysterically, and he grinned at her with a pride I had never seen from our own parents.

Banjo's partner, Lacey, watched them from a picnic blanket, her head in Colt's lap. Colt's family still lived next door to me, but I knew he lived with Lacey and Banjo and their fourth partner, Rafe. Almost everything I knew about my brother and the family he'd made for himself was through Colt's mom, Willa. Banjo had cut me off completely, and I couldn't blame him after the things I'd done. I wouldn't forgive me either, and I wouldn't ask him to try.

Banjo plunked Luna down on a swing and pushed her gently while Rafe called something to him and they both laughed. They were the perfect picture of family happiness.

I was so fucking happy for him.

And so damn jealous.

Colt called something to Banjo, and then suddenly, all four of them looked in my direction.

"Ah, shit," I muttered, slinking down on my seat.

But it was really too late for that. The smile slid off Banjo's face, and Rafe jogged over to him, both of them shooting glances in my direction. Rafe put his hand to the back of Banjo's neck, talking intently as they distractedly pushed Luna who didn't seem to have any idea that anything had changed.

I turned the bike on. I'd overstayed my welcome. Not that I'd ever actually been welcome in the first place.

Banjo strode across the grass toward me, face like a thundercloud. Behind him, his family gathered together, Lacey plucking up Luna from the swing and holding her close. Like she was protecting her from her asshole of an uncle.

Fucking hell.

I hugged my helmet as Banjo approached, and I tried to put in place the cocky asshole routine he knew me for. It was an act I'd perfected as a kid, and it kept the vulnerable parts of me protected. They'd been stomped on so hard lately; they couldn't handle another attack. I needed my walls up. Especially around Banjo because his rejection hurt more than any other.

"Hey, little brother," I drawled. "Fancy seeing you here."

He stopped a foot away from the bike and eyed me carefully. Distrustfully. He was right to do so. I wasn't the reliable brother. I was the one who fucked everything up and I couldn't blame him for not wanting me around.

He folded his arms across his chest. "You look like shit, Augie."

He was right, but it hurt anyway. I wouldn't show that though. "Luna is getting big."

He stiffened. "Stay away from her."

I laughed with my hands up, but the sound was forced. I hoped he wouldn't notice. "Don't worry, B. I'm not here to screw anything up for you. I know you don't want me around. I'm just killing time before I head into the city for an appointment. I didn't know you were going to be here."

His eyes narrowed, likely not believing my story because, frankly, it was weak at best. There was zero reason for me to be at a playground in Providence, apart from the fact I'd heard Colt talking with his mom on their front lawn the day before and heard him say they were having a picnic here this afternoon.

I winked at Banjo and pulled my helmet on. "Say hi to Lacey and the boys for me." I backed out of the parking spot, revving the engine, and peeled away. I didn't want to turn back, but I did.

The cocky smile slid straight off my face when my only brother walked back to his family, shaking his head.

The hurt of losing him was constant but one I was normally able to push deep inside. The reminder nothing had changed between us was a painful one. I was never going to be able to set things right with him. I knew that. But when Fawn had been around, that sibling void in my life had felt a little less lonely. She'd had no family either. So we'd kind of adopted each other.

Until I'd realized her feelings for me were more than brotherly. It had been a shock to find that out, but because we were such good friends, I'd tried to imagine what more would feel like. I'd spent sleepless nights, trying to force myself to feel more for her.

It would be so easy, if soft and gentle was what I needed.

But it wasn't. I would eat her alive, and not in a good way. I'd destroy her innocence. Drag her down into the mud and then drown her in it.

I'd never been a man who could be with someone

kind and sweet. I didn't understand love like that. I craved darkness. Attitude. Sass. Someone who could give me shit because God knows I deserved it. I needed someone who could take my bullshit, call me on it, and give me hell in return.

That woman wasn't Fawn. She was just too young to see it.

But I had, and instead of handling it like a mature adult in his thirties, I'd ignored her calls. I'd avoided having a real conversation because I hadn't wanted to hurt her.

And now she was gone.

I couldn't just let it lie. I'd done that with Banjo, and look where that had gotten me. With nothing and no one. Fawn was sweet and kind, and she was the first person besides Banjo who I'd ever truly loved, even if the love I felt for her wasn't romantic.

She couldn't just be gone. She had no one else to find her, no family hounding the police or starting search parties. That responsibility was mine. I owed her that much.

I drove into the city with a lump in my throat and a burning desire to remove it with alcohol. But the tattered photo of Fawn in my wallet stopped me from finding the nearest bar and drowning my loneliness in bourbon. At least for now.

I parked outside a seedy law firm on the edge of the city. I'd been here before. More than once, but something kept drawing me back. A feeling if I just searched harder, longer, I might find her. That if I studied the faces of each and every prostitute, maybe she'd be one of them, forced into work by her abusive ex. Or if I went into every strip club, I might find her there, swinging around the pole the way she had in Saint View. If I went through every homeless shelter, she might be there, too scared to come back to us because Eddie knew she'd run to us if she was ever set free.

I walked up and down the busy street, darting looks at every woman of the right age and build who passed. "Excuse me." I stopped a man passing by and thrust the photo in front of his nose. "Have you seen this woman?"

He squinted at the picture, then shook his head. "No. Sorry."

I stepped to the side and let him pass, only to try again with another man. "Have you seen her? Her name is Fawn. She's early twenties. Long blond hair—"

"Nope."

He hadn't even looked. Just brushed past me and kept going down the stairs to the subway.

"Thanks for fucking nothing," I muttered in his direction but then decided the subway probably wasn't the worst place to ask around either. I found a platform and showed the photo to every person waiting impatiently for their train.

One after the other, they all shook their heads.

No one had seen her. It was the same story every time I'd gone searching.

She'd disappeared without a trace. No clues to where she was. No leads to follow.

The police had given up, and it was time I did too.

The train pulled into the station with a whoosh of air and screeching brakes. I let the crowd move me along aimlessly, because where the hell did I have to go?

A woman staring out from the train, her chin in her hand, stopped me dead in my tracks.

I blinked twice, sure I was seeing things through the scratched-up windows, but I picked up the pace anyway, jogging alongside the train as it rolled to a stop.

Her hair was too dark, but her features...her eyes...

I was on the train before I could think about what I was really doing, shoving through the crowd of people trying to find seats. "Fawn!" I yelled, voice hoarse, drawing eyes my way. But I didn't care. I pushed past a guy about my age who grumbled at me. Hope grew with every step. It was her. It had to be her. It didn't matter that her hair was dark. I was sure Fawn's blond had been out of a bottle. She could have so easily gone back to brunette. Or been forced to. Heads turned my way, all except the woman who sat with headphones in her ears. My heart thumped.

I stopped at her seat. "Fawn." The word came out a choked plea.

The woman took the earbud from her ear and turned to face me. "Sorry, were you talking to me?"

My heart sank.

It wasn't her.

I sat down hard in the empty seat beside her as the train pulled away, and doubled over, head in my hands so no one would see the agony I was sure I had plastered all over my face. "Never mind," I said to the woman. "I thought you were someone else."

Fawn's photo was still clenched in my hand, and the woman peered at it, then paused. "This is the woman you're searching for?"

I glanced over at her, and this time, instead of being

struck by how much she resembled Fawn, I was struck by how pretty she was. Long, smooth dark hair was styled in loose curls around her face. Her eyes were the same shape and color as Fawn's, but while Fawn's held a naïvety that came from being so young, this woman's held a wealth of experience. There were tiny lines at the sides of her eyes, and I guessed her to be around my age.

She indicated the photo crinkling in my fingers.

I smoothed it out before handing it over to her. "Her name is Fawn. Have you seen her?"

The woman shook her head slowly, then her gaze returned to mine, wandering all over my face curiously. "Why are you looking for her? She your girlfriend?"

I shook my head. "No. A friend from work. She went missing a few weeks ago. We believe she's being held against her will by her ex."

The woman's eyes sharpened. "That's horrible. Where do you work?"

"Saint View Strip Club."

The woman raised one of her perfect, dark eyebrows. "You're a stripper?"

I wondered how I'd thought she was like Fawn. Her expressions were all wrong. Too full of confidence and curiosity. Fawn was just as beautiful but innocent and often unsure of herself. I would have never been able to tell her about my past or the things I'd done. She was too sweet to understand why. Her name suited her in that regard. She was as innocent as a baby deer.

"Yeah, a stripper. Among other things."

The woman crossed her long legs and twisted to gaze at me. "Like what?"

I wasn't in the mood to come up with a lie. Why

bother? I didn't know this woman. She could judge me all she wanted. "I sleep with women—men too, sometimes actually—for money."

I waited for it. The judgment.

It didn't come.

But the train driver's voice crackled over the intercom. "Next station is Providence."

The woman glanced out the window, then back at me. "That's my stop."

I stood to let her pass.

She cocked her head to one side, studying me while she waited for the train to slow. "Nice to meet you..."

"Augie," I supplied.

"Augie," she repeated back. "I hope you find your friend."

Our gazes held for a moment, and something flickered inside me. Something that felt a whole lot like attraction, but it had been so long since I'd felt that in any real way, I couldn't be sure. By the time I recovered, she was moving toward the doors.

"What's your name?" I called to her.

But she didn't answer. She already had her phone to her ear as the doors whooshed open. She'd clearly already forgotten all about me. "Vincent?" Her side of the conversation floated back to me. She paused, then her eyebrows furrowed together. "Scythe, then. Even better. We've got a problem, brother. A big one."

19

ZEPH

Sleep didn't come easy. I tossed and turned, catching a few minutes here and there, dozing on the couch with the TV on to keep me company. All I could think about was Lyric. What we'd done and how much I'd wanted to do more. It was an endless cycle of questions playing over in my head, making sleep nearly impossible. I'd tried watching a movie but couldn't follow the plotline, and eventually switched to the news station, needing something that didn't require concentration.

The first report was a murder at the other end of the country. I watched with vague interest; grateful they had moved on from reporting about the 'serial priest killer.' The second was a political report that was almost dull enough to send me off to sleep.

"Now onto the suspected abduction of three-year-old, Toby Innes. Police still have no suspects in the case. Toby was last seen at a Saint View park with his mother, Tammie, and her two other children, Daniel and Mathew. Grave fears are held for the young boy's whereabouts."

I sat bolt upright, staring at the TV and the image of the little boy, now familiar to me after meeting him and his family at the homeless shelter. "What the fuck?" That had to be a mistake. I'd only seen them a few days ago when I'd given them the money I'd acquired for them. Daniel had been healthy, he and Toby happily playing on the equipment. I pulled out my phone only to realize Tammie had never given me her number. I stood to go to her house, but I didn't know where she lived either.

I sank back down onto the couch and called the Saint View Police Department, who promptly gave me a canned response about not being able to divulge details of the case. A search party was already working around the clock, and even after I'd explained I was a friend of the family, I'd been told to sit tight and wait for an update.

I got out my phone and googled everything I could find, horrified Toby had been missing for twenty-four hours and this was the first I'd even heard of it.

Tammie had to be going out of her mind.

And there was absolutely nothing I could do to help.

I bounced my leg with nervous energy, sitting on my hands never something I'd been good at. I wanted to go search the streets, look in every alley, every home, until I found him.

This time, I had to be content with letting the police do their jobs.

But there was no chance of sleeping after that. I paced the halls of my house for hours after I gave up trying, but the walking back and forth was no better. Time moved at a snail's pace, the minute hand on the clock in my living room inching around at a sluggish pace that did nothing to calm the unease that had wrapped itself around me.

Thoughts of Lyric were less unsettling than wondering where Toby was.

I'd spent the last couple days on my knees in front of my altar, begging for some sort of clarity that never came.

Kissing Lyric had felt good. So damn good it was all I'd thought of since. Stroking my cock while watching her come had been better.

But both had awakened something inside me I'd so desperately been trying to dull for years, ever since Annie. That need inside me, dark and depraved, was the whole reason I'd agreed to joining the priesthood.

And it had worked.

Until her.

Because I didn't just want to kiss Lyric. I didn't just want to stroke my cock while she fingered her pussy.

I wanted things I could never say out loud again.

I squeezed my eyes shut tight, but it did nothing to diminish the desires. I wanted to chase her. To have her run while I followed close behind, an impending force at her back that would have her breathless. I wanted to grab her from behind. Pin her to a tree or to the ground. Take her hard and fast until her screams of terror turned to screams of pleasure. I wanted my hand around her throat when she came around my cock.

One short chase down a set of stairs, and all the work I'd put in at therapy came unraveled.

I couldn't see her again. She was the perfect temptation, made just for me, I was sure of it.

By one in the morning, I couldn't take it anymore. I

couldn't take the thoughts in my head, the guilt over what I'd done, the terror that I might do it again.

Because I'd done it once before. And it hadn't ended well.

I had to end this thing with Lyric now, before I hurt her. I knew exactly what I was capable of. I'd killed a man in cold blood. What if I did the same to her? That wasn't part of my desires, but I also didn't trust myself not to get carried away.

Hurting her was the last thing I wanted.

Hurting anyone wasn't it at all, and yet I knew that I could. I'd proved it more than once.

Every time I thought about what we'd done, the walls seemed to move in an inch until my house felt as small as a sardine can.

I needed out. I needed fresh air.

I slammed my way out of the house and ran to my car through the darkness.

"Zeph?"

Father Byron's voice stopped me in my tracks. I turned slowly to face the shorter man.

He was dressed in a full robe, and it baffled me as to why he'd be here and dressed as he was. "What are you doing?" I blurted out, slightly out of breath either from running or from my thoughts, I wasn't sure which.

He folded his arms over his chest. "I held midnight mass here tonight. Which you were supposed to attend."

Guilt slammed into me. I'd completely forgotten. "I'm sorry," I stuttered. "I don't know what happened. I just...forgot."

Father's eyes narrowed. "You forgot? That's not like

you, Zeph. You're normally very reliable. You miss mass and now you're running across the church compound in the middle of the night? Where are you going?"

I was responsible. It was something I was proud of. But my head had been elsewhere for days, and this was all the more reason why I needed to deal with it now. To go to her and tell her this had to end. So I could stop thinking and go back to just existing.

"I'm sorry," I muttered, feeling as small as a child.

"Go back to bed."

"I can't do that. There's something I need to take care of."

Father threw up his hands in frustration. "In the middle of the night? You heard the police; they want us to stay close to home. It could be dangerous."

I couldn't tell him I was the danger everyone feared.

Everyone but Lyric.

Though she would when I told her.

"I have to do this. I'll be back soon."

I turned and ran for my car again, Father Byron's shouts following behind me. He stared at me, completely bewildered when my car tires screeched across the parking lot and I left the church behind me.

I'd never allowed myself inside Saint View Strip Club. I'd sat outside many a time, watching from the outside, but I'd known I could never go in.

But now I needed to because if I waited a minute longer, I was going to implode. I handed the guy at the door a ten-spot, and he opened the heavy black door without a second glance.

Music blasted out of the club, surprisingly loudly for

a Wednesday night. Or Thursday morning, I guessed now. The room was dark except for neon lights that cast a pinkish glow and the white spotlights on the stage.

I stopped in the middle of the room, mesmerized by Lyric twirling gracefully around a pole. Her skin shimmered with some sort of product, and her eyes were made up with heavy liner and dark powders on her eyelids. She was topless, those perfect tits on display for every asshole in the club to see. A tiny pair of panties covered her pussy, while her bare legs looked longer than usual thanks to a sky-high pair of heels.

Lust jolted through me, hot and fast. I'd had those legs wrapped around me just a couple of nights ago. I'd had her beneath me, writhing against me, begging me for something I couldn't give for fear I'd take it too far. She'd shown me every inch of herself through the safety of a window, and yet now, every man in this room got to see her too.

I hated it. I hated their eyes on her. Their leering stares. When one reached out to tuck a dollar bill into her panties, dragging the material farther down than necessary so he could get a glimpse of her snatch, I saw red.

I stormed across the club, grabbing the man's wrist tight and yanking it away from her.

"Hey!" he yelped, hunching awkwardly to try to relieve the pressure on his wrist that I really fucking wanted to snap. "What did I do?"

His shout drew the attention of the bouncer, and I knew it would only be a moment before I was thrown out, but I couldn't seem to stop myself.

Mine, a voice in my head demanded. *My girl.*

"Zeph!" Lyric snapped.

Her eyes blazed with irritation as she jumped off the stage, not even wobbling in her heels. She got between me and the guy and glared at me. "Let him go."

I did, instantly, right as the bouncer arrived.

I braced for the impact of the big man, but again, Lyric put herself between us. "It's okay, Terry. He's with me."

Terry glanced at the guy howling about his wrist, then at me, and then at Lyric. "You sure?"

She nodded.

He pointed at me. "Don't come in here if you can't handle watching her dance, you hear me? Our patrons aren't here to put up with your jealousy."

His warning look at Lyric was slightly less pissed off. "You know the rules. Keep your boyfriends out of here if they can't handle it."

She glared right back at him, her voice full of sass. "If I had a boyfriend, I would. But this here is your friendly —or not-so-friendly tonight, apparently—neighborhood priest."

Terry blinked in surprise then cocked his head at me. "No shit?"

I didn't answer, but I could understand his confusion. There was nothing about my appearance tonight that would have given any indication I was a member of the clergy. No priest collar. No robes. Just a pair of my ripped and stained jeans that I wore when I was making a sculpture, a black hoodie, and a pair of boots. If he'd had X-ray vision, he might have seen the silver cross on a chain hanging around my neck, but to the outside world and to anyone who didn't know better, I was just some random asshole, throwing his weight around.

Lyric's fingernails imbedding themselves deep in my arm caught my attention. "Come," she hissed beneath her breath. Then louder, she called to a woman watching on with a frown. "I'm taking my break. Which room is free?"

I recognized the woman as the owner of the club. She was none too happy with me either, but she pointed at a door on the back wall of the club. "Take room one."

Lyric marched me in that direction, shoving me inside before slamming the door shut behind her. As soon as the lock clicked, she whirled on me. "What the fuck, Zeph!" she shouted. "You can't come to my place of work and act like some jealous douche canoe! We have rules about that which I didn't think I had to explain to you because, news flash, you're supposed to be celibate. Even if you're on some 'rebel against the priesthood' power trip, a little kissing and mutual masturbation does not make for a relationship!"

She was fired up, eyes blazing, tits heaving as she glared at me.

Everything I came here to say flew right out of my head.

I dropped to my knees in front of her and pressed my lips to her belly. I slid my hands up her naked thighs and over the curve of her hips, digging in there and holding her still.

I licked a path across her skin, down around the elastic of her panties while my hands kept traveling north to cup her breasts. She gasped, but it stopped her yelling at me.

Her nipples hardened beneath my fingertips and

desire for her raged through me. My dick hardened beneath my jeans, begging for attention. I squeezed her nipples, loving the way she sank back against the wall, the fight going out of her.

Her skin was so warm and soft, and I toyed with the edges of her panties with my tongue, until she made little whimpering noises of need.

I looked up at her and nearly came on the spot. She was the most beautiful thing I'd ever seen, and I wanted her more than I'd ever wanted any woman. She was worth it. Worth breaking every vow. Every promise. I'd been a fool to think I could walk away.

I lifted her thigh over my shoulder and pushed her panties to the side.

Her moan of pleasure when I licked her center had my balls tightening with need. Her pussy sparkled with her arousal, slick and just begging for my mouth. She grabbed my hair when I put my mouth on her again, tonguing her clit and up inside her until she ground against my face shamelessly.

"Zeph," she moaned. "Oh, fuck."

I needed more of those noises. Each one drove me crazy, higher and higher until I wanted to plow inside her and make her scream. I drove two fingers up into her, giving her something to ride, and she cried out in ecstasy.

"I'm going to come."

A fresh wave of her juices covered my tongue, and I lapped it up, fucking her with my fingers harder and faster until her body begged for more. I gave her three, and she screamed my name while the beat of the club outside vibrated through the door.

She was sugar sweet, wet and dripping down my

fingers. She coated my mouth and chin, and I drove to my feet, kissing her roughly, making her taste herself.

I waited for her to cringe away.

Annie would have.

But Lyric pulled me tighter, frantically grabbing at my hoodie, my shirt, my pants. She got her fingers beneath my T-shirt, and I hissed at the feel of her nails scratching over my abs. She ground her core against my erection, both of us frantic for more.

Like it had a mind of its own, my hand snuck up around her throat.

I froze when everything else I wanted to do roared in.

To have her on her knees, staring up at me, taking my cock deep in her throat.

To tie her up with the rope in my pocket.

To bend her over and take her tight little hole.

To have her anywhere, anytime, because she was mine.

I yanked myself away from her, spinning around and forcing myself to the other side of the room. I held myself rigid against the wall, while the two of us stared at each other, our breaths ragged.

"What just happened?" she asked curiously.

I just shook my head.

She took a step toward me, but I held up a hand, my voice hoarse when I said, "Please don't."

She stopped. "Don't what?"

"Don't come any closer." I swallowed thickly. "Please, Lyric. Don't."

She studied me for a moment, with her cheeks flushed pink, even beneath her makeup. "Why?"

I just shook my head again. I couldn't tell her. She'd look at me the same way my therapist in the church compound had. The same way my parents did when they'd found out what I'd done.

The same way Annie had looked at me. In absolute horror and disgust and fear.

"What's going on in your head right now, Zeph?" Her voice was quieter now. "I can practically see your brain whirring. You want me. I know you do. I want you too."

She closed the gap between us, and I was powerless to stop her from pressing up on me. Her tits felt so good against my chest. I wanted to wrap my arms around her, lift her from the floor, and feel her legs come around my waist. I wanted to sink my cock inside her warmth and feel her pulse around it. I pressed my head back against the wall, keeping my hands flat on the drywall behind me to keep from touching her.

"I joined the priesthood so I wouldn't do this, Lyric. So I wouldn't want anyone the way I want you."

Her fingers came up to stroke the side of my face. "Look at me."

I couldn't.

I knew I'd kiss her if I did.

"Zeph..."

I gazed down at her and gave up the fight, slamming my lips down onto hers.

She kissed me back but slowed me down, kissing softly where I was hard, gently where I was rough. Slowly, I caught on, following her lead.

My lips were swollen by the time she pulled away and walked me to a couch that sat facing a stripper pole built into the middle of the room. I sat numbly, and when she put a glass of a dark-brown liquid into my hand, I knocked it back in one shot.

"Every time I look at you, I want things I shouldn't want."

She cocked her head to one side. "Like what?"

I breathed out, knowing the only way to make her understand was to just tell her the truth. It had terrified Annie into never speaking to me again, and it would have the same effect on Lyric. It was the only way. I needed her to want to stay away from me because I couldn't keep myself away from her.

"The things I want are sick, Lyric."

"Doubtful."

I stared at her, frustration rising because I didn't want to spell it out. I didn't want her to hate me. To look at me the same way Annie had. Lyrics fingers traced over my thigh, inching ever closer to the bulge behind my fly.

I grabbed her hand before she could touch it. "Stop."

"Tell me why." She rubbed a firm hand along my erection. Precum wept from my tip.

In an instant, I had her on her back, her legs wide. With a single rip of my fist, her panties tore, baring her sweet pussy to me once more. I stared at her while she writhed beneath me. Then I put my lips to her ear and whispered, "Because I want every inch of you Lyric. I want you here..." I pushed my fingers inside her mouth, feeling her warm, wet tongue swirl around them. "And here." I trailed my wet fingers down between her breasts. Over her navel and mound and then up inside her.

She moaned loudly.

I dragged my fingers back to her ass. "Here too, Lyric." I spread her arousal all over the tight opening.

Her fingers dropped to her clit, and she rubbed herself hard and fast. "Yes! Please!"

I reared back. I couldn't do this.

Slowly, she sat up and sighed. She was still completely naked, but she didn't seem to notice or care. "Okay, clearly I'm not getting another orgasm until you talk about whatever is on your mind. And frankly, Zeph, I'm soaking this couch as we speak. So talk. You want me. I want you. I get it's complicated for you, but you're sending so many mixed messages—"

"I like dominating women."

She shrugged. "Okay, so you're a guy. I think we already had that established."

I shook my head. "Fuck, Lyric. You know what I think about? I think about chasing you. You running from me. I think about the adrenaline rush of catching you, pinning you down and spreading your legs. Taking you hard and fast, and not just in your pussy, Lyric. Your mouth. Your ass. Every part of you I want to mark. I want my fingers around your throat when you come. I want to tie you up. I want you to fight me while I fuck you until you're screaming in pleasure instead of in fear."

The words spewed out of my mouth in a tumble of angst and anger and disgust. I hated every syllable, and I couldn't even look at her.

"Have you ever acted on those impulses? To take someone against their will, because that's what it boils down to right, Zeph?"

I gazed up at her. "My high school girlfriend. Her name was Annie."

"You raped her?"

I flinched. "No. I didn't. But I scared her, Lyric. I was young and dumb, and at the time I was too naïve to realize she might not like it, because I did. I was rough when she needed gentle. I stopped when she said no. But that's no excuse. I scared her. She told her mom, who told mine, and then everything came out in therapy."

She stared at me in horror. "So you joined the priesthood?"

I knew she wouldn't understand. There was no understanding if you hadn't been there. "I'd been getting into trouble for years at that point. Fights. Gangs. I had a temper, that often got the better of me, and a chip on my shoulder."

"You ever hit Annie?"

"Never."

"You ever hurt anyone who didn't deserve it?"

I sighed. "That's subjective, isn't it? Pretty sure Jamie Alsen didn't think he deserved to get the shit kicked out of him for shoving my sister, but I disagreed."

A smile crept over her face. "You stuck up for your sister?"

I shrugged. "Of course I did."

She settled back against the couch. "And from those actions your therapist was horrified enough to suggest you go into the church?"

"The church has been good for me. I'm a different person now. Not the hothead I was when I first came here."

Lyric shook her head incredulously. "You ever thought that maybe you were just a dumb teenage boy full of hormones, and it wasn't the church that saved you? Maybe you just grew up, Zeph."

"Maybe," I agreed. "But it's irrelevant. I still want the things I want. You make me want them more than Annie ever did. I don't trust myself around you, Lyric."

"I'm naked right now and you're doing just fine."

I huffed at her. "My cock is so hard I'm probably going to need a surgical procedure to get it down. I don't call that fine."

She giggled but then sobered. "Zeph, listen to me for a minute. I know you've had a lifetime of churchy therapy that has clearly brainwashed you into believing there's something wrong with you for wanting the things you want. But can you please listen to me when I tell you there isn't a single thing wrong with you. You're kind and sweet and sexy as fucking hell. You aren't a danger to women or society. You made a mistake, and you've been punished harshly for it ever since. I bet Annie grew up to marry a nice lawyer, and now they live happily ever after somewhere in Providence. Am I right?"

He was an accountant, but Lyric was right in that they had a house in Providence. I'd found her on social media and I knew they'd gone on to have a couple of kids. The relief I'd felt when I'd seen that had been immense. I wanted her to be happy.

But Annie's current happy life was irrelevant. Lyric still didn't know about the men I'd killed, but she didn't let me get a word in edgewise. She was still intent on telling me off.

"You aren't some bad or evil person. You stop when you're told to stop. You don't want to hurt people. You just have kinks, Zeph. You ever heard of CNC?"

I shook my head. "Unless you're talking about machining..."

Her brow crinkled adorably. "Machining? What? No." She pushed me back against the couch and straddled my lap so she could look me in the eye. "CNC. Consensual non-consent. It's where I give you permission to do certain things...things like chase me, tie me up, be rough..."

With no permission from me, my hips jacked up off the couch, seeking her entrance.

"Down, boy. I haven't given it to you yet. There's terms that need to be agreed on. And safe words that really do mean stop." She rocked over me and leaned down to kiss me. "Because the things you want, Zeph? To Annie, they might have been scary. And maybe you went about it in the wrong way. These things can't be sprung on people in the heat of the moment, you know. Besides that, she was young. Even vanilla sex is scary to an inexperienced teenager. You tried to throw her right in the deep end without so much as a floatie."

I ran my hands up to her breasts again, taking handfuls. "Consensual non-consent is really a thing?"

She nodded, leaning into my touch, and pressed her lips against mine. "We'll talk about it some more. When I'm not naked and at work. But you can have the things you want, Zeph. With me. Without shame."

It was her last two words that hit me hardest.

Everything in my life had come with shame. From the circumstances of my very birth right through to joining the priesthood. I'd won back my parents' respect, and I lived a good life, one where I helped and made a difference.

That life couldn't exist with Lyric in it.

But I couldn't give her up either. I couldn't deny the things I wanted from her. The way I felt when she was near.

"You don't have to make any big decisions now, Zeph. I'm not telling anyone about any of this. I'm a safe space for you to try."

I nodded, falling for her a little more for the way she didn't judge. She was the only person in my life who didn't.

She nodded and got off my lap. "I've got to go back to work. And you need to leave and go home and sleep, okay? Whether we have a contract or not, you can't be here."

I nodded, letting her go. But as she got to the door, I spoke one last time. "Lyric?"

"Mmm?" Her long red hair flicked over her shoulder.

"The safe word is llamas."

She snorted on a laugh. "Llamas?"

"Least sexy thing I can think of. You say llama to me, and my erection just shrivels and dies."

We both focused on my crotch, and sure enough, the image of a buck-toothed, spitting llama had done the trick.

She laughed, but then she stopped to truly look at me. "You'll respect the llama?"

I bit my lip, trying to hide my own grin. "I'll respect the llama if you promise to say it when I'm too much. I mean it. You have to promise me. Because the last thing I want is to hurt you. It would kill me. I swear, I'm not being dramatic when I say that." The thought of her lying hurt somewhere because of my actions made bile churn in my stomach.

She stole back across the room to kiss me quickly. "You're being a drama llama, Zeph. But I promise."

I watched her go, wondering what the hell I'd just agreed to, and if I had the balls to actually carry it through.

20

———

LYRIC

The morning of Amelia's Edgely Academy interview, I had Peggy stay back to watch Gran so I could take Amelia out for a special breakfast. I sipped lukewarm coffee at a diner in Saint View, while she gobbled down pancakes smothered in syrup. Maybe it was partly the fact I'd been awake at the club all night and hadn't slept yet, but tears pricked the backs of my eyes remembering the tiny baby I'd brought home from the hospital, who was now grown up enough to be starting kindergarten next year.

I was grateful when my phone buzzed, distracting me from getting too maternally mopey about my baby's impending first day of school. Peggy's number flashed on the screen, and I answered it with a smile for my daughter with syrup smeared across her cheek. She might have been getting big, but she wasn't grown just yet. "Hey, Peggy. What's up?"

"First, I just need you to know your gran is okay."

I stiffened, gripping the phone tighter while trying to

keep a smile on my face for the little girl in front of me. "What happened?"

Peggy sighed. "She came for a walk to the mailbox with me and tripped on that cracked sidewalk that's needed fixing for the past few months. She fell just a few minutes after you left."

I checked the time on the diner's clock. "That was an hour ago!" I clutched my handbag, gathering up our things. "Where are you? I'm coming."

"No, don't. We're at the hospital. Her hip is broken—"

"What?" I gasped, sitting back down heavily. "Peggy, no!"

"I know, honey. It's okay. She'll be all right. I have her. The doctors have her sedated, and they're taking her in for surgery."

"Surgery! Why didn't you call me?"

"There wasn't even time until just now. She was scared and needed me to be the familiar face while the paramedics worked on her. I'm sorry, I know you want to be here. But that interview this morning is important, honey. There's nothing you can do for your gran until she's out of surgery and recovery. I know it's hard, but go do what you need to do and then come up to the hospital this afternoon."

I stared down at a napkin I'd been absently shredding into confetti. "Did the doctors say anything else?"

Peggy sighed. "No. But, Lyric, you need to brace yourself for this to be a long recovery, and not one that's going to happen in your home. Fractured hips in a woman her age take a long time to heal."

"But she will heal?"

"Damn right she will. She's a stubborn old goat. No fractured hip is going to keep her down, we'll see to that."

I smiled softly. I was lucky to have Peggy. She loved my gran and Amelia almost as much as I did. I knew Gran thought of her as a daughter. Peggy filled a space in all of our lives that my mother had left gaping when she'd abandoned us. She was right about Amelia's interview. If we cancelled, we may not be given another shot. Places at Edgely Academy were limited, and the waiting list was long. We needed to nail it on the first go. There wasn't any room for making a bad impression by cancelling at the last minute, even if we did have a really good excuse.

"I'm really glad you were with her, Peg. Please don't leave until I get there."

"Wouldn't dream of it. Take your time. I'll be here with my crosswords until she gets out. I'll keep you updated if the doctors tell me anything more."

I hung up and plastered on a smile for Amelia. "Ready to go, Slugger?"

"Yep!"

I wiped her sticky face and fingers with wet wipes from my purse and then drove into Providence, parking outside the impressive school building with ten minutes to spare before our early morning interview. I got Amelia out of the car and tugged at the hem of my knee-length, fitted business skirt, stressing over my gran and my appearance at the same time. I retucked the collared shirt and brushed off the uncomfortable jacket I'd picked up at a thrift store. A woman eyed me as she passed by with her young son and gave me an uncomfortable smile when I didn't turn away.

I didn't return it. I could see the judgement in her eyes

as clear as day. "Stuck-up snob," I muttered when she went on her way.

Amelia pulled on my hand and stared up at me with her big, round eyes. "What did you say, Mommy?"

I smiled and knelt in front of her, straightening her pinafore dress that I'd bought especially for the occasion. "Nothing, Slugger. You ready to do this thing?"

She grinned at me with her cute dimples. "Yep!"

I stood and scanned the school parking lot. "If only your father was ready…"

"There he is!" She let go of my hand and ran down the footpath to where her father and his girlfriend had parked her obnoxious car.

I had to give him credit. Lleyton scrubbed up nicely. His suit pants fit snugly around his waist, and his shirt was clearly expensive. Kat was always put together, and today was no exception. I was slightly annoyed he'd brought her, but I couldn't deny she might have been an asset when it came to getting my child into a private school. That was the goal here. To impress the principal enough that they accepted her application.

"You're so pretty, Milly!" Kat squealed.

Amelia did a twirl for her father's girlfriend with a big smile on her cherublike face.

"You ready to blow these people away with how smart and beautiful and talented you are?" Lleyton asked.

I frowned, not sure I liked the pressure he was putting on her, but she didn't seem to notice. "Mom says it's going to be fun!"

Lleyton looked at me like he doubted that were true, and I couldn't deny he was probably right, but what was I supposed to do? The kid was four. I shrugged.

If Lleyton noticed something was wrong with me, he didn't comment on it. I wasn't about to tell him what had happened to Gran. Not while Amelia was in earshot.

We all traipsed along the path, shadowed by the hugely imposing three-story buildings that made up Edgely Academy.

"It's so weird," Lleyton commented, watching a mixture of boys and girls run up the stairs around us, ready to start their learning day. "This place was boys only when I came here."

"I looked into it." Kat's heels clicked along the pathway. "The girls' school was partially destroyed by fire a couple years ago, and they never rebuilt it." She dropped her voice so Amelia wouldn't hear. "A man died. It was declared a murder."

"Shit," I muttered.

Lleyton shot me an amused look. "Don't be cussing here. I did many a detention for dropping an F-bomb."

I grinned at him. "I can imagine. I wasn't any better, but they don't care so much about things like that at Saint View High."

Kat shook her head. "You both have no class." But then she smiled down at Amelia. "But you will, my love. The teachers here are going to adore you."

Amelia beamed up at her and put her hand in Kat's. "I want to be like you."

Lleyton glanced at me with an apology in his eyes, which I ignored because I was too busy fighting back the hurt that my little girl's words had unintentionally caused.

She wanted to be like Kat. Not like me.

It hurt so bad because I could understand why. Kat

was tall and pretty. She wore expensive floaty dresses and accessorized with jangly bracelets, chunky rings, and sparkly necklaces. Her nail polish was always chip-free. She had an important, well-paying job in an office in the city.

Meanwhile, I got around in cutoff shorts, tops that showed off my midriff, and flip-flops. I worked in a strip club and owned a car that only started when it felt like it. I couldn't afford to give Amelia spur-of-the-moment vacations or pay for her to go to this uppity school. I had to swallow my pride and let Lleyton and Kat give her those things.

"Family of Amelia Torrenson."

I jerked my head toward the man who greeted us as we entered the office. I opened my mouth to say yes, then realized the man had used Lleyton's surname instead of mine. I narrowed my eyes at my ex. "That's not her name."

The receptionist's gaze bounced between us, his pen hovering over his clipboard. "It's not? That's the name I have on her enrolment papers..."

Lleyton seemed as baffled as I was. "I didn't fill them out."

Kat laughed, patting me on the arm. "Oh, Lyric." She turned to the receptionist and stuck out her hand. "Hi. I'm Kat. Amelia's stepmother. Torrenson is her father's last name. That won't be a problem, will it?"

The man smiled at her. "Of course not. Would you all like to come on through? Principal Williams will just be a moment, but you can wait in her office."

Kat reached for Lleyton's hand, linking her fingers

through his right hand and grabbing Amelia with her other. "Let's go, sugarplum."

I was left to trail behind them, too shocked to do anything else. But the moment the door closed, I whirled on them. "You know very well she has my surname, not Lleyton's. And stepmother?" I asked Kat incredulously. "Since when?"

Kat glanced at the door and then gave me a dirty look. "Lyric!" she hissed. "You're so loud! Sit down before the principal comes in here."

The hairs on the back of my neck stood up at her scolding me like I was a schoolgirl.

Lleyton must have seen the murderous expression in my eyes because he stood quickly, putting his hands on my arms. "Hey. Come on. We're all here for Amelia. We can discuss everything else later."

He was right, but it only annoyed me more.

Kat leaned over to him. "You didn't tell her we were getting married?"

My mouth dropped open. "What? Since when? You've barely been dating a year!"

"When you know, you know!" Kat held up a hand.

A diamond ring I hadn't even noticed before sat proudly on her finger. It probably could have paid for a house, and I had no doubt Lleyton had taken a large chunk out of his trust fund to purchase it.

"Amelia is going to be our flower girl."

Amelia screeched and jumped onto Kat's lap. "I am? I'm really going to be a flower girl? With a dress and shoes and hair and makeup?"

I stared at my daughter, bewildered that she was so excited about those things. She'd never expressed a specific interest in fancy clothes to me. She'd always been happy in comfy shorts and T-shirts and hoodies.

Kat twirled a lock of Amelia's auburn hair around her finger. "Of course. We couldn't get married without you! You're the most important person in our lives."

I swallowed down a lump in my throat. Not because I wanted Lleyton in any way, but because I could suddenly see a different life for my daughter. One where she had a stable family around her and all the money she could ever need. Not a mom who had to take her clothes off just to make the rent payments and a great-grandmother who confused and sometimes scared her. With Lleyton and Kat she could have her own room, nice clothes, expensive things. How long would it be before she didn't even want to come to my house? A teenager wasn't going to be okay sharing a bedroom space with her mother.

I botched the interview. Every time I was asked a direct question, the principal frowned at my jittery, distracted answers, and I just knew her scribbles on a notepad were about me and what a bad mother I was. But I couldn't come up with the words I needed to convince them we were the sort of family they wanted at their prestigious school. My head was too full of my gran, and the things I'd done with Zeph, and Kat and Lleyton becoming a family and Amelia leaving me for them.

Kat shot me exasperated looks and tried her best to cover for me, while Lleyton elbowed me sharply, and whispered, "Get it together," when I tried to make a joke about being a high school dropout who probably couldn't even help with first grade math homework.

I cringed beneath the woman's shocked expression,

and the *tsk* of disapproval that came from the receptionist, taking notes in the corner of the room.

"Just a joke," I explained lamely, face burning in
humiliation.

But the damage had been done, I was sure. I didn't fit
in at this school. Or with my ex and his new fiancée. How
long would it be before my daughter realized the same?

---

*L*eyton and Amelia said goodbye at the school
gates, and Amelia chatted my ear off happily as
I drove her back to her daycare at the church.
Excitement radiated from her little body and spilled over
when her teachers asked her how her interview had
gone. I probably should have told her about Gran, but I
left her happily babbling about the class play, their sports
teams, outings, clubs, and social events.

I didn't go back to my car. I didn't want to go home to
my cramped apartment, but it would still be a long time
until Gran was out of surgery. After I'd watched my
grandfather die in Saint View Hospital, the place held
nothing but horrible memories. I wasn't ready to go down
there and face them if I couldn't even see my
grandmother.

Voices from inside the church drew my attention, and
I found myself sitting in the back row, watching Zeph
address the other people around me.

His sermon was on forgiveness and repentance. I let
his deep voice wrap around me and the words sink inside
my brain. I thought about each of them, willing to give
this church thing a shot because I couldn't feel any worse.

Amelia was easy to forgive. The hurt she'd caused me today was unintentional and naïve. I couldn't blame her at all for the things she'd said. For the opportunities opening up for her. She was my baby, and there was nothing she did or said that would make me love her any less.

Kat and Lleyton, on the other hand...

I was sticking with my anger over them just enrolling Amelia under Lleyton's name without so much as even asking me. And I was angry at myself for letting everything get to me and making a poor impression on the principal.

"I'd like to call forth Father Byron. We'll both be in the confessional booths for the next hour if anyone would like to attend."

My mouth dropped open as an older man rose from his seat at the side of the altar. "Hairy hands."

I wasn't sure it was him. He'd been careful to partially shield his face with a baseball cap when we'd last met. But anger boiled up inside me at the reminder of the man who'd asked for a private dance at the club then taken things way too far. I shuddered at the memory of him asking me to plait my hair into schoolgirl braids, and his chode dick, purple in his fist as he'd come on himself.

Surely, I had it wrong. That guy couldn't be a priest.

I'd once said the same thing about Zeph though. I knew better now than to believe that anyone was who they appeared on the outside.

I stood, following the line of people lining up to take their turns in the confessional booths. I kept my gaze pinned to Father Byron.

Shock registered on his face when he spotted me. Okay, totally the same guy. Ew.

Unable to stop myself, I raised a hand and wiggled my fingers in a wave.

He hurried into his booth, quickly shutting himself inside.

"Fucking pervert," I mumbled.

The woman in front of me turned around and gave me a dirty look, but what was new? I was pretty used to being judged every time I came around here. Apparently, it didn't matter what I wore. Even in a business suit, these people could still see I didn't belong.

It was so tempting to go into Byron's booth when I reached the head of the line. I would have loved the chance at a private chat with him and to ask how God felt about him stealing money from me.

But I stepped aside and whispered to the man behind me. "I'm not quite ready. You go."

He nodded and made his way to the left, disappearing inside.

I waited for the woman in Zeph's confessional to leave and then slipped inside myself. I closed the door behind me, shutting us in together. "Hey."

The little peephole between us slid open. "Lyric?"

"Yeah. It's me."

"What's wrong?" His voice was slightly panicked, his gazed flickering all over my face.

"So much." I sighed heavily, leaning back on the hard wooden seat. "My grandmother is in the hospital—Peggy said she's going to be okay, but I need to get up there soon. And I screwed up Amelia's interview with that fancy-ass school. But I've got it all under control. Truly."

He wasn't letting me off that easy. "You're upset."

"I'm fine," I insisted on autopilot.

His knuckles cracked, but he didn't say anything.

I glanced over at him. "You mad at me?"

He still said nothing, but I could tell just from his eyes that he was.

I sighed. "Join the club, then. I'm pretty mad at myself too." Mad because I hadn't been there when Gran needed me. Mad at Kat and Lleyton. Mad because I let them get to me. Mad because I couldn't see a future that was any different from the present I was currently living. It was all just more of the same. My nights spent at the club, dancing for creepy old pervs like Byron, while my days were long and lonely and exhausting. "Seriously, Zeph. This is confession. You're supposed to say how you feel. So tell me."

"You aren't taking care of yourself. You never do."

I shrugged. "I do what I have to do to survive."

He paused for a moment. "I googled CNC."

I was sure my eyebrows shot right off my face. Not only that he'd googled it, but that he would bring it up here, of all places. But perhaps this really was the place to confess what was on your mind. And frankly, talking about sex was a whole lot easier than talking about any of my actual problems. "And?"

His voice dipped an octave until it was so deliciously deep I felt it inside me. "I learned more about what sorts of things can go in a contract. We need one."

I cocked my head to one side. "Agreed. What do you want in your contract?"

I expected him to defer to me, but he surprised me by having an answer ready. "That you look after yourself."

I frowned. "Explain what you mean by that. Because if you're being one of those alpha assholes on TikTok who like to carry on like they can't get it up for a woman who works out less than five hours a day, we're going to have a problem."

His eyebrows furrowed in. "What? No. That's not what I meant. I meant you run yourself ragged and take care of everyone but yourself. You're all sass and attitude to everyone, but it hides the fact you've always had to fend for yourself."

Despite the fact there was a partition between us, I'd never felt more seen. "I'm not sure that's exactly what they meant by a contract. I think it's supposed to be more like hard lines set out in writing."

"What's your hard line, Lyric?"

A tingle of anticipation lit up inside me. "You can take me by surprise, but I don't want to be truly scared of you. I can act it, if that's what you need, but if you jump out at me, I just need to hear your voice. I need to know it's you."

"What else?"

"That's all."

"There's got to be other limits, Lyric."

I said nothing.

"Public sex."

"Good with it. Actually, really good."

"Anal."

"Been there, done that. Use lube, please."

"Jesus fuck," he muttered, "I can't believe you just said lube in a confessional."

I cracked up laughing, which actually felt really good

after the morning I'd had. "Lube offends you? You're the one who said anal."

"I'm really glad these boxes are mostly soundproof."

I glanced around the wooden box, peering at the little gaps in the construction. I wouldn't have thought they were much good at muffling noise, but then the wood was thick and heavy. Maybe that was enough.

"We could test that theory..." I mused.

He groaned softly.

"You thinking about my lubed-up ass right now, Zeph?" I giggled.

"Yes. But you're avoiding the question. What if I climb through your window in the middle of the night, pull your panties to the side, and slow fuck you until you wake up?"

I clenched my thighs together. "Amelia is at her dad's this weekend, just in case you want to try that."

"Can I tie you up?"

"Yes."

"Can I put my hand on your throat?"

"Yes, but no choking unless you tell me you know how to do it safely."

"I don't want to choke you. I...don't want to risk taking that too far."

I glanced at him, not exactly sure what he meant, but he'd moved away from the peephole. I shifted so I could see him again. "Tell me I'm safe with you. That's all I really want to know."

He sat forward, gaze clear and earnest. "Always. I'm never going to let anyone hurt you. Not even me."

It was enough. It was all I needed. I leaned in. "Zeph. I give you permission to fuck me however you need to.

Hard. Fast. Rough. I'll remember the safe word. But the thought of you taking me anytime, anywhere? That doesn't scare me. *You* don't scare me."

He swallowed audibly. "You scare me though."

I nodded. "I know."

I was giving him permission to do the things no one else had. I was telling him he was normal and good and sweet, even though he had sexual desires that ran dark. But I needed things from him too. He provided a security I didn't feel anywhere else. He was someone I could let take the reins when I was too tired to steer. I didn't want a man who needed me to take over in the bedroom. I wanted to submit to him. To have a man who knew what I wanted and needed before even I did.

I got to my feet, hooking my purse over my shoulder. The distraction had been nice, but I needed to get to my grandmother. "I should go."

"I don't want you to."

I ducked my head so I could see him again and winked. "I know. But I think this booth has already gotten more than it bargained for. There's only so many confessions that should be said out loud in one day."

21

ZEPH

I waited for a few minutes after Lyric left the confessional, expecting another person to enter. But nobody did. I pulled my sleeve back to expose my wristwatch and realized we'd been talking a lot longer than the standard five minutes a confession normally took. Father Byron must have gotten through everyone waiting.

I opened the door and stepped out, stretching after such a long period of sitting.

"Do you know that woman, Zepherin?"

I spun, finally spotting Byron sitting in the back pew, eyes trained on the altar.

"Which woman?"

He folded his arms over his chest. "The redhead who was just inside your booth for over thirty minutes."

There was something off about him that made me wary. "I didn't time her, Father. I listened as long as she needed."

He stood and crossed the church to stand in front of

me. "And just what did she confess? A woman like her, it's not surprising she had a whole list."

I narrowed my eyes at the older man. "It's not our place to judge. We're all sinners."

The man's gaze flickered all over me. "Indeed, we are. But you didn't answer my question, so I'll ask again. Do you know her?"

"She's the parent of a child in the daycare."

He stroked the stubble growing across his jaw. "I see. And her confession was about...?"

"That's confidential. You know that."

He laughed suddenly, clearly trying to lighten the mood, and slapped me on the arm. "Just hoping for a bit of entertainment, Zeph. Nothing more. If you don't want to share, no problem. She's got a look about her that made me think she might have something interesting to say. Shame she didn't come into my booth."

I watched him walk away and ground my molars to keep from calling after him. I didn't like he'd noticed her. Singled her out. His interest in her sent a creeping sensation down my spine. It was the same feeling I'd gotten the night I'd stopped that man from following her home from the club. A man about the same build and shape as Father Byron.

I cursed myself again for not just revealing the man's face at the time. I couldn't confront him without being sure. If I were wrong, explaining why I'd been following a stripper home from work wouldn't be easy. It would draw attention to me, and worse, to Lyric. I didn't want to ask Lyric for fear of bringing up a memory she'd rather forget. And maybe a part of me didn't want to know. If Byron had been the one following her, I wasn't sure I'd be able to stop myself from making sure he never did again. How many men was I willing to kill? The other two had been easy enough, the proof solid, and I hadn't felt an ounce of remorse since.

But I knew Byron better. He'd taken me in when everyone else had turned their backs. He'd been a father figure to me when my own was too embarrassed to even be seen with me. The rumors that had circulated about Annie and me had left no stone unturned, and my father's golf club hadn't been spared.

My head was already so full of doubts and confusion. I'd picked a path for my life and now I was detouring wildly off it. The easy out would be to quit the priesthood. But what if things didn't work out with Lyric? I didn't know if I could handle what she was offering. I wasn't sure I even deserved to try, and yet I didn't know how to say no either. Wasn't this thing we were going to try better than watching her from a distance? I'd spent months *stalking* the woman, for Christ's sake. I was pretty sure that wasn't in the church guidebook. I'd broken so many rules, but I couldn't just leave. I didn't even know what I'd do on the outside. If I walked out now, I'd have no house. No job. No income. My parents would be ashamed; I couldn't go back to them. Lyric would be sympathetic, but I couldn't ask to sleep on her couch, she already had enough on.

No matter which way I looked at it, I couldn't see a way to leave. I had no college education. No money in the bank. From where I stood now, everything about the church felt like a trap, all designed to keep me here, to keep me quiet and obedient.

They were things I could work out, but only with time.

Until then, I needed to watch what I said. What I did. And who I trusted.

Frustration rose inside me. It was a constant state of being these days, one only relieved when I was around Lyric. The urge to find her was overwhelming, even though she'd only just left. She was a drug, and every hit of her only made me crave her more.

But there was once another way I'd dealt with these feelings.

Maybe a slightly less psychotic way than stalking a woman.

I got changed and grabbed my keys from my house and got in my car. I steered my way into Saint View, parking outside a place I'd once known well. Saint View Tattoo had been my first stop after I'd turned eighteen. But that had been a long time ago, so it wasn't surprising that when I walked in, I didn't recognize any of the guys working behind the counter.

"Got an appointment, bro?" one of them called out, glancing up from the calf he was working on. His tattoo gun was clutched between the fingers of his left hand. His gaze dropped to my collar, and I instantly wished I'd thought to not wear it. I didn't want to draw attention.

I shook my head. "Spur-of-the-moment thing." I wrung my fingers. "I really want to do this now. Please."

He gave me a slow nod. "Gotcha. We're pretty booked up, but if you hold your jets a minute—" He shoved his stool so it went sliding along the tiled floor. "Dax! There's a walk-in if you want to stick him in place of that cancellation you had."

Dax stuck his head out from a room off to one side. "Whatcha want done?"

I didn't care. I just wanted the pain. Something to focus my brain. "Whatever you want."

Dax raised an eyebrow in interest. "Yeah? For real? You aren't gonna make me do another fucking Koi fish or something?"

The other man laughed. "If you weren't so good at them, people wouldn't keep asking for them."

Dax ran a tattooed hand through his light-brown hair. It was on the long side, probably just enough to scrape into a rubber band if he'd wanted to. "Yeah, yeah. Sucks to be talented, right?" He peered at me. "Anything?"

"Anything."

"Them's dangerous words. Especially for a first-timer."

"Not my first time."

Dax squinted at me. "No? I just assumed tats don't fly with the church..."

I pressed my tongue to the side of my mouth and then decided it was easier to just show him. I pulled my long-sleeved shirt over my head, letting Dax and his friend see the work I'd already had done.

"Whoa." Dax stepped forward and then around me in a circle. "Who knew a priest was hiding all of this artwork beneath his robes?"

"No one," I admitted. "At least not all of it. Sometimes this one is hard to hide." I pointed to the bottom of my tattoo sleeve that had one image so low it snaked below my wristwatch.

Dax took my wrist in his hands and turned my arm over. "This is some nice work. Who did it?"

"Whoever owned the place about ten years back...I don't see him here..."

"Ah, no. That would be Chris. I bought him out not long after. I should have recognized his work. It's impressive."

I wasn't sure what to say. Thank you didn't seem right, since all I'd done was lie there while the artist had done his thing.

But Dax didn't seem to mind my silence. He was impressed enough with my existing tattoos that he slapped an empty padded bench. "Go on then. Get up here. I've got something sketched up that you might like."

I did as instructed, breathing a sigh of relief when the needle pierced my skin and a sharp throb of pain cleared my head.

22

LYRIC

I was proud of myself for biting my tongue when Kat and Lleyton came to pick Amelia up for their weekend with her. I let them walk away, ignoring how much they portrayed the perfect nuclear family with Amelia between them, holding both their hands.

With Gran still in the hospital, and staying there for the foreseeable future, too frail to come home, my apartment was quiet. I'd taken Amelia to visit her that morning, and she was doing a lot better than the last time I'd seen her. But even still, her tiny body tucked up in a hospital bed had hurt my heart.

As much work as it was to care for an elderly relative, she belonged here with me. There was no doubt about that in my mind. For as long as I could care for her, she'd have a home here.

I spent the day cleaning out her bedroom, wiping down every surface, changing her sheets, and throwing out trash that had collected. When I was done there, I continued with my and Amelia's room. Anything to keep myself busy. If I had nothing to do, I would dwell on either my gran's well-being, Fawn's whereabouts, or how I'd screwed up Amelia's interview at Edgely Academy.

Mom guilt ate away at me over the latter, reminding me I'd probably ruined her chances there. I couldn't get the principal's expression off my mind...the way she'd looked at me when I had managed to open my mouth. We'd heard nothing since, though Katherine had unhelpfully fretted to us that one of her friends had gotten her child's acceptance letter two days ago. I'd tried calling the school a couple of times during the week, hoping to catch Principal Williams so I could explain myself, but she was never available and didn't return my calls. I was one-hundred-percent certain I was the reason we hadn't received an acceptance letter. Lleyton was a past student, with parents who gave money to the school. Katherine was the put together, well-educated stepmom. The problem certainly wasn't Amelia, who was perfect.

I tried calling again, despite it being a weekend, but unsurprisingly, got the school voicemail. By the time I needed to get ready for work that night, the apartment sparkled and smelled of lemon disinfectant.

Disinfectant and crushed dreams.

"Shower," I said to the empty apartment, knowing I couldn't rock up at work as sweaty and gross as I was right now. "Stat."

I stripped off, humming something tunelessly beneath my breath. I checked out my reflection in the bathroom mirror and, remembering my promise to Zeph to take care of myself, I scrubbed my face with a cleanser I normally didn't bother with because—why be fancy when soap and water would do?

I was naked, cream smeared across my cheeks, and testing the water temperature when the room suddenly went dark.

"Ugh, no. Not now." The wiring in my apartment building was dodgy at best. A complete safety hazard at worst. It had a habit of fritzing out at the most inconvenient times. I cracked open the frosted-glass window, just enough to peer out, and groaned again. Okay, clearly not just the building. I couldn't see a single light on all the way down the street. "Shit."

I switched the faucet on and waited for the water to run warm. With the window cracked, I had barely enough moonlight to see.

The water never got warm. "Of course," I muttered. "Of course the fucking hot water system runs on electricity." I still had cream all over my face. The scent of disinfectant still clung to my skin, and I needed to get to work. I dove beneath the cold water with a shriek and scrubbed myself clean.

I'd never been so grateful for a dry towel. I wrapped it around myself, fighting off the shivers, and picked up my phone. A text from Eve had come in while I'd been in the shower.

EVE

Hey, gang. Club is closed tonight. Electric company says no power in Saint View until tomorrow. This show cannot go on by candlelight. Enjoy an unexpected night off. Be good. Or at least be careful. Augie, mainly talking to you here.

Augie had replied with the middle-finger-up emoji.

I really couldn't afford a night off, but Eve was right. There was no point being there with no power. We couldn't dance without music. Couldn't keep drinks cold. Eve had been right to close the place.

I shivered involuntarily, and it was a reminder I was still standing naked in my bathroom. I tiptoed down the hall and into my room, checking the time. Ten. It was normally when I was due to start work, but tonight it would be the time I went to bed. I dropped the towel, realizing with no one else home, I didn't need pajamas. Cold, I climbed beneath my sheets and pulled the comforter over my head.

It didn't take long for sleep to take me. It never did. I was always sleep deprived, and sleeping at night when the room was dark and as quiet as my place ever got, was so much easier than during the day when the complex was busy and noisy and bright sunshine streamed through the window coverings that were too cheap to really block anything out.

I fell asleep feeling oddly luxurious for a woman in a run-down apartment with one hundred and fifty thread count sheets. But at least I knew I could sleep all night, without Amelia waking me up, or half listening for my grandmother to go strolling about and burn the house down.

Instead, I woke to someone pushing my thighs apart.

Instinct took over, and I thrashed, kicking out at the dark man shape looming over me.

He caught my leg easily, like he'd been expecting it, and pinned it to the mattress. "Want to use your safe word?"

The terror flew out of me at recognizing the deep timbre of his voice.

"Say it now if you do."

I didn't utter a word.

His breathing quickened, and he finished what he started, opening my legs wide, so he could fit between them.

My body buzzed with anticipation, arousal pooling at my core. "How did you get in?"

He paused in his studying of me. "Your bathroom window. You need to keep that locked, Lyric. What if someone else had come in? What if they're in here right now, just waiting for their chance to pounce?"

I dragged him down on top of me. "Then I think they're about to get more than they bargained for."

He leaned down and kissed me, his lips hot and sure against mine. I opened for him, meeting his tongue, exploring and tasting him, completely turned on by the fact he was fully clothed and I was completely naked. I raised my hips, encouraging him to take me the way he'd obviously intended before I'd woken up.

"Needy," he whispered in my ear.

"Yes," I murmured back.

He pinned my wrists to the bed. "Wait."

I could have groaned in frustration. I already just wanted him. The anticipation was too great. But I did as I was told, lying patiently beneath him while he kissed my mouth.

Every lick and sweep of his tongue only made me want him more. When he dipped to the sensitive planes of my neck, it was all I could do not to writhe beneath him, completely desperate for more.

"I want you naked," I whispered to him. "I want to see you."

He lifted his head from worshipping my skin and pulled his long-sleeved shirt over his head. I gaped at him. Zeph didn't just have the one or two tattoos I'd seen sneaking out from beneath his clothes. Even the quick glimpse I'd had of him with his shirt off hadn't been long enough to truly take in the extent of his artwork.

The intricate designs swirled all over his chest and arms. I traced them lightly, my fingertips barely touching his skin. "I wish I could see these properly."

"They aren't that interesting."

"But they are to me. Everything about you is interesting to me." I scratched my nails up his back, stopping when I got to a bandaged section. "What's this?"

"New ink."

"How new if it still has a bandage?"

"A few hours."

I winced, feeling around the edges of the wound covering. "How big is this thing?"

"Big. I'll have to go back so Dax can finish it."

I smiled at the familiar name. "He does good work. He did this one."

I drew my hand between us and ran it down the swirling design that snaked onto my bare mound.

Zeph caught my hand. "Dax did this? He touched you here?" His words were practically feral.

"He was very professional."

"Don't. Fucking. Care." He lowered himself until he was halfway down my bed, his lips pressed to my belly. "I can't stand that he touched you there."

"He was hardly fingering me, Zeph."

He made a choking noise. "Stop talking."

I sniggered, but I did shut up because I wanted to pay attention to where his tongue was headed. It traced over my tattoo possessively, insistently licking away the memory any other man had ever seen it. His tongue prodded between my folds and swirled around my clit.

I grabbed the back of his head, arching my back and holding him to me. "Don't stop."

He lapped at the little bundle of nerves, stroking me so intimately. Each lick was pure perfection, moving lower and lower until he was fucking me with his tongue.

"More," I begged. "Please, Zeph."

I ground on his face, needing to be filled. Needing his hands. His cock. Every part of him I could get.

"I want to fuck you bare, Lyric. I want to feel how wet you are."

"Yes," I groaned. "I won't get pregnant. I've got that handled."

He reared back on his knees, gaze hot on my skin as he took in every inch of me splayed out for him. With agonizing slowness, he undid the button and zipper on his jeans, freeing a hard, thick erection.

I reached for him, sitting up so I could take his dick in my hands.

He groaned the moment I touched him.

"I haven't been with anyone in so long, Lyric. This is going to be embarrassingly quick if you keep touching me like that."

I pumped his shaft, teasing him, hips thrusting lightly against my grip. Precum beaded at his tip, and I touched my tongue to it, licking it away, tasting his tang.

The growl he let loose rumbled through me, and then

his arms were around me, hefting me up the bed, covering my naked body with his. I tried to thrust my hips toward his, but he wouldn't let me, pinning me down beneath him, but his cock prodding my leg instead of where I really wanted it.

He kissed my neck, sucking and biting the place it met my shoulder, leaving hickeys that would tell everyone what we'd been doing, but I didn't care. I wanted them. His mark on my body.

My nipples rubbed on his hard chest, and I cried out in pleasure when he dipped his head to take one between his lips. He sucked and licked me while his hand molded to my other breast, cupping and stroking.

The slick of arousal between my thighs was unbearable, an aching need for him that only worsened the longer he kept me still while driving me wild.

"I need to come, Zeph." I fought against his weight on top of me. "I need you inside me."

He kissed me again, shifting his weight so I could get my legs out from beneath him. They wrapped around his waist like they had a mind of their own, opening my core up to him, inviting him in. He crawled up my body so his dick could slide between my legs.

"You're so wet."

He coated himself in my arousal and rubbed his tip against my clit. It sent pulses of orgasmic ecstasy through me, the thick, blunt head so utterly perfect.

I twisted beneath him. Bucked my hips trying to get him inside me.

He bit down on my shoulder, and I yelped at the pain that then quickly turned into a searing pleasure as he drove his cock inside me.

"Oh!" I screamed, stretching to accommodate the size of him. "Oh, fuck, Zeph. More."

He drew back and then slammed back inside me.

I saw stars. The feeling of fullness hit home so perfectly. On the next thrust, I drove my hips up to meet him, letting his pubic bone grind onto my clit.

"Oh!" I shouted with every thrust.

The neighbors would hear, these walls were paper-thin, but there was nothing I could do to be quiet. He could have shoved my face into a pillow, and it still wouldn't have done anything to muffle my cries. Each pounding of his dick sent earth-shattering feeling through my entire body, until a wave crested inside me. He picked up the pace, grinding into me with a roll of his hips. I dug my nails into his back, and with the next thrust, I let go.

His name was a wanton breath of a word on my lips as I came. I gushed with arousal, mine mixing with his when he found his own relief with a groan of pleasure. We clutched at each other, fingers digging into ass and thighs, grinding and rolling, each of us using the other to draw our pleasure out as long as we could.

His cum was wet and sticky between my legs, but he tortured us both by continuing to thrust into me, mostly just grinding while I trembled beneath him every time he made contact with my clit. I was so desperately sensitive but at the same time, I wouldn't stop him.

Eventually, he pulled out, and I rolled over with a blissful sigh of contentment.

He fit himself behind me, warm chest at my back, thighs tucked up with mine. His wet dick was still semi hard against my ass. His palm trailed over the curve of my hip and then between us to cup my ass.

I moaned a little, pressing back against him as he massaged and molded my cheek. My eyes fluttered closed in a combination of exhaustion and pleasure when he pushed me over onto my belly.

I twisted my head to the side, looking back at him when he lifted my hips so my tits were still pressed into the bed, but my ass was on display for him.

His hands roamed all over both cheeks and dipped in between. "You're so beautiful with my cum dripping out of you like this."

I moaned at the dirty words. My knees shook and a second rush of need for him overcame me.

His fingers swiped the cum from between my thighs and spread it between my cheeks, lubing up my tight rear hole.

I turned my face into the mattress and fisted my fingers in the sheet.

"You like that?" He rimmed my entrance. "You're so tight."

"Yes," I moaned. My pussy clenched in on itself, another ache building as he worked a whole new erogenous zone.

He alternated between slow rubs and prodding my entrance, each one opening me up a little more. It had been a long time since someone had touched me there, but all the old feelings came rushing back. I rocked back, encouraging him, until he practically purred with satisfaction.

Through half-lidded eyes, I watched him wrap his fingers around his cock and pump it slowly until he was hard again. He slid inside my pussy, and I gasped at him plugging my ass with his finger at the same time.

"You said I could take your ass." His thighs slapped at mine as he rode me doggy style.

"Yes."

His breathing increased. "You want me here, Lyric?"

"Yes." I buried my face in the pillows. "God, yes."

"Touch your clit."

"There's a vibrator in the drawer."

He groaned and reached across me to open my bedside table.

"Beneath the underwear."

He rummaged through the drawer, producing the sex toy. I took it from him and touched it between my legs.

"Oh fuck," I shouted. I was still sensitive from my first orgasm, and now the second barreled down on me hard.

Zeph groaned when I pulsed around his dick. "You feel so good when you come," he murmured. "I've never felt anything like it.

Neither had I. I'd never had a man care so much about making it as good for me as it was for him. I braced myself for Zeph to fill my ass, but it never came. He kept it to his finger, building me up there while he slammed himself inside my core. Every stroke drew out my second orgasm until it turned into a third and sent Zeph over the edge as well.

"Lyric," he groaned, sweat beading on his skin. He dropped down on top of me once more, pushing me flat to the bed where he rode out the last of his orgasm on my weeping pussy.

When he finally stilled, the room was silent for a moment. Then he pulled out and got to his feet.

I was too exhausted to even wonder where he was going, and then the sound of water running in the bathroom answered that question anyway. He came back in, and a moment later, a wet cloth ran between my legs.

I rolled over, shuddering at the sensation on my already sensitive skin. Zeph gently pushed my legs apart and cleaned away the mess he'd made of my body.

It took me a minute to realize the power must be back on. I frowned at him. "What time is it?"

He'd obviously checked when he'd gotten up to get the cloth. "Nearly five."

My eyes widened. "I need to get to the church and get my cleaning done."

He lifted the covers up beneath my chin. "No. You don't."

I shook my head. "It's my responsibility, Zeph."

"And you're mine. We made a deal, Lyric. You let me have you how I need you. I take care of you when you're refusing to take care of yourself. I kept you from sleeping most of the night. So I'm going to go clean the church while you sleep."

There was no nonsense in his tone. He tucked me in, kissed me sweetly on the forehead, and then the front door was opening.

But it didn't close right away. There was a pause, and then he called back, "Keep that window shut, Lyric. Next time I need you in the middle of the night, I want it to be a challenge."

23

———————

ZEPH

I wasn't a virgin when I'd come into the priesthood, but the things I'd done with Lyric were nothing like the things I'd done with Annie. We'd had sex, but it had been the awkward fumbling of two teens, neither with any experience, and nothing about it had turned me on. She was beautiful, but it hadn't been enough. I'd had to use my imagination to get hard, but even my imagination hadn't done justice to what it felt like to be with a woman like Lyric.

One who knew what she liked. One who wasn't scared when I touched her in intimate places. While I liked the idea of chasing and pinning her and taking her anywhere, anytime, I liked she was loud with her pleasure. That she was enthusiastic. That she was alive beneath me, begging for more, wanting everything I offered.

I didn't want a timid wallflower. I wanted someone who challenged me, and Lyric was it.

I'd known it instinctively from the moment I'd laid

eyes on her outside my church, when her sass and attitude had been written all over her beautiful face.

Her scent lingered on my skin, pretty and feminine over the harsher smell of cleaning chemicals. I wiped over the church's stained-glass windows, rubbing at spots of dirt and fingerprints, pride swelling in my chest that my woman was at home in her bed, well satisfied and taken care of.

My woman.

I waited for the guilt to hit me. The things I'd done broke every vow I'd taken.

It didn't come.

I needed to leave. I couldn't be this person I was with Lyric while also being the priest who delivered Sunday morning sermons. I couldn't sheathe myself inside her, promise to fuck her ass, and then stand at the altar and preach stories I didn't believe in.

The church had been a haven for me. A place to hide.

But I didn't want to hide anymore. Not from her.

I pulled my phone out from my pocket and dialed my mother's phone number. She answered groggily. "Zepherin, do you have any idea what time it is?"

Early. But it didn't matter. "I've met someone."

She cleared her throat. "I don't understand. What does that mean?"

I tried again. "Mom. I've met someone. A woman."

There was a loaded pause on her end and then the scuffle of sheets being ripped off and a door closing. "What on earth, Zeph! You can't just say things like that, your father was in bed beside me."

"I don't care. I think I'm in love with her, Mom."

The noise she made was something of exasperation

and outrage. "Zeph! Are you drunk? High? You're a priest! Have you forgotten that?"

I sighed. "No, I haven't forgotten." How could I when she liked to remind me every five minutes joining the priesthood was the only proud moment she'd had with me.

"So, what? You're just going to leave?"

"Yes."

"Zepherin! You will not. I absolutely forbid it."

I rolled my eyes. "I'm not a child, Mother. You can stick your head in the sand if you want, but it won't change anything."

She breathed heavily into the phone, and I was quite sure she would have been beet red. "Who is this woman? The prostitute from the hospital?"

"Tammie? No. She's just a friend. I don't even have her phone number." I wished I did so I could reach out to her about Toby. I'd been trying to find her, and following every scrap of news I could find on the boy, but nothing had changed. He was still missing.

Mom didn't let me explain any of that. She just barreled on with her accusations. "If not the prostitute, then who, Zepherin? One of her trashy friends? She has no problems tempting a priest away from his calling? What kind of whore does that?"

I clenched my fingers around the phone. "Don't ever call her that again. We both know I never had a calling to join the priesthood. I was forced—"

"Forced? Nobody forced you, Zeph. Your own wicked desires were what got you there. Have you forgotten about what you did to Annie? Your counselors all agreed—"

"Excuse me, we're looking for Father Byron?"

I spun around to find two uniformed police officers at the entrance to the church. Covering the speaker on my phone with my cheek, I shook my head. "I'm sorry, he's not here at the moment. Can I help with anything?"

"We're here to pick up the HR files relating to the two deceased priests."

A trickle of worry worked its way down my spine. What could they possibly want with the church files of the two perverts I'd killed? It wasn't like there were written confessions in there that explained why they'd had to die. Did they have other evidence that had made them return? Or did they have no theories, and digging through the history of two old men was a shot in the dark? Either way, I didn't like that they were here, watching me with a quiet intensity. I needed a minute to think. I raised one finger in their direction. "One minute, Officers. I'll be right with you."

I turned my back on them and addressed my mother who was still squawking in my ear. "I need to go, Mom. I just wanted you to know that things have changed."

"I want to meet her."

That wasn't happening. Not after the way she'd acted the last time she'd met Lyric. It would be a thousand times worse if Mom thought Lyric was responsible for me leaving the church. "You already sort of did."

"What does that mean?"

"You met her once at church. The other day when she was here cleaning."

I waited for it. The explosion of my mother's brain. I was sure it would have an audible sound as it split in two from the steam her anger caused.

"Bring her to James's first birthday party on the weekend."

I raised an eyebrow at her inviting Lyric to my nephew's party. My sister, Kelly, went all out for her kids' birthdays, and they were more like wedding receptions than your average backyard party. They were always held at my parents' place because it was much grander than the place Kelly and her husband, who was a teacher, owned. I was sure my sister used the parties as a chance to show off to her Edgely Academy school mom friends.

Normally I went, because it was expected, did my unclely duty with a fun present, and then left as soon as the cake was cut because Kelly turned into a different person around the snobs from her kids' school. One I barely recognized and didn't always like.

But bringing Lyric would make it bearable. And Kelly had an in with the Edgely Academy crowd. The principal had been at her five-year-old's party last spring, chatting away with an attentive bunch of school parents. Lyric had been so upset after her interview at the school, this could be a chance for her to set the record straight. Her grandmother's accident wasn't so fresh anymore, so maybe the principal would give her a second, less formal, chance. I could ask Kelly to put in a good word for her.

The police officers tapped the door frame impatiently.

I didn't like that they were here. It felt like they were sniffing too close to the truth.

"We'll be there," I told my mother and ended the call and lowered my voice to a barely audible whisper. "As long as I'm not arrested in the next few minutes, that is."

24

LYRIC

I called Eve the moment Zepherin told me his family wanted me to come to a birthday party on the weekend. Worse, that the principal of Edgely Academy would be there. My palms had gone damp with nervous sweat, and my heart beat so hard I was sure I was having a heart attack.

Eve just laughed at me. "They're just people, Lyric. Same as you and me."

I wailed down the phone line. "You don't get it! His mom is a judgmental bitch. She already hates me. Why would they even want me at their probably beautiful home?"

"Uh, because their son is in love with you?"

I scoffed into her ear. "Uh, no. We're just... I don't know what we're doing, actually. But he's not in love with me."

I could practically hear her roll her eyes. "So let me get this straight. The man—a priest who has taken a vow of celibacy, no less—invites you to meet his parents because he's *not* in love with you?"

I waved a hand around in the air dismissively, even though she couldn't see it. "It's not like he's going to introduce me as his girlfriend."

She laughed. "Lyric! He doesn't need to. I've seen the two of you together. The chemistry is palpable. Like, you're going to have his mom's panties all wet just from the way you look at each other."

I screwed up my face in disgust. "That's revolting, and vaguely incestuous. Thanks for that mental image."

Her laughing at me would have been enraging if it were anyone but Eve. But as my best friend, she got a free pass on stuff like that.

"Okay, okay, but the real question is, what are you going to wear?"

I widened my eyes and spun around to my open closet doors. It was full of the sweatpants and old T-shirts on one side, skimpy stripping outfits on the other. There was very little in between. "Oh my God, what the hell am I going to wear? I don't have time to go shopping. My wardrobe is trash."

There was a clink of nail polish bottles from her end of the phone. "Want to borrow something of mine?"

"I don't have the booty to fill out anything you own!"

"Hmmm. True. Your ass could benefit from some squats."

"Oh, shut up. My ass is great. I'm just not blessed with your genetics, and my boobs were a more pressing problem. Can't afford ass implants as well."

Eve giggled but sobered when I wailed some more

about the party Zeph had somehow roped me into. If I hadn't really needed to talk to the principal and explain why I was so out of it at the interview, I would have refused to go.

"Since when do you care what other people think of you, Lyric?" Eve lectured. "This isn't like you. Zeph loves you in booty shorts and midriff tops. His parents will too."

I sank down on the couch, because although it was nice to know Eve thought I was amazing, I just knew Zeph's mom and I had already gotten off to a rough start. Zeph might like me, but I had something to prove when it came to his mother. I wanted her to eat her judgmental words.

Silence dragged out between me and Eve so long I thought she'd hung up. "You there?" I asked.

"Yeah. I was just thinking. What if we went over to Fawn's place and you borrowed one of her dresses?"

I sucked in a breath. Fawn's street style was much sweeter and more innocent than either mine or Eve's and would be perfect for a garden party with the Harts. Fawn and I were similar heights and builds, though my boobs were bigger. But she would definitely have something that would make a better impression than my current options. "I don't know how I feel about that..." My throat went oddly tight over even the thought of stepping inside Fawn's space.

"If she were here, you wouldn't think twice."

Eve sniffed, and I wondered if she was fighting back the same set of tears I was.

I missed Fawn. But Eve was right. We all borrowed

each other's clothes. Eve had two brothers, and I was an only child. If Fawn had family, they weren't in her life. So the three of us had become sisters.

Which was why it hurt so much she wasn't here with us now.

"I've got the keys to her place, and I haven't touched it. I can't bring myself to clear it out and get new tenants. Not until I know for sure she isn't coming back. The cops are finished with their investigations though, so there's no reason for us to not go over there and get you something to wear. You know she'd want you to."

I knew she was right. Because Fawn was the sweetest soul to ever have lived. Even now, she wouldn't have judged me for what I was doing with Zeph. She would have just sat and listened while I talked it out. "Okay," I whispered. "Can you meet me over there now?"

"Give me ten minutes."

I agreed, and we both hung up. I left immediately, even though I lived a little closer to the house Fawn had rented from Eve.

I sat in my car while I waited for Eve to get there. When she pulled up, Augie was sitting in the passenger seat. Eve got out and put an oversized cardigan around her arms like she was cold, even though it was still mild out. Augie followed, both staring up at the building like it held ghosts.

"What are you doing here?" I asked Augie.

Eve answered before he could. "He was at the club with me and overheard my end of the conversation. He wouldn't let me come alone."

Augie's gaze flared with defiance, just begging me to

have an opinion on his behavior so he could start an argument. But he wasn't going to find it with me. I knew Augie blamed himself for everything that had happened that night when Eve and Fawn had been abducted from this house and dragged into an unmarked van. I couldn't blame him for not wanting her to come back here without him.

Frankly, the empty property gave me the creeps. For all I was an independent woman, I didn't like the vibe. I wasn't upset we had him as backup. Eve and I had both grown up on the wrong side of the tracks and could put up a pretty good fight, but Augie had the brawn, should we need it.

"I haven't been back here since that night," Eve whispered.

I reached a hand toward her and squeezed her fingers when she linked hers with mine. I felt like a jerk for agreeing to this. She didn't need to be reliving those memories. "If it's too much..."

She shook her head. "It's not. I have to work out what I'm going to do with the place anyway. I've held it for her all this time—"

"But you can't do it forever," I filled in for her.

Eve turned sad eyes on me. "I can't afford it. If I could, I'd never set foot inside the house again. I'd just leave it exactly as it is until she comes home."

I didn't think either of us really believed that anymore. That Fawn was coming home.

"Come on." I tugged her hand. "Let's get on with it."

Eve followed me, but the tremble in her hand wasn't unwarranted. This was not only the spot where Fawn had been abducted, but Eve too. Eve had been freed, but if it had been me, I probably would have burned the house down already.

Augie strode ahead, keeping us tucked behind him. We didn't argue about who was going to take the lead, Eve giving up the key when he reached back for it. He fit it to the lock and pushed open the door.

None of us moved. We all just stared into the darkened space. I didn't know about the others, but I was waiting for something to jump out at us and yell boo.

There was nothing but the scent of must and dust though. Even still, Augie muttered for us to wait, and we did while he quickly scouted the house. His boots thumped down the stairs, and he jerked his head at us. "It's clear. No one is here."

My muscles relaxed, but Eve was still tense beside me. We moved slowly through Fawn's space, Eve running a fingernail over the smiley face tablecloth in the sunny kitchen. Fawn's laptop and an array of pens, papers, and a calculator all still sat spread out on the tabletop, like she'd just gone for a snack break and was coming back any minute now.

When I glanced over at Eve, she had tears streaming down her face. My own dam broke, and I joined her, the two of us crying and clutching each other, letting loose weeks of fear and sadness.

It helped. At least a little. Some of the weight on me eased just from releasing it. Eve, ever the mother hen, held out an arm to Augie, inviting him to join our huddle.

His eyes were glassy with unshed tears, but his jaw was tight. He turned away. "I'm going to the bathroom."

We both watched him go.

"He's not okay, is he?" Eve asked with a wobble in her voice.

"No," I agreed. "He's really not. None of us are."

But what else was there to do but go on with our lives? We had to. We couldn't stop living because life didn't make sense without our sunshine girl. I tugged Eve toward the stairs. "Come on. Let's just get this over with."

We both trudged up the stairs to the second-floor landing. On the left, the bathroom door was closed, and we left Augie to privately grieve. Eve and I slipped into the room on the right, Fawn's bedroom.

I couldn't look at her things too closely. Everything on her dresser was so her. A speaker for music on the thrift shop dresser. A tray full of colorful but cheap jewelry that she could add to any outfit. A Hello Kitty sweatshirt tossed haphazardly onto the end of the neatly made bed. Eve picked it up and clutched it to her chest.

I went to Fawn's built-in closet and smiled at the array of pretty dresses. It didn't even matter which one I picked. They were all adorable and would be perfect for Zeph's family party. I rifled through each one, trying to remember Fawn's face and her smile and her voice when I'd last seen her wearing each item.

I hated that her voice in my head was starting to fade. I dug my fingers into a yellow-and-pink sundress and forced myself to think harder, but it didn't help. I took the dress out, hanger and all, and laid it out on the bed.

Eve glanced over at it. "That's a good choice. She had shoes that match. You should get those too."

I nodded numbly, squatting to retrieve the cork heels

that had a pale-pink and yellow stripe painted across the wedge. I pulled each shoe out, gathering them into my arms, brushing off a bit of dust that had collected. Behind them sat a shoebox covered in cut-up photos, and I smiled, recognizing a younger version of Fawn in a lot of them.

"Look at this," I called to Eve. I straightened with the box clutched in one hand, the shoes in my other. "Check out baby Fawn with dark hair."

I passed the keepsake box over to Eve, and she grinned down at it, turning it over to see each of the glued-on images. "She was so cute. The dark suited her. I actually like it better than the blond."

I did too. Eve perched on the edge of Fawn's mattress, and I sat beside her as the toilet flushed across the hall.

"Augie! Come look at these," Eve called to him.

He leaned on the doorframe, crossing his arms over his chest. His eyes were red-rimmed and glassy, but neither Eve nor I mentioned it. She lifted the lid on the box and took out the photo on top.

I snatched it from her fingers. "Oh my, who is that?"

Eve peered at the photo with me. "Did she ever tell you she had a brother? That's gotta be a brother, right? He's so much like her."

"If he's her brother she's been holding out on us. He's hot." I pointed to the other woman in the picture. "This must be a sister, then."

Eve shrugged. "Or cousins, I suppose. She never told me about her siblings. Just that she wasn't in contact with her family and wanted it keep it that way."

In typical Augie fashion, he snatched the photo from my fingers without asking. I rolled my eyes but bit my tongue from commenting on his manners. Or lack thereof.

He glanced down at the photo, tracing a finger over a younger Fawn's image, and then his head jerked up, his eyes wide.

Eve reached for the old photo. "What? What is it?"

He turned it around, pointing at the woman standing beside Fawn. At the time, she was several inches taller than Fawn, with a womanly look about her in comparison to Fawn's gangly mid-teen self. The woman could have been mid-twenties, with the man at maybe twenty-one or twenty-two.

Augie's finger trembled slightly. "I know her."

I leaned in and stared at the photo again. The woman did seem familiar, but I was sure I'd never met her before. "Are you sure? She looks an awful lot like Fawn. Maybe that's why."

"I saw her on the subway, just the other day. I literally sat next to her. Fuck! We even talked about Fawn." Augie tugged at his hair. "What does that mean? She never said anything about knowing her. Just let me go on and on about her being missing."

A rising sense of dread crept up my spine. "Are you sure?"

"Of course I'm fucking sure, Lyric! You can see how much she's like Fawn! I chased her through the fucking subway because I thought she *was* her."

"There's a lot of people on the subway, Aug," Eve said gently. "And you're grieving—"

"It was her," he growled.

Eve held her hands up in mock surrender. "Okay,

okay. So, what? Are we assuming this woman is her sister? Her aunt? A cousin?"

I swallowed thickly, the uncomfortable feeling refusing to subside. "I don't know, but if Fawn was running from her family, the fact they're here in Saint View can't be for anything good."

25

LYRIC

Zeph's parents' place was in the richest part of Providence, where the houses had long, winding driveways, perfectly tended-to gardens, and expensive cars parked in the drive. I stared out the window as we pulled up behind a sleek silver Tesla and then gawked up at the house. "You grew up here?"

Zeph glanced over at me from behind the steering wheel. "First window on the second story was my bedroom until I was nineteen."

I gazed up to where he pointed and then shook my head in amazement. "Even that window reeks of money. All fancy with pretty curtains and as wide as I am tall. Makes my bedroom window look like a jail cell peephole."

"Speaking of, I had a visit from the cops yesterday."

My mouth dropped open. "Do they know?"

His gaze darted back up to the bedroom window. "About what?"

I dug my fingernails into his arm, heart hammering

nervously. "About your little habit of robbing the rich to give to the poor. Or in other words…" I lowered my voice, so it was barely above a hiss, even though there was no one else around, "*breaking and entering.*"

Though he had honorable reasons for doing the things he did, it didn't make them any less illegal. It had felt wild and exciting at first, but it suddenly felt reckless and dangerous. I didn't want him ending up in jail because of his Robin Hood fantasies. I was something of an accomplice after our night at Kat's place, even though the only thing we'd stolen was a few grams of her weed. But I knew that wasn't the case at the other homes he'd broken into.

An image of him being dragged off in cuffs had my stomach doing vomit-inducing backflips.

But he shook his head, his dark, almost curly hair bouncing around his face. "No, nothing like that. They just wanted some files that the murdered priests had worked on."

Relief rushed me. "Oh. Good. That's good." Then I peered at him. "Are you worried about that at all? Must be unsettling knowing there's a priest killer on the loose. It's still all over the news. I know you can take care of yourself, but still…" I smoothed out a wrinkle on my dress, trying to seem like I wasn't at all bothered.

I couldn't be bothered by him. I couldn't care. I had too much going on with Gran and Amelia. If I shouldered anything more, my entire house of cards would come tumbling down.

Feelings were too inconvenient. I wasn't going there. Especially with him, because falling for a priest would only end in heartbreak.

Zeph's lips turned up, and he reached over to pick up my hand. "You're nervous."

He'd completely misread my body language. "I'm not."

He ignored that I'd said anything. "You are, but it's cute. You're like a pissed-off kitten."

I sighed, because it wasn't really. "I'm not nervous. Not about you handling yourself. But your mother was a bitch last time I saw her. If she had wanted to see us, she could have called and apologized for calling me a slut."

His face darkened. "She'll apologize or we're leaving."

I glanced at him. "This is a big thing for your sister. I can leave. You don't have to. Shit. Maybe I shouldn't have come." But I needed this second chance with Principal Williams. If she wasn't taking my phone calls, then in person at a baby's birthday party it would have to be.

His fingers clamped down on mine. "I'm not here without you, you hear me? You want to bail, we both bail. But this is your chance to show Principal Williams you're funny and smart and intelligent. And that your daughter deserves a spot in that school. You don't need to worry about my family. They'll behave, and my mother will apologize."

Another car parked behind us, blocking us in, the party due to begin any minute now. I sighed, glancing over my shoulder at it. "Blocked in. No escape now."

The other couple called a greeting to Zeph and cast a curious look in my direction but didn't question who I was. A pretty, young, dark-haired woman greeted them at the door and welcomed them into the house. She spotted Zeph and I lingering on the drive, me debating on whether I could make a run for it in these heels.

She waved enthusiastically, a dozen or so bracelets clinking together around her arm. "Zepherin! You're here! What are you doing, sitting out there? Everyone is inside. I'm dying to meet your...friend. Hello there."

I swallowed thickly and raised a hand in greeting. Too late for running.

Like he could read my mind, he turned his back on his sister, his fingers tips brushing the back of my hand. "There's woods at the back of the property. You need to run, we don't need a car. You leave, I'll follow."

A shiver rolled down my spine, knowing that the chase was part of the thrill for him.

And apparently for me too.

We got out of the car, Zeph picking up my hand to tug me toward the door and his waiting sister. But when her gaze dropped to our linked fingers, I pulled away.

Zeph grabbed my hand back, squeezing my fingers possessively.

A warm glow radiated from the spot where our palms touched, even though his sister's smile fell.

She got herself together by the time we reached her though, and he let me go long enough for her to wrap her arms around him and squeeze him tight. "Why haven't I seen you in so long?"

"You've been busy with your brood." He hugged her back.

"Isn't that the truth!" She laughed and ushered us both inside, while rubbing her belly. There was a small baby bump there I hadn't noticed.

"Congratulations," I murmured to her. "Zeph said you already have four, so this is number five?"

The woman smiled widely at me. "Ridiculous, right?

In this day and age with how much it costs to feed each little person. But I just love being a mama. Kenny and I are truly blessed by God. I keep saying we're done, but God keeps giving us more."

I fought the urge to roll my eyes. Sounded more like Kenny and Kelly could just get on board with contraception, but each to their own. If the two of them wanted to repopulate the earth single-handedly, then who was I to stop them?

"It's Lyric, right?" Kelly asked, reaching a hand toward me. "You can put your purse in the cupboard here if you like."

I handed it to her with a forced smile.

Zeph jumped in. "Sorry, I forgot the two of you haven't met. Kel, this is Lyric. Lyric, Kelly."

I shook Kelly's hand, noting that her skin was buttery smooth and completely absent of the callouses that had become a permanent fixture on my hands, thanks to long nights swinging my G-string-clad ass around a stripper pole. "Nice to meet you."

To my surprise, Kelly tucked her arm in mine and abandoned her post at the door. "Zeph says the two of you work together at the church. You clean the toilets?"

I stopped walking. "Excuse me?"

Kelly gave me a sickly sweet smile I knew probably worked on most of the population but hid her wolf teeth and a bitchy undertone. "Oh, I'm sorry. Did I have that wrong?"

"No. That's exactly what I do there. Clean the toilets." I added silently in my head, 'And have mind-blowing sex with your brother when he climbs through my window on my nights off.' I imagined the horror on her face if I'd said it out loud.

It was satisfying.

Zeph chuckled, and I was surer than ever that he actually could read my mind.

His sister glanced between the two of us like we were crazy. I ignored her and wandered toward the sounds of the party in the back of the house, but slowly, taking in all the family photos on the walls. I recognized a younger version of his mother in many, with a man I hadn't met, but who was clearly her husband. In the living room were large photos of two babies, one boy and one girl, smiling gummily at the camera.

I pointed to the boy and nudged Zeph. "Is that you? So cute!"

But he shook his head. "It's my older brother, Jonathan."

"The girl is me," Kelly piped up completely unnecessarily since I knew Zeph only had one sister.

I frowned at the photos. "Why isn't there one of you as a baby?"

In fact, as I gazed around the room, there were no photos of Zeph until he was about kindergarten age. Then it was like he'd been birthed out of thin air, and he joined all the family photos.

"I was adopted," he said carefully. "When I was four."

I raised an eyebrow. "Really? You didn't tell me that."

"It never came up."

That was fair enough.

Kelly was more than happy to fill in the blanks, though. "Our parents saved him. He was born into a terrible family. His birth mom kept him in a tiny apartment in a terrible part of Saint View."

I reached for his hand, but he dodged my advances and walked stiffly away from us, toward the other room where the party was taking place.

"Oh dear," his sister murmured. "I didn't know he hadn't told you. He's very embarrassed about his early life, but we can't help the people we come from now, can we? Mom and Dad got Zepherin out, and it's been all hunky-dory since there." She fingered the single strand of pearls around her neck. "Do you have children, Lyric?"

"One. A daughter. She's four."

"Starting school in September?" Kelly clapped her hands together excitedly then grabbed my arm. "Oh, isn't that just the most exciting stage yet! You'll cry on her first day, of course. I sob like a baby when mine start school. But it's such an enriching and exciting experience for the child. She's going to Edgely Academy, right?"

It was a question, but she'd said it like there was no other choice and that the public schools barely even existed.

I nodded. "We're trying to get her in there. We had our interview but we haven't been offered a place yet." I was itching to go after Zeph, but his sister had me in her clutches, her fingers pressing into my arm. I spotted him on the other side of the room, staring out through the expanse of huge windows into the wooded area that lay behind the house. A young guy stood beside him, a grown-up version of the young boy I'd seen in the photos. Zeph's brother. He nursed a mostly drunk glass of whiskey while he talked quietly with Zeph. Or rather at Zeph, since he seemed lost in his own head.

Kelly took me in the opposite direction though, pointing toward a group of women. "You already know Kara then, the principal?" She waved in the woman's direction. "Kara! Do you remember Lyric?"

The heavyset woman turned and blinked at me in confusion. She clearly couldn't place me.

I cleared my throat uncomfortably. "Amelia Percival's...uh, Amelia Torrensen's mother. I'm Lyric. I had an interview in your office last week."

Kara smiled at me. "Oh, of course. Lovely to see you again. Are you a friend of Kelly's?"

I shook my head. "Of her brother's."

The woman's smile slipped a bit. "Jonathan?"

I shook my head, assuming Jonathan was the older brother whose baby photo had made it to the wall of honor. "No. Zeph's."

The woman laughed. "Oh, I'm sorry. I kind of just assumed priests didn't have female friends."

Kelly joined in, "Especially not one as pretty as Lyric here!"

The other women tittered, but I didn't crack a smile. I opened my mouth to ask Kara if I could have a private word, but Zeph's mom joined the group, glancing around at the laughing women.

"What's so funny?" Her gaze landed on me. Her delighted gaze turned frosty. "Oh. Hello."

I didn't say a word. Between the laughter that felt like it was at my expense and Zeph's mom's cool stare, I had nothing nice to say.

His mother cleared her throat. "So, Lyric. Zepherin has made me aware that there might be some air that needs clearing between us."

I froze. I didn't want to do that here. Not now, in front of Kara when I was trying to repair the damage I'd done with her the first time we'd met. The women around me quieted, all gazes bouncing between me and his mother facing-off. If they'd had any manners, they would have excused themselves and moved away, but they hung on Zeph's mom's every word like she was spilling the sweetest tea.

When I refused to answer again, the woman's smile grew. But it was that of a shark. Cold and hard. She glanced around at her friends. "I mistook Lyric here for a..." She dropped her voice to a conspiratorial whisper. "A prostitute."

The women around me gasped. One by one, they all swiveled to stare at me, mentally removing the pretty garden dress and heels and redressing me in G-strings and nipple tassels.

"You can't blame me though. She wasn't dressed as lovely as she is today."

My fingers twisted into fists, but I shoved them in the pockets of the dress, grateful it had them. This woman was the bitch I'd initially assessed her to be. But I couldn't say a word, because Amelia's school principal was watching my every move. My cheeks flamed with embarrassment and anger. I bit down on my tongue so hard I was sure it would bleed. I couldn't ruin this for my daughter. She'd loved everything about Edgely Academy, and she was so smart, she needed to be in that school where they could nurture her intelligence. She needed more than I had. So if I had to bite my tongue so fucking hard it fell off so my daughter could have the opportunities I never had, then I would.

But it hurt. Their words and judgment were like steel blades poking through my heart. I tried so hard not to care what other people thought of me, and mostly I succeeded. But I did care about Amelia's principal. If I was being honest, I also cared about the other moms at the school. I didn't want them telling their kids to stay away from my daughter because I was a bad influence. "I'm not a prostitute," I said stiffly. "And I forgive your assumption."

I just wanted this to be over.

But Zeph's mom wasn't even paying attention. She was looking at Zeph, who was watching me.

You okay? he mouthed.

It was so tempting to say no. I knew he'd sweep in and rescue me, but dammit, it was already bad enough I was taking this shit from his mother and sister. I didn't want him to have to save me too. I didn't even want him hearing the things they were saying because there was a nagging voice in my head that it was all true. I wasn't accepting money for sex. But the things I'd done with Zeph... The man was a priest, and I'd spent weeks flirting with him, testing his boundaries, pushing him to his limits until he snapped. Why? I kept denying there were feelings there, so why had I done it? For sport? That really did make me a whore.

I nodded at Zeph and turned away before he could study my expression too closely.

His mother's smile grew concerned. "I'm so glad you see it that way. Now. Tell us what you actually do for a living?"

Oh, she was good. I had to give her that. Twisting the conversation so I'd have to reveal the parts of me that weren't socially acceptable in a room like this. But I wouldn't lie. There was no point. She was hell-bent on outing me anyway. "I clean the church a few days a week. The rest of the time I work at Saint View Strip Club."

The way the women's eyes widened was almost cartoonish.

Kelly spluttered. "That dive of a place on the main road? Do you clean there too?"

I glanced over at Kara. Her expression was heart-breaking. I'd come here to try to prove I wasn't the disaster I'd been in her office, and all I'd done was cement that I was.

Then came the judgment. From all of them. Thick and heavy and slimy. They acted as if I'd just lifted my dress and taken a dump on the birthday cake.

I squared my shoulders. I wouldn't lie. I wouldn't mope. Wouldn't sit here and listen to any more of this. I couldn't fix the mess I'd made with Principal Williams and Zeph's family. It was clear any chance I'd had of getting Amelia into that school was over. But I could walk away from it with my head held high. They were all just waiting for me to admit it anyway. "No, actually. I take my clothes off and swing around a pole with my legs open so men can shove dollar bills into my panties. That what you want me to say, Kelly? There. I said it."

I spun around, but Zeph's mom caught my hand. "Your daughter deserves more than you can give her, Lyric. We have resources for women like you. Programs. There's a course at the church—"

I yanked my hand from her grip. "Don't tell me what my daughter needs," I hissed at the woman.

"I could report you. I'm sure Child Protective Services

would be very interested in knowing what goes on in your home."

Her threat sliced into a deep-rooted fear I had. The one where someone realized I wasn't good enough to raise Amelia and took her from me. Rage blazed through me, and I lashed out. "You're hardly the perfect parent, are you, Suzanna? Did you raise perfect children? Do your friends here know about…"

About how your son likes to dominate women? About how you pushed him into a role in the church but how he watches me masturbate? About how he fucks me bare and comes on my pussy, so I'm marked as his?

Her face went pale.

She knew. She knew the things he was capable of. She'd been the one to clean up his mess with Annie.

I would have never thrown Zeph under the bus like that, but I was more than willing to make his mother aware I knew her children weren't perfect either. At least not in her eyes, even though she tried very hard to hide that fact by bragging about them to everyone who would listen.

How the judgment would shift if I revealed that her perfectly priestly son was banging a common gutter whore like me.

"Lyric?" Zeph asked cautiously. "What's going on?" He took my elbow.

I jerked it from his grasp and spun on him. "I'm just fine, Zeph. Just fucking fine."

I stormed for the nearest door as fast as I could in my heels and wrenched it open, rushing out of the house and down the stairs that led to the pool.

"Lyric, wait."

I picked up the pace, running now while tears streamed down my face. My heart ached with everything I'd just lost for my daughter. I'd known my career choice would come back to bite me with her eventually. If not now, then when she was older and realized what I actually did.

Hell, maybe she never would have gotten in anyway, but now I would never know. Her rejection letter would be in my mailbox by Monday, I was sure of it. I seethed as I ran, angry at Zeph's mom and his sister, and myself for ever coming here. It reeked of a setup, and betrayal was bitter on my tongue.

"Lyric," Zeph snapped as I edged the woods. "Wait."

His heavy footsteps fell behind me, and I spun around to yell at him, only to find the entire party with their noses pressed to the glass, watching us.

Their gazes burned.

I didn't know when I'd become this person who cared about what other people thought of me, but I did. There were too many of them to ignore. Each and every one of them screwed up their face in disgust, all of it aimed at the stupid stripper who'd dared to come to their Providence home in the hope of giving her child a better life.

I couldn't stand the shame. Or the guilt. I kicked the heels off and ran, barely feeling the stabbing of pine needles beneath my feet. I ran into the woods until the house disappeared behind the thick trees. I ran until my lungs ached from overuse and forced me to slow.

I ran until all I felt was Zeph's presence behind me, slowly keeping pace, not gaining on me, but not dropping away either.

He said nothing. Didn't call my name or tell me to wait again.

The anger and hopelessness melted away, replaced by a different feeling all together. A breathless excitement, vaguely laced with danger. I sprinted around a tree, glancing back over my shoulder at him.

My heart leapt at the wild look in his eyes, at knowing I was playing right into his fantasies.

Maybe it was partially a 'fuck you' to his mother and sister and all the snobby assholes up in that house who had silently called me a slut.

But I liked that look on him. It made my heart race, not in fear, but in need.

A thrill shot through me, catching my breath. I slipped on some loose soil, tried to scramble back to my feet, but it was the opportunity he'd been waiting for. His big body came down on top of mine, sending me back into the dirt.

I tried to scream, an instinct rather than one of true fear because I wasn't scared. Just turned on. He clapped a hand over my mouth from behind though, pushing me roughly into the dirt once more, his stomach to my back, lips at my ear.

"Fight me."

I grinned behind his hand.

He flipped me to my back, pinning my hands above my head with his. His chest heaved, sucking in deep breaths.

I grinned up at him with a mixture of sass and defiance. "You're ruining my dress, Zeph."

He just shook his head and leaned down on me, grinding his hardened dick against my panties. He transferred my hands so they were held by just one of his, then swapped his dick for his fingers. "You already ruined these panties with how wet you are."

I moaned at his dirty words, and again when he ripped the panties straight off my body. The seams had no chance for the vicious way he needed me, and though the fabric dug into my thigh, the sting of pain before it tore only turned me on more.

"Sweet, bare, wet little pussy," he groaned. "So fucking tight for me."

I groaned, half twisting and fighting beneath him but sure I was really just thrusting my hips toward him, begging him to take me hard.

"Let me go," I demanded.

"No."

"Let me go, Zeph."

I said it as convincingly as possible, while knowing he wouldn't because I hadn't used my safe word.

"Not until you tell me why you're upset."

I wasn't telling him that. He could ask his asshole family. I struggled against his hold, fighting to get him off me. His fingers thrust up inside me, straight against my G-spot.

I cried out at the incredible rush of feeling.

He pleasured me with his fingers until I was panting and desperate, my dress rucked up around my waist, tits falling out, panties discarded in a torn mess beside us. His T-shirt had joined the pile at some point.

He let go of my hands long enough to undo his pants. "Don't move, Lyric."

Where was the fun in that?

I twisted and sprang to my feet, running again from him while he was distracted by his pants.

Twelve steps. That was as far as I got until he was behind me again and pressing me up against the nearest tree. The bark scratched my cheek, but I barely felt it, chest heaving from having Zeph's big body pressed so tight.

There was no escaping him this time. He had me exactly where we both wanted him. I waited, breathless with excitement, wondering what he'd do next.

I'd never had sex like this.

I'd thought I'd wanted other men. But none of them had ever been like this. None of them had ever made me want what Zeph instinctually knew I needed.

He lifted my dress, baring my ass, to no one but the trees and leaves and dirt. Even the birds had flown away, frightened by the way we'd crashed through the woods.

His palm cracked across my naked ass. "You ran from me, Lyric."

"You liked it," I sassed him back.

His palm cracked across my other ass cheek.

God, it felt good. I'd always liked it rough and hard. Public sex was nothing new. But Zeph made my legs tremble with anticipation. He was such an unknown, a surprise at every turn, so I never knew what to expect.

He shouldn't have wanted any of this. He shouldn't have known how to make me this wet.

The thick, blunt head of his cock slid between my thighs and straight up inside me.

"Oh," I moaned. "Yes!"

He withdrew and slammed back inside me,

bottoming out. I screamed at how full and thick he was, pleasure spiraling out of control.

"Don't you come," he warned in my ear, pumping himself in and out of my body. "Not yet, Lyric."

I shook my head, making a promise I wasn't sure I could keep because I was teetering on the edge. He slowed down though, his movements gentler, giving me a minute to bring myself back.

"Good girl," he whispered.

I shivered, enjoying his commands and praise when I obeyed him more than I should have.

He pulled out of me, and I whimpered at the loss of him.

"Turn around."

I did, and he picked me up, hands supporting my ass and guiding me to sink down on his cock once more. I wrapped my arms and legs around him, moaning while he bounced me on his dick. I'd never liked standing sex, but most men couldn't throw me around the way Zeph could. His biceps strained, and his abs flexed, but he carried me like I weighed nothing. I clawed at his back, scratching my long nails up and down the tawny, warm skin, muscles rippling beneath my touch.

"You're so deep," I groaned.

His every thrust rubbed his dark thatch of hair against my swollen clit, driving me higher and higher. He pushed me against the tree, using it as leverage to go faster and harder, his actions vicious and predatory, but each one lighting me up like I'd never truly known what it felt like to be turned on by someone until now. His thrusts were punishing, and I was sure I'd have bruises tomorrow. My back would be scratched, probably my face too. Eve was going to have a conniption if I went into the club looking like I'd gone a round with a porcupine. But she'd come around when I explained that they were sex injuries.

Really fucking good sex. The kind where you didn't feel pain, because the pleasure overrode every other sensation.

"You're close," he said into my ear.

I nodded desperately.

"You want to come, Lyric?"

I so did. All I could do was press my mouth to his and kiss him.

It was the only answer he needed. He growled into my mouth, fucking me hard, taking what I so freely offered, even if we were playing games. I clamped down around him, howling when I came, begging him to let me come again, because the orgasms barreled down, one after the other.

I closed my eyes, body going limp, unable to move for the sensation of the double orgasm. It dragged out for what felt like an hour but was probably only minutes, and Zeph mumbled praises and dirty talk into my ear as he found his own release. He shuddered around me, telling me I was too good for him, too perfect.

In the moment, I could believe it.

26

LYRIC

There was no way in hell I was going back into that house, and thankfully, Zeph didn't ask me to. With our clothes back in place, he led me through the woods with the sure steps of a man who knew them well. We skirted his parents' big house and emerged not far from where we'd left his car.

It was a relief to dive inside, slink down on the passenger seat, and wait while he retrieved my purse. If he announced we were leaving, nobody cared enough to come out and say goodbye to me.

I was grateful for that, because if I never saw any of those people ever again, I wouldn't be sad.

He tossed me my purse, and I sat it by my feet while he steered the car onto his parents' lawn to get around the cars parked behind us. Out on the road, I stared out the window at the big, pretty houses of Providence, knowing I'd never fit in here.

"I'm sorry we came," he said quietly. "That wasn't how I envisioned it going."

I really didn't want to talk about it. "Could you take me to the hospital? I want to check in on my grandmother."

"Of course."

We drove the rest of the way in silence, while I stewed. When we pulled into the grounds of Saint View Hospital, I pointed at the drop-off area. "You can just let me out there. I can walk home, it's not far."

"Not happening. I'll come with you."

I sighed. "Don't take this the wrong way, but can you not? Every time she mistakes you for my grandfather it breaks my heart. My heart is already a little battered today."

He slumped back in his chair. "I'm sorry."

I reached out for him. "No, don't be. It isn't your fault." I wanted to be with my grandmother. She was my safe space. The one who'd always seen through my bravado. She saw the hurt behind the tough front I put up and she had always known what to say to make me feel better. She'd spent my entire childhood years telling me I was more than what other people thought of me. That I was worth more than a mother who rejected me, boys who dumped me, a man who got me pregnant but didn't want a relationship. That I could be a stripper and still be a worthwhile human being.

Some days, you just needed your mom. And Gran was mine.

But Zeph was in my corner too. So I tossed him a bone. "Could you wait for me? Drive me home after?"

He leaned over and kissed me gently. "I'll be right here. Take all the time you need."

My heart squeezed.

I got out of the car, slamming the door behind me before I could analyze why.

I strode briskly through the maze of hospital corridors, the way to Gran's room already memorized from my previous visits. A nurse glanced up as I entered the ward, but I raised a hand in greeting, recognizing her face from the last time I was here, and she waved me on through.

"She's having a good day," the nurse called. "You picked a great time to visit."

I smiled at her and opened Gran's door.

She beamed at me. "Lyric!"

I perched on the edge of her bed, careful not to jostle it too much for fear it would cause her pain. But she waved a hand around dismissively.

"Get on up here and give me a hug. I'm doped up to the eyeballs on painkillers. Can barely feel a thing. They're good stuff. I'll try to steal you some."

I sniggered but did as she said, leaning in to gently wrap my arms around her frail body. "You seem a lot better today."

"Christ. Must have looked like death last time you saw me then. I asked the nurse to bring me some lipstick and blush. I looked in the mirror and thought I'd seen a ghost."

I swallowed thickly, emotion clogging my throat and tears filling the backs of my eyes. Because this was the woman I remembered. The one who was there for all my childhood memories.

The one dementia was cruelly stealing from me.

"Hey, why are you crying?" Gran squeezed my hand.

I shook my head, not wanting to tell her it was because I'd missed her so much. And I was grateful for her good days. But I knew they wouldn't last, and I was devastated over that at the same time. Tears dripped down my cheeks as I gripped her hand, wishing if I only held her tighter, she'd get to stay.

"Is it Zeph?" she asked gently.

And because I didn't want to upset her, and because it was partly Zeph, I nodded.

She brushed my hair back off my face, like I did to Amelia when she cried. "Oh, honey. You love him, don't you?"

I blinked at her. "Gran, no. He's a priest, remember?"

She gave me one of her no-nonsense looks that I knew well from my teenage years when I'd tested out lying on her. It hadn't flown then, and it apparently didn't fly now. "I think his profession is irrelevant at this point, don't you? Especially since you have a leaf in your hair."

I widened my eyes and swiped my fingers through my messed-up curls. Indeed, a leaf fluttered free, dropping to my lap. "Well, that's embarrassing."

Gran squeezed my fingers. "Maybe for you, but it makes me happy."

I stared at her, wide-eyed. "You aren't horrified I'm corrupting a priest?"

She scoffed. "You can't corrupt someone who doesn't want to be, Lyric. I've seen the way you act around him. The way he treats you. When has any man ever treated you so well? You finally picked one worthy of you. And that makes my old heart happy."

"Your heart isn't so old." I sniffed back tears.

She reached out to cup my cheek. "I know my days are numbered, Lyric. But I'm an old woman and I've had a good life. I knew true love, and when I pass on from this world, I'll meet my Harry on the other side. But I want to go knowing you're loved and taken care of."

"I can take care of myself. Always have."

She tskd me. "You can pay the bills, Lyric. You can put a roof over your head, food in your mouth, and give yourself orgasms."

"Gran! I'm horrified!" I half laughed through my tears.

She ignored me. "But having someone love you...truly and unconditionally... Maybe you don't need it to breathe. But I want it for you. I want you to know what it feels like to have someone care for your heart better than you ever could yourself. You need that, Lyric. You need someone to watch over you and make sure you remember it's not you against the world." She smiled fondly at me. "At least not the entire world."

I gave up wiping at my face with my fingers and rifled through my purse, searching for a tissue. My grandmother just watched me knowingly.

"Stop staring at me like that," I complained, hating she knew me so well. I dropped the tissue back into my purse then groaned, shoving aside my wallet and makeup bag and digging right to the bottom of my purse.

"What's wrong?" Gran asked.

"My phone. It's not in here."

"You left it at home?"

I shook my head. "I remember packing it into my purse before I went to this one-year-old's birthday party at Zeph's parents' place..."

Gran wrinkled her nose. "Ugh. I never understood why your generation are so hell-bent on having such elaborate parties for babies. It's not like they understand what's going on. All that fuss and time and money just for everyone to stand around and gawk at the sticky, poopy baby? Sounds awful."

I laughed at her. "It was."

"Save the money 'til they're twenty-one when they can actually appreciate it."

"Duly noted. Will wait until my kid is of legal age before doing any sort of fun celebration for her birthday. When she begs me for sleepovers, I'll tell her Granny was a spoilsport. But in the meantime, I need to go find my phone." I leaned in and kissed her again. "I'll see you tomorrow, okay?"

"On your way. I've got soaps to watch." She pointed at the little hospital TV mounted opposite her bed.

I left her to her shows and went back to the elevator, musing over everything she'd said. The doors opened, and I smiled at the little family already inside as I squeezed on with them. The woman was in a wheelchair, a brand-new baby on her lap, while her husband and maybe four-year-old son stood behind.

"Congratulations." I tapped the button for the ground floor and then snuck a peek at the baby swaddled in pink. "Girl? She's beautiful."

The woman smiled proudly. "Thank you."

The man opened his mouth to respond, but the four-year-old stomped his little foot. "She's not beautiful! She's ugly, and I hate her!"

The man cringed at me while patting the boy on the head. "Someone isn't taking too well to being a big brother," he said, like the boy couldn't hear. "You'll get used to her, buddy. And then you'll love her so much."

The boy wriggled away from his father's condescending head pats to stand at the front of the elevator and out of his father's reach. He crossed skinny arms over his small chest and glared at the elevator door, refusing to acknowledge his baby sister or his parents.

I felt for the kid. Change was hard.

The doors binged open.

The kid took off running, right for the hospital entrance, with the automatic doors.

And a busy main road on the other side.

"George!"

The man struggled to get out from behind the wheelchair and the bags piled up on the floor.

I was closer and not about to watch their kid get flattened.

But goddamn, he was a quick little thing. I ran after him, his parents calling after us.

The automatic doors swung themselves open as the boy approached, and despite his parents' calls, he just kept on going.

I doubled down, decreasing the gap between us with every stride but quickly and horrifyingly realized I wasn't going to be quick enough.

"George!" I added my own shouts to his parents.

From the corner of my eye, a truck trundled down the road, headed for the hospital's delivery entrance.

George was going to run right in front of it. It played out in my mind in slow motion and then sickeningly fast in real life.

His foot off the curb.

The blare of the truck's horn.

My fingers just barely grabbing the back of the boy's shirt and hauling him backward as the truck roared past us.

Someone screamed behind us, but I stood frozen on the very edge of the sidewalk, clutching the shaking, terrified, but completely uninjured boy to my chest.

"Oh my God, George!" His father had only been seconds behind me, but it had been seconds the boy didn't have. He grabbed the boy from my arms, wrapping him in his own.

I shook where I stood, frozen in place, imagining the boy had been Amelia. They were roughly the same age and size. All I could see was him stepping in front of that truck.

Two strong hands gripped my shoulders, spinning me around.

Zeph's terrified expression registered between the vague shake he gave me. "What the hell just happened? Are you okay?"

"The boy," I mumbled. "He walked in front of the truck."

"So did you!"

Had I? Had I stepped off the pavement, putting myself in the way of the oncoming vehicle? I didn't even know. And it didn't matter. "We're both okay," I told him. "It's fine."

He shook his head and pulled me to his chest, burying my face in his shoulder. "I thought I just watched you die. I was parked on the other side of the road. I didn't see you step back."

I squeezed him back, realizing how scary that would have been for him. "I'm sorry. I'm okay."

He guided me away, while George's parents called thank-yous to me.

Zeph put me in the passenger side, reaching over me to put my seat belt on for me.

His fingers trembled.

He got in behind the wheel and started the car. We slowly made our way home, Zeph parking in front of my apartment building.

I turned to him. "I think my phone might have fallen out of my bag at your parents' place. Can you ask them for me?"

He nodded. "But can you do something for me?"

I mirrored his actions.

"Can you please stop putting yourself in danger? Walking home alone at night in Saint View. Stepping in front of trucks—"

"You would have done the same."

"Yes, but you seem to make it a habit." He grasped my chin and twisted my head in his direction. "I don't want to bury you, Lyric. But you seem hell-bent on making that a possibility."

I leaned in and kissed him, hoping if I changed the subject he'd stop looking at me the way he was. That sort of intensity scared me. "I'll see you in the morning. I'm coming to clean the church after my shift at the club."

"No. Go home and sleep. I've got the church covered tomorrow. At some point before then, how close you came to dying is going to hit you. You're going to need to process that."

"I'll be fine."

"I want to remove that word from your vocabulary."

Gran's words about the entire world not being against me rang in my ears. So I gave in. An inch. And promised I'd think about it.

27

ZEPH

The next morning, I got up with the sun, and like I did every day, scoured the web for any fresh information on Tammie and her missing son. There was none, so with a sigh I went out and checked the church for Lyric. I fully expected to find her in there, exhausted after her shift at the club but vigorously scrubbing the stone floor.

There was no sign of her though. It felt like a damn miracle, but perhaps she'd actually listened when I'd told her to take the morning off. I did some paperwork, ate a quick breakfast, then sat on the park bench on the church lawn with my morning coffee, sipping it slowly while hurried parents dropped their children off at the daycare. Lyric would be one of them at some point, and despite telling her to take the morning off cleaning, I was still desperate to see her.

It wasn't Lyric's beat-up junk bucket that cruised into the parking lot, though. A sleek, new police cruiser, marked as being from the Providence department, stopped in between the church and the daycare, the two officers in the front seats gazing out at me and then talking to each other.

I didn't like how much they'd been hanging around. I'd given them all they could possibly need the last time they'd been here. Still, I put my priest face on and strolled through the early morning sunlight that dappled the grass and greeted them as they got out of the car. "What can I do for you, officers?"

"Zepherin Hart?"

I nodded in confirmation. I didn't recognize either of them. They were different from the men who'd come to pick up files. "Is this about Toby Innes? Did you find him?"

"We'd like you to come down to the station, please."

I frowned. "May I ask what for?"

The two looked at each other and then back to me.

"Best if we discuss it in town," the taller officer stated.

I raised an eyebrow, distracted by Lyric's car pulling into the gravel parking lot. She was supposed to be at home sleeping. I watched her run across the lot to drop Amelia at the daycare before I dragged my attention back to the police who were still standing there waiting for my answer.

"Is this the sort of thing I need a lawyer for?"

"We'd just like a chat."

Yeah, that wasn't going to happen, because I had a pretty good idea what they might want to talk about, and it wasn't Toby. If they were being cagey, it was definitely the sort of thing I wasn't going to discuss without representation. "I'll call my lawyer then."

The officer nodded. "You can call him on the drive over."

Not even letting me drive myself downtown. That couldn't be good.

"And if I refuse?"

The older man narrowed his eyes. "I would dislike having to arrest you. My mama is a devoted churchgoer. She wouldn't be happy with me."

Dread crept up my spine. They had something on me. I could feel it from the way they were staring at me.

"I call bullshit." Lyric strode across the parking lot toward us, her long legs eating up the distance. She had a pair of rubber gloves clutched in her fingers and her hair tied back with a bandanna. Clearly, she'd been planning on cleaning.

Brat.

"Excuse me?" the older officer said.

Lyric crossed her arms over her chest and glared at him. "You heard. You aren't arresting him."

"You his lawyer?"

She shook her head so her ponytail swished around her shoulders. "No. But I've been legitimately arrested enough times to know he hasn't done anything to warrant an arrest. So if you want to talk to him, it's under his terms. I'm pretty sure he doesn't want to go down to the station, because I know for a fact he's due at mass in an hour." She clucked her tongue in the direction of the church. "You know he's a priest, right?"

"We're well aware," the younger officer said dryly.

But Lyric must have been right because the older one let out a sigh. "Your fingerprints were found in the priests' quarters at Holy Trinity."

Lyric opened her mouth to sass him, but I quieted her with a stare.

She nodded reluctantly and shoved her hands in her pockets instead.

I'd killed the old pervert at that address. If they had my fingerprints, they were old. They were possibly even bluffing. "I've visited that parish before, yes. It wouldn't be abnormal for my fingerprints to be there."

"Were you in the room belonging to Father Simon Collier the last time you visited?"

I swallowed. I'd had gloves on the entire time. Hadn't I? Had I taken them off at some point? The entire night was a blur of adrenaline and anger and recklessness. Had that extended to doing something as stupid as leaving behind a fingerprint? "I'm not sure. I might have been. We were given a tour. I don't remember which room belonged to which person though."

That seemed vaguely plausible.

The two men nodded and noted something down on their notepads.

"That all, Officers? Father Zepherin really does have work to do this morning. Teaching the Lord's word and all."

The younger officer cracked his gum. "We're done. If we have any further questions—"

"I'll be here," I confirmed.

He pinned me with a hard glare. "I was going to say we'll come back with a warrant."

When I didn't respond, the two men turned away and walked back to their car.

Lyric sidled up next to me, and with a fake smile on

her mouth, she whispered, "What the hell was that about, Zeph?"

I didn't answer her either. I just watched and waited for the officers to leave.

The older one paused at his door and turned back. "Father Zepherin?"

I forced a smile and jerked my head up in response. "Yes?"

"Just out of interest, where were you on Friday the third between the hours of 9:00 p.m. and 4:00 a.m.?"

I had no alibi. Nobody had seen me that night. Nobody but the man I'd killed.

Lyric laughed like she didn't have a care in the world. "Same place he always is on Friday nights. Watching me dance at Saint View Strip Club."

Oh Jesus.

Lyric slapped me on the cheek. "Don't blush, Father Zepherin. The cops are just like you guys. Everything you say is confidential. They won't tell anyone." She turned back to the men. "Give me a notepad, and I'll write down the name of half a dozen other employees who can vouch for him."

The officer shook his head. "That won't be necessary. We'll be in touch if we have any further questions."

The two men finally got in their car and drove it away. Anger flickered deep in my chest.

As soon as they were out of sight, I grabbed Lyric's arm and towed her into the church, slamming the heavy wooden door shut behind me. I led her all the way up the aisle, trying to form the right words. When the altar blocked me from walking any farther, I spun on her. "What the fuck was that, Lyric?"

She blinked in surprise. "What do you mean?"

The anger got the better of me and came out in sharp words. "You just lied to those cops."

She shrugged. "So? You needed an alibi. I gave you one. What's the big deal?"

I widened my eyes at her. "What's the big deal? Lyric! Maybe you all cover for each other in Saint View, but if they find out you lied, you could be arrested! Thrown in jail for obstruction of justice, or worse, named as an accomplice! Do you realize you just gave me an alibi for a murder?"

Her face paled. "What?"

"Exactly what I said. You just put yourself in danger. The same thing you did yesterday. You did exactly what you promised me you'd stop doing. You put others ahead of yourself at the detriment off your own well-being."

"I put *you* ahead of myself."

That was worse. If it had been Amelia or her grandmother I could have understood. But I was not worth going down for. I cracked my knuckles. "Take your clothes off."

She recoiled. "What? No."

"Take your clothes off and get on your knees, Lyric."

She stared at me. "Have you lost your mind? Anyone could walk in here at any time and see us. Your entire life would be destroyed if anyone caught us."

"Maybe then you'd know how I feel right now, knowing you put yourself in danger for me. If you want to use your safe word, then now is the time. But if I don't hear that word on your lips..."

Heat flared in her eyes.

My dick hardened, a mixture of adrenaline and the

knowledge we could be caught. Lyric dropped her cleaning supplies and the took off her T-shirt and bra. I fought to keep my breathing under control, watching her bare breasts rise and fall gently as she peeled off her underwear and leggings. Completely naked, she stood in front of me and slowly pulled the bandanna from around her head, letting her auburn hair flow down her back. There was still a hint of defiance in her eyes that did nothing but turn me on.

"Get. On. Your. Knees."

She sucked in a breath but settled at my feet.

"Undo my pants."

She obeyed, undoing my belt and lowering the zipper. She dragged the fabric down my thighs, taking my black boxer briefs with them.

I brushed a strand of hair back from her face. "You are so beautiful."

"Thank you," she murmured.

I trailed my fingers to the back of her head and wrapped the long lengths of hair around my fist. She let out a mewling sound of desire as I tugged gently on her head, guiding it so her lips were mere inches from my dick. She pressed her thighs together, her fingers drifting over her mound.

"No." I grabbed her arm. "You don't get to do that. You don't take care of yourself out there, you don't get to do it in here either." At least not yet. I would wait until she was begging me to give her relief.

She moaned, and I took the opportunity to press my dick to her mouth.

She opened for me, sucking me inside greedily, her head straining against the hold I had on her hair.

"Deeper, Lyric. Take all of me."

I truly had no idea if she could, and I pulled out of her mouth so she could use her safe word, but she eagerly leaned in to take me in her mouth once more. I thrust shallowly between her lips, letting her get used to the size of me, then deeper, until I hit the back of her throat.

She took my size well, though all of me would have been impossible, despite my demands. But she took me with such enthusiasm that I wept from my tip, coating her tongue in precum.

She was everything I'd ever dreamed about. Every dirty thought that I'd been told I couldn't have was kneeling right here at my feet, letting me control her, at least for a while. She was too good, her mouth too wet, too warm, her tongue too seductive. She used her hands to cup my balls, massaging them as she worked me closer and closer to orgasm.

I groaned, a swell of need cresting deep inside me, ready to unleash in a surge. She made little noises every time she drew me deep, and every single one was like a shock to my system. A pure pulse of desire injected right into my veins.

"Need to come, beautiful."

She only sucked me harder, faster, jerking my shaft with her hand while she swirled her tongue around the head. She jerked her mouth away just long enough to say, "Need to taste you."

Then her lips were back on me, and I was coming before I could stop myself. I pulsed into her mouth for a second, the feel of her sucking me down almost too good to stop. But I needed more than just her mouth.

I pulled out of her wet heat and let the last of my orgasm spray across her tits.

She blinked in surprise but scraped up her hair and dropped her head back, offering me better access to mark her.

Spent, I knelt in front of her on the altar steps and stared down at her. She stared back, the defiance gone from her eyes, only desire and submission left. Her posture and expression left me breathless. Despite the fact anyone could walk in here at any minute, the calm in her body was clear. It was the most relaxed I'd ever seen her look. None of the stresses that normally weighed on her were there.

She'd laid them all down somewhere outside the church, and in here, all she had to worry about was being mine.

I swiped my fingers through the cum on her chest and used it as lubricant to rub over her hardened nipples. She leaned into my touch, her breath hitching with every roll of my fingers.

"Please, Zeph," she begged, breathing ragged. She circled her fingers around my wrist and dragged it down her body to her snatch. With desperate, jerky movements she moved my hand between her thighs.

I let out a hiss at how drowned with arousal she was. It seeped from the perfect lips of her pussy to coat the inside of her thighs. "So wet for me," I murmured. "Do you know how turned on I was because you were getting off on sucking me?"

She shook her head.

I pushed two fingers up inside her, and she gasped at the intrusion, clutching at my arm. She held on there while I gave her what she'd been begging for, each press of my fingers hitting her G-spot. Her head fell forward onto my arm and my fingers disappeared into her pussy, my thumb hitting her clit as she rocked her hips, taking what she needed.

Time moved too quickly, each tick of the clock taking us closer and closer to when people would arrive for the morning mass, and yet I couldn't force my fingers to move any faster. I wanted each thrust driving her higher, and every rock of her hips to make her wild. I worked her steadily until her breathing matching my pace and her fingernails dug into my skin.

"I need to watch you come, Lyric."

"The mass will be starting!"

I let out a growl in her ear. "Nothing is starting until you come for me."

Her breaths turned into pants. She reached up to cup her breasts and pinch her nipples. My dick hardened at my woman, knowing what she needed and taking it. This was no longer a punishment for her, but a punishment for me because I wasn't inside her.

With a growl of need, I scooped her up from the floor, carrying her to the altar and laying her across it.

"Zeph, people will..."

I didn't fucking care. I'd been pushed into this life. Shoved into a world I didn't believe in, because the people around me thought I wasn't normal. Lyric had shown me otherwise. Now everything felt tainted and wrong. The pews. The incense. The altar. All of it somehow designed to keep me trapped here when Lyric had shown me it was okay to want to fly.

I hefted myself onto the altar with her. Lifted her legs

and slipped one hand beneath her lower back to keep her pelvis tilted toward me.

I took her hard and fast, spearing inside her soaked core. My knees dug into the sturdy table, draped in cloths. They bunched and pooled around us, as messy as we were, Lyric's fingers twisting in them as I fucked her on the holiest of places.

Her legs wrapped around me, and we writhed together, her taking each thrust with a cry, the power of each one jolting the table until it creaked and groaned. I covered her body with mine, taking her lips possessively with my mouth, licking my way inside her, tasting the salty sweetness of myself still lingering.

She was close. So close her pussy fluttered around my cock, preparing for the clamp down I knew was coming. I broke off from her mouth to lick her neck and then her ear. She shouted my name, the word desperate and hoarse.

I slammed home once more, right as the church door opened.

Lyric's head swiveled to the door, a gasp of shock on her lips. I grabbed her chin, twisting her head back to me, plunging my tongue into her mouth once more, unable to stop, no matter who was watching.

It was too late for her not to come. She spasmed around my cock, immediately sending me over the edge too. We rutted together, a grinding slam of bodies, joining in the most carnal way, in a place that never should have seen it.

I finished inside her, whispering words I never thought I'd say to a woman. "I love you, Lyric. I love you."

She didn't answer. She let me finish and then pulled

the cloths from the table over her naked body. Her cheeks flamed, her head turned away from the door.

It was only then I remembered we weren't alone.

Father Byron stood in the doorway, his expression more leer than disgust.

The look on my mother's face, however...

Fuck.

She spun away, but too late for me to not see her horror. Her embarrassment. That's what I'd always been. The problem child who'd grown into a man she was mortified to call her son. Unless he had a priest collar on.

Father Byron just chuckled to himself as I clutched the cloths over Lyric's naked body so he wouldn't see. I stared at the older man, the man I'd known my entire life, and one of the people I'd gone to for guidance over the things I wanted.

He just clucked his tongue with a laugh I didn't understand. "What on earth are we going to do with you, Zepherin?"

A slimy, sinking feeling came over me. I didn't like the look in his eyes—or the way his gaze kept drifting to Lyric.

28

***

LYRIC

I lay there, completely horrified by what we'd done. Shame crept over me. As a stripper who had never pretended to be something I wasn't, if I'd taken every person's judgments on board, I would have never gotten out of bed in the mornings.

But we'd crossed a line here. Zeph and me. One he would now have to pay for.

I didn't want to be the person who destroyed him, and yet here I was, undoing a lifetime of therapy, ruining everything he'd worked for.

He'd been set on his path before me, and now he was whispering I love yous to a woman he'd fucked on an altar while his boss and mother watched on in horror.

That wasn't love. Not the true love my grandmother spoke of. That was some sort of messed-up defiance. A 'fuck you' to the two of them for denying him the things he'd wanted and making him feel less than.

I was his rebellion.

I wasn't sure when he'd gotten himself dressed, but

then he was scooping me into his arms, wrapping the cloths from the altar around me tightly and carrying me away from the scene of the crime. Bright sunlight blinded me, and I turned into him, burying my face in the familiar scent of his neck as he carried me to his home.

"No one can see you," he promised. "I'm so sorry."

I shook my head, not even knowing what to say. I was just as much to blame as he was. I could have used my safe word but I'd been too full of attitude and turned on by the games we played. With every gentle bump against his chest, I was reminded that playing with fire always ended up with someone getting burned.

Zeph and I had just exploded.

He paused at the door to his place, opening it and carrying me inside. He walked me straight to his bathroom, setting me down on the closed toilet. He cupped my face with both hands, tilting it up so he could look into my eyes, and then kissed me softly. "It'll be okay."

It wouldn't. Not if his mother carried out her threats to report me. Not if he and I kept doing things like this. I was beginning to think she was right. That I was no good for him. That together, we were destructive.

His bathroom was old-fashioned and overdue for a renovation. The floor tiles were a faded checkerboard, the white more an aged cream now from so many decades of use. But it was clean and tidy, and the ancient claw-foot bath was beautiful and twice the size of my tub at home. Zeph stepped over to it now, turning on the faucet and letting the water fall.

I watched him from my huddle, clutching the holy cloths we'd defiled to my chest. Steam rose off the water, and I didn't argue when Zeph took the cloths from my naked body and carried me to the tub.

The temperature was perfect, and I sank down into the warmth, letting it wash away not only the physical products of what we'd done in the church but also the sins.

Zeph undressed himself, dropping his clothes into a hamper in the corner before climbing in behind me. I scooted forward to make room for him, tucking my knees to my chest and wrapping my arms around them.

"Come here." He pressed a kiss to the curve of my spine.

Even though I was pretty sure our contract was done, I did as he asked because I wanted to. I leaned back into his embrace, the water sloshing around us. It warmed my oversensitive and tingly flesh that hadn't yet woken up to the fact the amazing sex we'd just had would be the end of us.

A sob crept up my throat at the thought of giving him up. But I had to. It was what was best for both of us. I didn't even know who I was anymore. Committing fraud. Screwing a man in the most inappropriate of places. Risking his mother calling CPS. I had thought I had no limits, and yet apparently, I did.

We'd crossed them.

I relaxed against his chest, dropping the back of my head to his shoulder as his arms came around me to rest beneath my tits. His thumb stroked the underside absently.

"I don't want you to worry about what happened just now. It's for the best."

I stared at the mirror on the wall opposite us. Stared

at my face and then at his. He watched me carefully in the reflection, his expression full of worry.

I couldn't answer him. Nothing that had just happened had been for the best. We were completely out of control. But when his lips pressed against my neck, there was nothing I could bring myself to do to stop him. One hand slid up to cup my breast, the other snaking beneath the water to my pussy.

I couldn't deny him. I wanted him too much, even after everything.

But this had to be the last time. There was no doubt in my mind any longer. Zepherin and I would only end in a hail of disaster. We were over before we'd even really had a chance to begin. Doomed from the start.

If I wanted to save myself the heartbreak, now was the time to cut him loose.

29

———

ZEPH

I made love to her in the bathtub then in my room, then in the bath again. We fucked, ate, slept, then did it all again, because it was easier than her saying words I didn't want to hear. If I could just keep her quiet—press my tongue into her mouth, steal her words with my touch—she wouldn't say the things I could see turning over behind her eyes.

I knew I'd gone too far. Taking her on that altar, not stopping when my mother and Father Byron had walked in on us. It had been too much for anyone to be okay with.

I'd wanted to blow my life up. Give them a reason I couldn't ever come back. But I'd hit the self-destruct button so hard I'd taken her out with me.

Shame poured in. Hate that I always did this. It had been the same with Annie. I'd got lost in her, used her as a balm on my jagged edges. Drew her in too tight only to strangle her. Not literally, but the death had been the same. Her out of my life forever.

Now I'd done the same with Lyric.

I watched her from the bath while she got dressed with her back to me, dragging one of my T-shirts over her head and then pulling out her long hair, the ends damp from the bath.

"Lyric."

We'd barely spoken all day. Every time she'd tried, I cut her off, pleasuring her until the only words she'd uttered were, "I'm coming."

If she was getting dressed, she was leaving, and I needed to talk to her before she walked out that door. But she'd completely shut down. Wouldn't speak. Wouldn't turn in my direction.

"Lyric. Look at me."

"Llamas."

I froze. The water in the bath around me may as well have been ice-cold. "What?"

She finally turned on me. "Llamas. I'm done, Zeph. This is finished. Safe word activated."

I stood too quickly, water spraying off my body. She flinched away. I wasn't entirely sure it was the water she was avoiding, and my suspicions were confirmed when I reached for her and she avoided my touch.

"Don't, Zeph."

With her shorts back on and tied around her waist, she shoved her feet in her sneakers and strode through my house. I followed her, not caring I was stark naked or dripping water everywhere. She yanked open the front door.

"Wait." I caught the door, stopping her from opening it fully.

"I can't do this right now. I need to go pick up Amelia. It's late. She's probably the last one there."

I blinked and looked over at the clock on my wall only to find she was right.

She used the momentary distraction to slip out beneath my arm, and then she was running across the lawn toward the daycare.

"Shit," I muttered. I didn't even have so much as a towel. I couldn't run after her. But I needed to talk to her. Explain. Come up with some sort of plan to move forward, because letting her go wasn't something I could do. Not again. Not with her. I ran back to my bedroom, found the nearest pair of sweats and a T-shirt, dragging them on over my still-damp body. Without bothering to find shoes, I ran barefoot across the lawn, sprinting because the only woman I'd ever loved was about to slip through my fingers.

I slammed my way inside the daycare, my heart stopping when I heard Lyric's shouts.

"You fucking pervert! Get away from her!"

Father Byron looked up from a beanbag, Amelia reading a story on his lap.

Lyric leaned down and snatched her daughter from him, clutching her close and backing away.

Pamela, the only educator left in the room, rushed to Lyric's side, but her tone was admonishing. "Lyric, Father Byron is one of the other priests. He was just reading Amelia a story while we waited for you since you are quite late. We called you, but you didn't answer. Eventually, we had to call Amelia's father to come down here."

Lyric's eyes flashed at the older woman. "I don't care how late I was or who you had to call. What you failed to see while you were lecturing me about being tardy is that your priest friend here is reading her a story with a fucking hard-on, Pamela."

Pamela covered her mouth with a gasp.

I looked to Byron's lap, but he'd conveniently twisted away so no one could see a thing.

"I was just trying to help the child learn to read. Nothing more to it than that. Kara told me she didn't do too well on her Edgely intake tests. I didn't want her disadvantaged because she isn't getting the support she needs at home." He pushed to his feet, brushing his hands off on his pants like all of this was no big deal.

Pamela gave a wobbly smile, trying to keep the peace. "See? Just a misunderstanding—"

Lyric whirled to me, covering Amelia's ear with one hand and pressing her other to her shoulder, muffling our conversation. "He's the creep who followed me home from the club that night. Stalked me with a mask on, but I know it was him. He had me plait my hair into pigtails so I would look young enough to be in school."

Unlike Pamela who frowned at Lyric with a disgusted expression of betrayal, I believed every word Lyric said.

I'd buried my head in the sand. Refused to see what was right beneath my nose because Byron had taken me in and set me straight when I'd been a lost kid, reeling in a storm of confusion. I'd suspected Byron myself and then nixed the idea because I didn't want it to be true.

The thought of him watching Lyric dance, stalking her, intent on violence, sent a shudder through my body. I wished for the rope I'd taken from him. Wished it were in my pocket right now so I could wrap it around his fat neck.

The punch connected with Byron's nose before I even really knew what I was doing. Pamela screamed, scuttling for the exit. Amelia's cries rang in my ears, but I couldn't stop. Another punch had the man howling in pain and blood spurting across the room, splattering against fingerpainting and stuffed animals.

I drew my foot back and kicked him in his flabby gut. Over and over again, completely out of control.

"Jesus, Zeph. Stop."

Lyric's words fell on deaf ears. All I could see was this asshole making her play dress-up, touching himself while she danced, then following her home, intent on no good. I'd regretted letting him go ever since that night, and now I hated myself even more. Because Lyric might have been a grown woman who had proved she could take care of herself.

But Amelia was a child.

A child I was terrified was being groomed right in front of me.

Bile rose in my throat, and the anger left my body the only way it could. In kicks and hits and punches.

"Fucking stop, man. You'll kill him." Strong arms wrapped mine from behind, his hands pressing to the back of my neck while he dragged me away.

I twisted and turned, catching glimpses of Lyric and Amelia, huddled in a corner, expressions terrified.

Not of Byron. But of me.

The fight went out of me, and I let Lleyton drag me away, out the door into the waning evening sunlight.

"Go check on him," Lleyton said to Pamela, who was staring at me like I'd lost my mind. Probably because I had. "He might need an ambulance."

Lyric came out with Amelia held tight in one arm. "What the fuck was that, Zeph! Are you insane?"

"He followed you. Could have hurt you. Or Amelia."

"And your response is to try to kill the man in the middle of a daycare? You have no proof!"

I shook my head, trying to clear my foggy brain. "You said... Wouldn't you have done the same?"

She was furious. Angrier than I'd ever seen her. "I know what I said. I know what is true. Fuck, I wouldn't have minded getting a punch or two in either. But what you were doing in there...you scared me! You could have killed a man. I've got a child to think about, Zeph. One who needs me to not be in jail. You told me off for putting myself in danger just this morning, and then what? You try to kill a man right in front of us? How is that keeping us safe, Zeph?"

"I love you. I'd do anything for you. For her. If I find out he's touched any child in that center, I'll put him six feet under."

Lleyton finally let go of me and stormed across to Lyric.

Amelia leaned to him, frantically trying to get to her father.

Lyric's face fell at her daughter's reaction. She let her go when Lleyton lifted her from her arms, saying, "Come here, little girl. I got you."

He pinned Lyric with a disgusted look, holding his daughter tight while she trembled. "I don't know what the hell is going on, but this whole thing is messed up. Our daughter is terrified, and the two of you clearly have some shit to work out, that is if Zeph isn't in jail tonight."

Lyric only had eyes for her daughter. "Amelia. I'm so sorry, sweetie."

Amelia only buried her face in her father's neck, her little body shaking.

I wanted to vomit. Knowing it was me who'd scared her like that...I doubled over, hands to my knees, trying not to be sick.

Lleyton's voice softened at Lyric's distraught expression. "I'm taking her tonight, okay? I need her with me, and I think she needs it too."

Lyric trailed after them as they moved toward Kat's car, parked in the lot.

Kat got out of the passenger seat, her eyes wide and full of concern, flicking between Lleyton and Lyric. "What's going on?"

Everyone ignored her.

"Lleyton, please. Just give her to me. Let me talk to her," Lyric begged.

But Lleyton was firm, his voice gentle. "Not tonight, okay? She'll be okay. Just let me take this one. We can sort this out tomorrow. Or in a couple of days. However long you and Zeph need to work yourselves out."

Lyric's shoulders slumped, but she nodded. "Okay. You're right. You take her tonight, but tomorrow..."

"I'll bring her home when everything has settled down. Go take care of yourself."

She nodded, but I could see the heartbreak on her face when Kat took Amelia from Lleyton and hugged her tight before climbing into the back seat with her.

Helplessness radiated from Lyric as she watched them drive away.

"Lyric," I croaked out. "I'm sorry."

She didn't move when I cautiously approached her. But when I touched her elbow, she flinched, spinning around to glare at me.

"Lleyton was right. We're messed up, Zeph. Amelia was terrified just now. I was terrified. You're scary when you lose control."

"I'd never hurt you. Or her. I did it for both of you."

She shook her head miserably. "You've lost sight of what's actually right, Zeph. Byron is a creep, but you would have killed him if Lleyton hadn't shown up."

Byron's leering expression while he'd watched me and Lyric on the altar was all too fresh in my mind. "I don't like the way he looks at you."

She threw her hands up in the air. "Neither do I. But you can't murder people, Zeph! I don't know what you're doing, taking vows of God and then sinning like you were sent straight from Hell. And I'm not helping things any! I encourage you. We aren't good together, Zeph. We lie to each other and ourselves. If we can't even be honest, what future do we have?"

"I killed a man."

She stared at me. "Say that again."

"I killed a man. The priest who died a few weeks ago in the city. It was me."

She held up her hand, closing her eyes. Her tone changed to one of complete exhaustion. "Say less. Fuck, Zeph. Say less."

I grabbed her arm, desperate to make her understand why I did the things I did. I'd always hated men who hurt women. I hated when the rich took advantage of the poor. Something inside me needed to right those wrongs, and I couldn't find it in me to be sorry for killing a man who'd hurt a young woman the way he had. I needed her to understand that. "Lyric. I had a good reason."

She snatched her hand back like I'd burned her. "You always do, Zeph. But you're toxic. I'm toxic. Together we're a fucking chemical spill that spreads its poison to everything it touches."

I shook my head. "Don't say that."

Her shoulders slumped in defeat. "It's the truth. We aren't good for each other. You've just made me an accessory to murder, and I don't even know what to do with that."

She was right. I'd been so hell-bent on not losing her I hadn't even considered what telling her truly meant. "I'll go to the cops. Whatever you want me to do, I'll do it."

But she was slipping away. I could feel it in the anguish of her words, the tears rolling down her cheeks. I hauled her into my arms, wrapping her tight, inhaling the scent of her, desperate for her to stay.

She sobbed against my chest for the briefest of moments, her fingers curling into my shirt. But then she shoved me away. "Please don't make this harder than it has to be."

"I'm turning myself in. This isn't going to blow back on you."

She stared up at me with glassy, miserable eyes. "I'll keep your secrets, Zeph. I'll take them to the grave. Just... no more. We're done."

She was right.

I had to let her go.

30

LYRIC

The apartment was too quiet with Amelia at Lleyton's and my grandmother still in the hospital. There were no cartoons on the TV, no little girl laughter, no records on the player Zeph had stolen for us. I ran a finger over it idly, then yanked the plug from the wall, bundled the thing up, and stormed out to the junk pile at the side of the building. Without ceremony, I dumped it on top of a stained mattress. Someone would probably claim it, or it would sit out here and rot with the other things the people in our building no longer wanted. I didn't care either way. It just couldn't be in my home.

Time ticked by too slowly. I didn't have my phone to ring Lleyton, and logically, I knew that was probably for the best. But I did need to get it back. There was no way I could ask Zeph to get it from his mother though. I'd already asked him once, but then everything had blown up between us, and I wasn't even sure he remembered I didn't have my phone. I wasn't about to go to his house and ask him about it. At this point, I'd rather deal with his mother than have to face him again. So I filled in time by driving into Providence to get it myself.

The house sat empty though. I walked to the back where the big glass doors and windows were, but I couldn't see my phone sitting out on a countertop or coffee table. As tempting as it was, I was already trespassing on their property, I wasn't going to try breaking in. They very probably had alarms that would send the police here in minutes. Wouldn't that just make Suzanna's day?

I left empty-handed and drove past Lleyton's place instead, since it was only a few blocks away. His car wasn't in the driveway though, so I kept going, knowing that even if it had been, I couldn't stop. He'd been right to take Amelia. I appreciated he was watching out for her and I wanted him in her life. I didn't want her growing up with the parental issues Zeph and I had.

But I counted the minutes until he would bring her back. Nothing felt right in my world without my daughter. I went to work at the club, went through the motions of the routine, did what I was paid to do. But I didn't go to my shift at the church.

That was as done as Zeph and I were. My resignation surely assumed after everything that had gone down. I couldn't go back there, knowing he'd be there. I couldn't enter the church and see that altar, or the confessional booth, or his living quarters, knowing everything we'd done.

But it hurt. Every part of me ached for missing him. For knowing he was hurting, and maybe even doing something stupid, like turning himself in. I couldn't be the one to save him when I couldn't even save myself. Yet nothing about being without him felt right either.

I couldn't sleep. I sat in my cold, lonely apartment with a blanket wrapped around my shoulders, watching time tick by, just waiting for my daughter.

After two days without hearing her sweet little voice, I caved. I couldn't stand it anymore. I finished my shift at the club in the early morning and drove to Lleyton's house. Adrenaline coursed through me. His parents and I had never really seen eye to eye, but I rapped my knuckles across their door.

Nothing happened. Lleyton's car was in the driveway though, parked behind his parents' cars. It didn't necessarily mean he was home, since he had a penchant for driving Kat's convertible, but goddammit, somebody was. Somebody who would know where he and my daughter were.

I thumped my fist on the door again. "Lleyton!"

There were footsteps on the tiled entryway foyer, and a bleary-eyed Lleyton dragged open the door.

I pushed inside, gazing around for a little redhead in cozy pajamas stumbling down the stairs with her stuffie, or for her to be playing with Barbies on the living room floor. "Where is she?"

Lleyton rubbed his eyes. "Good morning to you too. What time is it?"

I finally looked at him properly. His long legs were clad in suit pants, and a crinkled button-down shirt hung half open off his shoulders. There was a tie discarded on the living room floor, but no sign of Barbie dolls.

"Not that early," I answered him. "I stayed back after my

shift until it was a decent hour, but I can't wait any longer, Lleyton. I need to see her." I looked past him to the couch, eyeing the cushions all over the place and his shoes and socks discarded haphazardly. "Did you sleep down here?"

He ran a hand through his golden hair and squinted over at the couch as well. "Yeah, I guess I did. Didn't mean to. This new job is kicking my ass. Didn't get in until so late."

I blinked at him. "When did you get a new job?"

"I told you about it."

I shook my head, unable to recall him even mentioning it. But then, I'd been absentminded lately, too caught up in Gran and whatever Zeph and I were to really notice what was going on with my baby daddy. "I don't remember. But congrats. Did your parents watch Amelia last night then?" I strained toward the stairs, wanting to rush up them. "I need to see Amelia, Lleyton. Now."

"Chill out, she's at Kat's. She had her last night while I was working. I'll call her." He found his phone in the pocket of his pants and then pulled it out, blinking sleepily at it. His eyes widened, and he stared up at me in horror.

I grabbed his wrist, straining to look at the phone. "What? What is it?"

"Kat has a flight back the UK today. I completely forgot, she's been calling me all morning. My phone was on Do Not Disturb." He glanced around for his keys while I trailed him. "Shit, if she misses her flight because I wasn't there to get Amelia then I'm never going to hear the end of it. She's gonna be so pissed. Where the hell are my keys?"

I didn't much care about Kat's flight, she could catch the next one. "My car is behind yours anyway. We'll just take mine. You can call and beg your girlfriend's forgiveness on the way."

He nodded, chasing after me without putting shoes on because he probably rightly realized I wasn't waiting for him. I got behind the steering wheel while he slid into the passenger seat, screwing his nose up at the state of my car. "Jesus, Lyric, this thing is a death trap if ever I saw one."

I just glared at him and revved the engine. The car zoomed backward out of the driveway, tires squealing on the blacktop.

Lleyton clutched the holy-shit bar dramatically, but once I'd straightened the old girl out and was headed toward Kat's place, he called her.

It went to her voicemail. Over and over again, his calls went unanswered. A growing sense of unease prickled at the back of my neck, growing because he wasn't saying anything.

"Lleyton. What time was Kat's flight?"

His teeth were mashed together. "Ten minutes ago."

My breath caught. "Where is Amelia if Kat is on a plane? Would she have just left her at the house?" I fought back tears at the thought of my little girl waking up alone in that big house, scared and feeling like we'd abandoned her.

But Lleyton shook his head. "Kat loves Amelia. More than she loves me probably." He cleared his throat. "She can't have kids of her own, Lyric. It's why she clings to Amelia so hard. She wouldn't just leave her in the house alone."

It did explain how motherly she was to Amelia, and I would have felt sympathy for her. But I couldn't feel anything until I knew where Amelia was. "So where are they, then?"

Lleyton scraped his hands through his hair. His white teeth sank down on his bottom lip.

It was his tell. His giveaway that he was lying. I'd grown used to it over the early years of Amelia's life, whenever he promised he'd be there for us when he knew very well he wouldn't. But I hadn't seen it lately, not since he'd started dating Kat and they'd become a more permanent fixture in Amelia's life. "What aren't you telling me?"

"Kat wants to move back to the UK. She wants Amelia to go with us."

I glanced over at him sharply. "What? You aren't taking my daughter to live in England, Lleyton!"

He held his hands up. "I know. I know. I already tried to tell her that. I'm not willing to move there either and be apart from Amelia. But what if...?"

I was ready to steer the damn car right off the road. "What if what? Speak, Lleyton! For God's sake."

"We got her a passport so she could come to the UK. It was just supposed to be on a holiday! I swear. Kat wanted Amelia to meet her parents."

I shook my head over and over, reading between the lines. "No. No, she wouldn't have."

Lleyton didn't answer. He just kept calling, redialing every time it went to Kat's voicemail.

"I don't know where to go," I mumbled to myself helplessly. Did I go to Kat's place, hoping she'd left Amelia behind? Did I go to the airport and demand they ground the plane? "We need to call the police, Lleyton! If you're right, it's kidnapping!"

"It's ringing!"

My heart thumped. I drove aimlessly now, circling the streets of Providence, desperate for Kat to pick up the phone and tell me my daughter was safe.

Kat's screech of anger was so piercing even I flinched on the other side of the car. She yelled so loud Lleyton jerked the phone away from his ear.

Even still, he and I both heard every word Kat screamed down the phone line. "I was nearly late for my flight, Lleyton! You're so lucky it was delayed or I wouldn't have made it! You are the most inconsiderate, immature, irresponsible man I have ever met. You swore to me you would be there on time, but I couldn't get a hold of you, no matter how many times I called. I had to call Lyric, and even she wasn't around. What is wrong with the two of you? What if there'd been an emergency with Amelia? Do you have some aversion to phones or is it just when it's me on the other end? If Lyric's grandmother hadn't answered and come to get Amelia, I would have had to drive her back to you and then I definitely would have missed my flight. You really are a piece of shit sometimes, you know?"

I froze.

Lleyton carried on like Kat hadn't just rocked my entire world. All that was in his voice was relief that he'd been wrong. That his girlfriend hadn't abducted our child. "I'm so sorry, baby. I swear, when you get back, I'm going to make it up to you. Dinner. Candlelight. The works."

Kat sniffed on the other end. "You'd better."

But all I could hear was her saying my grandmother had picked up Amelia. "Kat," I choked out, strangling the steering wheel. "Who picked up Amelia?"

Lleyton looked over at me like I was stupid, but put Kat on speakerphone "She said your grandmother, right, babe?"

"Yes," Kat huffed. "The one person willing to answer a phone call apparently."

My heart thumped behind my ribs. "My grandmother is in the hospital."

Lleyton twisted to me, the corners of his eyes crinkling as he squinted at me. "Are you sure? How did she pick Amelia up then?"

"She didn't."

"What?" Kat snapped. "Of course she did. I called you, she answered, and then she was at my house. She most definitely did not have a broken hip."

Panic clawed up my veins, and I fought to keep the car straight on the road. "Kat, my grandmother is currently in a hip cast and most definitely did not drive to your house. She doesn't even drive at all."

Kat fell silent. "Oh no."

I couldn't breathe. "Didn't Amelia tell you it wasn't her grandmother?"

"It was so early, she was still asleep! I just bundled her into the woman's car…"

"I'm calling the police," Lleyton bit out. "Fuck!"

Kat bawled into the phone, hysterically sobbing down the line. "I'm so sorry! I'm so, so sorry. I didn't know. I was just in such a rush to get to the airport and I was so angry at Lleyton…"

I hit the 'end call' button on Lleyton's phone, cutting off Kat's barely coherent babble.

I knew who had my daughter. I just never thought she'd stoop this low.

Terror laced Lleyton's voice. "I'm calling nine-one-one."

I shook my head. My phone was still at Zeph's parents' place. There was only one person who hated me enough to answer that call, drive over to a stranger's house, and impersonate my grandmother. "Don't bother," I bit out. "Call Zeph instead. Tell him to meet us at his mother's house. She has my daughter."

31

ZEPH

A small crowd had gathered outside my parents' house when Kelly and I arrived. They were a group of nosy neighbors, each of them staring wide-eyed as Lyric picked up a stone and threw it through the front window, screaming my mother's name.

"What on earth is she doing!" Kelly squawked, hand over her mouth in shock at the broken glass all over the driveway.

I wished I'd been anywhere but at her house when Lyric had called, completely frantic and hysterical, accusing my mother of unspeakable, but not terribly surprising, acts. Kelly had insisted on coming with me and had pissed me off the entire way here, babbling excitedly like this was the most exciting thing to happen in her bored-housewife existence.

Tasha, the older woman who had lived next door to my parents since I was a kid, hurried over to my side. "Oh, Father Zepherin. Kelly. Thank goodness you're here. We've called the police."

I ignored her, running past Lleyton who stood helpless on the grass, watching Lyric scream up at the silent building.

I collided with her as she drew her arm back to hurl another stone.

She struggled against my hold, tears streaming down her face. "No! Let me go! She has my baby!"

"Stop. It's me."

She instantly went floppy in my arms, her knees giving way. I caught her, hauling her up into my arms and cradling her.

"Shh. It's going to be okay. We'll get her back."

"What kind of evil is your mother, Zeph? Where is she? They aren't here! They aren't here! They've taken her somewhere."

She sobbed into my arms, and I carried her to my car. Lleyton followed, face white with shock.

"Drive," I barked at him. "Hurry, before the cops get here and arrest her for the damage."

He nodded numbly, getting in behind the wheel. I got into the back with Lyric, not bothering with seat belts, so I could pull her onto my lap and rub slow circles on her back. "I've got you. I'm going to fix this."

I let her fall apart, holding her together while a storm of hate swelled in my heart. This was the woman I loved. No matter how broken we were, none of that mattered in the moment.

"Where is she, Zeph?" Lyric sobbed into my shirt. "I know your mother hates me and thinks Amelia is better off without me, but Amelia doesn't know her. She's going to be so alone and scared..." The rest of her words were muffled by her cries.

My heart ached. Lyric was everything that was important to me, and Amelia was everything important to her. I'd promised to protect them and I thought I had. Beating up Father Byron was what I'd done to keep them safe, but he hadn't been the only threat. I'd missed the one living in my family home.

Her words struck something in the back of my mind. "What do you mean she thinks Amelia is better off without you?"

"She told me that. That no child should grow up in poverty with a prostitute for a mother or something along those lines. That the church had programs in place to help whores like me."

"You aren't a whore."

"I am in her eyes."

My mind whirred. Toby was still missing.

Tammie had been sleeping with men, trying to make ends meet.

My mother had been there that day in the hospital, where Tammie had admitted it to me.

I was sure the color drained from my face, and my expression had changed to one of pure horror.

It was confirmed when Lleyton glanced in the rearview mirror and caught sight of me. "What?" he asked. "What is it?"

Lyric sat up and looked at me.

I shook my head. "Toby. The son of a woman I met through the homeless shelter. One of the last people to see him was my mother. And she knows Toby's mother was sleeping with men for money."

Lyric's mouth dropped open. "You think...?"

I shook my head. "I don't know what to think. That

she took two children from their families and is holding them somewhere is crazy. And yet…"

Kelly twisted in the front seat and stared at me. "Zeph…your mom…I mean your biological mom…"

I stared at her. "What about her?"

"She was a prostitute."

I blinked. I'd been reminded many a time my parents had rescued me from my birth family. But there'd never been any mention of who they were or what they did. Just that they were too poor to care for me. "What do you mean? How would you know? I haven't seen my biological mom since I was four."

Kelly twisted her fingers in her lap. "Jonathan and I weren't ever allowed to talk about it. He probably wasn't even old enough to remember. But I was fourteen when you came to live with us. I remember seeing you at church every week with your biological mom. You were this skinny kid who seemed like he never had enough food. But your mom always came to church, no matter what."

"Why didn't you ever tell me?"

She shook her head. "We all learned pretty quickly that any mention of Juliette set Mom off, unless we were saying how horrible she was and how badly she treated you. Even you, at four, stopped crying for her quickly after seeing the way Mom reacted to it. It wasn't pretty."

A repressed memory of my mother's palm slapping across my face appeared in my head.

"She used to hit me."

Kelly nodded. "Only when you talked about her though."

"Why did Juliette give me up?"

Kelly sighed. "I don't know the full story. I only caught dribs and drabs. But it was after Mom convinced her to take that parenting course she runs at the church."

Lyric lifted her head curiously. "She tried to get me to do a course through the church."

Kelly grimaced. "My mother is the last person on earth anyone should take parenting advice from. Just look at Zeph and Jonathan and me. None of us are exactly the poster children for healthy, thriving adults. I'm having babies to feel the love I never felt from her. Jonathan is a full-blown alcoholic, though he hides it well. And Zeph..."

There was no need to go into my sins. We all knew them.

Kelly reached back and squeezed my knee. "I think she talked your biological mom into thinking you were better off without her." She shifted to aim her words at Lyric. "And I think that's probably what she would have tried to do with you too. You remind her of Zeph's mom. Low-income family. A small child who she perceives to be in danger..."

Lleyton had been particularly quiet, taking all this in, but now he spoke with conviction. "Lyric is the best mom in the world. It doesn't matter where she lives or how she makes her money. She loves Amelia. She sacrifices everything for her so she can have the opportunities she never had. Hell, if anyone is the shitty parent here, it's me."

Kelly patted him sympathetically on the shoulder, but I just shook my head. "It doesn't matter how good any of us are as parents if we can't get them back. Where the hell would Mom stash a child, possibly two?"

Kelly shook her head. "I don't know. She runs the

meetings in the church meeting room, but there's no way you wouldn't have seen Toby if she were keeping him there somewhere. They aren't in the house. That would have been too risky with all of us there for the party."

"Call her," I demanded. "If she's taken Amelia, she won't answer a call from me. But she'll answer one from you. There's no reason for her to think you're with us."

My sister nodded and rifled through the bag on her lap, pulling out her phone. She punched the screen a few times before holding it to her ear. She put a finger to her lips, telling the rest of us to keep quiet.

Lyric sniffed, and I gently wiped tears from her cheeks. "We're going to get her back. I promise," I whispered to her.

She didn't get a chance to answer, because Kelly's voice sharpened. "Mom! Hey, what are you doing?"

There was a pause, and I strained to hear my mother's reply, but there was nothing. I imagined she wasn't confessing to kidnapping though. Kelly nodded a few times, then tried again. "I really need to speak to you. No, it needs to be in person. And now. Please, Mom, I'm desperate. I really need your advice. I'm already in the car, just tell me where you are, and I'll be there in a few minutes."

There was more talking on my mother's end, and then Kelly burst into tears. "Mom! Please! I need you. I'm scared I might do something I'll regret. Again."

Until that moment I'd had no idea my sister was such a good actress. The anguish in her voice accented the tears suddenly welling in her eyes. But then she froze, a smile widening her mouth. She flipped us a thumbs-up. "I'll be there soon."

She hung up, and her smile flattened into a grimace. "She's at the Saint Paul of God mental institute the church runs. Apparently working a shift, but I don't believe that for an instant. I could hear a child crying in the background. What would a child that age be doing somewhere like that?" She twisted her fingers around on themselves. "That's no place for children. I spent a week there as an adult, and it was terrifying."

I glanced at her in shock. "You did?"

She nodded, pulling back a sleeve to reveal a scar across her wrist that made my stomach turn. I'd never noticed it before. If she wore short sleeves, she always had an arm full of bracelets.

She ran her fingers idly across the old, faded scar. "See? I'm just as messed up as you are, little brother. I just hide it better."

I ground my teeth. "I wish you'd told me. I would have been there for you."

She gave me a soft smile. One that showed me the sister I remembered from when I was a kid, before she'd gotten married, moved out, and we'd drifted apart. I remembered something else about the mental institution run by the church. "Father Byron is the head priest assigned to running Saint Paul of God. He knows everything that goes on there. Whatever Mom is doing, he's in on it too."

"Then we have a place to start," Lyric said, determination straightening her spine. "If I find out he had anything to do with it, I won't stop you twice."

I nodded at her, making a silent promise.

If Byron had even the tiniest part in any of this, then he was as good as dead.

32

——————

ZEPH

Saint Paul of God was about as pretty as the local prison. It was a long, rectangular building in dire need of a high-pressure wash and a gardener. Dirt and mold covered the once white walls, and weeds grew wild in what had once been garden beds. The complex was on a large block of land, hidden away down a narrow private road. Nothing about it invited people to come too close. I'd been told more than one ghost story about the place as a kid growing up. Even as an adult, the place gave me the heebie-jeebies. There was little happiness here. It was the place people dumped family members when they were at their wit's end and couldn't take the pressure any longer.

"This does not seem like the sort of place that would be good for anyone's mental health," Lyric murmured, staring out the window.

"Almost ironic that this is where Mom would bring your daughter, considering she has got to be having some sort of mental episode to be kidnapping children." Kelly shook her head sadly. "I'm so sorry for my part in all of this. I was so horrible to you."

Lyric looked away. "Now isn't the time."

Kelly nodded, dropping her head. "I understand. If it were one of my kids, I wouldn't forgive me either."

Lleyton parked the car in the visitor parking lot and twisted around. "Do we have a plan? I doubt your mom will come out if she sees you or Lyric. Maybe you should stay in the car."

A growl rumbled through me, but Lyric spoke over the top of me.

"Not a chance in hell. I'm getting my daughter back."

I completely agreed. I couldn't sit by and do nothing. But Lleyton had a point. My mom wouldn't just waltz out and hand over Lyric's daughter. I scanned the long building, bypassing reception because there'd be too many people there, including security. My gaze came to rest on an emergency exit at the end of the building. It was no doubt locked, probably from both the inside and the outside to stop patients leaving, but Mom would have an access pass. It was our best bet of luring her out. I pointed at it. "Kel, ring Mom and tell her you're at that exit. Once she comes out, we'll be able to get in."

She called Mom again, this time on speakerphone so we could all hear.

"Kelly? Are you here?" Mom snapped without so much as a greeting. She sounded irritated more than sympathetic to her daughter's cry for help.

I made a mental note to tell Kelly to call me if she ever truly did feel like hurting herself again, because Mom was not the person to talk you off a ledge.

"I'm at the emergency exit to the left of the parking lot," Kelly fake sobbed into the phone.

Mom sighed. "Come to reception."

"No!" Kelly yelped. "I don't want anyone to see me like this. Please, can you come out?"

A child cried in the background. I didn't think it was Amelia, but it was young enough to be Toby. Lyric's fingernails dug into my thigh. The cries grew fainter, like she was walking away from the little boy, and then came the sound of a door slamming. "Fine. I'm on my way. I'll be one minute. Kelly, if this is another ridiculous bid for my attention, I will not be happy."

Kelly hung up without replying. But I saw the way she swallowed thickly, hurt by our mother's words.

"Apparently one suicide attempt is all you get with her. Any more than that and you're just being an attention-seeker."

We all got out of the car, closing doors behind us. I gave Kelly's hand a squeeze of support, grateful for her help and hating that this was probably resurfacing bad memories for her. All four of us ran across the parking lot to the building, hightailing it for the emergency exit where we were supposed to meet my mother. Lleyton, Lyric, and I stood to the side, where the open door would conceal us.

Kelly waited in plain view, glancing at us nervously. "What if she doesn't come out?"

I shook my head. "Then we'll find another way in."

I wished for darkness. It had always been my friend. I wanted its whispery fingers to cloak us, hide us from the security cameras and guards. It wouldn't be long before we were spotted and guards sent to investigate what we were up to. Or worse, police called.

"Come on. Come on," Lleyton muttered, bouncing on the balls of his feet like a track star ready to race.

Lyric put a steadying hand on his arm, but he shook it off, too wired to be comforted. I knew a little about how that felt.

The sound of locks disengaging had us all freezing. A moment later, the handle turned.

None of us wasted a moment.

I grabbed the solid wooden door, yanking it open wide. Kelly sprang forward, catching my mother by the arm, and hauled her out of the doorway.

"What on earth?" my mother squawked. She stumbled, caught unaware and unprepared. "Kelly!"

Her gaze landed on me and Lyric.

I expected guilt. Maybe a babbling apology now that she'd been caught. But she just narrowed her eyes, seething at the two of us.

"What are you doing here?" She lunged toward us, pulling out of Kelly's grasp.

Lleyton caught her before I could. "Where's our daughter?"

Mom didn't answer, she just stared at me and Lyric with an almost feral snarl. I barely recognized the woman. She had never been particularly warm or caring, but the hate on her face now wasn't her either.

"You have some nerve, coming here, pretending to be good parents when you abandoned your child."

Lyric trembled with barely concealed rage. "Where's my daughter?"

But Mom wasn't done with her rant. "It should be

illegal for people like you to walk the streets. Just look what you did with my boy! Corrupted him with your ungodly filth. I spent years cleansing his soul, wiping away the filth his mother left him with. But it was clearly too late for him. One glimpse of you, and all my hard work with him was like it never happened." She threw her head back and screamed out her frustration.

Kelly let out a sob. "Mom. Stop. Please. You need help. You took this woman's child. You can't do that! No matter what you think of her."

Mom strained against Lleyton's grip on her to face off with her daughter. "Can't I? I walked right up to that house, and the woman there *gave* me that little girl. Put her right in my arms. There was no kidnapping involved. She willingly gave her up."

"After you tricked her into believing you were her grandmother," Lyric accused, ice in her tone.

Mom smiled coldly. "Tell the police that, sweetheart. Who do you think they'll believe? An upstanding, church-going woman who volunteers at hospitals?" Her gaze rolled up and down Lyric's body. "Or a gutter whore who should have never had custody of her in the first place."

I didn't even know the woman standing in front of me right now. It was like I'd never met her. Was this how she'd spoken to my mother? How she'd convinced her to give me up? "And Toby? Did his mother just willingly give him over to you as well?"

Mom pinned me with a dark stare. "Why are you asking me all the questions, when the real question is, Zepherin, why do you continue to surround yourself with prostitutes? Is it because you were born to one? Your mommy issues are showing, son."

I shook my head, done listening to her rubbish. I yanked the security pass from around her neck and handed it to Lyric. "Don't let her go," I barked at Lleyton, referring to my mother.

He went to argue, but Lyric was already storming inside the building, opening each door to the left and the right of the corridor, searching each one for her lost daughter.

I had no idea what my mother had done to Amelia, and I wasn't about to let Lyric face it alone. I caught up with her halfway down the hall, and she turned wide, wild eyes on me.

"Where is she, Zeph? Where?"

I didn't know either, but I joined the hunt, running down the hall, opening doors. This entire wing of the hospital didn't seem to be in use, each room empty of patients, and a musty, abandoned smell permeating the air.

A cry rang out, muffled but sad and desperate. A keening wail that broke my heart.

In unison, Lyric and I sprinted for the room at the end of the hall. She slammed the electronic pass against the card reader. The second it took for it to register felt like an hour, the little light finally going green, allowing her to push down on the handle and open the door.

On the inside of the dark room, pads lined the walls.

A tiny figure ran to the corner of the room in fear.

"Toby," I choked out, kneeling so I was the little boy's height.

He had his face buried in the corner, trying to hide

from us. But at my voice, his cries quieted, and he raised his head.

"Hey, buddy. Remember me?"

On tiny toddler legs, he ran across the mats and threw himself into my arms.

I scooped him up, clutching him close, and then turned to Lyric, panicked. "Is he hurt?"

She scanned his body, lifting the dirty T-shirt, checking his arms and torso for any signs of injury. "No, I don't think so."

Fury filled my veins. I strode from the hospital corridor, out into the sunlight, leaving the suffering of patients behind me.

"Oh, Mom," Kelly gasped, taking in the sight of Toby in my arms. "You didn't. That boy has been all over the news for weeks."

"It was for his own good. He needs rehabilitation after living with that prostitute so long. The church can turn him into a good man."

"Like they did with me? Where's Amelia?" I spat out at her.

But she'd clammed right up.

I passed Toby over to Kelly who went straight into Mom mode, shushing him and carrying him away from our mother. I grabbed the woman who'd raised me by the shoulders, giving her a solid shake.

"So help me God, Mom. If you don't tell me what you've done with that little girl, I will not be held accountable for what I do next."

Police sirens started up in the distance. I didn't know who'd called them. It could have been Lleyton or Kelly, or maybe it had been one of the staff members. It didn't matter. But Lyric and I needed to get out of here before they arrived. I wasn't losing hours of searching time while I filled them in on what was going on.

Some of the fight went out of Mom's stance, her head twisted toward where Kelly had Toby's head tucked tight to her neck, rocking him from side to side and singing lullabies to comfort him.

"She's in class, being cleansed of her family sins. The boy was to join them, but he wouldn't stop crying."

"Where?" I demanded.

She finally looked me in the eye. "Father Byron has her."

33

LYRIC

"I'm going to be sick." I doubled over, putting my head between my knees, trying to ward off the vomit feeling that swirled in my stomach every time I thought of what that monster might be doing with my daughter.

From behind the steering wheel, Zeph glanced over at me. "You're not. She's going to be fine. We're going to get there in time."

I wrapped my arms around myself, holding tight, trying not to fall apart. We zoomed down the road that led to the mental institute, passing cops on their way in, hopefully to arrest Zeph's mother and reunite Toby with his. Lleyton had stayed behind to restrain Suzanna, and Kelly had promised not to give Toby up to anyone until his mother got there.

"I should have let you kill him," I muttered. "This is all my fault."

Zeph shook his head. "This is no one's fault but my

mother's and Byron's. Don't you dare blame yourself, even for a second."

But I couldn't get the image of him hurting her out of my mind. My sweet little girl. Suzanna had been right. Amelia was tainted by who I was. I loved her and sacrificed for her, but I was still raising her in this town, where bad things happened to good people. It wasn't what I wanted for her, and yet the dangers she was currently in were because of two people from Providence with money and influence.

Nowhere felt safe. This world was cruel, and no matter how I tried to shield my daughter from it, it just kept creeping in, dark shadows blocking out her sunshine.

Zeph's face was a storm cloud. Full of anger and hate but still so stunningly beautiful. I hated that I'd pushed him away.

"I'm sorry," I muttered.

He looked at me sharply. "What for?"

"The things I said to you."

He sighed. "They were warranted, Lyric. I'm not the good guy, even when I try to be. I don't know how."

"I don't either." I raised my head and watched him speed through the back streets of Providence. "What your mom was doing back there...is that what they did to you too? Took you from your mother? Brainwashed you into believing she was bad and God was the light or some shit?"

He shrugged. "Honestly, I don't know. I don't remember any of it. Nothing except..."

I waited for him to go on.

"My mom...my biological mom, I mean. She used to

sing to me. At night before she left the house. She would tuck me into my bed and lie beside me, singing while she brushed back my hair. She would wait for me to fall asleep, then leave me alone in the house. I know because a couple of times I woke up and she wasn't there."

"She was working?"

"I guess so."

My heart squeezed at his pained expression. "I think she loved you. Those aren't the actions of a woman who didn't care. I think she loved you enough to give you up, thinking you would have a better life without her."

He shook his head. "I think my mother convinced her I was better off without her."

"We can look her up?" I reached over and stroked my thumb down the back of his neck. "We can find her. Let her know that we know she tried her best."

He glanced over at me. "You're a fucking amazing mother, Lyric. You need to know that. Don't let anything my mother says get to you. You are the only person who can raise Amelia into the woman she is supposed to be."

I nodded, buoyed by his heartfelt praise. I wanted to believe it. I wasn't sure I could. Not until I had my daughter back.

Zepherin pointed at a mansion looming ahead of us. "We're here. That's his place up there. I haven't been inside but I've driven him home before."

I squinted at it. "It's huge."

"Perks of being high up in the ranks, I guess." Zeph's tone had a hint of bitterness.

I couldn't blame him after seeing the tiny place he lived in.

I gazed at the big house. "I don't understand how such a pretty building can house such evil."

He parked the car, jerking the handbrake up and unclicking his seat belt. His eyes darkened. "Let's go relieve it of its burden."

It was a look I'd seen before, but this time, it made me shiver.

Zeph noticed, and when he rounded the car, meeting me at the front, he wrapped me in his arms. "I don't want you to be scared of me."

"I'm not," I said truthfully. "I know you won't hurt me."

But I couldn't say the same for the man inside.

I didn't care.

Zeph clamped his fingers around mine and stormed up the short driveway. He didn't bother knocking. Didn't even bother checking to see if the door was unlocked.

One hard kick from his booted foot, and the door splintered, breaking in two, one half jammed on the lock, the other flying open and hitting the wall behind it.

Screams came from somewhere down the hall. A woman stuck her head out into the hallway, took one look at the two of us, and hurried back inside.

"Hey!" Zeph shouted, storming forward but then glancing over at me, eyes wide. "I fucking remember this place. Not with Byron running it, but I remember that room. I came here while they preached at me. How long has this shit been going on?"

There was no time to unpack his childhood trauma. Not if my daughter was in that room. I ran ahead, skidding to a stop in the open doorway.

"Please!" the woman begged, arms stretched out, with

several small girls huddled behind her. "This is a house of God! They're just children! Take what you want, but leave us alone."

"Mommy!"

From behind the woman's leg, my little red-haired daughter peeped.

I broke in two, slumping to my knees, relief pouring through me at the sight of her. I opened my arms, and then she was in them, both of us crying and clutching at each other.

"I'm so sorry, Mommy. I'm so sorry. I didn't mean to be bad. I didn't mean to make you angry. Please don't send me away."

I pulled back from her, studying her worried face. The pinch of her fair eyebrows. The big eyes that begged for forgiveness.

I stroked my hand over her hair, shaking my head. "What are you talking about? You aren't bad, Slugger. I would never send you away."

"The lady said…"

I stood to my full height, glaring at the woman. "What lies did you feed my child?"

The woman shook her head. "I don't understand. These girls are from foster care. Their parents abandoned them."

"Is that the story they've been spinning? You've been sorely misinformed."

The woman covered her mouth, true shock on her face. "I don't understand. I'm so sorry. I need to get Father Byron, and we can sort this out."

"Where is he?" Zeph growled so deeply the woman flinched.

She silently pointed upstairs.

Zeph slammed his way up the stairs, shouting Byron's name at the top of his lungs, his voice as sharp as razor blades.

I gathered Amelia into my arms, checking her all over. "Did anyone hurt you, baby? You aren't in trouble. I just need to know."

She shook her little head. "No. I'm okay."

She truly did seem to be fine. There wasn't a scratch on her. She was wearing pajamas I knew Lleyton had bought for her.

I glanced up at the other girls in her 'class.'

They were all older, ranging in age from maybe eight to twelve.

I didn't think any of them were okay. They had the sad, shut-off look I'd seen on too many kids. We might have gotten to Amelia on time, but I didn't think we could say the same for the three girls who stared back at me.

I eyed them. "Are you okay?"

They all nodded quickly. Too quickly.

I wanted to reach out to them. Pull them behind me like I had with Amelia. Protect them from the people who hid their evil behind a fake veil of good. "I don't think you are. But you will be, okay. I'll make sure of it."

The woman tutted. "Let's go, girls. To my car immediately. You aren't safe here."

I blocked the doorway. I wasn't sure whether to believe this woman or not when she made out like she didn't know what was going on here. But it didn't matter. I wasn't letting her take these girls. "No."

But I knew I wouldn't be able to hold her back forever.

I took out my phone to call the police, then glanced up the stairs. Zeph could be killing Byron up there right now. Shouts floated down the stairs, too muffled by walls and floors to be discernible.

But I couldn't leave these girls here with their abusers any longer. I had to do what was right.

I called nine-one-one and waited for the sirens to wail.

34

ZEPH

 found Byron in an office at the top of the stairs, half crouched, hiding behind his desk. His fingers still worked furiously over a keyboard though, banging keys so frantically he barely lifted his head when I entered.

Like he'd been expecting me.

Like I'd given him a head start by shouting his name as I'd taken the stairs two at a time.

He should have been running. Scared of what he knew I was capable of. I'd already given him a taste, leaving him black and blue, he had to know I could kill him if I wanted to.

There was nothing that should be keeping him in the room.

Nothing unless he was hiding his tracks.

"What are you doing?" My voice was as cold as I'd ever heard it.

The man I'd once admired didn't answer. His

continual clicking of keys filled the small space, mixing with panicked, too-quick breaths.

I yanked the screen around.

The clicks went silent.

The images on the screen were something no one ever wanted to see. No one but dirty, filthy perverts like Byron and his online friends. My eye caught on one image, and I recognized the young girl as one who had been downstairs.

My stomach rolled.

I let go of the computer screen, averting my eyes to things I wished I could erase from my memory forever.

This was what would have happened to Amelia if we hadn't gotten here in time. She would have been another child, in an innocently named folder, that contained the most unholy of sins.

Blinding anger took over me. It blazed through my body like lightning, obliterating everything except for a solitary thought.

Never again.

Never again would this man be allowed to ruin a life. Never again would he get away with exploiting those weaker than he. Never again would he use the cover of being a man of the cloth so people trusted him.

The urge to leap across the desk and strangle the life out of him rose quick and sharp and satisfying. I clenched my fingers into fists, just begging to be unleashed on the piece of scum cowering behind his desk, begging me with his hands up.

His words fell on deaf ears.

"Shut up."

He didn't. He babbled hysterically. Blaming anyone

but himself. The church. God. Random internet strangers. His own disgusting biological 'needs.'

I couldn't bear to hear it. "Shut up," I bellowed again.

He cowered beneath the force of my words and closed his mouth.

I pointed at the desk chair. "Sit."

He did.

"Pick up a pen."

The man's fingers trembled as he slowly picked up a blue pen from his desk.

It was so tempting to tell him to shove it in his jugular. But I had the opportunity to kill two birds with one stone here.

Or two priests.

And I was going to take it.

"Write down what I say. Word for word."

His bushy eyebrows inched up on his forehead. "And if I say no?"

I leaned in, resting my hands on the edge of the desk, gripping it so tightly my knuckles went white. "Then I cut off your cock and feed it to you. That would be more than you deserve, you filthy piece of shit."

He pressed the nib of the pen to a notepad of paper. "What should I write?"

I didn't even try to get the snarl out of my voice. "The things I've done are unforgivable."

I waited, watching him slowly move his pen across the paper before I continued. "The images on my computer will explain, but there's something else I wish to confess to."

I paused while he reluctantly wrote the words I'd dictated. He looked up at me, waiting for me to continue.

I couldn't help the smile that flickered at the edges of my mouth. "I killed a man. Strangled him in his bed while he slept. Father Simon Collier died at my hands. I'm the serial priest killer."

Byron shook his head violently. "No. I never did that. That wasn't me."

I winked at him. "I know."

"I won't write it."

"Oh, you will. Because I think by now we both know what I'm capable of if you don't."

He stared at me, shaking his head.

I took a single step toward him.

He cowered away, covering his head. "Okay! Okay! I'll write it!"

His letters were slightly squiggly from how bad his hand shook. I didn't think it mattered. Nobody would be analyzing his handwriting when they saw the sick images on his hard drive. His shoulders shook with silent sobs.

Almost like he knew. He finally knew what it felt like to be powerless.

I wanted to throw my head back and crow with victory and the power that had transferred from him to me.

But that power belonged to those little girls. I could hold it for them in the meantime, but them being safe was the real win here.

I craned my neck, reading the words he'd written. When he finished, he dropped his pen. In the distance, a wail of a siren came, and I knew my time for playing with my prey was over.

He knew it too.

"Just do it." He sniffed. "Get it over and done with already, Zeph."

I forced out a laugh and cocked one eyebrow. "You misunderstand, Father. I'm not killing you."

Hope flashed in his eyes. "You aren't?"

From the pocket of my hoodie, I pulled the rope he'd tried to strangle Lyric with. The one I'd kept in my pocket ever since.

He gasped, recognizing it.

I dropped it into his lap. "Long enough to hang a man, don't you think?"

He shook his head. "I won't do it."

My hand shot around his throat quicker than I realized I could move. My lips came to his ear. "You will, or it will be your dear sweet mother whose neck I have my fingers around. Don't you worry. Before I kill her painfully, I'll be sure to tell her she raised a sadistic pedophile. Then you'll die as soon as you hit the prison gates. I'll make sure of that. All it will take is one mention to another prisoner, and he'll pass it on to the rest of them. I'm sure you've heard how men who hurt children are treated in prison."

Resignation came over him. He knew I had him. He knew there was no way out. Not after what he'd done. There was no sparing the man's life. I was never letting him hurt anyone again.

Writing a wrong I should have fixed a long time ago, when I'd first intercepted him trying to attack Lyric.

I turned on my heel and left the room.

At the bottom of the stairs, the police had arrived. They'd separated the girls from their "teacher," and Lyric stood with Amelia on her hip, giving her statement.

Lyric's beautiful light-colored eyes shot to me the moment I emerged.

Panic rippled all over her expression along with silent questions. The biggest one being, is he dead?

I walked over to them and calmly put my arm around her shoulder. "My name is Father Zepherin Hart. I'd be happy to give my statement too."

She relaxed beside me, trusting that I had this. That I had them.

I did. I occupied the police with questions and drawn-out statements, until I knew enough time had passed. When they finally made their way upstairs, and a shout came for a medic, it was already too late.

Lyric looked up at me, and I just squeezed her shoulder in reassurance.

The ambulance wouldn't make it here in time. We'd distracted the cops long enough.

Lyric called Lleyton, and he arrived in minutes, rushing across the grass to engulf his daughter in his arms. He walked her over to me and hugged me quickly. "Thank you," he murmured.

I shook my head. "It was my fault in the first place. You should be hitting me, not thanking me."

"You aren't your mother. You got her back, unhurt. That's all that matters."

I grudgingly accepted his praise, while keeping an eye on the door beyond which paramedics worked to bring Byron back to life.

"Zeph?"

I turned back to Lleyton, giving him my full attention. "Yeah?"

He sighed. "No matter what Lyric says, don't give up

on her. I've never seen her as happy as she's been with you. I don't know why she thinks the two of you together are no good, but fix it. Whatever is broken can be repaired. Because Amelia hasn't been calling you Daddy Zepherin because she's confused. It's because she can see her mom loves you."

I opened my mouth to answer, but I didn't have words to get out.

Lleyton just slapped me on the shoulder. "Look after her. She and I would have murdered each other if we'd tried to be a couple, but she's a great mom and an impressive woman. Treat her well."

I was so desperately in love with her that it was an easy promise to make.

He drove away with Amelia and Lyric, taking them both home.

I stood on the grass for hours, waiting and watching the comings and goings of police and the sun moving across the sky as morning turned to afternoon turned to evening.

I was still standing there, tiny smile on my face, when the police brought out Byron in a body bag.

35

———

LYRIC

*A*melia in her Edgely Academy uniform was the cutest thing I'd ever seen. Navy knee-length pleated skirt, crisp white blouse with the school crest embroidered on the pocket, and a red tie around her neck. I'd brushed her hair until it shone, and it fell in waves down her back, held off her face with a matching red headband.

I'd paid for her expensive uniforms with the money Lleyton had been paying into my bank account. I'd confessed to him the fraud Zeph and I had committed, tricking Lleyton into paying me when he thought he was paying for Amelia's daycare. Maybe I'd picked a good time to lay my soul bare, right after everything had gone down with us working together to rescue Amelia, but Lleyton hadn't been mad. If anything, he'd looked a little guilty and told me to keep the money, for all the child support he hadn't paid over the years.

He'd even continued his payments, never being late with even one.

He'd grown up. We both had, and we were working together better than we ever had, both of us just wanting the best for our daughter after how close we'd come to losing her.

Gran clapped frail hands together, in approval as Amelia did a twirl around Gran's rehab room. She was still struggling to regain the movement she'd had prior to her accident, but she liked the rehabilitation center. It wasn't terribly different than a nursing home, and Gran seemed to be enjoying the social interaction. When I'd commented on it during one of her more lucid days, she'd waved me off like I was talking nonsense. But then I'd found some nursing home brochures in her drawer, and the nurses had whispered she'd asked them for some information.

We still had time before she would be healed enough to go anywhere, but we'd pursued legal action against the owners of my building, arguing that the neglected state of the building had caused Gran's fall. They'd settled out of court for an amount that had covered her medical expenses, with a little to spare which was all we'd wanted. With Zeph and I both bringing in an income, we could afford anything extra required to set Gran up in a care facility if that's what she wanted.

When Amelia ran off to twirl for Gran's physiotherapist, Gran leaned in and whispered to me, "How did you get that school to agree to take her? You were so sure she wouldn't get in."

I'd already told her this story a couple of times, but she kept on forgetting. "The school had a change of heart, I guess." Or more accurately, the church had asked us what they could do to help make amends for the ordeal we'd been through. Anything to stop us going to the press.

I might have suggested they make a sizeable donation to Edgeley Academy to fund scholarships for four young girls so we could make sure their traumas didn't stop them from receiving a quality education. The church had readily agreed, and Amelia and the three girls we'd found with her were given full tuition scholarships. There was one ready for Toby as well, once he was old enough.

It was the goddamn least the church could do, after failing so badly to see what was right beneath their noses.

Zeph had been one of those who'd donated in the name of a scholarship for the girls, hating that he'd been blind to it all too. He'd signed the check for the complete amount of his savings as his last act as a priest.

Then he'd gotten in his car and driven to the home we'd rented together. It was still in Saint View, but a nicer part than where my apartment had been. It was three bedrooms. One for us, one for Amelia, and one for Gran, should she decide to come back to us.

Gran kissed Amelia's head. "Off you go to school now, Slugger. Thank you for coming by to show me your pretty uniform."

Amelia kissed her back, and then we were in the car once more and delivering Amelia to the gates of Edgeley Academy.

"You going to cry?" Zeph asked, a small smile playing around his mouth as we got out of the car and joined the stream of families walking their little ones through the gate for their first day.

I shook my head determinedly, smiling down at Amelia, skipping along beside me, full of excitement.

"Nope. I'm too happy for crying. I'm just so glad she gets to be here. And that the other girls do too."

Zeph nodded then pointed up ahead. "Look who's up there. You sure you're not going to cry?"

Amelia squealed with excitement and let go of my hand, running ahead. She ran straight past Lleyton and Kat, who frowned in confusion, but my girl had eyes for someone else. "Aunty Eve! Uncle Josh!"

Eve and Boston stood at the gate, frantically waving at Amelia. Amelia threw herself at Eve's legs, and Eve put her hand over her heart and mouthed, "So cute!" at me.

Boston squatted and offered Amelia a high five, and she slapped his hand with everything she had.

"What about me, kid?"

Amelia gazed up at Augie, grinned at him, and then stuck her tongue out. "Nope!"

Farther along the fence, Kelly waved to Amelia, calling her over. "Come have a first-day photo with your cousins!"

Amelia skipped over, and Kelly's eldest daughter put an arm around Amelia's shoulders.

Zeph had been right. Seeing all my friends and our family come out to support my girl meant a lot. Tears pricked at the backs of my eyes, and I blinked furiously, trying to keep them at bay.

I couldn't keep them in when I realized there was still one person missing.

Eve knew. I think Augie did too. Eve picked up my fingers and wordlessly squeezed them while Augie turned away, hiding his own emotion.

The school bell rang, and we all hugged Amelia

before she went racing off with Kelly's kids, not looking back once.

We all stood there, watching her go. A tear slipped down my face.

Eve elbowed me. "Stop or I'll bawl and I'll never be able to stop."

I nodded.

She cleared her throat and raised her voice. "Family dinner at the club tonight, everyone. I expect all of you to be there. It's been too long since we had one."

I glanced at Zeph and then nodded to Eve. "We're in."

Lleyton and Kat nodded when Eve raised an eyebrow at them. Kelly smiled happily when the invitation was extended to her as well.

"All of us," Eve repeated. "Family isn't blood. It's the people you choose. And the people your people choose. See you all at six."

Augie was the only one who hadn't replied. The silence drew out.

"It's Amelia's first day of school, Aug. You have to come to dinner. We need to celebrate. Please?" I begged.

He seemed like he might prefer to poke his eye out with something hot. But Eve reached out and tickled him.

He batted her away, but I joined in, jumping on his other side.

"Come on, Augie. Please? Please? You gotta."

He squirmed and twisted out of our grasp, but there was a smile on his too-handsome face. "Fine. Fine! If I come, will the two of you knock it off?"

I grinned and pushed up on my toes to kiss his blond stubbled cheek. "Thank you, Augie. It'll be fun. I promise." I swallowed thickly. "Maybe we can make it a celebration too. Fawn's birthday…"

Augie stiffened. "Is tomorrow. I know."

I nodded. "We gotta keep living, Augie."

"I know."

And for the first time in a long time, I believed him.

There was nothing we could do to help Fawn now. Nothing except live our lives the way she would have wanted us to. Without any new information on her case, life had to go on.

36

LYRIC

After saying goodbye to Amelia's first-day cheer squad, Zeph and I strolled hand in hand back to the car. I hugged his arm, humming beneath my breath.

He gazed down at me, that adoration he always had for me shining in his eyes. "Happy?"

"Mmm-hmm. Very. I love knowing she's at the very best school. And from that she'll have opportunities I never had. We're breaking the cycle. That's important to me." I squeezed his biceps affectionately. "I love you took the day off to be here for it."

Zeph had picked up a carpentry job with a local builder in desperate need of anyone willing to swing a hammer. I'd agonized over him taking a job like that, worried he was just doing it because we needed a paycheck to pay the rent on our new house. But to my surprise, the hard work suited him. He came home smiling each afternoon, talking of big plans to build houses for the homeless one day when he'd learned the trade. With him home at night, we'd been able to let

Peggy go to another family who needed her services. The money I saved on her wages meant there was funds for things like bills and new clothes and even a weekend trip away.

Zeph dropped a kiss on my head. "Wouldn't have missed it for the world. But do we have plans for the next few hours?"

I let go of him and got into the passenger seat, pulling on my seat belt. "Nope. No plans. We are free as a bird until school pickup time and dinner at the club."

He settled behind the wheel and started the engine. "Good. Because if you're up for it, I wanted to work some more on my sculpture."

When he'd resigned from the church, I'd tried to convince him to take a job with an artist. But art was a luxury most people in Saint View could not afford, and while Providence had a small art gallery on the main street, they mostly brought in artists from the city. Positions with sculptors were few and far between, paid terribly, and even if he had been able to secure a spot, Zeph had refused to be that far away from me and Amelia on a daily basis.

But he hadn't stopped creating. In our new home, we'd turned the attic into his studio. It had the most light, spilling in from a large window, and had been big enough for his table and tools and the pieces he'd already created.

Last week, he'd asked me to model for him.

I grinned at him now. "Take me home and sculpt me like one of your French girls, Zeph."

He squinted at me, confusion on his face, and I slapped his arm.

"*Titanic*? Rose laid out on the couch and Jack behind the artist's easel?"

His face was still blank.

"You are so sheltered. I'll put it on so we can watch while you work."

He pulled into our driveway and leaned over to kiss me. "You're the only thing I watch when I work."

His grumbly words sent tingles through me. I was the only thing he watched almost all the time. It was a heady feeling, his gaze on me. Sometimes it was full of love and admiration. Sometimes it was with a smile because I'd sassed him and he liked it. Sometimes it was with nothing but pure, unadulterated lust.

Right now, it was verging on the latter.

In the doorway, he put his arms around me and ducked his head to steal my lips. A blistering kiss of need that had us both stepping away to run up the stairs to the attic, eager to get on with this so we could get to other things.

In the attic, we closed the door, and he locked it, even though that wasn't really necessary with Amelia at school.

I lifted my dress over my head and unhooked my bra, peeling it down my arms.

Zeph's eyes flared, taking in my tits and the curve of my hips.

With a teasing grin, I shimmied out of my panties as well until I stood in front of him completely naked.

He did nothing to stop his gaze wandering all over me, languishing on my nipples hardening and the junction of my thighs. With effort, he pointed at the couch on the other side of the room.

"Couch."

I knew the drill by now, after several nights in a row of this. But it still made me breathless with anticipation.

Because it was obvious where this would lead.

Even still, I kneeled on the couch with my back to him, resting my hands on the frame for balance.

"Spread your knees a little wider," he instructed.

I did, shifting on the soft couch cushions.

"Look over your shoulder at me."

I flicked my hair out of the way and twisted the way he'd asked.

Heat flared in his dark eyes. But he held himself firm in his seat, picked up his tools, and got to work.

I held the pose, loving the way his hands moved as he molded and shaped the clay with various tools I didn't have names for. Every tiny movement seemed insignificant, and yet as time ticked by, the clay changed from a lump of nothing to the curves of a woman.

My gaze strayed to the other pieces around the room. His work was dark. Erotic. All the newer pieces based on him or me or the things we did together.

Me on my knees for him.

Him covering my body, wrists pinned above my head.

A close-up of our torsos, his dick buried deep inside me.

They were beautiful. Sexy. And so was he.

It was too much for me to be naked in his presence without wanting him. A building need for him rose deep inside me. I let my hand drift to the ache between my legs and rubbed my clit gently.

"Don't move, Lyric."

I flashed him a sassy grin and trailed my fingers lower,

pushing two of them up inside me. I closed my eyes and moaned at the intrusion.

He dropped his little spatula-like instrument on the table, leaning back in his chair and watching me finger myself. "That how you want me to sculpt your fingers? With you riding them?"

I rocked my hips, tempting him a little more. "Unless you want to give me directions otherwise."

He groaned, reaching down beneath the table to palm his cock. "Squeeze your nipple."

I dragged a palm up my belly and cupped my breast, rolling the nipple. He couldn't see that, because my back was still turned to him, but he could hear my breaths morph into pants at the new sensation.

I knew what I liked. I knew how to touch myself to get me to the line in a matter of minutes. But I also knew he'd stop me.

He stood, washing his hands in the bucket of fresh water he kept here for that sole purpose. But his gaze never strayed from what I was doing, how I writhed, the noises I made.

"Not yet, Lyric," he said gruffly. "There are other things I want to do today before I let you come. Stop moving."

With a whimper I slowed down, taking my finger off my clit and dropping my hands to my side. I trembled in anticipation as he put one hand to the back of his shirt and dragged it over his head. My gaze dropped to his abs, wandering all over them, visually tracing the ridges and curves that were only more pronounced now he had a more physical day job. His biceps were solid muscle, popping and flexing as he stalked across the room to me, undoing his jeans while he walked.

Free of his jeans and underwear, he stood at the edge of the couch behind me, in the gap between my feet sticking over the edge. He trailed his hands down my arms, leaving goosebumps in his wake until his fingers interlocked with mine. He brought both our hands up, guiding me to rest mine on the back of the couch once more.

His breath was warm on my neck when he leaned in, trailing his tongue up the sensitive flesh to my ear. "Do you remember your safe word?"

I nodded, breathless.

"Good girl. Hold on. Don't let go unless I tell you to."

Excitement pounded through me. We'd done this so many times now. So many decisions fell to me during our day-to-day lives, especially as a mother. Zeph and I weren't at a place where he could make decisions about Amelia. Not yet. She had Lleyton for that, and she and Zeph were taking their relationship day by day, building a friendship first, more than a father/daughter bond.

Outside this room, I was the boss. I'd been single too long and liked my independence too much to ever fully give that up.

Inside it, he had full control.

The power to dominate me.

The permission to take what he needed.

And the ability to blow my freaking mind.

I trusted him.

Loved him.

My breath hitched at the words scalding my tongue.

He knew. I was sure he did. With the way I created a

home for all of us. With the way I encouraged him, comforted him, built him up when he faltered.

I showed him every day with the way I gave myself up to him.

"I love you, Zeph," I murmured as he kissed my neck. "I love you so much. Not just the way you make me feel in here, but the way you make me feel every day. I hope you know that."

He reached around and grasped my chin with two fingers, twisting my head to the side so he could peer down at me. Behind the lust and desire was the love that was always there, no matter what. Even when I was giving him a hard time. Even when I didn't deserve it. That love had been there almost since day one. It had never faltered.

"I don't need your words, Lyric. I never have. I just need you. Your heart. Your mind. I know you love me."

I breathed out a shaky sigh of relief.

He smiled against my lips. "I'll always love you more."

I tried to argue because it simply wasn't true. The man filled my heart to overflowing with every tiny thing he did. It was always about me and Amelia. He was so inherently selfless, giving his time to the homeless shelter and making me a better person for it. I volunteered there now too, along with Amelia, the three of us working there side by side.

I could barely remember the woman I was before him.

I didn't want to.

She was unhappy. Lost. Sharp.

He softened my jagged edges. He was the balm to my crazy, and I was his.

We'd put the illegal stuff behind us in order to give Amelia a safe and stable home. But we would never stop trying to help those who needed it. Those who society forgot.

He kissed me deeply before I could explain any of that, and the words floated away, not needing to be said, because they were felt.

He guided my fingers around the solid back of the couch once more, reminding me not to move. He cupped my breasts and then kissed his way down my spine, dragging his fingers along with him to massage my ass.

He placed a kiss on my lower back, swirling his tongue in circles over my heated skin while his fingers kneaded into the tight muscles of my cheeks, well-toned from long nights on the pole. "I want you here, Lyric. My cock buried in your tight little ass when I come."

I nearly came on the spot. I pressed back against him instinctively, wanting what he'd been working me up to for weeks but never quite delivering on.

He slapped a palm across my behind, using the other hand to grip my hip and hold me still. "Not yet. Not until I get you good and wet."

I'd be a freaking waterslide if I got any wetter, but I knew better than to argue with him.

He drew my hips back as he kneeled on the wooden floorboards, putting his face right at my ass height. My knees were already wide apart, and I was sure he could see my pink pussy glistening between my thighs.

I slumped forward, ass out when he buried his face between my legs and licked. He groaned at the taste of my arousal and then used his fingers to spread it to my tight rear hole.

He'd been doing this for weeks, edging me until I begged for him to fuck me there. I ground back against him now, taking the tip of his finger.

He bit down on my ass cheek, the sting of pain only heightening the pleasure.

I moaned and whimpered until he knelt behind me and fit his cock to my pussy, fucking me deep and slow while my head spun. The added pleasure his finger brought heightened every feeling, until I was gasping, an orgasm building inside me, searching for a place to escape.

The pressure of his finger disappeared, and he pulled out of my pussy, sliding back until he was notched where I really wanted him.

"Play with your clit while I fuck you here, Lyric. Touch it like I would."

Which meant don't just go hard and fast to get to the finish line.

It meant play slowly, roll and rub, tease it gently until my knees shook and I begged for release.

I didn't dare disobey for fear he wouldn't give me what I wanted.

He pushed inside me, the place only his fingers and toys had explored so far.

I shouted, and he stilled, taking a handful of my hair to tilt my head back.

"I'm going to keep going unless you use your words."

"Fuck me," I begged. Then grinned. "Are those the words you were waiting for?"

He bit down on my shoulder. A punishment but a weak one, because he knew it felt good. There was a chuckle in his voice when he said, "Exactly what I wanted to hear."

The first full slide of him there was ecstasy. Exactly what I needed. I rubbed my clit while he grabbed my hips and took me with gentle slides, each one giving me time to get used to the size of him, but with the added benefit of driving me wild. After four or five thrusts, I was taking him easily, no resistance, all pleasure. I ground back against his base, letting him bottom out inside me, and panted around my moans. I drove my fingers up inside myself, my pussy tight with him inside my ass. I stroked my G-spot and then my clit, alternating while his dick drove me higher and higher up the pleasure scale, my building orgasm so intense my legs shook.

"Zeph!"

The orgasm curled around the places we were joined, spreading out like wildfire when I stroked myself. I moaned and shouted and shook, barely hanging on while he picked up the pace, fucking me fast, taking me hard.

Bright spots swam in my eyes when he pushed my hand away and took over control of my clit, his dick spasming inside me. I came again, everything squeezing tight around him and sending him over the edge with a shout that drowned out mine.

His chest came down on top of my back, covering me with a light sheen of his sweat. He waited until he was limp inside me and then pulled out, his cum coating us both in a sticky mess.

I didn't care. I would never care. All I wanted was him and the way he made me feel. Safe. Secure. Loved. I'd once thought I was too independent to want a man in my life, but Zeph had always made me want things I shouldn't.

He was no longer forbidden. There was no hiding the love between us.

He was the unholy sin I'd never be ashamed of.

EPILOGUE
AUGIE

Family night at the club was never a quiet or small event. Even before the cop had come along and whisked Eve off her stripper heels, family night had drawn a different crowd each week. Sometimes Lyric brought Amelia and her gran. Sometimes Terry relaxed from guarding the door to twirl his wife around the dance floor while Eve and her musician friends jammed. Terry's kids always looked horrified when they did that, which I quite enjoyed. Dylan, Eve's younger brother, had started hanging around in recent months, he and Phoenix sitting side by side, watching the action from the edges of the room. It was a free-for-all. If you knew someone, you would be welcomed with open arms.

Because there was always room for more in Eve's heart.

Mine was dead.

Black.

Cold.

But I hadn't been in the mood for one of Eve's lectures, and the idea of one of her homemade feasts was too good to pass up. My house was a mess of takeout wrappers, and the only thing in the refrigerator was a bottle of Coke to go with the bottle of Jack on the countertop.

But Lyric was right. I had to stop living in this fucking limbo Fawn's disappearance had created. And I would. I was here, wasn't I?

Something felt different lately. When I watched my brother with his family, I'd once felt nothing but anger because they were tying him down, saddling him with responsibilities he was too young for. It was the same stupid shit my parents had done. Fall in love young. Have babies before you were ready for them. Then get sick of them when the responsibilities got too much.

That was how Banjo and I had been dumped in foster care. As soon as I'd turned eighteen, I'd started the fight to get him out. That had meant a job. A house. I'd gotten those things, but the job barely paid the rent. It wasn't enough to feed myself, let alone a growing ten-year-old kid.

I couldn't let him go back into care.

Not after the shit that had happened to me in there.

So I'd done what needed to be done. I'd sold drugs. My body. My entire fucking self-worth.

None of it mattered, as long as Banjo was out of the system.

Now I didn't even have him.

All I had was the knowledge he was safe and happy. He seemed to love his girl and their baby. I had no idea what was going on with the other two guys they lived with, but if he was also getting off on being with them, more power to them.

I fought off the bitterness that happiness wasn't in the cards for me. After Fawn, I was done trying to be anyone's anything. Not their big brother. Not their friend. Not their lover.

I'd been distancing myself from Eve and the others, knowing that hanging out with me was sure to bring the darkness to their door too.

Eve and her band friends finished up their song, and Lyric let out a wolf whistle from her perch on the bar. She had her arms wrapped around Zeph's neck, who stood in front of her in the gap of her swinging legs. She rested her chin on his shoulder, and he rubbed her thigh absently, drink in his other hand while they watched Eve on the stage and Amelia running around on the dance floor with Zeph's sister's kids chasing her.

Everyone else clapped, and Eve held up a hand. "We're celebrating tonight. It was our little miss's first day, and she nailed it, didn't you, Milly girl?"

Amelia stuck both her thumbs up in the air, and everyone smiled or clapped for her.

Fuck, she was a cute kid. I had no experience with kids her age, or really kids at all, but her gappy-toothed grin was infectious. My cold, dead heart gave the occasional thump of happiness when she called me Uncle Augie, before it tucked up in on itself once more.

Eve cleared her throat. "It's also Fawn's birthday tomorrow." Her bottom lip trembled, but she forced it into a smile and held up her glass of water. "To you, Fawn. Wherever you are. Happy birthday, girl. We love you."

Everyone raised their glasses. Lyric glanced over at me, and slowly I raised mine too.

Her smile was wobbly, but at least she managed one. I couldn't say the same for myself.

Up on the stage, Eve opened her mouth, presumably to finish her toast to Fawn, but a thumping on the club doors put a halt to that.

Eve frowned over at the door practically vibrating off its hinges with the force of the pounding thumps from outside.

She didn't have to say a word. In unison, Cop, Terry, Phoenix, and I all moved to the door.

We'd had too much shit go down here. Street races. Protests. Brawls. If there was someone out there wanting to start something, then they could bring it. I cracked my knuckles, ready for a fight. My muscles rippled with the need to fucking hit something. Someone. Anything to feel alive again, because all I'd felt since Fawn had disappeared was dead.

Terry yanked open the door, while Cop, Phoenix, and I stood shoulder to shoulder, a wall these outsiders would have to go through before they got to anyone behind us.

I blinked at the woman on the other side.

So like Fawn and yet so different. Taller. Dark hair where I'd always known Fawn to be blond. Curvier to Fawn's slimmer build. But the eyes. Eyes Fawn shared with both the woman I'd seen on the train and the man who stood beside her now.

He leaned on the doorway and eyed the four of us.

If we worried him, I didn't notice.

All I could see was her.

That same intense crackle of chemistry I'd felt when

our gazes had met on the train lit up again. She looked me up and down, held my gaze, and then lifted her head in acknowledgement. "I'm Ophelia." She pointed at the man who was so clearly her brother. "That's Vincent."

He rolled his eyes. "Scythe."

She huffed out a sigh. "Fine. Sorry. He's Scythe today. It's a long story."

"It's a private party," Terry barked, none too friendly. "We ain't open. Come back tomorrow."

He went to close the heavy door. Before I could even say a word, Scythe stuck one big, booted foot in the way and pinned Terry with a glare that sent a frost into the air.

"I don't think we'll be doing that." His hand clapped around the door, and he pushed it open, gaze bouncing around each of us, eyeing off who was the biggest threat.

Voice like ice, his gaze finished on me. "Where the fuck is my sister?"

There's more from Saint View Strip in book 3.
Get it here: https://mybook.to/SaintViewStrip3

ALSO BY ELLE THORPE

Saint View High series (Reverse Harem, Bully Romance. Complete)

*Devious Little Liars (Saint View High, #1)

*Dangerous Little Secrets (Saint View High, #2)

*Twisted Little Truths (Saint View High, #3)

Saint View Prison series (Reverse harem, romantic suspense. Complete.)

*Locked Up Liars (Saint View Prison, #1)

*Solitary Sinners (Saint View Prison, #2)

*Fatal Felons (Saint View Prison, #3)

Saint View Psychos series (Reverse harem, romantic suspense. Complete.)

*Start a War (Saint View Psychos, #1)

*Half the Battle (Saint View Psychos, #2)

*It Ends With Violence (Saint View Psychos, #3)

Saint View Rebels (Reverse harem, romantic suspense. Releasing in 2023)

*Book 1

Saint View Strip (Male/Female, romantic suspense standalones. Ongoing.)

*Evil Enemy (Saint View Strip, #1) - March 10, 2023

*Unholy Sins (Saint View Strip, #2) - May 10, 2023

Dirty Cowboy series (complete)

*Talk Dirty, Cowboy (Dirty Cowboy, #1)

*Ride Dirty, Cowboy (Dirty Cowboy, #2)

*Sexy Dirty Cowboy (Dirty Cowboy, #3)

*Dirty Cowboy boxset (books 1-3)

*25 Reasons to Hate Christmas and Cowboys (a Dirty Cowboy bonus novella, set before Talk Dirty, Cowboy but can be read as a standalone, holiday romance)

Buck Cowboys series (Spin off from the Dirty Cowboy series. Complete.)

*Buck Cowboys (Buck Cowboys, #1)

*Buck You! (Buck Cowboys, #2)

*Can't Bucking Wait (Buck Cowboys, #3)

*Mother Bucker (Buck Cowboys, $#4)

The Only You series (Contemporary romance. Complete)

*Only the Positive (Only You, #1) - Reese and Low.

*Only the Perfect (Only You, #2) - Jamison.

*Only the Truth - (Only You, bonus novella) - Bree.

*Only the Negatives (Only You, #3) - Gemma.

*Only the Beginning (Only You, #4) - Bianca and Riley.

*Only You boxset

Add your email address here to be the first to know when new books are available!

www.ellethorpe.com/newsletter

Join Elle Thorpe's readers group on Facebook!

www.facebook.com/groups/ellethorpesdramallamas

ACKNOWLEDGMENTS

I knew the minute a hot priest with tats showed up in a Saint View book I wrote in 2021, that eventually, he'd get a book of his own.

I was so sure that when I saw the cover photo that same year, I bought it, even though the book had no title, no plot, and I didn't even know which series it would be in.

I'm so glad Zeph got to have his moment in the sun! I really hope you guys loved him.

Who's next?

Augie.

He was one of the very first Saint View characters, first appearing in the very first Saint View book, Devious Little Liars. He's been an asshole since day one. But I think you can see from this book that things are changing for Augie. And he's finally ready to find his HEA.

I promise, if you still hate him, I'll convince you otherwise. Because that man has experienced a lot. And there is a heart beneath the cold shell.

As always, huge thanks go to my editors, Emmy and Karen. To Wander Aguiar for always taking such beautiful photos. To Soj for the perfect hot priest pose. To my beta readers, Shellie, Louise, Sam, and Dana for your early feedback. To my ARC team for last minute typo hunting and all your reviews. And my to my readers group for being the best place to hang on the internet.

And last, but never least, Jira, Thomas, Flick, and Heidi. Every ounce of hard work is for you guys. I love you.

ABOUT THE AUTHOR

Elle Thorpe lives in regional Australia with Mr Thorpe and their three kiddos. When she's not at the local cafe writing stories full of kissing, you'll probably find her throwing a ball for her slobbery dog Rollo, or chasing one of the seventy alpacas on the family farm.

You can find her on Facebook or Instagram(@ellethorpebooks or hit the links below!) or at her website www.ellethorpe.com.

If you love Elle's work, please consider joining her Facebook fan group, Elle Thorpe's Drama Llamas or joining her newsletter here. www.ellethorpe.com/newsletter

facebook.com/ellethorpebooks
instagram.com/ellethorpebooks
goodreads.com/ellethorpe